TEMPTING FATE

"There's a cellar over here. I'm gonna go check it out."

"Negro, get back here!" Coach yelled, but Rice ignored him, and stepped down into the small dark passageway. The door slammed closed behind him with a loud creak and a swirl of dust.

The cellar door sparked a memory from one of Sunnie's crazy dreams. Her stomach did a flip. Not knowing what else to do, she said a quick prayer for Rice.

Coach shook his head. "Famous last words from the ignorant brotha in every horror flick: 'I think I'll go check it out.'" Coach mocked Rice in a doofus voice.

Sunnie grabbed both Geffen and Coach by the arm. Her eyes were big, her voice shaky. "Guys, I've got a real weird feeling—"

A strange, low rumbling sound cut Sunnie off. It was coming from beneath their feet and causing the whole ground to vibrate. The low growl grew loud and diabolically raucous, like a hockey match in Hades. Sunnie, Coach, and Geffen stood still and waited until it stopped.

"What in *Sam Hill* was that?" Coach asked.

Also by Lexi Davis

THE AFTER WIFE

Pretty Evil

Lexi Davis

POCKET BOOKS

NEW YORK LONDON TORONTO SYDNEY

POCKET BOOKS, a division of Simon & Schuster, Inc.
1230 Avenue of the Americas, New York, NY 10020

This book is a work of fiction. Names, characters, places and incidents are products of the author's imagination or are used fictitiously. Any resemblance to actual events or locales or persons, living or dead, is entirely coincidental.

ISBN-13: 978-1-4165-2706-0
ISBN-10:   1-4165-2706-0

This Pocket Books paperback edition October 2006

10 9 8 7 6 5 4 3 2 1

POCKET and colophon are registered trademarks of Simon & Schuster, Inc.

Cover design by Janet Perr

Manufactured in the United States of America

For information regarding special discounts for bulk purchases, please contact Simon & Schuster Special Sales at 1-800-456-6798 or business@simonandschuster.com

To my parents, Leon & Bertha,
my foundation, my inspiration.
I am eternally grateful.

Acknowledgments

It is said that songbirds learn to sing in the dark. Through my dark days, I thank God for the special people who shined their light into my life and helped me to see.

Lawrence, God knew I needed someone exactly like you. Thanks for being my safe place, my anchor, my love of a lifetime. Treasure, I asked God for you, and I couldn't be happier with what He sent me—a snuggly, little pretty package and a bundle of laughs called you. You're priceless. Don't ever forget it. Lisa, I won't say anything corny like, "You are the wind beneath my wings." But you are. Without you, my dreams would not have taken flight.

Mother, you define the meaning of the verb *love*. Unselfish, self-sacrificing, loving beyond limits, you are the glue that holds this family together. Dad, thanks for being a foundation of love, support, and assurance. In fifty-two years of marriage, you two personify true dedication and commitment.

Keith and Byron, thanks for always having my back.

Rhonda (LaRhonda) and Diane (Alex), thanks for reading my stuff early on. Whatever's mine is yours (just don't try to walk outta here with my car keys). Dream courageously and never settle for less than God's best. Aaron Mays, ditto.

Lawrence II and Brenda, thanks for your "gift" to me. Chris, Wendell, much love. Aunt Lois, Christine and Dena, thanks for always encouraging me. My Pasadena and Altadena family, Aunt Norma, Daisy and Ralph, thanks. Ronald J., Rebecca, Shyniece, Monwilla, Marcus, Betty, Herbert, El, Brittany, Demetrius, Cassandra, Gwen, Elnora H., Johnny and Doris, Sam and Eula, Jan, Cherish (my goddaughter), Little Byron, Crystal and Christian, Elise and Diamond, Jovanna Kay, LaLa, DeMarco, all of my peeps, little peeps, in-laws, friends, cousins (Hey, e'erbody down in Alexandria and Natchitoches, LA!), and in Compton, L.A. and Southern Cali—much love. For your encouragement—the Palmdale Barnes & Noble Book Club and staff (Joyce A., Nila U., Lynn F., Sonja W., Lisa Ann J., Peggy B., Paul S., Pam L., Dawn) and the AV Writers Group. For prayers and support—Aaron and Nita D., Timika S., Mrs. Pledger, Erma B., Izetta H., Evangelist Flakes, F. Fly, Gwen S., The Terrells, The Samuels, Delores A., and my churches—First Missionary (Bishop Hearns), Agape Community (Pastor Todd), Christ Missionary Bible (Pastor Hudson), Shining Light (Pastor Benson), Greater Ephesians (Pastor Payne), and Desert Christian Vineyard (Pastor D. Parker).

Of course, much gratitude to Sara Camilli, agent

extraordinaire, and Selena James, editor supreme. You saw the vision early, picked it up and ran with it.

To my author friends, especially Eric J. Dickey for doing what you did way back when, and Leslie Esdaile-Banks (big shout-out to ya, girl!). Also, Zane, Brenda L. Thomas, Kim Roby, Reon Laudat, Marissa Monteilh, Jacqueline J. LaMon, Brandon Massey, Debra Phillips, Angela Henry, LaTonya Williams, Geri Guillaume, Pam Samuels, every writer who shared info, but especially, Cydney Rax. Girl, you helped pull me through this whole process—tugging, clawing, laughing, crying, and thanking God the whole way. You're my girl!

To all the bookstores, radio stations, book clubs, and websites (especially BookRemarks.com) I say thank you—but especially to each and every reader. When you open my book, you open up the possibility for us to connect on a creative, emotional, or spiritual level, and that's always exciting and a privilege for me. If I've forgotten anyone, I'll get you in here next time. As long as God continues to shine His light on this songbird, I'll sing through a hundred more books. Remember to always dream courageously!

Chapter

1

WHEN GEFFEN CAGE ENTERED THE CRUSTACEAN, AN upscale French Colonial Vietnamese restaurant in a section of Beverly Hills known as the "Golden Triangle," he had one thought: *I wish this was the* Bermuda *Triangle so my date would disappear.*

Usually Geffen felt comfortable in high-profile places like this, but tonight he wanted to hide. As one of "the beautiful people" among the L.A. socialite circles, he was known to have impressive taste in women, but tonight all of that was blown to hell. He was looking good as usual, but his date was another story. If she stood on the side of the freeway, people would stop because this woman looked like a wreck.

Geffen hoped he wouldn't run into anyone he knew, but that would be hard because Geffen knew a lot of people. His date had suggested this place. The restaurant had an indoor, under-the-floor stream filled with black and gold koi and covered by glass. A floor-to-ceiling aquarium, waterfall, and copper-topped bar added to its breathtaking ambience, but all Geffen could do was hold his breath as he walked his date over the small wooden bridge, ready to duck if anyone recognized him.

"Sorry for the inconvenience, Mr. Cage," the maître d' said, as Geffen and his date stood waiting in plain view of the whole restaurant while an attendant cleaned up a spill near their table.

Aw damn, Geffen thought, as he brushed nonexistent lint from his Versace suit's lapel. Geffen was superclean and always *GQ,* dressed sharp like a razor with not a hair in his thin, trimmed mustache out of place and not a fingernail unfiled. He just needed a distraction, a reason to put his head down and try to hide, but he was too late.

Three women sitting at a table a few feet across the marble floor spotted him. He didn't know them, but they were talking loudly, sipping on martinis and ragging on people as they walked by. Both Geffen and his date could hear every word they said.

"Why is he with *her,* as fine as he is," one woman said.

"Maybe the young brotha likes older women—nothing wrong with that," said the second.

"I *know* she gets a lot of candy on Halloween."

"Quick, call the zoo and see if they're missing a llama."

Geffen shot the attendant a hurry-your-ass-up look.

When their table was finally ready, Geffen's date walked closer to the ladies' table. At first, Geffen thought she was showing off her 5 carat oval-shaped diamond ring, but turns out she was giving them her middle finger. Then she sat in her seat.

Geffen tried to concentrate on reading the menu, and put his mind over the matter. The fellas were counting on him to convince this woman to give them a cut-rate investment loan to buy property.

Geffen pulled a long-stemmed red rose from the table piece and handed it to her. "Tonight you look . . . *indescribable*."

She batted her fake eyelashes and grinned at Geffen like he was a piece of meat and she hadn't eaten in twenty years. All Geffen could think about was how much older she looked here in the candlelight compared to when he had first met her at the bank that she owned. She had been dressed better, too, with not so much sagging skin showing. And who had done her makeup tonight? Cirque du Soleil? He tried hard to think of something positive. *Umm, okay, nice, expensive teeth.*

"You really know how to treat a lady, Geffen, my sweetheart," she said in a low, guttural voice intended to be sexy but that sounded like a toad croaking. She opened her menu. "Umm, I'm so hungry. What looks good to you?"

Not you, that's for sure. "The roasted lamb is always good," he said out loud.

She asked the waiter, "What's your catch of the day?"

While his date irritated the waiter with too many questions, Geffen smiled and tried to look patient. *Don't order the baked potato. It'll take too long.*

Finally, she placed her order, then added, "Oh, and add a baked potato to that."

After ordering his meal, Geffen asked the waiter to bring a Moët & Chandon right away. Then he started the conversation. "So tell me, how does a woman like you end up owning United Financial Funding Corporation, the second-largest lender of venture capital in Southern California?"

"Geffen, that's business. I *never* mix business with pleasure. And just so there's no misunderstanding, tonight is strictly for *pleasure.*" She slipped off her shoe, raised her foot beneath the table and rubbed the inside of his calf with her bare toe. She continued her exploration even as the waiter brought and poured their drink.

"You're quite a flirt, too, I see." Geffen sipped his Moët.

"I don't believe in wasting time, Geffen, my dear. Did you know they make a Viagra pill for women? I purchased a two-month supply."

I bet your husband is glad he's dead right about now. To his relief, the waiter arrived with their food. But the meal's arrival did little to distract Geffen's horny dinner partner.

"I'm hoping that a young man like you will be able to keep up, if you know what I mean."

She reached over and rubbed his hand. Her fingers felt like withered tree branches. He set his fork down and politely withdrew his hand to use his napkin. "You are full of surprises," he said with a smile.

"Yes, I *am* full of surprises. I bet you didn't know

this about me." She leaned in close and whispered in his face, "I like *rough* sex."

Oh, that's just nasty.

Geffen cleared his throat to try to keep his dinner down. He emptied his champagne glass and smiled at her. She did a little shimmy-shake, another attempt to be sexy. *I need some weed and a blindfold.* She opened her mouth and wiggled her wrinkled tongue at him. *Hell, hit me with a dart gun. Tranquilize my ass.* "Waiter, check, *please.*"

In her town car, on their way to her Palisades home, she made it clear to Geffen what he would have to do in order to get the loan he wanted at half the interest rate that other banks had offered. Desperate for a moment alone to rethink his strategy, he asked her driver to stop at a 7-Eleven. He said he wanted to get a *Wall Street Journal,* but really he wanted to buy a pint of vodka and a *Penthouse* magazine for sexual inspiration. But mainly he wanted to call his friend, Rice Jordan.

As he paid for his items, he flipped open his cell phone and called Rice. When his buddy answered, Geffen broke down, saying, "I can't do this shit, man."

"Hold on. Calm down. Where's she at right now?"

Geffen knew Rice would take his call, even though he was in the middle of his book signing at Barnes & Noble in Palmdale, California. Geffen had already told Rice about the bank owner who was sweet on him, and that tonight he was going to try to get them an investment loan *by any means necessary.*

"She's in the car. I had her driver stop at Seven-

Eleven so I could get some things. I'm trying to stall, man. I'm telling you, she ain't just old, she's an old freak. 'Bout the same age as that mummy on *Tales of the Crypt.*"

The cashier gave Geffen a weird look as he handed him his change. Geffen picked up his purchases and ducked into a corner of the store. "Rice, man, stop laughing."

"Gef, I'm signing books, so I can't really talk right now—"

Geffen cut him off—his problems were more important. "You ever spanked a skinny *old* freak before? Rice, what if something falls off her, man?"

"*Whaaaat?*"

"You know, what if I try to spank that ass and one of her old, skinny, wrinkled legs pop off?"

"Man, you trippin'."

"No, I'm serious. She's *old.* Her Social Security number is probably one."

Rice could hardly talk for laughing. "This whole setup was *your* idea, remember? I told you it was wack, but *you* said you'd get us that loan by any means necessary."

"But, Rice, *pahtna,* I can handle most any kind of pressure, but I didn't think it'd be like *this,* dawg. This woman right here would give Freddy Krueger nightmares."

"Gef, you are straight-up trippin'. But, hey, if you can't do it, then call it off. Let's forget about that investment loan, forget about purchasing investment property, forget about making that money."

"Money?" *Money* was always the buzzword for Geffen—it never failed to pump him up and motivate him.

Rice played him like a Spanish guitar. "Yeah, that *money.* You're the one who swore you'd do whatever it takes to become a multimillionaire in the next two years."

Geffen closed his eyes real tight and thought about the money and all the things he wanted to do with it. Geffen had plans, big plans. He got his confidence back.

"Okay, man, I can *do* this. I'm going to get us that loan—I don't care what it takes. I'll spank her till her legs, eyes, teeth—everything—pop off."

Rice said, "Don't get carried away now."

"I'm going to get us that investment loan so we live like the royal-blooded Africans that we are. I can't give up on my dream of owning a Fortune 500 company, and this is the first step."

"Right. Think about that when she asks you to bite her."

"What?"

"I'm just messing with you. Hey, Gef, just do the damn thang," Rice said.

Geffen straightened his Versace collar and strutted back down the aisle of the 7-Eleven, cell phone to his ear. "I got this. I'm going to buy some ACE bandages."

"Bandages? For what?"

"To wrap her old mummy-ass up, so won't nothing fall off." He called to the checker, "Hey, Saddam, where're the ACE bandages?"

Rice couldn't stop laughing. "Gef, go handle your business. I gotta go. Call me later, but spare me the gory details. I ain't tryin' to hear about you getting busy with the Crypt Keeper. Oh, and don't forget, tomorrow's Sunday. We promised our girl Sunnie we'd show up for church, right?"

Geffen asked anxiously, "She found us a place?"

"She said she did, but I don't know if I believe her."

"She can't lie to get us in church. That'd be sacrilegious or something like that."

"Let's just show up and see," Rice said. "We'll know she's lying if she gets too close to the altar and spontaneously combusts."

Geffen threw the ACE bandages on the checkout counter. "Man, if I go through this, she'd *better* have us a property tomorrow. Yeah, I'll be at church."

"Okay, cool. And hey, you might wanna pick up some superglue, too, in case those bandages don't work."

"Yeah, you got jokes. What*eva*." Geffen hung up, paid the cashier, and walked out the door. He stopped and thought about his mother, and how he'd move her grave site to a better place if he got this loan and some property. *This one's for you, Ma.*

He pulled the pint of vodka out of the bag, opened it, and kicked back a fourth of the bottle. Geffen never drank strong alcohol—he valued his brain cells too much—but this qualified as special circumstances. He was willing to sacrifice one or two brain cells for a multimillion-dollar venture.

•　　•　　•

The Barnes & Noble in Palmdale, California, was bustling with customers, mostly women who had driven past the Antelope Valley Mall and the Wal-Mart superstore to come see if author Rice Jordan was anything like the main character in his books. The fictional "Mathis Shade" was a forthright, moral, upstanding family man who had no trouble at all opening himself up and expressing his most intimate feelings to his woman. Mathis was the type of character who believed in honest communication, even if it meant laying his heart open and getting hurt. Women readers assumed Rice *must* be like his main character in order to write him so well. *Yeah, right.*

After listening to him read from his latest novel, *No Game, No Shame,* book-toting readers waited in a long line to have Rice autograph their books.

Rice sat behind a table with a stack of his novels, a permanent marker, and a bottle of Evian. He had on the same plain blue shirt and whitewashed jeans he'd worn for his book cover photo shoot. He was strictly a T-shirt-and-jeans kind of guy, leaving the dressing up for folks who were trying to impress other folks. He wore his hair closely shaved to camouflage those few pesky gray hairs that wanted to spring up and scream *I'm getting old!* even though he was only thirty-two. Despite 20/20 vision, he wore glasses as a tiny shield between him and the women who always tried to look into his eyes to see if he was telling the truth, which half the time he wasn't.

Rice was uncomfortable around people and longed to be back home in his private study. He wished Sunnie were there with him because she had a way of putting him at ease, even amid hoards of strangers milling around staring at him like he was a damn monkey in a cage, expecting him to say something clever and witty every ten damn seconds.

Rice smiled and handed a freshly autographed book to a lady, then waited for the next lady in line. Without looking up, he took her book and opened it. Inside the front cover was a glossy photo of the woman *stark naked*.

He thought to himself, *Okay, now things are getting interesting*. Rice closed the book and looked over his shoulder to see if anyone else had noticed the picture. He looked up at the lady standing in front of him. She looked like Jada Pinkett-Smith with auburn locks.

"Uh, hello," Rice mumbled.

"You're blushing," she said. His eyes immediately fell on her small, perky breasts underneath her thin cashmere blouse. They looked like two acorns trying to push their way out.

He squirmed. "I was, uh, trying not to."

"But you were. Does that mean you like what you see?" She arched her back. The acorns saluted. He broke into a full-fledged grin. A group of bookwormy women with buns, bifocals, and bunions grunted impatiently behind Miss Acorn Breasts.

He cleared his throat, picked up his pen, and opened her book again, but this time he kept the cover halfway closed, hiding the nude photo. "Where should I sign?"

The woman leaned across the table. "Right here."

Her finger landed on her sweet spot in the photo. She leaned closer and whispered a proposition in his ear. He signed the photo and watched her as she walked out of Barnes & Noble, her book tucked under her arm.

Rice signed books for about ten more minutes, but the line remained long and he was eager for his rendezvous with Miss Acorn Breasts, so he began coughing. The store manager rushed and brought him more water. He took a sip and started coughing louder in long hacking, fake coughs.

"Mr. Jordan . . . are you all right?" the manager asked nervously.

"I gotta go," Rice said, coughing and collecting his things.

"But, Mr. Jordan, we need you to keep signing books." Rice pointed to his throat and hacked louder. He threw his coat over his shoulder and waved apologetically at everybody.

The manager was desperate. "But, Mr. Jordan—"

Rice was gone.

He jumped in his car, drove across the parking lot to Baja Fresh Grill, and blinked his headlights twice, just as she'd requested. Miss Acorn rushed out, hopped in his car, and they drove to her condo in West Palmdale, where she let him sign a whole lot more than her photo. At the height of their "signing" session, she screamed out the name of Rice's fictitious male character. "Oh, *Mathis.*"

Rice paused for a second. *What did she just call me?*

Her eyes were closed. "Oh, Mathis Shade, do it, baby. Don't stop."

This was not the first time an enraptured fan had confused him with Mathis Shade, the main character in his novels. Mathis was not only good-looking, he was strong but vulnerable, rough but gentle, worldly but homey—the kind of oxymoronic guy all women claimed they wanted. Rice, the novelist, was nothing like that—not even close. He opted to hide his true self behind the pages of his novel while he reaped the sexual benefits on Mathis Shade's behalf.

Acorn Lady screamed out again, "Don't stop, Mathis. Don't stop."

"Okay, *Mathis* won't stop," Rice said, and did his best to make sure his completely delusional fan was satisfied with his work.

The second she fell asleep, he whipped on his clothes, grabbed his keys, and tiptoed out of her condo.

Rice chuckled, trying to play it off like it didn't really bother him to be called someone else's name as long as he was the one who got the nookie. But underneath his chuckle, that shit really bothered him, made him feel like he was the Invisible Man or something.

During his sixty-five-minute drive south on the 14 and 405 freeways, Rice checked his voicemail. As he passed over the Santa Monica Mountains heading back to his home in Baldwin Hills, he replayed Sunnie's message several times, listening closely: *"Rice, where are you? You're supposed to always answer when you see my caller ID no matter what you're doing. What if this was an emergency? Rice, just be careful, okay?"*

He tried to figure out if Sunnie was actually worried

about him or just taking him for granted, as usual. He called her back but got her voicemail.

He decided to stop by the gym on La Cienega Boulevard, knowing that his boy, Franklin Brass, better known as "Coach," would be there. He needed to remind Coach to show up for church tomorrow.

Coach felt at home amid the muggy smell of rubber mats, damp towels, and body sweat at the 24-Hour Fitness Magic Johnson Sports Club. The gym was packed with well-toned bodies in various shades of brown sweaty skin even after 11 P.M. on a Saturday night. The clinkety-clank of metal machines and iron weights was music to Coach's ear. He was in his usual spot in the southeast corner of the weight room, pumping iron while watching his biceps bulge in the floor-to-ceiling mirror. This was the only place where Coach's beefy chest, muscular buttocks, and bulging thighs blended in with the rest of the athletic bodies.

Coach wasn't expecting to see Rice. Rice looked out of place in his loose-fitting shirt and baggy jeans compared to Coach's muscle shirt, bandana, and sports shorts.

Rice stepped in front of the mirror, and shouted over the noisy equipment, "Nigerian, *please*. Stop looking at yourself."

Coach kept pumping. "What you doing here, Ethiopian? Thought you was out signing romance novels or some girly shit like that."

Rice ignored the comment. "Came by to remind you that tomorrow is Sunday."

"Who are you, the calendar cop?" Coach knew perfectly well what Rice was getting at, but he liked giving people a hard time. Sunnie, their closest female friend, was also a real estate broker and she had coerced them into going to church in exchange for finding them an investment property. But Coach preferred to spend Sunday morning in the gym rehabilitating his injured leg so he could get back out on the football field.

Rice said, "Man, you forgot? We promised our girl Sunnie we'd show up for church."

Coach grumbled. "I ain't going."

"Got to. Sunnie's been trippin' lately. She thinks we're going to get into some kind of trouble."

"What kind of trouble?"

"I have no idea. Anyway, you know our deal—we go to her church, she shows us the property. Besides, we wouldn't want to disappoint Sunnie."

"Like I give a rat's ass 'bout that."

"You know you do. Sunnie's our girl."

Coach didn't deny it. He changed arms and continued doing reps. When Coach worked out, he liked to get into a zone and tune out the rest of the world. It was like intercourse between his mind and his body; his mind told his body what to do and it obeyed, no matter how hard or how painful. He got off on pain and roughness, and he liked to dominate, whether it was on the football field making a tackle or in the bedroom making love, as long as he conquered the task.

Right now his mind was on conquering the leg injury that had sidelined him this season. If he wasn't out there playing, he was nothing. That's the way he saw it.

After a hundred bicep curls, he set the barbell down and lay flat on the bench. He strapped the weight's belt to his left leg and started doing leg curls, pressing his leg muscles against two hundred pounds of iron weights.

"Hey, Big Zulu, that's a lot of weight to put on your injured leg."

Coach gasped for breath, but didn't stop pumping the leg machine. "I-gotta-get-back-in-uniform."

Coach figured Rice couldn't relate to how it felt being a pro athlete sidelined by an injury. He needed to stick to what he did best—type.

Rice kept butting in, messing up Coach's zone. "I know you trying to get off the injured list, but, *whoa*, you're overdoing it."

Coach slammed the weights down and stood up. "It's pro football! There's fifty guys straight outta college itching to put on that Chargers jersey and take my place."

Coach was explosive like that, and when his volcanic temper flared, he was truly intimidating. Rice backed up a bit. A few people around them stopped and looked. Everybody knew Coach and knew what he was about, and nobody would ever get in the big guy's face and question him unless they wanted a beatdown. But Rice wasn't just anybody, he was Coach's lifelong friend.

Rice raised his hands. "You ain't got to yell."

Coach continued, "I ain't 'bout to be replaced. I'm thirty-two years old, man. I still got good years in me, but I gotta get back out on that field. So I gotta *do* this!"

"Okay, okay. I feel you."

Coach calmed down and went back to his leg presses. He knew he shouldn't have blown up like that, but sometimes his adrenaline surged so strong, he couldn't help it.

Coach stopped. "Hey, what time is it?"

"It's eleven thirty. Why?"

"Aw, hell. I gots to get outta here." He unstrapped the weights.

"What's your hurry?"

Coach swooped up his sweaty towel and headed for the showers. "I'm supposed to be somewhere. I'm late."

Rice yelled after him, "Where you going?"

Without pausing, Coach answered, "To a beauty pageant."

Thirty-five minutes later, Coach drove his big black shiny Chevy Suburban to the front of the Embassy Suites Hotel on Airport Boulevard near LAX. He jumped out, tossed his keys to the valet, and grabbed his overnight bag. He hustled through the mustard-colored lobby with the eight-story atrium, swooshed past the elevator, and bounded up the stairs.

Fifteen minutes later, he was lying faceup on a king-size bed with his fingers interlaced behind his head and a thousand-watt smile plastered on his attractive bearded face. Even though he was late, the show couldn't have started without him.

Out walked Miss Tennessee. She pranced across the

berry-colored carpet in the elaborate hotel suite wearing a white ribbon with gold letters diagonally across her chest and nothing else. She sashayed on six-inch-high stiletto heels across the large room to where Coach lay in a black silk robe, his huge bare chest exposed.

"Show me whatcha working with, Ma," he said, bobbing his head to the Ludacris CD playing on the stereo. A fake diamond-studded tiara was on the bed next to him.

She turned around, did a pose, turned back around, did another pose, and dropped it like it was hot. Her lively breasts bounced up and down like crazy on each side of the white ribbon.

"How'd you like that, Daddy? Do I get that crown now?" She reached for the tiara, but Coach quickly snatched it away.

"Slow your roll, woman. You can't win yet—not until you've had a little competition." Miss Tennessee poked out her cranberry-glazed lips, pouting. Coach said, "Move to the side, darlin'," then clapped his hand loudly twice. Out walked Miss Nevada and Miss Indiana. Each wore similar white ribbons, stilettos, and nothing else. Coach turned up the music with the remote while all three contestants did their runway routines across the hotel room floor just for him, droppin' it, poppin' it, and making it clap.

Coach judged all aspects of their routines—physique, confidence, and poise—but it was hard for him to remain objective because Miss Tennessee's breasts reminded him of his two most favorite things in the whole world—two firm, brown, round footballs. And they were pointing straight at him.

He announced, "And the winner is Miss *Titty-See*. I mean, Miss *Tennessee*."

Miss Tennessee jumped up and down, her pigskins scoring one field goal after another in Coach's mind. The other two contestants complained. "How can she win? Her boobs ain't even *real*."

Coach declared, "If I can touch them, then they're *real*. But hey, at this party everybody wins. And to prove it, I'm gonna let all of you share this crown. Now, when I say '*go*,' I want all three of you to dive in and get, but you gotta keep your hands behind your back, okay?" They agreed.

"On your mark." Coach untied his silk robe and opened it. His massive bare chest and muscular body glowed in the red strobe light.

"Get set." He placed the fake crown around a strategic part of his anatomy.

"Go."

All three beauty contestants, a.k.a. groupies, dove in face-first to get their crown.

Chapter 2

BRIGHT AND EARLY SUNDAY MORNING, ALISON DEMILA Clark, better known as "Sunnie," stood on the steps of First Angeles Church of West L.A. checking her watch. It was 7:50 A.M. and she saw no sign of her best friends, Rice, Coach, or Geffen.

"Those three knuckleheads stood me up *again*," she muttered to herself, but kept smiling at the other worshippers as they rushed inside to get a good seat. Sunnie straightened her black pin-dot skirt suit and adjusted her small matching hat over her dark brown permed hair. She popped a Tic Tac in her mouth and checked her watch again.

A loud voice behind her startled her so bad that she swallowed her Tic Tac.

Coach yelled, "Is this supposed to be a church or the Staples Center?"

He swaggered up the church steps, Geffen and Rice

trailing behind him. At the sight of those three lovely gentlemen, Sunnie's heart leapt for joy.

"I was beginning to think you guys weren't going to come."

Coach grumbled, "If it'd been up to me, we wouldn't—"

Rice interjected, "—miss being here. Good morning, Sunnie."

"How you doing, Sunshine?" Geffen added.

"I'm great now that my three favorite guys are here." Sunnie hugged each of them real tight, ending with Coach, who grumbled again.

"Back up off me, woman. Stop interfering with my action," he said, as his eyes latched on to a woman walking by in a tight dress. When the woman noticed the handsome famous pro football player watching her, she dropped her Bible. As she bent over to pick it up, her cleavage burst out the top of her dress. All three guys mouthed a silent *Damn!*

Sunnie cleared her throat loudly to regain their attention. The guys looked handsome, but worn out. "Guess I wasn't the only one who didn't get much sleep last night. You all look tired as heck. Rice, where were you last night?"

"At a book signing in Palmdale."

"How did it go?"

"You know, same ol', same ol'," Rice said evasively. Sunnie knew Rice was hiding something, probably something naughty. She made a mental note to coax it out of him later.

"Coach, what about you?"

Coach yawned, and frowned. "Why are you all up in my business?"

Sunnie gave him a don't-make-me-pinch-you look.

Coach, remembering his night, started grinning. He conceded. "I went to a beauty pageant."

"A *beauty pageant?* Since when do you attend beauty pageants?" Sunnie asked.

"I'm a bit curious about that myself," Rice added.

"I was a judge." Coach grinned even harder. "And I can honestly tell you, every last one of those girls earned that crown. Yes, Lordy!"

"Shush, Big Mouth, and stop using God's name in vain. Besides, I seriously doubt the *Lord* was involved in whatever you did last night." She turned to her other best friend. "Geffen, what about you? Did you get any sleep last night?"

Rice looked at Geffen and smirked like he knew a secret. "Yeah, Gef, tell us, did you *get any* last night?"

Geffen brushed the already clean lapel on his Versace suit, ignoring Rice's insinuation. "You know me, Sunshine, it's always about business." Then he changed the subject. "What did *you* do last night? You look a little stressed yourself."

Coach butted in. "I know what she *didn't* do last night."

Sunnie rolled her eyes, she knew what was coming.

Coach continued, "Plastic Man still ain't hittin' it, huh? That ain't even normal." He shook his head.

The guys had nicknamed Sunnie's boyfriend "Plastic Man" because he was a plastic surgeon. They didn't like him and thought he was a fake, as his nickname suggested. And the fact that he was willing to go along with Sunnie's proclaimed celibacy made them even more suspicious of Marvin, especially Coach, who thought a man's true manliness lay somewhere south of his belly button and north of his knees.

Sunnie protested. "Coach, a man and a woman can enjoy each other's company without '*hittin' it*,' as you so crudely put it. And yes, it is normal. It's called *abstinence*."

Coach played dumb. "*Abstinence?* What's that? Some kind of new disease? They got a cure for that?"

Sunnie defended Marvin. "My loving boyfriend just so happens to share my decision to abstain from sex until after marriage."

"Either he's lying or something's wrong with him," Coach said flatly. He nudged Rice and made a crude hand gesture. "Either the gun ain't loaded or it don't shoot straight, *ya-know-what-I'm-saying?*"

"Don't start with me, Coach." Sunnie looked to Geffen and Rice for help, but they shrugged, tending to agree with Coach. "Not *all* men think with their *little* head."

"Sho' you right," Coach said, appearing to agree with Sunnie. "Like me, for instance, I don't have a little head. Both of mine are *big*." Coach laughed and knocked knuckles with the guys.

Sunnie huffed. "Okay, look, I know you guys think Dr. Marvin Stubblefield is a fake, but—"

Rice interrupted. "As fake as Michael Jackson's face."

"—but he's not. He's just—"

Geffen interrupted. "Fake as a ten-dollar Rolex."

"—sensitive, he's understanding, he's—"

Coach interrupted. "Fake as an albino with a suntan."

"—considerate, he's patient. . . . My boyfriend is not a *fake*," she yelled. A few people stopped and looked at Sunnie, who covered her mouth, embarrassed. Finally, she gave up. "Fine. I don't care if you guys don't like Marvin. He's *my* boyfriend."

Geffen said, "You're right, Sunshine. All that matters is that you believe in him." But she could tell he didn't really mean it.

Rice put his hands in his pocket and hesitated before saying, "Hey, Sunnie, I've been meaning to ask you about something. I saw Plastic Man down at the Fox Hills Mall the other day. He was shopping—"

"—for a nookie sale." Coach interrupted, laughing.

Sunnie slapped his arm. "Hush, Coach. Go on, Rice. You saw Marvin shopping—*and?*"

Rice suddenly looked lost, like he wished he hadn't brought it up. "Nothing." He looked at his watch. "Shouldn't we head inside?"

Sunnie agreed. "Yes, let's go in." She tucked her purse under her arm and caught Rice and Geffen by the hand.

Coach dragged his feet behind them, complaining the whole way in. "I hope this ain't one of those churches that last all damn day long. I ain't staying up in here past ten, that's my limit. So you can tell the preacher right now, don't get carried away. It ain't like they serving us lunch up in here. Shoot, I'm already hungry. If they hook us up with some BBQ ribs and some pinto beans, now that's a different story. . . ."

• • •

The sanctuary inside First Angeles Church reminded Sunnie of a concert hall. The theaterlike seating consisted of over a hundred ascending rows of cushiony seats in a semicircle around the center stage. The floor was covered in thick, plush carpet and tasteful arrangements of white flowers with lush green foliage lined the steps leading up to the altar. Seating for a large choir was located behind the podium.

But Sunnie didn't come for the choir, she came for the preaching. She was hoping the preacher would say something to convince these guys to stop chasing women and playing with their emotions. This Sunday was particularly special because Bishop T. D. Jakes was the guest speaker, visiting from his home church, The Potter's House, in Dallas, Texas.

The place was packed. Sunnie was glad she'd asked Mother Roby to save four seats in the front row. As they walked to their seats, Coach complained. "Why we gotta sit so close? What if this guy spits when he preaches?"

Coach absolutely refused to sit in the front row. He made a man who was sitting in the second row get up and exchange seats with him.

Sunnie sat down quietly with Rice and Geffen on the front row next to Mother Roby, while Coach sat directly behind Sunnie, purposely bumping the back of her seat with his knee.

The guys greeted Mother Roby, then made uncomfortable small talk among themselves and waited for the service to begin.

"Give me some sugar, Alison, baby," Mother Roby

said. Sunnie leaned over and kissed her cheek. She laughed. "I see some things never change," she said, referring to Coach who'd always given Sunnie a hard time, since high school.

Mother Roby was the sweetest, most caring person Sunnie had ever known. She had stepped in and mothered Sunnie when Sunnie's adoptive parents failed to find time for her. Mother Roby lived on the same block in Compton as Sunnie, Rice, and Coach's parents.

As Sunnie grew up, Mother Roby was the one who taught her about life's intricacies, such as love, friendship, sex, and God. And when Sunnie stepped out of line, it was Mother Roby who cared enough to scold her. Sunnie was by no means a perfect adolescent—she did some rebelling. Even in her twenties, she took a while to finally come around on the "sex" and the "God" part, but Mother Roby was as happy as a bowl of jellybeans when Sunnie finally started coming to church with her last year.

Mother Roby asked Sunnie, "Have you told your friends about your gift yet?"

"Shh. They'll hear you." Sunnie peeked around to see if the guys were listening. They weren't. She shook her head. "No, they'll think I'm crazy."

"Child, tell them anyway. You have a very special gift of discerning spirits. You can sense evil that other folks don't even know exists. And since you think those three guys are heading for trouble, you may be the one who saves their behinds." Sunnie exhaled real hard. Mother Roby scolded her. "Child, stop acting like your gift is a curse. It's a blessing."

"But it scares me."

"Well, look on the bright side. It ain't like you see dead people," she joked. Then added, "But seriously, Alisun, those strange feelings you get is the Holy Spirit speaking to you. And you'd better listen, for your sake and for theirs."

Sunnie sighed. Mother Roby took her hand. "Just slow down and learn to listen to those inklings. Okay?"

Sunnie smiled despite her confusion. "I'll try, Mother Roby. I'll try."

A half hour into the service, Bishop T. D. Jake's baritone voice boomed through the giant auditorium. Beads of sweat dripped off his thick forehead, his burly neck bulged over his crisp white collar. He purposely stuttered on certain phrases to emphasize his point.

"Some of you think that what you don't know *can't* hurt you? Well, you'd better think again. Sometimes it's the things that you *don't* see that can hurt you the most."

"Tell it, preacher!" the crowd shouted.

"You think you're sinning and getting away with it, but you ain't getting away with nothing. Things are going on behind the scenes. It's only God's grace that's keeping things from erupting right in your face. But don't mistake God's grace for a dirty old doormat that you can wipe your feet on and keep on truckin'." The bishop hoisted his robust body over the smooth velvety carpet in a feet-wiping motion, like the moonwalk. The crowd went crazy.

The bishop's words were powerful and penetrating,

like bullets from a machine gun as he spit out truths and held nothing back. "Sin has consequences. Sometimes you reap what you sow."

Wow, that ought to catch the guys' attention, Sunnie thought as she peeked at them. Rice was chewing gum and had a detached look on his face. Geffen kept fiddling with his PDA on the sly, checking his appointments. She looked back at Coach. When he saw her looking, he yawned real big and loud.

After a while, the bishop slowed his tempo. He told everyone to sit back down and to listen carefully. He lowered his voice, wiped his sweaty forehead with a white handkerchief, and walked in slow, labored steps toward the center of the stage. His expression, serious and somber, was like God was whispering in his ear and he was translating.

He stopped directly in front of Sunnie. He seemed to be looking directly at the guys. Sunnie blinked. He *was* looking directly at the guys.

The bishop leaned forward, exhaled real hard, and looked over the top of his wire-rimmed glasses at them.

He said, "Slow your roll, *playas.* Life ain't one big game. Some of the things you do just for fun can backfire on you."

Sunnie's stomach did a somersault. The weird vibe she would get lately when the guys bragged about their sexcapades was back. *Is this preacher feeling the same thing about these guys as me?* she wondered. *This is spooky.*

The bishop continued. "Don't keep going down that same path. Turn around before it's too late." Then he left them with these ominous words: "If you keep knocking on the wrong door, eventually the devil's gonna answer."

After what seemed like a hot eternity, they were dismissed.

After kissing Mother Roby good-bye, Sunnie walked with the guys to the parking lot. When they got to her yellow Saab, her heart was still pounding.

"Was that dude talking to *us?*" Coach asked in his overdefensive way.

They all stood silent, thinking. Sunnie wanted to speak up and to tell them about her *gift*, but she was too nervous.

Finally, Geffen clapped his hand and got everybody's attention. "Hel-*looo*, Africans, let's snap back to reality. That man was not talking to us."

Rice agreed. "Right. He doesn't even *know* us."

Sunnie turned to Rice. "But maybe he had a feeling or something. Sometimes a person can have feelings . . . like me. I've been having, uh, feelings about *you.*"

Surprise flashed across Rice's face. "You have feelings . . . about *me?*" He stuck his hands deep inside his pockets and started rattling his keys, a nervous habit.

Sunnie explained, "I've been having feelings about *all* of you." When she said that, Rice looked disappointed. Sunnie didn't know why, and at the moment she was too preoccupied to try to figure it out. Rice popped a gummy bear in his mouth and looked away.

Coach frowned. "What you doing having feelings 'bout me?"

"Not *that* kind of feeling. I mean, I feel like you guys are heading for danger, the way you guys chase women and always follow your lusts."

"Oh yeah?" Coach rubbed his chin like he was thinking real deep, then he shrugged. "Sorry. I don't see nothing wrong with that."

Sunnie was getting frustrated. "Listen, this is *serious*. I'm telling you this because I *care* about you guys. And I'm scared."

Coach wasn't taking her seriously, Rice was ignoring her, and Geffen was looking impatient.

Geffen said, "Hey, Sunshine, we know you care, but stop worrying about us because ain't nothing going on but the rent. Whatever that preacher was selling, we're not buying." He looked at his watch. "And speaking of buying, it's about that time. Let's go see that property you found for us."

"Property?" Sunnie was so caught up, she'd completely forgotten about the property she hadn't found for them.

Geffen flipped open his PDA to check off this appointment. "That was the point of us coming here, right?"

"Uh-uh . . ." Sunnie stammered.

Coach slapped his hard abs. "Yeah, let's go 'cause I'm getting hungry."

Geffen walked around to the passenger side of Sunnie's yellow Saab. "C'mon. We'll take your car." She stood there, mouth open but nothing coming out.

Rice was the first to pick up on her body language. Of all the guys, he knew her signals the best. "You lied, huh? You didn't find us a property."

Geffen froze. Coach stopped, too. All three guys stared at Sunnie.

"Okay, look, guys. It's not like I intentionally lied, I just—"

Geffen cut to the chase. "Did you find us a place or not?"

"Well, I found a—Well . . . No, not exactly, but—"

"Then you did lie." Geffen flipped his PDA closed and shook his head, looking seriously disappointed in her.

"Gef, I didn't find the *right* place, but I still wanted you to come to church. Don't be mad at me."

"I just wasted a whole morning." Geffen started walking away.

Coach put his finger in her face. "You're wrong, woman." He started walking away, too.

Rice stood a moment longer, locking eyes with Sunnie. He was disappointed, too—about more than just the property—but all Sunnie could think was that her friends were mad at her and leaving.

"Rice, I—"

"Go home, Sunnie," he said, and starting leaving, too.

"Guys! Wait! C'mon, don't just leave me like this." Sunnie couldn't stand when they were mad at her, and she really hated being left alone.

In desperation she said, "Okay, stop!" She walked into the middle of the parking lot and failed to notice the red Jaguar XK8 convertible fast approaching behind her. "I'll take you to the house!"

As soon as she said "house," there was a loud

screech. The red Jag slammed on its breaks and skidded. Sunnie turned and screamed. All the guys jerked around.

Rice ran for Sunnie. "Watch out!" He grabbed Sunnie and the Jaguar swerved, missing Sunnie by inches. Rice held her real tight, shaking from fear and anger. The car came to a stop, but Rice continued holding on to Sunnie.

He yelled at the driver. "Hey! Watch where you're going, you stupid son of a—" He recognized the driver. *"Charlotta?"*

Coach recognized her, too. "Were you trying to hit Sunnie? Woman, have you finally lost your mind?!"

"Isn't that one of her old friends?" Geffen asked.

Rice told him, "That's Charlotta Haynes, and they're not friends. She's been Sunnie's rival since the tenth grade, competing over dudes and stupid stuff like that."

Charlotta hopped out of her brand-new, shiny red Jaguar wearing a rabbit-skin skirt that hugged her slim hips like a glove. "Why are you all yelling at me? Sunnie stepped out in front of *my car!*"

"Slow your ass down!" Coach yelled. "This is a parking lot, not the damn 405 Freeway!"

Sunnie hadn't seen Charlotta for months, but as soon as she laid eyes on her Barbie doll–sized figure, her naturally red wavy hair, her brownish yellow skin, and hazel eyes, all of those old feelings of female competition and rivalry came rushing back. Here she was, a grown-ass thirty-year-old woman, successful in her own right and pretty darn good-looking herself in a

Gabrielle Union sort of way, yet she wanted to run up and yank Charlotta by her hair and scratch her eyes out for stealing her first boyfriend back in the tenth grade.

Sunnie screamed, *"You tried to run me over."*

Charlotta razzed, "Believe me, if I'd wanted to hit your big bubble butt, I would've done it *easily.*"

Sunnie scrambled away from Rice and tried to grab a fistful of that wavy red hair, but Rice grabbed her again.

"Sunnie, hey. Stop it. Why do you let her get to you like that? This isn't high school. Grow up." Rice turned to Charlotta. "You too. You're still jealous of Sunnie."

"Jealous?" Charlotta huffed, "Of that cleanup woman?"

"Cleanup woman?" Sunnie pulled her arm out of Rice's grip. She took a deep breath and tried to remember that she'd given her heart to God, but Charlotta was bringing out the old *unredeemed* Sunnie right now, and *that* Sunnie wanted to kick her ass. "Let's get one thing straight—you didn't leave Marvin, Marvin dumped *you* because of your ho-ish ways. I didn't clean up behind you."

Charlotta yelled, "Sloppy seconds."

Sunnie lunged for Charlotta again. Rice grabbed hold of Sunnie.

Coach told Rice, "Let her go handle her business, man." He motioned to Sunnie. "Go put shorty in a headlock—you know, how I taught you." He made a WWF locking move with his big forearm. Sunnie looked ready to do it. Charlotta took off her right shoe and reared it back, pointing the spiked heel at Sunnie, ready for her.

But Rice wouldn't let go of Sunnie's arm. "Sunnie, stop selling yourself short. Charlotta is jealous of *you*."

Charlotta waved her long nails at him. "No, Rice, you've got it twisted. Sunnie's jealous of *me*."

Rice moved Sunnie behind him. "No, Charlotta, I got it straight. Yeah, I admit you look good on the outside in a *shallow* sort of way. But Sunnie's the real deal, through and through. Her problem is she don't know it."

Charlotta scowled at Rice, making her attractive face ugly. "Everybody *luuuuvs* Sunnie. Puh-*leese*. Sunnie ain't all that. Y'all are just blinded by the light."

Sunnie noticed people had gathered in the parking lot to watch them. She hoped Mother Roby hadn't seen her acting a fool and ready to fight right after getting out of church. Embarrassed, Sunnie calmed down, smoothed down her suit, and straightened her small hat.

But Charlotta had no shame and wasn't finished yet. "Well, let me tell all you folks. She's not a *real* as you think. Sunnie's done her share of dirt."

Uh-oh. Sunnie knew Charlotta was right, but no one was supposed to know about the dirty prank she'd pulled that finally convinced Marvin to leave Charlotta. Sunnie didn't feel good about what she'd done, and she knew the way they competed for a man's love was crazy, but Sunnie *needed* to win.

Rice said to Charlotta, "You've got no dirt on Sunnie."

"I can't prove it yet, but just wait." Charlotta pinned her hazel eyes on Sunnie. "I'm going to get you back, and believe me, it's going to hurt worse than what you did to me."

Charlotta put her shoe back on, tugged her rabbit-skin skirt and glanced at Geffen to see if he was watching. As she got back in her Jag, she paused.

"Oh, one more thing. Everyone knows how bad you want to marry Marvin, but don't get your hopes up, girly. Marvin's never gonna marry you. *Never*, as in 'It *ain't* gonna happen.'"

Charlotta puckered her lips and blew Sunnie a sour kiss, then turned to Geffen and blew him a real one. She peeled out of the church's parking lot, burning rubber.

Charlotta's words hit Sunnie hard. She *did* want to marry Marvin, more than anything. They'd been together six months, and she was happy. The kind of love that goes deeper than friendship was finally within reach after years of fumbling, and she wanted to seal the deal with marriage. She'd been giving Marvin clues, dropping hints, cutting wedding pictures from magazines, but he didn't seem to be getting it. Charlotta was right. Sunnie stood in front of Rice and the guys and tried hard not to cry.

Rice saw how hurt she was. He buried his hands deep inside his pockets and looked away.

Geffen rubbed her shoulder. "Hey, c'mon now, Sunshine, cheer up. You don't need that guy. When I make my first mil, I'm going to buy you a brand-new Jag ten times sportier than hers."

Coach shook his head. "You shoulda put that trick in a headlock when you had the chance."

In a somber voice, Rice asked, "Why do you want to marry that guy?"

"'Cause I don't want to be alone anymore." She sniffed back a tear.

"*Alone?* You think you're *alone?*"

"I *am* alone. I don't have anyone who loves me like *that.*"

"Like *what?*"

"Enough to marry me." Sunnie started to cry.

Rice put his head back and gazed up at the sky. Looking back at Sunnie, he said, "Don't cry, Sunnie. Congratulations," he said.

She sniffed. "What do you mean?"

Rice paused. "I saw your boyfriend at Fox Hills Mall inside Zales Jewelers. He was buying you an engagement ring."

Sunnie's eyes widened and she stopped breathing temporarily. Finally, it sunk in and she grabbed Rice, hugging him and jumping up and down at the same time.

Rice sighed. "Guess you can finally stop chasing after what you think you're missing."

Chapter 3

A TYPICAL SUNDAY MORNING DRIVE FROM THE LAID-BACK strip malls of West L.A. to the fashion-conscious, avant-garde boutiques of Beverly Hills would normally take about twenty minutes, but it only took Sunnie fifteen. She was excited, yapping all the way about marrying Marvin. She sped north on Santa Monica Boulevard through Westwood, rushed past the twin towers in Century City, and ran a red light near the Los Angeles Country Club.

She asked Rice, "Why'd you take so long to tell me Marvin bought me a ring?"

Rice didn't have an answer. In fact, he wasn't saying a whole lot of anything since they'd left the church. He slouched in the backseat, looking out the window, giving fictitious names to people waiting at corners and bus stops. Sunnie knew that was his habit when something was bugging him.

Rice looked out the window at a homeless woman

standing near the corner of Camden Drive. She was drinking Evian and carrying a raggedy old overstuffed Yves St. Laurent bag. "Phoebe," he called out, thinking the name appropriate for her snooty posturing, despite her predicament.

"An upper-class transient," Geffen joked. "Only in Beverly Hills."

Hearing the words *Beverly Hills* brought back images of the creepy old mansion and killed Sunnie's mood. She had only agreed to take them there out of desperation, but now she regretted her quick decision. Something about that house made her feel uncomfortable.

Slowing the car Sunnie said, "Hey, fellas . . . about this house. I don't think you'll like it. I mean, it's old, it's run-down. Heck, I don't even know if I'll be able to find the owners who abandoned it, so let's just turn around, okay?"

Geffen objected. "Are you kidding me, Sunshine? I'm loving this location, so keep driving."

She continued up Coldwater Canyon into the true hills of Beverly. The road wound alongside trees and woody shrubbery. The multimillion-dollar estates grew sparser the farther they went up into the mountains.

Just when it seemed that the inhabited area had run out, Sunnie made a sharp left turn. She drove her yellow Saab slowly along a narrow, gravelly road teetering on the edge of the Santa Monica Mountains National Recreation Area. This road-less-traveled covered with fallen leaves and overgrown brush snaked its way up toward the old mansion. The area was dark even in the daytime due to the tall, dense trees, and it was so secluded it felt cut off from the rest of the world.

Coach asked, "Are we still in Beverly Hills?"

"Are we still in *civilization?*" Rice asked.

Geffen said, "These canyons were here long before Rodeo Drive existed. In fact, those streets were built around these mountains. A man named Edward L. Doheny discovered oil in L.A. in 1892, then bought a four-hundred-acre parcel of land, now known as Beverly Hills, in 1912." Sunnie wasn't surprised that Geffen knew a thing or two about the topographical history of Los Angeles. Geffen knew a thing or two about a lot of things, especially if money was involved.

"Thus the infamous Doheny Drive," Sunnie said, flatly.

"Yeah. They had oil, but they needed water. A few years later, a cat named William Mulholland brought the DWP up here and built a reservoir bringing water from the Owens Valley."

"Mulholland Drive." Sunnie stared straight ahead.

"No doubt. And that water and oil is what transformed L.A. from a small town into a major metropolis."

Coach grunted and rubbed his stomach. "I didn't ask for a damn history lesson, Bro-Fuscious. You wanna impress me, show me a freakin' Fatburger's up here in these damn canyons."

Rice sat up in his seat and strained his neck to look around. The darkness and the trees had gotten his attention. "Sunnie, how the heck did you find this place?"

"By accident. I took a wrong turn."

When the mansion finally came into view amid the bent trees and dense foliage, Sunnie's gut leapt. "There it is," she said real low, holding her stomach.

Rice strained to look. "Where?" Rice couldn't see it. Neither could Coach or Geffen.

Coach said, "I don't see nothing but trees."

"Right *there*." Sunnie pointed straight ahead as she drove several feet closer. "Look."

Finally, the guys saw the house. The old, enormous structure was crammed into the hillside and buried beneath tall pines, overgrown oaks, and bushy evergreens. Dense foliage climbed along the sides of the old house and clung to its walls like a stubborn disease. Riotous weeds prevented any would-be walking path, and a small conglomerate of the droopiest weeping willows Sunnie'd ever seen shielded the front of the house like they were trying to hide it.

"Damn. Can hardly see it till you get right up on it," Coach said.

Rice frowned at all the shrubbery. "There's got to be a whole lot of spiders in those bushes. I *hate* spiders."

Sunnie just sat there staring at the mansion, hoping it would disappear.

Geffen was eager. "Turn off the car so we can get out."

"No," Sunnie said, without taking her eyes off the place. Geffen laughed and reached over to try to turn the engine off, but Sunnie blocked his hand and hit the automatic door locks, locking everybody in. "Look, fellas, this was a bad idea. I don't know what it is, but I've got a bad feeling about this place."

Geffen tried to reach over her to unlock the doors, but she blocked his hand. "C'mon, Sunshine, stop tripping. Open the door."

"Wait. You guys wouldn't listen to me earlier when I tried to explain my gift to you, but—"

Coach pushed the back of Sunnie's seat. "I'm too hungry for you to be playing games. Let's go see this damn place so we can go eat."

"Turn the engine off, Sunshine." Geffen said calmly, then switched off the ignition, took the keys, and grabbed a flashlight from her glove compartment. Geffen jumped out of the car.

"Gef! Wait!" Sunnie tried to stop him. Geffen hurried up to the front door. Coach and Rice got out and followed him, crunching dried leaves and twigs the whole way.

Sunnie didn't want to get out of the car, but she didn't want to stay out there by herself either. "Guys, wait!"

She looked to her right and to her left. The tree branches were so long and scraggily they looked like hands reaching out to grab her. She got out and ran, tripping through the thickets, to catch up with the guys. By the time she reached them, Geffen had already pulled a small metal lock pick from his shirt pocket and had begun picking the old rusty padlock on the front door.

"Gef, I haven't even contacted the owner yet," Sunnie said. "We can't go any farther than this. Without the owner's permission, we could get in serious trouble."

The padlock fell open, and Geffen smiled. "Who'll know?"

"I could lose my real estate license over this."

Geffen pushed the door. It creaked on its dilapidated hinges and slowly opened. He motioned for Coach to go in first. "After you, Big Zulu."

Coach grumbled, "Negro, you trying to get me arrested for TWB?"

They all looked at Coach. "TWB?"

" 'Trespassing While Black.' This is Beverly Hills, man. They've got their own little police force, drive their own fleet of BMWs, and every last one of them looks like Mark Fuhrman."

"Relax, Big Man." Geffen had a cool smile on his face. "We'll take a quick look around, then be out."

Geffen stepped inside first and clicked on the flashlight. Coach followed him. Sunnie and Rice both paused at the doorway, with Rice waiting on Sunnie.

"Rice, don't go in there."

"Why not?"

"Because . . . you just shouldn't."

Rice starting stepping in. "Guess we all do things we shouldn't do."

"Wait." Sunnie pulled his arm. "Remember what that preacher said: 'If you keep knocking on the wrong door, eventually the devil's gonna answer.'"

"And?"

"I think it applies here."

"That's crazy."

"Why is it crazy?"

" 'Cause Gef picked the lock, we didn't knock." Rice

pulled away and started walking inside. "Besides, *you* don't take everything in the Bible seriously."

"How can you say that? I *do*."

"Yeah? Well, maybe next week they'll preach about casting your pearls before swine."

"What's that supposed to mean?"

"Ask Marvin." Rice went inside.

Sunnie refused to cross that threshold. Something churned and shimmied deep down in the pit of her stomach, and it wouldn't let her step forward. Rice doubled back. "You coming?"

"No." Sunnie stood outside the door and tried to look brave.

Rice glanced over her shoulder. "Suit yourself. But be warned, I just saw something move in that bush behind you."

Sunnie jumped and ran inside, straight into Rice's arms. He chuckled and pulled her the rest of the way until they caught up with Geffen and Coach.

Geffen and Coach were standing inside the huge dusty foyer, letting their eyes adjust to the darkness.

"Guys, I feel funny, but not ha-ha funny," she said, but no one was listening to her. They were too preoccupied with what they saw.

Geffen was mesmerized. "This place is huge."

He led the way out of the foyer and into an enormous receiving room. A humongous vaulted cathedral ceiling loomed above their heads. The house's interior looked as if time had lapsed at an abnormally fast pace and had taken its occupants by surprise. A thick, grayish white layer of dust covered the once classic brothel-type furniture. Elaborate velvet curtains, now moth-ridden and threadbare, covered each eight-foot-high window. Hoary spiderwebs stuck like cotton candy to the fancy candelabras and chandeliers.

"Damn," Rice said, looking at the layers and layers of spiderwebs. "I *hate* spiders."

"It's cold up in here," Coach grumbled.

Sunnie shivered, and without waiting to be asked, Rice draped his arms around her. But that didn't help much because the cold that Sunnie felt went more than skin deep; it was a bone-chilling cold.

Trying to stay calm, she whispered, "I don't think this house is particularly warm and friendly."

Geffen pressed through the atrium and went deeper into the house.

"Nonsense, Sunshine. Any property that can bring a five, or possibly ten, percent return on our investment automatically qualifies as warm and friendly."

They followed him up a massive set of stone steps. Sunnie was watching the shadows extra close. "I don't think this place wants to be disturbed."

Geffen turned and made a *duh* face at Sunnie. "It's a *house,* Sunshine. Houses don't have emotions."

He entered a capacious room and shined his flashlight on an old brass bed frame. "What have we here?"

It was draped by an oversize, moth-eaten red velvet bedspread. The once-thick red carpet had withered to threadbare. Four red lamp shades sat atop old metal lamp stands that stood in each corner of the room.

Geffen walked over to the bed. Hanging on the bedpost were a pair of deteriorating lace women's panties, the old-fashioned kind with the garter belt attached, along with a wire-cup bra with holes at both nipples. He used his lock pick to hold up the bra and shined the flashlight on it.

Geffen wisecracked, "Guess they used this room for Bible study."

Coach walked over to the table between the bed and an old-fashioned corner sink. "Gef, shine that light over here. There's some stuff on this."

Rice joined them in inspecting the items on it. There were an antique oil lamp, two empty vintage brandy bottles, an old cigarette pack, an ashtray containing butts with traces of red lipstick, Cuban cigars, an antique Vaseline jar, an opium bottle, an antique condom tin, and a timer.

"Whoa." Rice picked up the condom tin. "There was some serious conjugating going on in here."

Coach tapped the timer. "No overtime without penalty. Dang. A whorehouse."

"Correction, a high-class, private brothel," Geffen said.

"Like I said, a whorehouse." Coach threw the timer on the bed frame.

"Let's get out of here." Sunnie tried to grab the flashlight, but Geffen quickly changed the hand he held it in.

"Wait," Geffen said, "this is getting interesting. No shame in free enterprise. Let's see what other secrets this place has."

Geffen was as excited as a little boy in a toy factory. He left that room and went into the hallway, quickly moving from one room to the next while the others followed close behind.

Rice yelled, "Slow up, man. You got the light and we can't see."

Geffen led the way down a dark hallway, up more steps, and into another long hallway with eight doors. Geffen opened one of the doors.

"Bedrooms. Look at these babies." He opened more doors. "This is unbelievably perfect. We can turn this section into an upscale bed-and-breakfast for execs who fly into L.A. for business. This place is close to everything and it's private enough for those paranoid bourgeois celebs who think the paparazzi are after them. Their delusions of grandeur can put money in our pockets."

"Geffen," Sunnie said, huffing, out of breath and feeling woozy. "You are getting way ahead of yourself. We don't even know who owns this place. Let's just go before—"

Before she could complete her sentence, Geffen left that hallway and darted into a main room that was larger than all the others put together.

"Africans, picture this." Geffen shined his flashlight along the walls of the oval-shaped room and up toward the indoor 360 degrees of balconies that overlooked it. "A dance floor down here, a DJ booth up there. Bar over there. This is *perfect*. We can rent it out for exclusive, private parties and charge a grip. With my connections, I can book rappers, record execs, and PR people who are always looking for a private place to throw parties. With the right ambience and word of mouth, we can make a killing in this baby."

Coach threatened, "If you don't hold up with that flashlight, I'm about to make a killing."

Geffen ignored Coach's threat and hurried down a corridor and into what looked like a recreation room. Coach grumbled but quickly followed.

Geffen told Coach, "Hey, Moroccan, here's your future gym. Look over there. A sauna. Over there, an indoor pool room. We can rent all this out."

Sunnie saw Coach start to grin. "Yeah, now I can get with this right *here*. Sex and exercise. The old owners had their priorities straight." Coach stomped around the room crunching pieces of plaster under his foot.

Rice pointed up at the high ceiling. "What're those things up there?"

A series of elaborate wooden beams crisscrossed a massive center and formed five triangular points around the edges of what appeared to be a star.

"It's a pentagram," Sunnie said, the words making her stomach quiver.

Rice shook his head. "No, not that. Those things up there hanging underneath that beam."

Rice guided Geffen's flashlight up to what looked like a bunch of oblong Christmas ornaments hanging below the rails. They were black.

"I thought I saw one move," Rice said.

"Yeah, right," Sunnie said. "I'm not falling for that trick again."

Coach picked up a piece of plaster and pitched it like Sammy Sosa, hitting one of the small black objects. They all began to fly.

"*Bats!* Oh, shit!" Coach yelled.

Umpteen dozen red-eyed, wet-fanged bats let out a high-pitched squeal and took off flying in a wild, mad frenzy above their heads.

"Aaaahhh!" Coach, Rice, Sunnie, and Geffen screamed and took off for the door.

Coach beat everybody out. They barreled down two sets of stone steps, through three hallways, and ran out an old creaky side door that Coach didn't bother to open—he just rammed his shoulder into it and took it off its rusty hinges.

They spilled outside into a courtyard on the east side of the property, breathing hard and hanging on each other.

Coach's big chest heaved up and down. He looked around, lost. "Where the hell are we?"

The cobblestone brick clearing was filled with park benches and trellises, probably once beautifully draped with climbing flowers, but now strangled by angry-looking dead, thorny weeds.

Coach demanded, "Sunnie, take us back to the front. It's time to get the hell outta here."

"For once, I agree with you, Coach." Sunnie turned to go, but Geffen caught her arm.

"Wait a sec. Those were only bats. So what?"

Coach put his finger in Geffen's face. *"So what?* Negro, let me tell you something. When I was ten years old, I spent the summer with my uncle Rufus in the projects. He had rats. Big-ass *rats*. One night I woke up, one was on my arm. That *mug* was about to *bite* me. The next night I slept with Uncle Rufus's cane and waited. When it showed up again, I swung the hook part of that cane so hard, I tore up that whole god-damn apartment, but I got that mug. I *hate* rats. As far as I'm concerned, a bat ain't nothing but a pissed-off rat with wings. A goddamn rat with *wings*. It don't get no worse than that."

Geffen backed away from Coach. "Whoa, Samson, you're obviously having a flashback. All I'm saying is, don't let a few winged rodents keep you from seeing the big picture. Bats can be taken care of. All we need is an exterminator."

"More like a *terminator*." Rice corrected him. "Those were some mean-looking suckas."

Geffen tried to get them to refocus. "Whatever we need, we can get it. But right now, let's think of the moneymaking potential here."

Sunnie cleared her throat. "Look, guys, let me remind you of two things. First, this place is beyond creepy, it's one step above purgatory. Second, it's a mess."

Geffen, Mr. Optimistic, objected. "It's a fixer-upper. It needs a little work."

"It needs a wrecking ball," Sunnie said.

Rice pried Sunnie's hand from his shirt. "Sunnie's right. This place is whipped."

"And it's got *bats*." Coach said, his gaze scanning the weeds.

"More important"—Sunnie stepped out of Coach's way—"it has a really, really bad vibe to it."

Geffen checked his pocket to make sure he hadn't dropped his PDA. "No, Sunshine, houses are concrete, brick, wood, nails, that's all. They don't have vibes.

You're a businesswoman, a top-selling real estate broker. You should be able to *smell* the potential pay dirt here."

Sunnie sniffed. "All I smell is dirt."

Coach kicked over a bush. "Yeah, dirt and some damn *bats*."

Geffen reasoned, "Okay, then think about your fat commission check if you pull this deal together."

"Some things are more important than a commission check." Sunnie smoothed down Rice's shirt where she'd scrunched it. "Like friends."

"Aha." Coach pulled a big stick out of the bushes and gripped it like a baseball bat. "I got something for those damn bats."

Geffen punched numbers into his PDA, mumbling, "Friends help friends get rich."

Coach took a few practice swings in the air with the stick. "I'm ready now."

Rice asked Sunnie, "Why'd you bring us here if you thought this place had bad *vibes?*"

"So you wouldn't think I lied just to get you to church. I *had* found a place, just not the right place. But I figured once you guys took one look at this dump, you'd want to leave. I didn't think you'd actually break in." She threw Geffen a look.

"I agree with old-girl," Coach said, looking over his shoulder. "This place is a shit hole. And I ain't trying to get bit by no bat."

Geffen pointed his stylus at Coach. "Big Zulu warrior chief, I'm disappointed in you, man. Buggin' out over a few little bats. Thought you wasn't scared of nothing." Geffen, the college psychology minor, played his pal.

"I *ain't* scared of nothing. If it can bleed, I can kick its ass." Coach flexed his biceps. Geffen ducked as Coach took another practice swing. "But I ain't trying to get bit by no bat."

Sunnie noticed Rice starting to wander away. "Rice, where are you going?"

"There's a cellar over here." Rice pulled open the small creaky door and peeked inside. "I need inspiration for my next mystery novel. Gef, toss me your flashlight. I'm gonna go check it out."

As soon as Sunnie saw the cellar door, a strong surge jolted through her body. She couldn't move. She was speechless.

Coach yelled at Rice. "Negro, get your ass back here."

Rice ignored him and stepped down into the small dark passageway. The door slammed closed behind him with a loud creak and a swirl of dust.

Coach shook his head. "Famous last words from the ignorant brotha in every horror flick: 'I'ma go check it out.'" Coach mocked Rice in a doofus voice.

Geffen noticed Sunnie's sudden paralysis. "Sunshine, you all right?"

Coach looked back at her. "What the hell's wrong with you, woman?"

Two words spilled from Sunnie's mouth. "My dream."

Geffen asked, "Your dream?"

Sunnie swallowed hard. "I've been having bad dreams. I think it's connected to my gift."

Geffen patted her back. "C'mon, Sunshine, quit trippin'."

Coach said, "Dreams don't mean nothing. I dreamed about Beyoncé last night." He held up his hand and looked around. "Where she at? She ain't here 'cause it wasn't nothing but a dream."

Coach turned and pointed toward the cellar. "Now, your boy going down there in that cellar like a damn fool—that's real." Coach shouted after Rice, "Hey, Kumba, don't you know the colored guy is always the first to get his head bit clean off?"

Geffen reminded Coach, "We're all colored here."

"A dark meat buffet, that's what I'm talking about." Coach hit the trellis with his stick. His stick broke.

Sunnie grabbed both Geffen and Coach by the arm. Her eyes were big, her voice shaky. "Guys, I've got a real weird feeling about this."

"Stop worrying, Sunshine," Geffen reassured her. "Nothing's going to happen to—"

A strange, low rumbling sound cut Geffen off. The sound grew louder and echoed through the courtyard. It was coming from beneath their feet and causing the whole ground to vibrate. They stood still, listened, and waited until it stopped.

Coach balled up his fist. "What in Sam Hill was that?"

"Shhh, it's starting again," Geffen said.

The low growl grew loud and diabolically raucous, like a hockey match in Hades.

Geffen said, "It's coming from the cellar."

Sunnie ran to the cellar door. "Rice!" He didn't answer.

Geffen pulled on the door. "It won't open."

Sunnie panicked. "Oh no!"

Coach pushed through them and pulled hard on the steel latch, grunting and straining his huge biceps. The latch popped off, but the door still wouldn't budge.

"It ain't Halloween and I don't need this Stephen King bullshit." Coach wasted no time and kicked his foot through the cellar door, busting it off its sides. He hollered inside, "Rice! Get your ass out here! *Now!*"

Still no answer.

Sunnie's spiritual spook-o-meter began beeping off the hook. She swallowed real hard. Even Geffen, a.k.a. Mr. Cool, looked nervous. Coach was sweating, his biceps twitched, and his fists were tight.

They looked at the entrance to the cellar, then at each other.

Sunnie said, "We gotta go down there and get Rice."

Chapter

4

As soon as Sunnie saw the cellar door, she felt as if a bolt of lightning had struck her in her gut and set her stomach on fire. Images of those scary dreams rushed back, and for a moment she couldn't move. She remembered that dizzying blackness, the sensation of vertigo and the feeling of falling into that thick, ungodly darkness. She also remembered feeling like she wasn't alone, like there was another *presence* in there, something bad.

Now she was feeling all those things again, but this time the feeling was much stronger and she wasn't dreaming.

As she, Geffen, and Coach prepared to go down into the cellar to rescue Rice, a quick, new, haunting image flashed in Sunnie's mind. She saw the dark blurry outline of a woman. But this was no ordinary woman. She was dark like the night and hauntingly seductive. Sultry, sensual, and sinister, this woman was the shape of beauty, the silhouette of evil. And she was wearing all white.

Down in the cellar, in the earth beneath Sunnie's feet, a woman draped in a flowing white dress hovered next to Rice, who'd gotten lost in the wine cellar's corridors. More like a cavern than a wine cellar, it was a multi-tunneled hiding place for God knows what. The air was so thick with darkness that no human could survive down there for long. This woman lived there, and had done so for many years. The cellar was her home, and trespassers, especially men, were strictly forbidden.

"Crèp, look. We have a visitor. It's a *man*." Vixx walked next to Rice as he stumbled in the dark, unaware of her presence.

Crèp jumped up and nearly fell off his perch. Crèp was Vixx's sidekick, her old, fiendish partner in crime, and they hadn't had a visitor in ninety-nine and three-quarters years.

Vixx scolded him. "Calm down, old ghoul. Squat low so he won't see you, and don't speak out loud. Talk to me through your thoughts. You do remember how to do that, don't you?"

Vixx was a caustic beauty, untouched by age. Her darkness was delectable, but it wasn't a skin-deep darkness—it was more of an aura and it penetrated down to her soul. Swarthy, smoldering, and sexy, she had the face of an angel and the heart of a hellcat.

Her old companion, whose crinkly skin and crooked torso looked every minute of his one hundred twenty years, needed a moment to get over his shock.

He had to readjust and try to remember how to use his rusty preternatural powers. He hadn't done that tele- pathy thing in decades. Compared to Vixx, who was still as sharp and vicious as she had been nearly a hun- dred years ago, when she was the head demoness of the brothel, Crèp was awkward and pitifully clumsy.

Unlike Crèp, who was a ghoul, Vixx was a she-devil, a spectral being who didn't have to hide. Vixx was right up on Rice, peering in his face, walking alongside him, and he had no idea.

Crèp squatted low behind a wine barrel and peered through the murky darkness at Rice, who, with his arms outstretched like a zombie, tried to feel his way through the dark cellar. Rice coughed and gagged on the foul humid air, then held his nose.

Vixx let him pass her so she could check out his tush. *Hmm, nice and round.* She gestured with her hands like she was squeezing a tomato. *I could have some fun with this guy before I kill him.*

Despite everything that happened ninety-nine years ago that caused Vixx and her assistant, Crèp, to lose their brothel, she still had an uncontrollable horniness for human men. At the same time, she hated every- thing they stood for, especially the good-looking ones. Hers was definitely a love–hate relationship.

Crèp squinted his jaundiced eyes and gritted his teeth, trying to telepath accurately despite his panic.

But, Vixx, there's no time for that. His presence here jeopardizes what we've been waiting ninety-nine years to regain—our house of ill repute. Only a few more months, and our hundred-year sentence will be over.

Vixx spoke aloud knowing Rice couldn't hear her while she was in her spirit state, though he'd be able to hear Crèp, who was merely a ghoul with less supernatural powers than Vixx.

"Oh, stop your blubbering, old ghoul. I know all that. There's no way I'd let this man get in the way of our long-awaited plans to resurrect this whorehouse back to its original grandeur."

I'm just reminding you that your uncontrollable horniness got us in all this trouble in the first place. You violated The Rule, *remember?*

"Shut up, you little twit, before I pluck off one of your crooked toes and make you eat it. I know what I did." She turned back to Rice. "I'm going to properly dispose of him, but first I just wanna have a little fun. Hell, ninety-nine years is a long time to go without cable and a little nookie."

Vixx stepped squarely in front of Rice and snickered. "Tsk, tsk, the little man is scared, and oh, what's this I'm picking up on?" She read his mind. "He's paranoid about spiders. Here, let me see if I can make him feel better."

Vixx swept her fingers lightly across Rice's left hand. He jumped and slapped at his hand as if he were brushing something away.

"Ooops. My bad," she laughed. "Okay, let's try *this.*"

She backed up, got down on her hands and knees, and turned into a giant tarantula. She jumped up on Rice's face.

"Ahhh, shiiit!" Rice hollered, as he felt something big and furry pounce on his face. Frantic, he whirled

around and ran face-first into the stone wall of the cellar, knocking himself unconscious.

Vixx busted a gut laughing.

Back in her original form, she squatted and looked at Rice as he lay faceup on the dirty, muddy, stinky cellar floor. His eyes were closed, mouth open, and he was moaning.

Crèp peeped up from behind the wine barrel. "What's he thinking?"

"Shhh." Vixx kept her face close to Rice's, studying him. "He's calling someone for help."

"Who? His mama?"

"Shhh. No." Vixx frowned. "He's calling somebody named . . . *Sunnie.*"

"*Sunnie?*"

"He's hoping that she knows he needs her, hoping that she'll come and find him down here."

Crèp panicked. He darted from behind the barrel as fast as his slow, decrepit legs would take him. His crooked stick cane wobbled and creaked as he leaned on it. "There's more of them. They'll find us. They'll take our house. If they take our house, we won't regain our brothel. If we lose our brothel again, we'll be banished again."

Vixx grabbed Crèp by his tattered collar. "Shut your face, you blubbering twit." She shook him to bring him back to his senses. "I swore, by the blood of every unholy she-devil hell vamp in the land of FemDom in Hades, that I would never allow anyone, especially a man, to cause me to lose this house again."

"But, but—"

"No *buts*. This place belongs to us. It's our last and only hope to regain the life we had. I swore to the Great Council of the Underground SPA that I'd protect it against any invasion, and they agreed that after our hundred-year sentence is up, they'll grant us our brothel once again. But only if this house is vacant."

Vixx let Crèp go and walked back over to Rice. She cringed thinking about how the Council of the Underground SPA, Supernatural Powers Association, had banished her for violating its rules. "We've done ninety-nine years. We've only got a few more months to go in exile before we can gain the house back. I'll be double-damned if I lose it now."

Crèp still wasn't at ease. "But, but—what if more humans come?"

Vixx stood up over Rice and straddled him. "Let them come. Any humans foolish enough to trespass on this property will meet their Maker much sooner than they expected. Give me my blade."

Crèp reached somewhere in the darkness and pulled out a three-foot-long, razor-sharp, scythelike weapon. He handed it to her.

She gripped the blade's handle and planted her bare feet in the muddy dirt on both sides of Rice's body. He was faceup, lying on his back, his eyelids fluttering in the dark. If they had opened, he would have had a clear view straight up Vixx's flowing white dress.

Knowing this, Vixx paused, aroused. The thought kind of turned her on.

She lifted her foot and pressed it into Rice's crotch, grinding her toe in a slow, rhythmic motion. Even slightly injured and unconscious, Rice's body responded with a very competent hard-on.

"Hmm, impressive, but what a waste." She smiled naughtily and thought to herself, *He looks a little like . . . Bruce.*

Crèp was old and his powers of mental telepathy and mind-reading were rusty, but he heard that, and he knew that the naughty thoughts she was thinking might lead them into even more trouble. He couldn't let that happen. He had to zap her out of her horniness. He was risking her ripping his head off, but he had to say it.

"Vixx, do you remember how Bruce *played* you?"

Vixx froze.

Crèp went on. "Remember how you fell for him? How he was a smooth, suave playa-playa human man who came to our private brothel looking for the fantastic otherworldly sex he'd heard about, and how you were so curious you took him yourself, and he rocked your world?

"Remember how he kept coming back and telling you that you were his boo? Before anybody even knew what a boo was, you were falling for him. Remember how you violated The Rule that had been set by the council: 'Screw their brains out but never get attached'?"

Vixx gave a deep, guttural groan. The cellar floor started to vibrate. Crèp went on.

"Remember how you decided you'd risk everything just to be with Bruce? You sat him down to tell him you weren't a normal woman and that this sex house wasn't a normal sex house but was staffed by she-devils on loan from the Underground SPA who were doing research and recreation, learning how to destroy men's lives and mess with their minds through sex, and that you were willing to give up your position as head demoness-mistress in order to run away and be with him? And how he told you he had to go take a leak but ended up crawling out the bathroom window?"

Vixx groaned louder, the rumble in her chest so strong it shook the whole cellar.

Crèp went in for the kill: "Remember the 'Dear Boo' letter? The one he wrote on a piece of toilet paper."

Vixx grunted. "That . . . damn . . . 'Dear Boo' letter."

Crèp recited it from memory: " 'Dear Boo, The sex was good, but ain't no booty worth all this. I'm at the top of my game and ain't about to turn in my player's card to settle down with a bitch from hell. Catch me later. Peace out. Bruce.' "

Vixx hollered, "That no-good, dirty, lyin', cheatin' dog."

Crèp added, "The council punished you for violating The Rule, stripped you of your brothel, threw you down here in the stinkin' cellar for a hundred years, after which time they'll grant you your brothel again, but *only* if you guard it from invaders. All of this happened because of *Bruce*. A typical, trifling man."

"Men. Grrrrr-rrr." Vixx hollered so loud the entire ground beneath the courtyard shook.

Crèp cautiously tapped his cane on her shoulder, and when she looked, he pointed it at Rice. "That's a man right there. He even looks a little like *Bruce*."

Vixx snapped back. Her resentment and desire for revenge on Bruce remained strong. The real Bruce was dead, so she'd never be able to carry it out, but *any* man who crossed her path would suffer her wrath.

Still straddling Rice, she raised her blade high into the air. "Okay, you maggot man, enough foreplay, get ready for the climax."

Vixx swung the blade down hard on Rice's chest, but it clanged loudly and bounced back, vibrating in her hand like a brass cymbal. She flinched and looked down at Rice. His head and body were still intact.

Crèp had covered his eyes to shield them from the anticipated blood splatter. He spread his fingers and peeked at Vixx. "What happened?"

"I don't know." She gripped the knife again and swung it with all her might. Again, it bounced back with a loud clang.

"It's an invisible barrier!" she said.

Rice squirmed beneath her, unharmed. His eyes fluttered. The clanging bell-like sound was waking him from his stupor.

"A *barrier*?" Crèp clutched his sticklike cane, his knees quivering in fear. "The only thing that can cause a barrier like that is—"

"Prayer." Vixx finished his sentence. She dropped her arms to her side, the blade hanging loosely. "Somebody's praying for this guy."

She backed away from Rice.

"Prayer . . . uuuugh." Crèp cringed. "But who's doing it?"

"If I had to guess, *Sunnie.*"

Crèp sighed, then asked in a hoarse voice, "What does this mean?"

"It means I can't kill him—at least, not right now. Not like this." Vixx flung her blade across the cellar. It stuck into the wall.

"But if you can't kill him, how will we protect our home?"

"Shush. Listen. Someone's coming."

Chapter

5

SUNNIE SAID ANOTHER QUICK PRAYER FOR RICE JUST BEFORE she, Geffen, and Coach stepped down into the dark cellar to find him.

The air grew denser with each step they took down the narrow, creaky stairs. Coach reached back toward Geffen. "Gimme your flashlight, Gef."

"I don't have it. Rice took it, remember?"

"Damn."

Sunnie flipped open her cell phone and handed it to Coach. "Here, use this." The faint light from its small screen gave off a low glow that allowed them to see just a little.

Coach grumbled, but took the cell phone anyway. Sunnie gripped the back of his jacket as he led the way. Geffen followed close behind Sunnie.

"I don't want to run into whatever made that noise," Sunnie said.

"If it can bleed, I can kick its ass," Coach repeated

like a mantra, until Sunnie asked, "But what if it *can't* bleed?"

Coach paused. "Shut up, Sunnie."

They descended a few more steps in silence. Coach stopped. "What in Sam Hill is that *smell?*"

Sunnie had noticed it way before, but hadn't said anything. She didn't know if she was the only one who smelled it, because lately strange smells, sounds, and feelings were a part of her life. "It smells like burning—"

"—shit." Coach finished her sentence.

Sunnie corrected him. "No, like . . . *darkness.*"

The thick air made it hard to breathe. Finally, they reached the bottom of the stairs and found themselves in a small, cavelike space about the size of a closet. The close quarters were a nightmare for Coach, who was a bona fide claustrophobic.

"Man, it's too goddamn small in here. This must be what hell is like."

"I got a feeling hell is much worse." Sunnie huddled closer to the guys. By the weak light of the cell phone, they saw the grimy concrete walls covered with moldy, rotting leaves and bat droppings.

"What's *that?*" Sunnie gripped Coach's jacket even tighter and pointed to a small black thingamabob creeping across the muddy ground in front of them.

"How the hell do I know? And stop pushing on me, woman."

"I'm not pushing on you."

"You are."

"I'm not."

They looked around. Sunnie spotted something

else. "Look, tunnels!" She pointed to three narrow passageways leading in three different directions, none of which they wanted to go. "Which way did Rice go from here?"

"Rice!" Geffen yelled.

"Rice!" Coach yelled louder. "Negro, get your ass out here." His big voice echoed inside the small cave loud enough to wake the dead. He muttered, "He'd better hope nothing ate his ass, 'cause when I get my hands on him, he's gonna wish it did."

"Coach?"

"What?"

"That didn't make any sense."

"Shut up, Sunnie!"

They waited, afraid to move. Finally, Geffen broke the silence. "We gotta go through one of those tunnels and look for him."

Sunnie's stomach lurched. "I really don't think we should do that."

"But we gotta find Rice, right?"

"Of course. There's no way I'd leave without him, but everything inside of me says 'Don't go in there.'" Sunnie had a feeling that whatever was in those tunnels, she wasn't ready for it. Both Geffen and Coach started walking into a tunnel.

"Wait! I got an idea." Sunnie took the phone from Coach and dialed Rice's cell number, hoping he had his. It rang three times. Rice answered on the fourth ring.

"Hell-lo?" He sounded like he'd been asleep and was just waking up.

Sunnie was so glad to hear his voice. "Rice, where are you?"

Rice lifted himself up on his elbows and looked around the dark cellar. "I don't freakin' know."

"Are you lost?"

"Sunnie, I just told you I don't know where the fuck I am. Yeah, I'm lost."

"Stop cursing and calm down. Which way did you turn at the bottom of the stairs?"

"Left. No, right. Left. Hell if I know." He stopped. "Damn."

"What?"

"My forehead hurts like hell, like somebody clocked me with a brick." Rice tried to remember what happened, and why was he on the floor? He struggled to sit up. He was sore and *stiff*. He ran his hand over his crotch, noticed he had a hard-on. "What the hell is *this?*" He was sitting on the floor of a dark, funky-ass cellar, scared as hell, *with a boner*. It didn't make sense.

"What's *what?*" Sunnie asked. Coach and Geffen were trying to listen.

"Nothing." Rice scuffled to his feet and stood up, wobbly.

"Rice, listen. I'm gonna have Coach yell. When you hear his big mouth, follow his voice. Okay?"

Coach didn't wait for his cue. He started hollering like a quarterback calling plays. *"Riiiice!* Get your colored behind out here *riight noowww*. You got ten seconds or we're leaving your dark-meat fool ass behind. *Oooone! Twooo!"*

Rice heard Coach's voice booming through the tunnel and started trotting as fast as he could without running into a wall again.

"Fiiiive!"

Sunnie listened carefully in between Coach's yelling. "I hear him. He's coming!" They all turned toward the sound of footsteps.

"Siiix. Seveeen."

Rice called out, "Hey, y'all out there?"

"Yeah, we're here—keep coming," Geffen said. Coach kept leading Rice with his voice.

Suddenly, Sunnie's smile left. She doubled over with a pang in her stomach. *"Oooaah!"*

Geffen turned toward her. "What's wrong?"

Coach kept counting. *"Eeeight! Niiiinnne!"*

Sunnie's eyes widened, she whispered painfully, "He's not alone."

Coach shouted, *"Ten!"*

Sunnie jerked up the moment Rice came barreling out of the tunnel, her attention caught by the shadows behind him.

She yelled, "Rice, something's behind you!"

At first, Rice seemed not to believe her, thinking she was trying to pay him back, but when he saw her eyes, he knew she wasn't playing. Before he could turn around to look, Sunnie saw the shadows erupt in a frenzy of motion and heard a loud cacophony of noise and confusion.

Sunnie screamed, "Oh, God!" and pointed up at the shadows that only she could see moving behind Rice. "Watch *ouuuut!*"

Rice hollered and kept running. Geffen jumped.

Coach started swinging, throwing punches in midair. Rice ran headlong into Sunnie, who kept screaming.

"There's something in here!"

Coach jabbed wildly at the air. "Where they at? Where they at?!"

Geffen caught Rice and hung on to him as he fell forward.

Sunnie heard the *whoosh*like sound of something slicing through the air like a large knife, then a clanging sound like metal against metal, followed by cymballike vibrations. Sunnie grabbed Coach's back.

"What was that? What's happening?" She felt an unnatural heat. "There's someone here, I can *feel* it!"

Coach yelled, "Let's get *outta herre!*" He grabbed Sunnie around her waist and practically dragged her up the cellar stairs like a rag doll, her feet barely touching the steps. Geffen and Rice were both on his heels.

They flew like bats out of purgatory up the stairs, out the cellar, through the courtyard, and out the side gate on the east side of the house, trampling over weeds, crashing through bushes, and ripping through vines until they somehow miraculously found their way back to the front of the property.

Down in the cellar, Vixx pulled her blade out of the wall and surveyed the damage. "Awww, daaay-yamn!" Her favorite weapon was all banged up and dented at the tip.

She complained, "I couldn't get a straight shot. I kept hitting that stinkin' barrier. All three of those men had it around them. As for the girl, the force of energy surrounding her was so powerful it almost melted my blade."

Tired, Crèp leaned against the wall for support. "I tried to help, but—"

"Help my ass, you worthless old fart! I ought to stick you with this." Crèp moved back a safe distance from her. "I told you to stay low and try to scare the shit out of them so they won't come back."

"And that's what I did."

"Is that what you call it? *Aaaaoooh!*" she said, mocking him. "What's that supposed to do, Crèp? Is that supposed to *scare* somebody? You sounded like a broke-down bogeyman on crack. Aaaoohh." She threw her weapon on the ground. "You might as well have just said, *'Boo!'* You couldn't scare the Easter bunny."

Crèp felt bad. "Vixx, I'm not as young as I—"

"Aww, save the drama for your mama. I took up the slack for you. I had them hollering and bumping into each other like fools. They'd have to be idiots to ever come back here again."

Crèp disagreed, but didn't tell Vixx that for fear of getting slapped. Vixx sat on the cellar steps and rested from the battle. She hadn't had that much excitement in a long time. It had stirred her up, got her juices flowing in more ways than one. But still, something was bothering Vixx.

"Crèp, I'm a demoness, a she-devil, a hell vamp," she said.

"Uh, I know that, Your Highness." Crèp had no idea where she was going with this.

"No *ordinary* human sees me unless I *want* them to. I didn't want those people to see me."

"Uh, yeah . . . ?"

Vixx frowned, her jet black eyebrows furrowing into checkmarks, worried. "That woman—I think she *saw* me."

Chapter

6

WHEN SUNNIE AND THE GUYS CAME RUNNING AROUND TO the front of the house, Sunnie never was so glad to see her little yellow Saab. Sunnie jumped into the driver's seat. Geffen got in next to her. Coach and Rice jumped into the back.

Panting, Coach said, "Start the car, Sunnie!"

Sunnie fumbled through her pockets for the car keys. She prayed, "Our Father, Who are in Heaven . . . forgive us for our trespassing." She knew she was using it out of context, but it was all she could think of.

"Start the dang car, Sunnie. *Now! Let's roll!*" The more Coach yelled, the more flustered she became.

Then she saw Geffen pull the keys out of his pocket.

"Give me those," Sunnie said, and tried to grab them out of his hand, but he pulled them away.

"Let's all calm down for a sec," Geffen said.

Coach slapped the back of Sunnie's seat. "Calm down, my ass. Start this car, woman. Let's bounce!"

"Geffen won't give me my keys."

Geffen raised his hand. "Let's all calm down. Now, what just happened in there?"

Rice's head throbbed from when he ran into the cellar wall. The back of his clothes were muddy and sticking to the car seat. "I think I heard some noises."

Geffen rationalized. "Some noise. That's all it was, just some noise."

Coach slapped the back of Geffen's headrest. "It was a freakin' *poltergeist*, that's what it was!"

Sunnie kept her eyes pinned on the house, expecting something ghoulish to leap out at any moment.

Geffen turned around. "Listen to yourself. *Poltergeist?* That was a *movie*, it wasn't real."

Coach leaned forward. "Okay, you take your ass back down in that cellar and you tell that to the poltergeist. In the meantime, give Sunnie the damn keys so we can get the hell outta here."

Geffen insisted, "Since when do grown-ass men run from noises?"

Rice, forehead throbbing, looked at his watch. "Since about a minute and a half ago. Let's *goooo*."

Geffen grew incredulous. "I can't believe this. You warriors are actually going to run away from a little *noise?*"

"You weren't exactly *walking*, brotha man," Rice informed him.

Coach agreed. "Yeah, you ran like a bitch, too."

"That's because you all didn't give me a chance to investigate."

Coach reached up between the seats, pinned Geffen's chest with his forearm, and took the keys. He tossed them to Sunnie. "Let his fool ass out so he can go *investigate*. In the meantime, start this damn car and let's book."

"Okay. Okay," Geffen conceded. "I admit, I got caught up, too, but that's because Sunnie was acting like she'd lost her mind."

Sunnie slapped his arm. "I *saw* something in there."

Geffen challenged her. "Yeah, what did you see?"

"I saw, uh, uh . . ." Sunnie couldn't put it into words. Just like in her dreams, the events were dark and confusing.

Geffen cut her off. "*I* didn't see anything." He turned around. "Did you, Rice?"

Rice rubbed his forehead. "It was dark. That's all I know."

"What about you, Coach? Did you actually *see* anything?"

"Yeah!" Surprised, everyone turned and looked at Coach. "I saw *me* getting the hell up outta there. Now, let's go. We can talk about the details after we put some miles between this house and my ass."

Sunnie fumbled the keys and started the car, but Geffen jumped out before she could go. Sunnie yelled, "Gef, what're you doing? Get back in here!"

Coach whispered to Sunnie, "Hit the pedal, woman. Leave his ass out there."

Sunnie said, "You know we can't leave him."

Coach huffed and kicked the seat.

Geffen stood by the car and gazed at the house,

thinking, adding up numbers in his head. Rice rolled down his window.

Geffen said, "An opportunity of a lifetime, blown, and for what? Some *noise*. Could have been a trapped animal from these mountains."

Coach muttered under his breath. "That's some bullshit."

Geffen continued. "Even if we had to rebuild this whole house from the ground up, the land itself is worth twice the money we'd spend."

Rice got out of the car and stood by Geffen. He looked at the house, too, reconsidering. "I've got to admit this place *is* huge."

Coach rolled down his window. "If something comes hopping out that cellar and starts kicking y'all's asses, I ain't even gonna get out the car. I'ma just kick back and watch."

Sunnie was exhausted. Her spiritual spook radar had beeped so much it needed recharging. She knew something had happened in that cellar, but she didn't know what. She had nothing solid to go on, just a feeling, some noises, and a shadow.

She opened the door to get out. Coach touched her shoulder. "Leave the keys." She took the keys with her. Coach got out, too, grumbling.

Sunnie stood alongside the guys and they all looked back at that mysterious old house. Sunnie had found it purely by accident. She'd made a wrong turn, ended up on a dirt road too narrow to turn around on, so she had to keep going straight and ended up at this mansion. When she saw it, curiosity made her get out and peep through the window. Now she regretted that curiosity.

Sunnie wanted to leave, go to a restaurant with the guys, celebrate her anticipated engagement, and forget she ever laid eyes on that house. When she turned to Geffen to tell him this, Geffen had a sadness in his eyes.

Geffen bit his lip. "My mother died poor. She was—" His voice cracked.

Geffen hardly ever talked about his mother—it was too painful. The only reason he was talking about her now was because getting this mansion was not only about the money, it was personal for him. If he owned a place like this out in the mountains, he could move his mother's grave site here.

Geffen continued, "She was beautiful. She deserved a whole lot more than what life gave her."

Sunnie moved to hug him, but he stepped away. He explained, "My mother had one wish."

Rice put his hands in his pockets, lowered his head, and listened to Geffen. Sunnie knew that Rice didn't have the same sentimental feelings toward his mother, who was still alive, but she knew Rice was a very sensitive person. Coach, for once, remained quiet out of respect.

Sunnie already knew, but she asked anyway. "What was your mother's one wish, Geffen?"

"For us to be together." He'd let Sunnie read some of his mother's letters. He'd been away in Germany at a boarding school, and his mother had been in the United States, sick. It was obvious. She knew she was about to die because she wrote, "If not while I'm living, then maybe when I'm dead, we can for once be together. . . ."

Geffen wanted to move his mother's grave site from the low-budget, unkempt cemetery in the inner city to someplace nice, someplace close to him, maybe even to his own property, if he owned a place like this.

Sunnie said, "Geffen, I know what you're thinking and I understand, but this place is not—"

"This place is perfect. The location, the land, the size, and I bet the price is right, too. Sunshine, if you understand, then help make this happen. Find the owner, negotiate a sale."

"Geffen, I can't. I just don't feel right about this place. Let me try to find you guys another place."

"There's no time." Geffen exhaled.

"Sure there is. Just give me another month or two."

He snapped, "No. If we're going to do this, we've got to do it *now*." Geffen was adamant.

Sunnie asked, "Why the rush?"

Geffen announced to everybody: "I got us that loan."

Rice laughed. "I didn't think you'd pull that off, man."

Coach frowned and said flatly, "I wouldn't have done it."

For a second, Geffen looked uncomfortable and embarrassed. He smoothed down his wavy hair and straightened his collar.

Sunnie didn't know what they were talking about. "What loan?"

Geffen cleared his throat. "United Financial Funding Corporation has agreed to back us one hundred percent on a full venture capital loan up to four million at half the going rate, with no points. Construction and improvement costs included."

Rice congratulated him. "Wow, brotha, you must have really been on your game last night."

Sunnie couldn't believe it. "No way. Geffen, a loan that good is totally unheard of. You'd have to practically sell your soul to get a deal like that."

Geffen swallowed hard like he had a bad taste in his mouth. Rice shook his head, grinning.

Coach said again, "I wouldn't have done it."

Sunnie didn't know what was going on, but she knew the guys weren't telling her the whole story.

Geffen added, "But there's a catch."

"What?" Sunnie asked.

"The offer expires in thirty days. We've got to at least get a signed contract and put a property in escrow by that time."

Sunnie bucked her eyes. "Geffen, that's impossible."

"Nothing's impossible, Sunshine. Find the owner, make this deal happen."

Sunnie saw seriousness and desperation in Geffen's eyes. He turned to the guys for support. "Fellas, I can't do this alone. Are you with me on this?"

Rice was the first to step up. "Gef, man, you ain't alone, pahtna. We got your back."

Coach nodded. "Yeah, we all in this thing together. I mean, I ain't gonna lie—there's some weird shit going on in that basement—but we can get an inspector to go down there and check things out. Get animal control out here, a fumigator, an exterminator—"

"—a *terminator*," Rice laughed. "Call Governor Arnold to come down here."

Everyone laughed except Sunnie. She didn't like this whole idea.

"Assuming I can find the owner, what if he doesn't want to sell?" she asked.

Geffen was back to his ambitious self. "We'll *make* him sell. We'll force him to sell, threaten to get the place condemned if he doesn't. I've got friends down at City Hall. Look at this place, it's abandoned. Whoever owns it deserves to lose it. If he won't sell, we'll find a loophole—get it through an auction or foreclosure or something. Big-time real estate tycoons acquire property every day through loopholes. I'll find a way to get this place or die trying."

Sunnie knew Geffen meant every word. He had a business and law degree from USC. He'd studied abroad and had all sorts of success with entrepreneurial endeavors. He was shrewd and knew how to outfox his competitors. Plus, he knew a lot of influential people in key positions who could pull strings and who owed him favors. Geffen was as smart as he was driven. Sunnie believed him when he said he'd find a way to get that house, or die trying.

Sunnie said, "Fellas, everything inside of me is against you buying this house. I can't explain it, I just feel it. But"—Sunnie paused—"if you insist on doing it, I can't stop you."

"But are you going to *help* us?" Geffen asked. Rice and Coach also awaited Sunnie's answer. Sunnie remained silent.

Geffen asked again, "Sunshine, *please?*"

Sunnie's heart felt ready to cave in. She was torn. She wanted to help Geffen and the guys, but her stomach wanted nothing to do with that house.

In his gruff manner, Coach said, "Don't even think about referring us to another realtor. We don't trust nobody but you."

That touched her. Sunnie closed her eyes.

Geffen added to her dilemma. "You said it yourself. This type of loan is unheard of. I may never be able to swing a deal like this again. We've got to jump on it. *Now.*"

Rice reminded her, "We don't have time to search for another house."

Geffen said, "Besides, this place right here is a gold mine, based on just the land itself. We want *this.*"

Rice said, "You got what you wanted—you wanted Marvin to marry you. Now, what about me? I mean *us?* We want this house. We've always done everything together." Rice took a minute, remembering. "Why stop now?"

Sunnie saw that same look in Rice's eyes that he'd had when they were kids and she'd told him her parents were thinking about moving away. Rice didn't say a word to her the rest of that day, stayed home sick from school the next day, and stopped talking altogether. When Sunnie told him that her parents had changed their minds, Rice started talking again and was back at school the next day.

The memory brought a smile to Sunnie's face. That's how Rice had always been, and would probably always be—as deep as still waters.

Coach's gruff voice brought her back. "You gonna help us, woman?"

Sunnie ground her heel into the rocky dirt. "Let me ask you guys this: If I say no, are you still going to try to get this house without me?"

Geffen nodded in the affirmative, like she knew he would. Coach and Rice agreed. Geffen said, "But we'd rather do it with you, so you can share in our profits, in our success, in our lives. You're not just our realtor, Sunshine, you are our *girl*."

Sunnie threw her head back and gazed up through the tree branches. Why can't everything be as clear as the sky? It was no use trying again to explain about her gift, or all the weird stuff she felt. They wouldn't understand. She didn't really understand it herself. At least if she were with them, she could look out for them.

Sunnie exhaled. "One condition, fellas—you get a house inspector in there to do a *thorough* investigation before you step one foot inside this place, okay?"

"Does that mean you're with us?" Geffen asked.

Sunnie looked at Rice and smiled. "Aren't I always?"

Coach raised his big arms and Sunnie took her cue, joining the fellas in one big group hug. Instead of a home inspector, Sunnie wished they were planning to call a priest or an exorcist.

"Hey, guys," she grunted. "I can't breathe," she joked. But they didn't let up.

Sunnie had her three best friends surrounding her, and it felt good. Still, she wondered, *What kind of trouble are these guys getting themselves into?* And more important: *Will I be able to help them if they need it?*

Chapter

7

BRIGHT AND EARLY MONDAY MORNING, SUNNIE DIDN'T drive to her office at SoulMates Realty in West L.A., she floated. Thinking about Marvin's upcoming proposal made the sky seem bluer and the traffic lighter.

Sunnie told her secretary, "Clear my schedule. I'll be working on a special project today." Sunnie still couldn't believe she'd agreed to help the guys get that house. "And if Marvin calls, put him through right away."

She'd wanted to have dinner with Marvin last night, but he had another late patient consultation. The man was so dedicated, he worked even on Sunday nights. When she'd called him last night, he'd told her, "Sunnie, I have something very, very important I want to ask you, but I can't do it over the phone." Sunnie's heart had stopped beating and she'd wanted to scream *Yes, I'll marry you!* But she'd remained silent and calm. Marvin said, "My schedule lately has been unpredictable, so I don't know exactly when I can see you, but hopefully soon, okay?"

"That's fine," she'd told him. "I look forward to it." She could hardly wait.

Sunnie hadn't even turned on her computer yet when Geffen called her private number. "Hey, Sunshine, what did you find out about that house?"

"Can I sit down first? I just walked in the door."

"C'mon, now, it's already seven fifteen. This is no time to be slacking on the job. Give me the parcel number and assessor's ID number. Do you have the owner's name yet? How about a phone number? Did you call him? What's his price?"

"Geffen, calm down. Geesh." Sunnie watched the Windows logo come up on her computer screen. "I'll start gathering the information, and then I'll call you, okay? Bye, Geffen."

"Sunshine."

"What?"

"Why don't I just hold while you look."

"Bye, Geffen." Sunnie hung up.

She spent the next two hours searching through the L.A. County Assessor's records, parcel maps, and other public records, but all she came up with was one big question mark. She called Geffen back.

He answered right away. "What do you have for me?"

"This is strange. It's as if that house doesn't exist."

"Please, Sunshine, don't play games. I've been up all night thinking about that house, this loan, and—"

"No, really, Gef. It's like the information for both the house and the lot has been erased from public records. Every time I try to pull it up, I get 'Information Not Available' or 'Record Obsolete.'"

"That's impossible."

"Nothing's impossible. Remember, you said that." Sunnie logged off her computer and shoved printouts into her briefcase. "I'm heading out to Culver City to the Assessor's West District Office. The clerk said he'd let me search manually through the microfiche. Maybe when the system was computerized, somehow that parcel's information was not entered correctly."

"The West District Office is on Bristol Parkway, right?"

"Un-huh," Sunnie confirmed. "I'll call you and let you know what I find." Sunnie hung up, hopped in her yellow Saab, and drove south on Sepulveda Boulevard to West Slauson Avenue to Bristol Parkway. When she pulled up at Assessor's West District Office in Culver City and parked her car, Geffen was waiting beneath the flagpole, pacing and looking at his watch.

"What took you so long?" He had his briefcase, too.

"Good morning to you, too. It's so good to know that my client has enough faith in me to let me handle things by myself."

Geffen opened the front door for her. "It's not that I don't have faith in you, Sunshine. I just don't want you to screw this up." He winked at her. They went inside together.

Five hours later, with no lunch break and eyes sore from staring into the blurry microfiche screens, Sunnie and Geffen were told by the clerk that the office would be closing in forty minutes.

"Un-freaking-believable." Geffen removed a fiche from the machine and tossed it on the desk. "Nothing."

Sunnie and Geffen had searched every parcel entry within a twenty-mile radius, thinking maybe the parcel information with the mansion on it had been misfiled.

Sunnie rubbed her eyes. "I've never experienced anything like this before. Every single square inch of dirt in the state of California is supposed to be accounted for in these records." Her stomach growled. She took a sip of her warm Dr. Pepper, her third one from the vending machine. "Maybe we didn't really see a house out there. Maybe it was all a figment of our imaginations."

Geffen picked up her Dr. Pepper and sniffed it. "I hope for your sake there's alcohol in here, or else you really are losing your mind."

Sunnie got up and stretched. "Well, Gef, dear, I'm sorry. We gave it our best shot."

"Sit down," Geffen said. He flipped open his cell phone and voice-dialed a two-way with Rice and Coach. "Nairobi chiefs, listen up. . . ." Geffen gave them the 411 on what was happening, gave them the address of the Assessor's office, then gave them both ten minutes to get down there. "We've got one more box to search, and this place ain't closing until we're done."

Rice got there first. Judging by his wrinkled white T-shirt and loose jeans, he'd been napping.

Coach had on red sweats and had a bandana tied around his big head. He came in complaining. "I don't know nothing about no microfeet."

Sunnie corrected Coach. "It's micro*fiche*."

Coach huffed. "Whateva. Somebody needs to turn on a computer and push Control and F."

At three minutes until closing, Sunnie and the guys were down to the last two microfiche in the box, and they still hadn't found anything.

The clerk came into the room. "It's five o'clock. We're closed."

Geffen spun around in his chair. "It's not five o'clock. It's three minutes *until*. You are not closing, and we are not done yet." Geffen snatched the last two microfiche from the box. He tossed one to Sunnie, who quickly loaded it in her machine and began reading. The clerk left.

"I found it." Sunnie said. Her nose was practically touching the screen.

Geffen didn't believe his ears. Neither did the other guys.

Coach said, "Quit playin'."

Sunnie kept her eyes glued on what she'd found. "It's right here. I found it. It matches the parameters exactly. But you're not going to believe what else I see here."

Geffen sprang over to Sunnie's machine and looked in the screen. Rice and Coach tried to look over their shoulders. Geffen squinted, read the entry, and froze, as did Sunnie. Both were sitting there speechless.

Coach complained, "I can't see *nothing* with y'all heads in the way."

Sunnie told him. "We found the parcel, but it's like someone took a permanent marker and blacked out all of the owner's information."

"What?" Rice squeezed his way in and looked.

"You're right. Look, there's something scribbled on the side. It looks like two letters."

Sunnie zeroed in on them. "Yeah, that's a *V.* And that looks like an *x.* It says 'Vx' near where the owner's name goes. 'Vx.' That's all we've got—no address, no phone number, no former mortgage company—just 'Vx.'"

They all looked at each other.

Coach asked, "What the hell is a 'Vx'?"

Sunnie and the guys left the Assessor's office and went straight to eat, at Coach's urging. The Greek restaurant in Westchester was crowded, mostly with suited-up professionals who worked near LAX and had just gotten off work. They bypassed the people in the lobby and walked to the private booth in the back that Geffen had called ahead and reserved for them.

Geffen, preoccupied with finding a way to get that property, immediately took out his PDA and started looking up his contacts at City Hall.

Sunnie, tired and light-headed from skipping lunch, leaned over on Rice's shoulder, daydreaming out loud. "I wonder how I'll look in my white chiffon wedding dress. Do you think Marvin is thinking about me?"

Rice pushed her gently but firmly back to her side of the booth. "Yeah, I'm sure he's shoving silicone into some flat-chested woman's boob and thinking about you the whole time."

Coach looked at the menu. "Where are the BBQ ribs? Don't Greeks know how to BBQ?"

Geffen found the contact he was looking for and set

his PDA on the table. "Now, Ashanti descendents, let's get down to business."

"Hold up." Rice saw their waitress walking toward their table. He quickly picked up the menu and buried his face inside. "She's a *bitten apple*."

The guys knew exactly what the term meant, and so did Sunnie, who rolled her eyes. The waitress, a pretty petite girl with a slight gap between her front teeth and a nice figure, smiled at everyone and began taking their orders. When she got to Rice, he kept his nose pressed so close inside the crease of the menu, she couldn't see his face.

Geffen intercepted on Rice's behalf, made up a fake name and ordered for him. "And Ed Smith here will have the kabob on pita with bougatsa."

When the waitress reached for the menus, Rice refused to let go of his. He tugged back when she tried to pull it away. She tried to see who was behind the menu, but could only see Rice's hands. Everyone else at the table acted as if nothing was wrong and went on making small talk. Sunnie only hoped the situation wouldn't get more embarrassing than it already was. After a moment, the waitress gave up, gave them a funny look, and walked away.

Coach thumped the back of Rice's menu. "Gone."

Rice lowered the menu. "We go."

Sunnie objected. "We stay. I'm hungry and I refuse to leave this restaurant just because you screwed the waitress and didn't bother to call her back."

Rice ducked in his seat. "Lemme get those Ray-Bans, Gef."

Geffen handed him his tinted sunglasses. Rice put them on, pulled up his shirt collar, sank low in his seat, and used his napkin to cover his face, pretending he was coughing.

Rice said to Geffen, keeping his voice low, "You know I hate bougatsa."

Geffen snickered, "That's why I ordered it, Mustafa."

Sunnie shook her head at Rice. "Poor girl. Why didn't you call her back after you'd taken *a bite,* Rice? Or should I call you *Ed Smith?*"

Rice gave Sunnie a deliberately blank expression. "For what?"

Sunnie rolled her eyes again. "To get to know her. *Duh.*"

Coach laughed. "He already did that in the *biblical* sense."

"You know what I mean," Sunnie said.

"Call her back for what?" Rice asked, seriously. "Best-case scenario: We date, we get along for a while. Then she starts getting comfortable, starts getting in my personal business, wants to get all up in my head, know everything. Before you know it, I'm avoiding her, she's tracking me down like the CIA, and I'm not wanting to go through the drama or end up in therapy. Next thing you know, I'm changing my phone number, borrowing Coach's Rottweilers to keep her from ringing my doorbell at midnight, flying to Cancun. Sunnie, I don't feel like flying to Cancun *again.*"

"Gee, Rice," Sunnie said. "And the most amazing part about all of that is, you actually think it makes sense."

"I agree with Sunnie. That's some bullshit."

"You agree with me, Coach?" asked Sunnie.

"No, just the part about having to fly to Cancun. That's bullshit. I ain't flying nowhere to get away from a woman. When I hit it once, that's it. I ain't trying to hide. If I see her again, I'm bold with mine," Coach said cockily.

"Oh, so when you run into a woman you mistreated you're not ashamed?" Sunnie asked.

"*Hell* naw, 'cause I don't mistreat women. I treat them real *good* and that's why they always want seconds." Coach slapped hands with the guys.

Geffen explained this theory like he was a CNN correspondent. "That's how the game's played, Sunshine. Players keep moving. That's the rule."

"Gee, Geffen, you say that as if it's written down in section 101 of *The Playa's Handbook.*"

Coach gulped his water down in one swallow. "He's right. As long as there's still time on the clock, you keep moving the ball, keep scoring touchdowns."

Rice adjusted his sunglasses. "If you slow down, you're gonna get your ass tackled and end up all twisted over somebody."

"So, that it? It's all one big game? That's sad. I'm glad I'm settling down and getting married. All that game playing is getting old."

Coach reached over, took her glass, and gulped her water down, too. "Don't try to act all innocent. Women play the game, too. The only time they complain is when they lose."

Sunnie frowned. "Why play games at all? Why can't men and women just be honest with each other?"

"Because people lie, Sunnie." Rice moved his collar up a little higher. "They'd rather hide and evade the truth because dealing with the truth is scary. You could end up all bent out of shape over somebody who doesn't give a dang about you."

Sunnie looked at Rice hiding behind the sunglasses. "That's sad."

"Sad but true." Rice's napkin fell. He quickly put it back up to his face.

Geffen said, "In my own defense, not all players play the game because they want to. Some of us do it out of necessity."

"Necessity? Oh, give me a break, Geffen." Sunnie tried to pull the napkin from Rice's face, but only managed to tear off a small piece.

Geffen explained. "No, for real. I'd love to find a beautiful woman who can turn me on, make passionate love all night long, and the next morning get up and discuss stock options."

"Stock options?" Sunnie frowned.

"Yes, or her views on the future financial performance of the Dow Jones. Either one."

"Get outta here."

"I'm dead serious. I need someone who stimulates my mind as well as my body. I haven't found that yet. If she's beautiful, she's got the brains of a fried green tomato. If she's financially savvy, then she *looks* like a fried green tomato." The guys laughed.

Sunnie waved her hand dismissively. "Geffen, that's so stereotypical and a pitiful argument against monogamy."

Geffen smiled. "I'm all for monogamy, as long as I can have more than one monogamous woman at a time." They laughed again.

"Monogamy?" Coach said in his usual deadpan style. "What's that, some kind of disease? They got a cure for that?"

The waitress came and refilled the water glasses. Rice adjusted his napkin on his face and waited for her to leave, then spoke. "Limiting yourself to only one woman is the first step to getting messed up."

"*One* woman?" Coach frowned. "That ain't even natural. God made too many women to expect a man to have only one. Besides, *one* woman can't satisfy all of my needs. It takes a whole lot of different types to turn me on."

Sunnie grabbed her water glass before Coach drank from it again. Coach broke down his theory for them. "I need a Janet Jackson on the dance floor. A Tyra Banks to take out to dinner. A Serena Williams when I need to sweat a little bit. And a Halle Berry when it's time to get *Monster's Ball* freaky in the bedroom."

All three guys slapped hands.

Sunnie interrupted. "As much as I'd like to sit here all night and hear about you guys' debauchery, I do have a lovely, loyal man waiting for me to call him when I get home and perhaps discuss our glorious monogamous future together."

Rice accidentally tore the napkin across his face and had to get a new one.

Geffen checked the clock on his PDA. "She's right. Let's focus here. There's a hurdle we have to jump over in our path to financial success, and I've got a plan."

After the food arrived and they were an hour into their dining, Geffen had completely laid out and was wrapping up the details of his plan. He had already excused himself from the table and made several calls, and now he was even more confident that his plan would work.

Sunnie always admired Geffen's intellect and the way his mind naturally maneuvered itself around obstacles and worked toward its goal. But even so, this latest plan of his was a bit far out there.

Sunnie said, "Let me get this straight. Your contact, who is on the Urban Redevelopment Committee, is going to put this property on the list of properties declared abandoned, condemnable, or uninhabitable by the city, and therefore eligible for special investor's auction purchase under the redevelopment program."

"Exactly. The property would bypass the normal purchasing procedures wherein the owner or, in this case, the absentee owner, would not have to participate or give their consent. In these special cases, the city steps in and assumes ownership."

Rice asked, "Like eminent domain?"

"Kinda, sorta," Geffen said. "In the interest of rebuilding the community."

Sunnie held up her finger. "But, Geffen, that committee is set up to serve the inner-city area. This property is in *Beverly Hills*."

"Right, Sunshine. But you must understand, this is where a little bit of creativity comes into play."

The waitress came and placed the bill on the table, gathered some dishes, and left.

Rice lowered his napkin and murmured, "Creativity, a.k.a. lying."

Geffen justified, "One man's lie is another man's artistic expression." He leaned forward in his seat and lowered his voice. "It's just a matter of a typo."

Coach asked, "A *what*-o?"

"A type-o. Someone, probably a part-time, academically challenged high school office clerk—and if there's not already one working in the redevelopment department, we'll get one—just happens to mistype the Zip code on one of the properties (a.k.a. ours) while entering data into the computer when compiling their urban blight list."

Sunnie gets it. "And this *student* transposes a number in the zip code—instead of '90210' for Beverly Hills, she types '90220,' for Compton."

Geffen seats back in his seat again. "You're a smart girl, Sunshine. You catch on fast."

"Geffen, that's fraud."

"No, Sunshine, that's *business*."

"It's unethical."

"It's necessary."

Geffen straightened his cuffs. "The next auction is in two weeks. We wait until the very last minute to slip this property on the list. That way it gets overlooked by other potential investors. And believe me, there aren't many because nobody's really looking to invest in the inner-city neighborhoods that really need cleaning up, unfortunately."

Geffen sipped his Perrier and continued. "These auctions are low key, unadvertised. We bid low on the property. Nobody's expecting anything to be in Beverly Hills, so nobody's going to compete with our bid."

He turned off his PDA and slipped it back into his pocket. "Once a bid goes through, the Redevelopment Committee checks it off their list. After that, the mistake will have been corrected, and by the time the committee gets ready to do any follow-up, this property is not even on their list. And as far as anyone knows, it never was. My contact on the committee handles the other details for us, ties up all loose ends. We cut him a nice check for his troubles."

Geffen took out his platinum card and slapped it on top of the bill. "Escrow closes instantly. And it's ours."

Rice shook his head and chuckled. "I've got to give it you, Gef. You are one crafty muthamustafa."

Sunnie drummed her fingers on the table, digesting it all. There was no way she could be a part of this scheme. Not just because she'd risk losing her real estate broker's license if they were ever investigated for fraud, but because Sunnie had been trying to walk the straight and narrow path lately. Though she'd teetered here and there, she wasn't about to fall completely off the mountain for the sake of her realtor's commission. But Geffen had brilliantly worked it so that she wouldn't have to be involved. She had given her assistance as promised, had done her part with clean hands, and now this *dirtier* deal was between the city, the guys, and God, and perhaps whoever once owned that house.

"Geffen," she finally said. "I don't know whether to turn you in to the police or vote you into Congress."

The next two weeks went by snail slow for Sunnie. She felt like someone had broken the hands off the big clock in the sky. Every day was spent waiting for Marvin to call and tell her he was on his way, but instead he'd call and tell her his patient log was backed up and that he couldn't get off work.

Sunnie would try to tell the guys how anxious she was for Marvin to propose, but Geffen, who was so sure they'd win the house, was too busy interviewing prospective contractors to listen to her. Coach was busy at the gym rehabilitating his leg. And every time she mentioned Marvin's name to Rice, he would either change the subject or he wouldn't say anything at all.

She was relieved when auction day finally arrived. The auction was exactly the way Geffen said it would be. It was low key with not many people present in the small, dingy downtown City Chamber. There was no fast-talking auctioneer at the microphone and none of those bidding signs for buyers to hold in their hands. One Urban Redevelopment Committee member went to a table in front of the room. There were only about nine barely interested people, and about three of them worked at the City Chamber and were just taking their lunch break.

A bifocaled lady read off properties from a list. Some properties she skipped over altogether because no one had signed up to even preview them. She was about to skip over the house in Beverly Hills for the same reason. Geffen's "contact" had made sure the Beverly Hills property called no attention to itself.

However, Geffen stood up in his crisp navy blue Armani suit. He announced a bid that was ridiculously low for the Beverly Hills property, but seemed very generous compared to other properties on the list. Geffen's contact had done research prior to the auction, and they'd settled on a figure that would be acceptable without raising any red flags.

But the bifocaled lady halted as soon as Geffen stood up and made his bid. She took off her glasses and temporarily delayed the auction. Sunnie held her breath. *Uh-oh, they are so busted.* The lady acted very suspicious of Geffen, questioning him unlike she had any of the other bidders. Then she left Geffen hanging, standing in the middle of the room, his bid still in question, while she took a minute and left the table to confer with another woman, who looked equally suspicious of Geffen.

Sunnie looked up at Geffen, who'd been sitting next to her. He saw her looking, he also saw the near panic in her eyes, but he didn't reciprocate it. He remained confident, glanced at his watch as if he had somewhere more important to be. Rice and Coach were sitting in the chairs behind Sunnie like statues.

Finally, the bifocaled lady returned to the front table. She gave Geffen a final look, put her glasses back on, and unceremoniously said, "Bid for said property goes to the buyer in the blue suit."

Geffen nodded coolly to Sunnie, Rice, and Coach as he picked up his Italian leather briefcase, straightened his Fendi tie, and walked out of the room. They followed him down the lackluster corridor, out the city building, all the way to the parking lot before Geffen even turned and said one word to them. When he got a sufficient distance away from the auction, Geffen let out a whoop like Sunnie had never heard him do before. The guys spent a good fifteen minutes clasping hands, bumping shoulders, hugging Sunnie, and celebrating their accepted bid.

Sunnie was happy to see them so happy, but she still didn't like the idea of them getting that house. Over the past two weeks, her dreams had intensified. Instead of her dreams becoming more clear, they were getting more confusing. The blurry outline of that mysterious woman continued to haunt her. Even when Sunnie was awake, she could recall the woman's darkly enigmatic, shapely figure oozing with sensuality and lust. At times Sunnie recalled the woman's lusty scent. It was dense and fetal, like darkness had a smell. And the woman was angry, like she had a vendetta. Perhaps the worst part was that now the guys were in Sunnie's dreams also. They were in some sort of danger, but Sunnie didn't know how, when, why, or from what, especially since in real life they appeared so happy, safe, and content.

"Tonight we celebrate in style," Geffen said, as they all piled into his Hummer.

Later that night, when the celebrating had finally ended, Sunnie went home to her one-bedroom West L.A.

condo and lay across her multicolored art deco bedspread, alone. She stared up at the ceiling. Loneliness gripped her around her chest, and held her with cold arms. She wanted to get married. She wanted that one true and meaningful love. She wanted to get married so badly that she hadn't stopped to ask herself if Marvin was the man who was meant for her. She thought about it. *Of course! Who else?*

She turned off the light on her nightstand.

As she lay there, she thought of that song by Babyface—"What If?" The one where the guy runs into a friend of his old girlfriend and starts asking if he was the one she was supposed to have married.

Sunnie had drifted off into a fuzzy slumber when the phone rang. She barely woke up and glanced at the glowing green caller ID. She saw Rice's name. She wasn't surprised he was calling, figuring he wanted to apologize for acting so strangely toward her lately. She'd catch him looking at her, but when she looked at him, he'd turn away. He was also in one of his nontalking moods, hiding something from her. She picked up the phone. "It's about time you called."

"Hello, Sunnie?" It wasn't Rice. Sunnie looked again at the caller ID. It was Marvin's name. *But I could have sworn—*

"Hi, Marvin." She figured her eyes were playing tricks on her. "I didn't mean to say—"

"No. It's fine. You're right. I know. I need to apologize for the delay. I cleared my schedule so that I can concentrate on you. You're special to me and you deserve my full attention." He paused. "How about Thursday evening?"

She sat up on her bed. "Yes. Yes."

"Okay. I'll see you then. Good night."

Sunnie plopped back down on her pillow, giddy with happiness. She had been humming a song before she drifted off, but now she couldn't remember what it was. Now all she could think about was, *Yes, yes, I'll marry you, Marvin.*

Chapter

8

TUESDAY MORNING, BEFORE RUSHING OUT THE DOOR OF HIS
Burbank bungalow-style house, Coach threw bloody
slabs of red meat onto Tabitha and Samantha's plates.
"Eat up, girls," he said to his two full-grown Rot-
tweillers as they tore into the bloody meat. His phone
rang again. Sunnie had been calling him all morning.
He didn't have to time to talk because he was running
late.

Coach jumped into his custom-built black 4WD
Chevy Suburban and checked the clock on his dashboard. *Damn. J.B.'s gonna be pissed.*

Bouncing on twenty-four-inch rims, he drove his
shiny black truck south on Interstate 5 while blasting
Ludacris on his customized Bose sound system. As he
hopped off at the Rosecrans exit in Compton, his cell
phone rang. He checked the caller ID. *Sunnie again.*
He turned down the music and answered through his
truck's speaker system.

"What do you want, woman?"

"Guess what? Marvin called last night. He's going to ask me to marry him on Thursday."

"Tell him no."

"Coach, c'mon be serious."

"Tell him *hell* no."

"You may not like Marvin, but you love me and should want me to be happy."

Coach mumbled, "Whateva. Is that what you called me for?"

"Yes . . . no . . . I also called to tell you to be careful."

"Is this some more of that Miss Cleo bullshit?"

"Images have been popping into my mind, even when I'm awake, like flashes."

"Maybe it's that metal plate in your head."

"I don't have a metal plate in my head."

"Maybe you need to get one."

"Coach, stop it. Listen, I see images of you, Rice, and Geffen in danger."

"I gotta drive."

"Wait! An old white truck."

"What?"

"That's what I saw. An old white truck and you were in danger."

"Bye, Sunnie."

"Hey, be careful, okay?"

Coach hung up and took a quick left onto Wilmington, then right onto Alondra, and turned into a small community of houses just south of the small airport. He didn't have time to trip on Sunnie—he had other things on his mind, like buying that house yesterday, dealing with J.B., and finding Joey.

When Coach pulled into J.B.'s yard, he saw him standing in the driveway in his overalls. "'Bout time you got your ass here, boy. Now come help me with this pit."

J.B. was the only man who could call Coach "boy" and not be introduced to the pavement. Joe Brass, better known as J.B., was Coach's father. Coach hopped up on the back of J.B.'s white 1985 Ford truck and grabbed the opposite end of the half-barrel BBQ pit.

His father was nearing sixty, but was determined to take his gladiator mentality with him to the grave. With his testosterone level elevated, especially around his beer-drinking domino buddies, J.B. never missed an opportunity to demonstrate his tough manliness.

"Haul ass, boy. What you waitin' on? I got meat to cook." J.B. flexed his no longer solid muscles and stuck his chest out as far as it would go. He was still in reasonably good shape thanks to his stubborn regimen of exercise, which included pushing people around, and no booze. Coach sometimes wished his old man would sip on a Hennessy just so he'd chill.

Coach helped him unload the pit from his white truck, which was backed into the driveway. Coach's parents lived in a quaint stucco frame house with a detached garage. On Coach's pro-football salary, he could easily afford to move them into a newer house, but J.B. was in his comfort zone in this Compton neighborhood where he knew most everybody and everybody knew him, though not necessarily fondly.

Coach pushed the pit next to about five similar pits lined up along the side of the house. "Which one of these you selling?"

"None."

"It's getting kinda crowded. In case you change your mind, I can—"

"I ain't *never* changing my mind, boy. I'm keeping my pits. All of 'em!"

J.B. ripped open a bag of charcoal and dumped it into his new pit. His fellow gray-haired friends picked up their folding chairs and scooted the flimsy folding card table a comfortable distance away from the new pit. J.B. seemed unconcerned that he might light his friends on fire.

Old Slim said to Coach, "Hey, what about them Chargers, huh? Y'all going all the way this year?"

J.B. spoke for Coach. "Damn right they going all the way."

Coach hated the fact that his father hadn't told his friends that he was on the injured reserves list this season. When he'd first told J.B. the news, J.B. looked like he wanted to take a swing at Coach just for saying the word *injured*. "What the *hell* do you mean, you ain't playin'?" J.B. had yelled, and balled his fists. Coach had backed up and pointed to his left leg, which was in a cast. "That ain't no escape. Be a man and get your ass back out there and play, boy." J.B. didn't speak to Coach again for weeks, until he wanted Coach to do things for him, like unload his BBQ pits. Coach knew J.B. had issues, but he thought, *Fuck it, that's my father.*

J.B. shifted his cigar between his front teeth and

poured way too much lighter fluid over the coals. He boasted, "The only way that sorry-ass team got as far as they did last year was because of Badass Brass Number Fifty-eight." He said Coach's jersey number like it was bigger than Coach himself.

As if daring the gods of fire and getting-your-ass-burned-up, J.B. stood over the fluid-soaked pit and lit his cigar. Nobody dared say anything to J.B. as he dangled the chewed cigar loosely from his fingers, letting the ashes fall into the pit. Coach knew his father was fronting and trying to look extra tough, but at times like this he questioned his old man's mental faculties.

Stoney, Buckshot, Old Slim, and Snow got up and moved their chairs once again. J.B. saw them and called out, "Wimp-dick, punk-ass bitches," then went on bragging about his son's football career, as well as his prowess when it came to getting women. Coach stood by listening to J.B. talk as if he wasn't standing there.

"My son's got that Brass blood flowing through his veins, and we some hard-ass sons of bitches. Where you think the phrase 'brass balls' came from? We one hundred percent men, and women know it."

Coach patted J.B. on the shoulder. "You too much, Pop. Ma inside?"

J.B. nodded and kept boasting. Coach went inside the house. The house he grew up in always seemed smaller than he remembered. He went into the kitchen where his mother was marinating pork ribs for the BBQ.

"Hey, Ma."

"You hungry, Franklin?" she asked.

"Always."

"Stick around. These'll hit the spot."

"Can't. Just came by to help J.B. unload the pit. You heard from Joey yet, Ma?"

Joey was Coach's younger brother. His mother had called and left a message saying that J.B. had been beating on Joey again, and that Joey had left.

She answered, "No, but I saw him drive by earlier. He saw J.B.'s truck in the driveway and kept going." Her voice was sad. Coach didn't know how to comfort her. J.B. was always doing things to make her sad, but what could he do? He'd been raised to respect the man of the house, even if he was an asshole.

Coach stepped into the narrow hallway where Ma kept framed pictures on a glass stand. One was of Coach in his high school football uniform right after the Homecoming game. He was standing between a much smaller Rice, who looked funny in a Jheri curl, and Sunnie, who was all smiles and dressed in her cheerleading uniform. She and Charlotta were the cutest girls on the squad. Rice's parents and Mother Roby still lived down the street, but Sunnie's adoptive parents had moved on.

Coach picked up their family portrait. He and J.B. stood tall in the back, while Joey kneeled in front close to his mother. He and Joey looked just alike, except that Coach was much more muscular. Joey wasn't athletic at all. He preferred hanging out with his less-popular friends to attending Coach's football games. Growing up, Coach did his thing, which consisted of football, girls, and parties, and Joey did his, staying out of the way while his father gave all this attention to Coach, the star athlete and ladies' man. Only recently did Joey seem to always do something to piss off J.B.

"Gotta go, Ma," Coach said. He took the platter of ribs from his mother and carried it outside to J.B., who was still boasting on the Brass men's virility.

"Here's the meat, Pop. I gotta go."

"Where you rushing off to, boy? Going to see one of them fine-ass women you got?" J.B. grinned, further proving his point about Brass men.

"Naw, I'm meeting my boy, Rice, for lunch."

J.B. shot Coach a hard, mean look. He'd rather Coach had lied about meeting a woman than to have said that, especially in front of Old Slim and them.

Old Slim poured dominos out onto the card table. Snow the Albino whispered something to Buckshot, who laughed, but stopped when he saw J.B. looking. "What's that you say, Snow?" J.B. asked.

Snow turned red. "Nothing."

Coach set the rib platter down on the domino table and turned to leave.

J.B. persisted. "What he say, Buckshot?"

Buckshot was reluctant. "Snow was just joking 'round. He ain't really said nothing."

J.B. came up to him. "I asked you, what did he say?"

Buckshot hesitated. "He said he hopes Frankie's buddy ain't like Joey's buddy—a *bed* buddy."

J.B. lunged on top of Snow, knocking the card table over, and sending dominos and pork ribs flying through the air. He tackled him and both of them went cartwheeling backward over his chair.

As Coach turned around and ran back, J.B. put Snow the Albino in a headlock and tried to choke the whiteness out of him. Coach did his best to pull his father off Snow, but the old man was stronger than he thought. Finally, he got J.B. off Snow.

Once J.B. calmed down and Coach saw that Snow had soiled his pants but was otherwise okay, Coach left, glad to get from around J.B. He climbed into his Suburban, thinking about all the stuff J.B. pulled. He shook his head. *Fuck it. That's my father.*

Coach drove to Vernon's Fried Catfish Shack on Wilmington, about five minutes away. Rice was sitting outside at one of the rickety tables ducking droppings from the fat pigeons sitting on the edge of the roof.

Coach walked up, found a clean spot on the rusty splattered bench and sat. He said, "Tell me again why we come to this busted joint?"

"Because they've got the best fried catfish," Rice answered.

"That ain't why." Coach and Rice both forgot about the pigeons and hooked their eyes on two sistas walking up. One looked like a young Janet Jackson and the other had a badunka so tight you could bounce a penny off of it. "That right *there* is why," Coach said, staring while Rice fished in his pocket for a penny.

Coach grabbed his chest, faking a heart attack and whooped at them. "Hey, Ma, c'mon over here and give me some CPR." The women smiled and went inside.

Rice pushed the white greasy bag toward Coach. "I

ordered you the chicken, greens and cornbread. They ran out of catfish."

Coach frowned. "How is a place with catfish in its name gonna run outta catfish?" Coach ripped open the bag. "Throw me that hot sauce." Rice threw him a packet, and they started eating. "She's home right now," Coach said, without looking up, already devouring his second chicken breast.

Rice picked at his candied yams. "Who's home?"

"Don't play, Nigerian. You know who. I just passed your mom's house. Her LeSabre is parked curbside."

Rice didn't say anything. He left the yams alone and picked at his roll.

Coach kept eating. "You going by there?"

Rice's demeanor was flat. "For what?"

"'Cause you ain't visited your moms in over a year, yet you always find a reason to come down this way."

"Told you, man. I come for the food and the sight-seeing."

"The hell you do. You come right around the corner from your mom's house, but you won't take those few extra steps and go see her."

Rice said, "Who are you supposed to be, Dr. Phil? Hey, just shut up and eat."

Coach finished off the last of his greens and sat back. "You ain't got to get all defensive. You think I *like* going to J.B.'s? But that's my father, so I go regardless." Coach stood up and picked up his keys. "That's your moms, regardless."

Rice stuck his fork back into his yams. "Later, Coach."

Coach walked away, but not before sticking his head inside the door and taking another peek at Miss Badunka. "Lawd haf mercy!" Coach left Rice sitting on the metal pigeon-blasted bench.

Rice finished his food, got in his car, and drove around to his mother's block. Her gold LeSabre was parked out front, just as Coach said, but he couldn't even do a driveby. He stopped before he reached her house and parked in his usual spot, leaving his engine running.

He knew that if Sunnie were there, she'd tell him to go ring the doorbell. She was the only person in the world who knew why he couldn't do that. His mother came outside and stood on the porch smoking a cigarette. Mid-fifties, in good shape, young-looking, she was wearing one of those Willona-on-*Good-Times* scarves around her head. She looked the way she always looked—confident, aloof, self-absorbed.

She flicked her cigarette in that movie star quality she had about her, though she'd been an extra in a Folger's commercial. Rice wondered if she was smoking outside because of his father's bronchitis. Naw, she'd toss him a cough drop before she'd make that kind of sacrifice.

Rice put his car in reverse, about to leave, when a car blew its horn behind him, scaring the crap out of him. It turned into a driveway near him and blew at him again. He was pissed and ducked down in his seat before his mother saw him. Rice heard his name, peeked out, and saw Sunnie's yellow Saab. *Damn, Sunnie!* He looked back at his mother. She was looking at him. She flicked her cigarette, dropped it on the porch, snuffed it out with her princess slippers, turned, and walked back inside.

Sunnie parked and came over to his car. "Hey, Rice. What are you doing out here?"

He didn't answer. She glanced down the street at his mother's house. He didn't have to answer, she knew.

Rice had parked right in front of Mother Roby's. Sunnie was all smiles like this was a damn happy occasion. "I'm here visiting Mother Roby. Guess what? Marvin called last night. He's going to propose to me on Thursday. Finally! Yeah!" Sunnie did a cheerleader step from back in the day.

"Great. See ya" was all he said. Rice made a U-turn and left.

On his way home, he passed by the rinky-dink cemetery shoved between a donut shop and a liquor store on Avalon Boulevard. It was littered with broken beer bottles and donut wrappers, and the grass was not kept up. That's where Geffen's mother was buried.

Out of respect, Rice slowed down as he passed. He caught the tail end of Geffen's money-green Hummer, license plate CORP BIZ, turning into the cemetery's cracked driveway. Rice didn't stop, knowing that his friend was too embarrassed to bring anybody to his mother's trashy grave site.

Geffen drove his Hummer up the bumpy entrance of Kringle Cemetery, almost scraping his side door on the donut shop's cracked cement building that sat too close. Everything around there needed fixing—the driveway, the buildings, the sign that had fallen down years ago. Geffen had been so embarrassed by it all, the only person he'd ever brought there was Sunnie. He'd planned to bring her with him today because she had a calming way about her that helped him deal with it, but she was so ecstatic about Marvin proposing to her on Thursday, he didn't want to spoil her high.

Geffen got out and walked a few yards over patches of yellow-green grass interspersed with small flat, faded grave markers. The cemetery wouldn't allow him to buy his mother a decent gravestone, saying there wasn't enough space.

Geffen hated coming here. The only thing he hated more than visiting his mother in this place was the man responsible for her being there. His father could have afforded to bury her someplace nice. Geffen's father never married his mother, but he had money and provided for Geffen's school and board until he was eighteen. He didn't give Geffen's mother a penny. Sometimes she didn't even have a place to call her own. Geffen had to send her letters to his uncle, so he could give them to her. His uncle, a doctor, would let his mother stay with him on occasion.

Geffen's Ferragamos crunched the dried twigs around the simple grave marker inscribed with his mother's name. Geffen couldn't bring himself to talk to his mother the way some people talk to their buried loved ones. Something about talking aloud to a dead person's grave seemed irrational to him. Geffen valued his brain too much to compromise it in any way. He felt that keeping his mind sharp and focused would ultimately lead to his wealth and success.

If he had talked to her aloud, this is what he would have said: *Mom, I bought investment property yesterday. I've got land now, and with the first money I make, I'm going to bring you home to live with me. I love you, Mom.*

Chapter

9

ON WEDNESDAY MORNING, AS SOON AS SUNNIE FINISHED with her client, she rushed out of SoulMates Realty in West L.A., jumped in her Saab, and sped up to Beverly Hills to meet the guys at their new mansion. Geffen had called her the night before after she'd gotten home from Mother Roby's house.

"I got bad news," he'd said. "My financier just reneged on the renovation costs."

Geffen filled her in on the details of how he got that great loan in the first place. He told her that the horny financier wanted seconds . . . and thirds . . . and fourths of Geffen's undivided "attention." Not only had Geffen never promised her that, but he refused to be railroaded into doing it. The loan had already been funded, but she had reneged on the renovation costs.

After first seeing the house two weeks ago, Geffen was so excited and confident that they would get it that he immediately started interviewing and hiring contractors, architects, landscapers, interior designers, painters, plumbers—you name it—and had kept them on standby. After they won the house on Monday and the city bypassed the normal escrow procedures, Geffen's crews began renovating it on Tuesday morning. His goal was to transform the decrepit old mansion into an ultramodern, high-tech bachelor's pad suitable for posh celebrity parties, filming locations, and a bed-and-breakfast for out-of-town execs.

But now the guys were going to have to come up with a substantial amount of cash out of pocket. Sunnie knew Rice would freak when he heard the news, with his cheap self, and Coach would probably want to throw somebody through a wall. But Geffen had a plan, as usual, and he said it involved Sunnie's help, so he told her he wanted her to meet them there this morning.

Sunnie drove her yellow Saab up the winding, narrow dirt pathway that snaked up to the house, and that gnawing feeling in the bottom of her gut returned. It had never really left, but every time she went back there, it got worse. The road had been expanded so that large machinery could pass through. A few trees had been chopped down, brush cleared away, and a makeshift gravel road built.

Geffen and Coach were already standing out front waiting for her. Construction workers walked around in hard hats carrying power tools. Rice had been tailing Sunnie in his car since she turned left off Sunset Boulevard. She parked her Saab between two large pickup trucks and got out. Rice parked directly behind her.

Sunnie waited for him to catch up. "Good morning, Rice."

He caught up and walked right past her to Geffen and Coach. "Hey, what's up?"

As soon as they all gathered at the fountain in front of the house, Geffen wasted no time telling them the bad news.

"Hey, tribal warriors, we've encountered a slight glitch. We've got to come up with $660,000 cash for renovation costs."

Rice asked, "You're joking, right?" Geffen shook his head.

Coach said, "A glitch? Did you say a *glitch?* $660,000 ain't no *glitch!*"

Rice panicked. "You said our loan included renovation costs."

"The banker reneged," Geffen said.

Coach balled his fists. "Reneged? *Reneged?* Where she live?"

Sunnie butted in. "Coach, you can't intimidate that lady into paying renovation costs."

Rice's voice went up two octaves. "Well, what the hell are we supposed to do? It's not like I got that kind of money lying around in a cookie jar. You told us there'd be no out-of-pocket expense."

Geffen said calmly, "I got a plan."

Coach exploded. "A *plan?* What you need to have is *$660,000!*"

A crewman slipped and fell off a ladder near the entrance, crashing through some trees on the way to the ground. His foreman went to handle it.

"Hear me out." Geffen kept his cool while Coach fumed and Rice was about to go into shock. "We sell our homes, all three of us, liquidate our assets, and we move in here." Geffen motioned toward the house.

Coach looked at him like he was crazy. "That's your plan? You want me to sell my house and come live here? This place is a shit hole."

Geffen went into his sales pitch mode. "This place is about to become a palace. With all this square footage, we'd still have more than enough room to rent it out as we planned. Under a corporation, we can use our business property as our residence, too, with a hefty tax write-off."

Geffen, skilled in the art of persuasion, gradually let the idea sink in while the noise from buzz saws, hammers, wrecking machine, and forklifts drowned out their doubts.

Geffen went on. "We select three out of the eight bedrooms and make them into our own private master suites. After Sunnie sells our homes and we pay for renovations, we'll have plenty left over to customize our spot like African royalty. Picture it, fireplaces, Jacuzzi tubs, lofts, sunroofs, balconies, private wet bars"—Geffen looked at Coach—"stripper poles." Coach's eyes widened. Geffen went on. "We'll write off the money we put into it as an investment into the corporate business."

Rice ran his fingers down his mustache. The prospect of living virtually tax free off a corporation caused the blood to slowly drain back into his face. Coach folded his arms across his chest, grinning to himself. ". . . Stripper poles?"

Sunnie knew this was a done deal, and once again she felt as though she'd just been sucked into a very bad idea.

A crashing sound and a commotion erupted near the east side of the house. A few crew members ran to investigate.

Sunnie was growing more uncomfortable by the minute. "Hold on, guys. Buying this place was bad enough, but actually moving into it is absolutely, downright dangerous."

Geffen defended his plan. "It's a good idea, Sunshine, a win–win situation."

Three plumbers hollered when a main valve burst and sent water gushing.

"My team of lawyers are putting together the details as we speak. I fly out at six A.M. to meet with them in Sacramento tomorrow." Geffen dusted a leaf off his Hugo Boss shirt from a tree that accidentally fell in the wrong direction a few yards away.

A man in white overalls ran past them slapping himself, yelling, "Hornet's nest!"

Sunnie watched the man run past them just as a bulldozer fell into a ditch. She said, "I *really* don't think you guys should move in here."

Coach stopped humming, Rice snapped to attention, and so did Geffen, but not because of anything Sunnie had said. They all squinted their eyes and covered their noses. Coach frowned, "Da-um! What's that smell?"

Sunnie smelled it, too. A green fog arose from the east side of the house. It crept along the ground, then circled around the legs of the guys, rising slowly and attacking everyone's nostrils with a smell so putrid it brought tears to their eyes. The crewmen were gagging, falling on the ground, wiping their eyes. A few grabbed their lunch boxes and left.

The head inspector emerged from the east side of the house and staggered toward Geffen, Sunnie, and the guys. He could hardly see, blinded by the funk. He said to Geffen, "It's coming from the cellar."

"What is it?" Geffen demanded.

"I don't know. Something's blocking the cellar door. My men can't get in there to find out." The inspector put his hand on Geffen's shoulder. "And you know what, Mr. Cage? You can't pay us enough to try to find out. Find yourself another house inspector. We quit." The inspector stumbled away.

Sunnie watched as more crew people left, some walking, some running. Much more than a stinky smell assaulted Sunnie's nose. It was a sign—a funky signal that something much more serious was going wrong in that place. Sunnie scrunched her nose and looked at Geffen, hoping he'd finally call this whole thing off. Disaster after disaster was occurring right under their noses, workers were quitting, and now the cellar was jammed shut and emitting a putrid smell. *That cellar.* As soon as Sunnie thought about it, she got a vivid flash of that dark, shadowy woman, mad, shouting, and surrounded by green smoke. Sunnie shuddered, but kept it to herself.

Coach, coughing, said, "I'm outta here. Let's go." Coach and Rice started heading for their cars—Sunnie, too. Everybody was leaving when Geffen said, wheezing, "Hold up, Africans. I got another plan."

Vixx ran back down into the cellar, holding her hand over her nose, stomping through green, putrid smoke, mad as hell and screaming.

"Crèp? What did you *do?*" she yelled.

Crèp jumped, dropping his cane and fumbling with the roots, bones, and bloody bat wings he had in his hands. He was standing over a huge black kettle that was boiling over with bubbly green slime. "You told me to cast a spell on them."

Vixx stumbled toward Crèp, fanning the green fumes. "I said a *spell,* not a *stink bomb.*" The stench was so strong, she wiped tears from her eyes and sat on the muddy floor. "You'd better be glad I can't see you in all this green funk, or I'd kick your ghoul ass."

She pounded her fist on the ground. "This is ridiculous. I've been up there pushing ladders over, breaking pipes, crashing things around—I even got into some hornets and stung some butts. Still they won't leave."

Crèp put a lid over the kettle and turned down the flame underneath it. He shook with worry. "How'd all this happen? We were so well hidden."

Vixx snapped. "That little Sunnie girl, she sees more than she's supposed to. I overheard them talking. She spotted this house by accident. Then those greedy man fools bought it at an auction."

"An auction?"

"Yeah." Vixx scowled. "They're as conniving as they are good-looking—especially that writer one. I could just grab him and pin him on the ground and jump his bones." She spat.

Crèp said with a sneer, "Why? Because he looks like Bruce?"

Vixx snatched the lid off the kettle and bashed him upside his head. "I got your *Bruce*."

"Ooow-ooh-*wee!*" Crèp sloped over like a falling tree and ate dirt.

Crèp's comment was enough to rile up Vixx and remind her of how much she hated men and why, remind her of how her penchant for sex with them had gotten her into all this trouble in the first place and how badly she wanted to take revenge.

But even more important, it reminded her how necessary it was for her to get those three guys out of her house before her hundred-year sentence was up, or else she'd never be given her brothel back by the council, and she and her sidekick would be banished and homeless for eternity.

Vixx paced the cellar floor, talking to herself. "I'd have smoked their asses a long time ago if it weren't for that prayer sheath protecting them. *Sunnie*. I'd like to strangle her pretty little neck for praying for those guys, but I can't touch her. She's got serious *connections*." Vixx's flowing white dress swished around her shapely dark legs as she turned and paced.

She kicked Crèp. "Wake up, you old fart. This is no time to be sleeping."

Crèp moaned, regaining consciousness. The first thing he saw when he opened his eyes was the kettle lid. He jumped again.

Vixx said, pacing, "We've got to find a way to destroy these guys. Help me think."

Crèp rubbed his branchlike fingers over his bumpy, bruised scalp. Patches of his long gray hair came out. He thought about hitting Vixx in the head with the lid like she'd done to him, but he was a ghoul, not a fool. Instead, he tried to assist his demoness mistress. "In all of my ghoul years, I've never known any way that one of us from down here can harm one of them up there if somebody's praying for them."

"Shut up. I ain't trying to hear that. Who asked you anyway?" Vixx continued pacing. "There's got to be another way to get to those fine-ass, sexy sons of b—" Vixx stopped in her tracks. "I've got a plan."

Crèp got up and put the lid back on the kettle. "What's your plan?"

"I'm going to ask for help from the Dark Sisterhood. I'm going to do a ritual and summon them up right now." Vixx ran to her altar and started gathering up all of her ritual stuff—her silver chalice, her cast-iron cauldron, pouches of bat eyes, bottles of spider legs, and a mirror to check her makeup.

"Those evil bitches spend their whole immortal life vexing and tormenting human men. They should know how to bypass a protective prayer covering them." Vixx ran a comb through her thick black hair right quick. She wanted to look presentable.

She drew a pentagram in the mud, sat in the middle of it, and went into a deep meditative state. Her head flew back, the ground vibrated, and flames burst up all around her. In the midst of the flames, she chanted, calling up her spiritual half sisters from the great black abyss below.

In a dramatic ritual voice, she said, "Oh, great and evil sisters of the great chasm, I beseech thee, in the name of all that is evil, fierce, and kicks ass, please, I beg thee, answer my *caaaallll*."

Vixx fell silent. Crèp came closer, but with caution. Vixx's eyes were closed, her forehead was sweating, her face was in deep concentration. Crèp watched her through the flames. Seconds passed, then minutes, and still Vixx remained perfectly still and silent.

Finally, Crèp leaned in a little closer to the flames and asked in a hoarse whisper, "Vixx, what's going on?"

Vixx opened one eye and whispered to Crèp, "They put me on hold."

After being placed on hold for over two hours, Vixx was pissed. "Oh, no, they didn't just diss me like that." She got up, stamped out the flames with her bare foot, and put her ritual stuff up. Then she grabbed a suitcase and started packing.

Crèp scratched his old dried-up head. "Where are you going, your majesty?"

"I'm going to hell."

Crèp gasped. "It's kinda dangerous down there, don't you think?"

Vixx threw her flatiron in the suitcase and kept packing. "I'm going to bypass those jealous tricks. I'm going to the Underground SPA to see Queen Domina personally. She'll tell me how to destroy those men." Crèp held her tampons out to her. She snatched them, threw them in the suitcase, and slammed it shut.

Crèp was worried. *"Queen Domina?* But, Vixx, the last time you faced her was ninety-nine years ago in front of the council, and she threatened to skewer you like a Peking duck for falling for a man, getting played like a deck of cards, getting kicked to the curb like a dented beer can, getting twisted and—"

"Shut up already! Dang. I *know* what I did." Vixx stuck her feet in her Nikes. "But I have to go and take my chances. I can't risk losing this brothel after waiting ninety-nine years to get it back."

Vixx rushed around the cellar trying to get ready to go. She grabbed her suitcase and reached for her jacket.

Crèp stopped her. "I don't think you'll be needing that."

Vixx left the jacket and grabbed her small purse and makeup pouch.

As she walked to the stairs toting her suitcase and glossing her lips, she gave instructions to her sidekick. "I want you to lock up this place, keep the cellar door sealed off, and don't let anyone in here while I'm gone. I won't be long, and when I get back"—Vixx paused by the door, tossed her white scarf over her shoulder, and struck a dramatic pose—"I'm gonna make those guys wish they'd never messed with a hot-blooded hell vamp like me."

Chapter

10

SUNNIE DIDN'T HAVE MUCH TIME LEFT TO PREPARE FOR Marvin's proposal, and she sure didn't want to waste it standing in front of the mansion in the midst of what smelled like a stink bomb, listening to Geffen's next plan.

"Hold up a second," Geffen said, following Sunnie, Rice, and Coach, who were all holding their noses and heading for their cars. "We can bomb the cellar. Get a demolition crew to come in and place strategic explosives at that east-side entrance and blow away that wall. That way, whatever is blocking the door will be removed and whatever is causing the smell can be cleaned out."

They decided to climb into Rice's car since it was the closest, and they wanted to get away from the smell as soon as possible. Geffen got in with them and sat in the back with Coach. Rice started his car and began backing out.

Sunnie gave her opinion of Geffen's plan. "Geffen, maybe you should let whatever is in that cellar *stay* in that cellar."

"We purchased it and now we *own* that *whole* house. We're entitled to use every square inch of it," Geffen said cockily.

Sunnie turned to look at Geffen. "Your *over*confidence amazes me. Don't you ever stop and wonder about the real owners—where they are, what they'd think about you taking over their property?"

"Who are the real owners, Sunshine? We found no information on them. I don't believe they exist," Geffen replied.

"But we did see a name, or at least some initials, on the microfiche, remember? It said 'Vx.'" Just saying the initials sent a hot wave through Sunnie's belly, but she didn't know why.

Coach, in his deadpan style, said, "What the hell is a *Vx?*"

Geffen didn't even respond—he dismissed the whole notion of an original owner with a wave of his hand.

Rice drove a little ways down the private road, far enough to escape the smell, then pulled over and stopped. "I agree with Gef. It's *our* house now, and we can't live there with that smell, so that smell's got to go."

Coach puffed. "Man, what could have caused funk like that? Something ain't right."

Sunnie threw up her hands. "That's what I've been trying to tell you knuckleheads about this *whole* thing—something *ain't* right. C'mon. Did you notice how many freak accidents happened while we were standing there?"

"All coincidental." Geffen rolled down his window and checked the air.

Coach asked. "How long we gotta wait for that smell to leave before we go back?"

Geffen tapped the window, contemplating his plan to blow up the cellar. "I don't know. Let's give it a half hour or so."

Sunnie watched the rest of the crew members drive past in their trucks, leaving. She started getting antsy. "I can't wait a half hour. I've got to start getting ready."

Rice turned toward her. "Getting ready for what?"

"My *proposal*, of course. How could you forget about something as important as that?" Sunnie started wiggling in her seat. "I'm taking off work the rest of today. Since Marvin wants to meet at my place, I figured I'd prepare a special dinner; that way we can stay in and keep the evening intimate. So, I need to go grocery shopping, as well as go shopping for the perfect 'proposal' outfit, and that could take some time."

Rice straightened up in his seat. "Dinner? You're cooking him dinner? What are you going to cook?"

"I'm thinking sweet-and-sour chicken. Do you think he'll like that?" Sunnie valued Rice's opinion because he'd taught her how to make it, though she'd changed the recipe a bit.

Rice thought about it a minute. "Yeah."

Coach grumbled. "Stop talking about food. I'm getting hungry."

Geffen was preoccupied with his plan. "Does any-body know of a good explosives company?"

"No," Sunnie said, then turned to Rice. "I have to leave now. Take me back to my car."

Rice drove them back up the winding road. "It probably still stinks," Rice said, as he parked.

Geffen stuck his nose out the window. "No, it's cool. Let's get out."

Sunnie was the last to get out the car. She looked around. The green smoke had ceased, as if someone had put a lid on it. She felt something else, too. Strangely, she no longer felt that thick, muggy, menac-ing presence that she always felt at that house. But she didn't get her hopes up. Her gut instinct told her it could return at any minute.

Geffen followed behind her. "Hey, Sunshine, get the paperwork started. We need to get our houses on the market. I've only got sixty days to make that payment on the renovations."

"Don't rush me, Geffen—I have to get ready for my proposal." Sunnie got in her car. She saw Rice coming.

"Okay, I won't rush you." Geffen turned back toward the house. "Just have it ready for us to sign first thing tomorrow morning ASAP."

Sunnie shook her head and started her car. Rice walked up to her window and leaned on her door as if she wasn't in a hurry. "Hey, you want me to help you fix that sweet-and-sour chicken?"

"Aw, that's real sweet of you to offer, but no. I should fix this myself."

Rice kept leaning on her car, purposely holding her

up. "You know how sometimes you get in a big hurry, and you mess things up."

Sunnie revved her engine, giving him a subtle hint. She said, defensively, "No. I got this."

Rice stayed on the car. "I could come over and—"

"Rice, get off my car." He leaped up. "I'll see you later." Sunnie drove off.

Rice said to himself, "Yeah. Later."

Chapter

11

WHEN SUNNIE WOKE UP THE NEXT MORNING, SHE WAS glad that her dreams had been relatively peaceful. The dark, looming presence seemed to have been lifted. She didn't know how long it would last, but she was happy. She had needed a good night's rest before this special day. It was *Thursday*.

She jumped out of bed and rushed to get ready. She had errands to run before she could start getting ready for tonight. The main thing was to get the guys' sales contracts signed. She'd stayed up last night inputting the information on Rice's, Geffen's, and Coach's homes. She turned on her home desktop computer, printed out the sales forms on her laser printer, and rushed out the door. All she needed were their signatures, and then she could post them on the MLS and get them sold. Even though he was in Sacramento meeting with his lawyers, she could almost hear Geffen's voice in her ear: "Hurry up, Sunshine. We need that money!"

She called all three guys to set up a place to meet and sign. Geffen gave her his lawyer's fax number in Sacramento. She stopped by her real estate office and faxed it; he signed and faxed it right back.

As for Coach, he was at the gym, as usual. She met him in the parking lot. "Hey, watch that sweat," she said, trying to shield her documents as he signed them with his sweaty hand.

But Rice was nowhere to be found. He wasn't answering his phones. She left two messages. She drove to his home in Baldwin Hills, near the Fox Hills Mall. He lived in a nice area with a good view of L.A., but he'd bought the smallest home on the block. *With his cheap self,* Sunnie laughed to herself, wondering if it would sell slower because of it.

She knocked on his front door. Compared to Coach's brazen Burbank bungalow, which always had loud music playing, and Geffen's highly stylized condo in Fox Hills, Rice's house was the most unassuming. The front façade looked more like a retired school-teacher lived there than a bachelor.

When he didn't answer, she went around to the back and reached inside the ceramic toad where he kept his spare key. She'd used it frequently to water his plants and feed his goldfish when he was on his book tour. It wasn't there. He'd taken the key out, for some reason. She knocked once more at his back door, thinking she'd heard him sneeze. There was still no answer, so she left.

She swung by her office and entered Geffen's and Coach's houses on the market, but Rice's would be delayed. She knew Geffen wouldn't be happy about that. But she had more important things to do than track down Rice. She had to go home and prepare for the big night.

The aroma of sweet-and-sour chicken breasts glazed in pineapple and brown sugar filled Sunnie's condo. That warm, sweet, sticky smell matched the way she felt inside. *Finally,* she could trade in her lonely one-bedroom condo for a multiroom family home.

She jumped out of the shower, whipped on her *proposal* outfit—a white cashmere sweater and matching skirt.

The doorbell rang. Marvin was twenty minutes late, and that wasn't like him, but she was not going to complain. She opened the door and smiled at her knight in shining FUBU. Marvin looked as nervous as a poodle in a pack of pit bulls.

"Come in, Marvin. Are you okay?"

"I'm fine." He kissed her cheek. She felt his lips quiver. His hands were empty. She was expecting a bottle of the finest champagne for this momentous occasion, but that was okay. He was so nervous, he forgot about etiquette.

Marvin was no Denzel, but he was adequate. He wasn't as smooth and suave as Geffen, as buff or as irresistibly rambunctious as Coach, nor did he have that quiet, pensive charm that Rice had, but he was, well, . . . adequate. Four years of med school might have given him a sprinkle of nerdiness, and those old-fashioned glasses and pants that were always three centimeters too short didn't help any, but all in all, he was a good guy. Sunnie would talk to him later about his consistent choice of cheap aftershave lotion. *Old Spice? C'mon, let's be serious.*

Sunnie sat him down at the dinner table and they ate while listening to smooth jazz on 94.7 FM, The WAVE. Sunnie was trying to ease Marvin's nerves. He kept dropping his fork.

"How's the chicken?" She sipped her wine, hoping he'd do the same so he could relax.

"Chicken's fine. Nothing's wrong with the chicken. Why'd you ask?"

"No reason, Marvin. It just seems like you're hardly tasting it."

He said, "Mm-mmm," and began to chew more enthusiastically.

"You know, I'm not really hungry either. Let's go sit on the couch and talk. Okay?" Without waiting for his consent, she put their plates in the refrigerator and carried their glasses to the couch, where Marvin really started fidgeting.

"Marvin, you said you wanted to ask me something important tonight." She wanted him to propose before she had to strangle it out of him.

He sucked in a deep breath. "Yes, right. Sunnie, I've never met anyone like you. You're everything I've always wanted in a woman." *Great start.* Sunnie tried to stay calm and was planning to look surprised.

Marvin continued. "Lately, I've been thinking a lot about us. This morning I called my parents and told them about you. They've been married over fifty years and taught me to do the right thing, you know—start a family the *right* way."

A family. Wow. Tears of joy welled up in Sunnie's eyes. She hadn't even thought about their kids yet.

"I love you, Sunnie."

"Oh, Marvin." She reached over for a Kleenex. That's when she saw it in his pocket. The *ring box.* She froze.

"Are you okay?"

"Yes. Go on." Sunnie's heart raced like a horse in the Kentucky Derby.

"Sunnie, I love you, and I want you to—"

The doorbell rang. Sunnie was so caught up in his proposal, she didn't want to move. Marvin hesitated.

"No, go on. You were saying?"

The doorbell rang again. Sunnie got up and ripped the door open. "Rice, what're you doing here?"

Rice walked in, hands in his pockets, whistling. "You told me to come by."

"No I didn't."

Rice stepped around Sunnie, "Hey, Marv, what's up?"

Rice sat on the couch next to Marvin and started talking to him like he was his old buddy, when Sunnie knew he couldn't stand the guy. "So, wha's up, G? You still chopping off noses and blowing up boobs?"

Marvin got tongue-tied. Sunnie interrupted. "Rice."

Rice picked up the remote and clicked on the TV. "I'm just messin' with you, man. You look a little nervous, a little wrinkled. You could use some of that Botox yourself, doc."

Sunnie couldn't believe this. "Rice, what are you doing?"

Rice looked totally innocent. "You told me to come, Sunnie. Remember? You left two messages on my voicemail saying you need me to sign my sales contract."

Sunnie took the remote from his hand. "That was this morning. I didn't tell you to come here, not right *now*."

Sunnie tried to give Rice eye signals, and even pointed to her ring finger on the sly to jog his memory about the *proposal*, but apparently he wasn't getting it.

Rice leaned back, put his arm up on the sofa, and relaxed. "Well, I'm here now. Might as well sign them. Ain't like I got nothing better to do."

Sunnie clenched her teeth. "*Now* is not a good time."

Rice saw how uncomfortable Marvin looked, wringing his hands, sweating. He looked up at Sunnie, who was glaring at him, fire practically shooting out her nose.

Rice made a very innocent, puzzled expression and feigned ignorance. He asked, "What's wrong with now?"

Sunnie lost it. She screamed, "*Riiice,* what has gotten into you? I told you I had *plans* this evening. You can sign those papers tomorrow. Why are you . . . ?"

Marvin stood up. "Look, it's no problem. Go ahead, let him sign the papers. We can do this, uh, another time. I've got to go anyway."

Sunnie stepped toward Marvin, who was practically out the door already. "Marvin, wait, you can't leave yet. You haven't—"

Marvin turned around. "No, really, it's just . . . bad timing." He glanced at Rice, who was sitting on the couch, just kickin' it.

Rice leaned up. "Too bad you gotta rush off. Hey, how was the chicken?"

Marvin's face went blank. "What chicken?"

Rice stood up. "Man, Sunnie fixed you her special sweet-and-sour chicken glazed with pineapples, and you don't even remember eating it?" Rice looked directly at Sunnie as if the statement was for her benefit.

Marvin, thoroughly embarrassed and tongue-tied, gave Sunnie a weak smile and left.

As soon as the door closed, Sunnie laid into Rice. "What in the *hell* was that all about?"

"C'mon, Sunnie, you know you don't cuss." He sat back down on the couch and put his feet up on her coffee table. "But if you gotta cuss at somebody, cuss at *him*. He ate your chicken and didn't even remember it. Now *that's* a damn shame." Rice changed channels.

Sunnie stood motionless and counted to ten. Rice pretended to look at TV but watched her out the corner of his eye. "You a'ight?" he asked.

She took a deep breath. Blew it out. "Yes. I'm fine. Just great."

She went into her bedroom. He tried to peek around the corner, but she came back around the corner carrying her portfolio briefcase. She stood in front of him and very calmly asked, "You want to sign the papers now?"

Surprised by her calmness, Rice looked around, hesitated, then said, "Yeah, okay. Let me have them."

Sunnie swung her whole briefcase by the handle and hurled it straight at him. He barely had time to duck. It hit him, open, papers flying everywhere.

"Sign that, you proposal wrecker!" She grabbed her purse and her car keys, and headed for the door.

Rice, covered from head to toe in legal-size contract paper, asked, "Hey, where you going?"

"To get my *damn* ring!"

After Sunnie left, Rice got up, went to the kitchen, and opened the fridge. He knew which plate was Sunnie's because she always sprinkled a little extra brown sugar on hers. He took it, put it in the microwave, and punched the numbers. He and Sunnie had been sharing stuff since fifth grade—laughs, bags of Doritos, secrets. That's why she was the only girl in the world he was comfortable around, because she knew the secrets that made up his life.

He took the plate to the couch knowing how much Sunnie hated for people to eat on her sofa. *Sorry, babe.*

He *was* sorry. Sorry he'd ruined her special night. Sorry he wasn't secure enough in his own skin to let her know exactly what she meant to him. Sorry she was out there running after a man who didn't appreciate just how good her chicken really was. But that was Sunnie, always running after something, never stopping to look around at what she already had. He licked his fingers. *Hmm, this chicken is kicking!*

Chapter

12

SUNNIE STOOD OUTSIDE MARVIN'S GRANADA HILLS HOME, banging on the front door in the middle of the night. She'd gotten a flat tire while zooming through Van Nuys. Since she had rushed out and left her cell phone at home, she'd had to walk a few miles to find a working payphone to call the Automobile Club, then she'd had to walk back and wait for them to arrive, a two-hour delay.

She saw a faint light in Marvin's upstairs bedroom window, but he wasn't answering. She stepped beneath the window and called, "Marvin!" The curtains moved. Finally, he opened his front door.

"Sunnie, what are you doing here? I wasn't expecting you." Marvin had on his robe, but didn't look like he'd been asleep.

"I wanted to come apologize for my friend, the way he barged in on us. He's been tripping lately, and I don't know why." Sunnie waited. "Aren't you going to invite me in?"

Marvin clumsily stepped aside and let her in, but didn't move after that.

She asked, "Did I disturb you? Were you busy?"

Marvin stuttered. "N-no, I was just, uh, upstairs."

"I know. I saw your bedroom light." Sunnie noticed him avoiding her eyes. "What were you doing, Marvin?"

"I was—uh—uh—"

Sunnie was a lot of things, but she wasn't a fool. She walked closer to the stairs and peered up into the hall-way where she could see his bedroom door. "Are you alone? Why is your bedroom door closed?"

"Because, uh—uh—"

"Wrong answer. Marvin, please tell me that there's not a woman up there."

"No, no. It's not like that." He was so jittery, his teeth clicked together.

"Look me in my eye." He tried to, but kept blink-ing.

"That's it." Sunnie headed up the stairs toward his bedroom door. "Of all people, I thought I could trust you. I came here thinking we were about to start a life together, and this is what I find?"

Marvin caught up to her, but she didn't stop. "Sun-nie, wait. Before you open that door, let me explain."

Sunnie threw the door open. There was no naked woman lying in his bed. There was no one in the room at all. The light was coming from his computer moni-tor. She went to the computer. He'd been online mak-ing travel reservations through Paradise Honeymoons. She saw her picture lying close to the monitor. She was speechless.

Marvin tried to explain. "I didn't want you to see this until—"

Sunnie threw her arms around him. He was still shaking. Obviously, this man had a nervous disorder and Sunnie wasn't helping any. "Oh, Marvin. I'm *sooo* sorry."

Marvin took her hand and sat her down in the chair. That's when she noticed his pants lying across the back of the chair and the square-shaped ring box still inside the pocket. Marvin got down on one knee in front of her. Her heart skipped two beats.

"Sunnie, I'm not good at this sort of thing. I've been trying to do this for two weeks, but I've been too nervous."

Sunnie clasped her hands around his sweaty face. "Marvin, I should have been more understanding."

"Sunnie, you mean a lot to me. It's hard to find the right words. I love you, Sunnie."

"I love you, too, Marvin." Sunnie started to cry soft tears of joy. Marvin's eyes welled up, too.

He took a final deep breath. "Sunnie, will you—will you *forgive* me? I slept with Charlotta."

Sunnie paused. "You, you—come *again?*"

Marvin stood up and walked across the room. "It happened two weeks ago. I got weak. I'd been struggling with this celibacy thing. Charlotta knew. Oh boy, did she know. She showed up on my doorstep Sunday night around half past booty call. I know I shouldn't have let her in, but that—that thong—"

"*Thong?*"

"The one she had on underneath her fur coat. We

went at it right there on the stairs, like jackrabbits on Viagra."

Sunnie felt the room spinning. She clasped her hand on the chair. "You—you—had—had—had—ssss—"

Marvin helped her say it. "*Sex.* With Charlotta. But just once—well, twice if you count the hallway."

Unable to speak, Sunnie made a squealing sound. Marvin threw himself at her knees. "But I love *you,* Sunnie, not Charlotta. Charlotta was only a quick fix in a weak moment. *You* are the woman I want to spend my life with. Please, forgive me. *Please.*"

Marvin pleaded, clutching her hands and trembling while she tried to make sense of it all. *So this is what Charlotta meant when she said she'd get me back.* Even Sunnie had to admit, Charlotta had gotten her back good. This hurt. This really, really hurt.

Sunnie had wondered if Marvin could remain celibate and faithful to her. Now she had her answer. *No.* She almost had to laugh when she thought about how right Coach and the guys had been about him.

Marvin was crying and slobbering all over her new white cashmere skirt. She wanted him to stop. She wanted this whole competition thing between her and Charlotta to stop.

Marvin pleaded, "Please, Sunnie, please forgive me."

Forgiveness. She'd been reading about it in her Bible, studying about it in Sunday school. *Is this a test, God?* Sunnie took a deep breath, unsure of what she was about to say.

"I trusted you. You betrayed me. There is no excuse for what you did."

Marvin started slobbering harder on her skirt. Sunnie tried to move her leg, but he was too heavy. "Marvin, look at me. I am so tired of playing these no-win games with Charlotta, competing over men. I'm going to ask you one more time, and tell me the truth—do you love *me* or *her?*"

Marvin looked up at Sunnie through red guilty-looking eyes. "I love *you.*"

Sunnie closed her eyes, released her breath. "This is not easy, but I—I forgive you."

Marvin was so happy, he buried his face in her lap. She would have the skirt dry-cleaned tomorrow. Right now she had to deal with this mixed-up situation. Angry, hurt, disappointed, she still wanted to get married. She still wanted to put an end to her lonely days.

Elated that she'd forgiven him, Marvin pulled her down on the floor with him, repeating, "I love you, Sunnie. I never intended to hurt you."

Caught up in emotion, he began kissing her hand, her neck, her face. Sunnie, caught up as well, was dizzy from having her emotions yanked around.

"Um, Marvin, I—we shouldn't—" Despite what he'd just put her through, it felt good to be held and kissed like that. Marvin was beside himself. He stretched her out on the floor and pressed into her, devouring her with sloppy, wet kisses.

"Ooh, I've wanted you so baaad," he moaned.

"Marvin, hey—wait—slow down. Let's still do this right. We'll have a short engagement and plan a quick, simple ceremony, okay? Then we can go on that honey-moon you're already planning for us."

Marvin, aroused and distracted, mumbled some-thing and kept devouring her. Sunnie was feeling the heat as well, but was trying to be good.

She said, "Go ahead, give it to me." Marvin started undoing his belt. Sunnie said, "Whoa! Not *that*, silly. I mean my ring."

Marvin murmured, "Mmm."

Sunnie repeated, "Go ahead and give me my ring."

Marvin's "Mmm" turned into more of a "Hmm?"

Sunnie playfully pushed him over, reached up into his pants pocket, and pulled out the ring box. She gave it to him. "Go ahead, propose."

Marvin, a raging ball of passion a minute ago, now looked stumped, holding the ring box.

Sunnie repeated, "Propose to me."

"Propose what?"

"Stop playing, silly boy, and just do it."

When Marvin wouldn't cooperate, she took the ring box, smiled real big, and opened it. It was empty. "Where's my ring?"

"Your what?"

"My *ring*? Where's my *ring*?"

Marvin backed up with an incredibly stupid look on his face. "Um, I guess I left that part out."

"What part?"

"The part where I had to give your ring to Char-lotta. She's pregnant. I have to marry her. You know, *do the right thing*."

Sunnie felt all the blood drain from her face. She felt weak and numb. She wanted to scream, cry, shout—anything—but all she could do was kick Marvin. She kicked and kicked and kicked until she couldn't kick anymore. And all he did was sit there like the blubbering idiot that he was and cry.

Chapter

13

On FRIDAY, COACH SAT BEHIND THE WHEEL OF HIS BIG, black shiny Suburban, blasting Chingy on his CD player. He was stuck in traffic gridlock on Manchester, trying to get to LAX to pick up Geffen.

As soon as Coach pulled up in front of the American Airlines terminal, he saw Geffen standing curbside decked out in a black tailored suit, carrying his Louis Vuitton briefcase like he'd just flown in from *Ebony* Fashion Fair rather than a meeting with his lawyers. Coach mumbled to himself, "Overdressed mutha-Ghana."

Geffen hopped inside Coach's Suburban and immediately checked his Rolex. "You're late, man. You know how I feel about punctuality—it's a sign of intelligence."

Coach cut his eyes at him. "Man, I know you didn't just hop into my ride complaining about my punctuality. Your ass could've caught a cab."

"No, I needed you to come because something's up with Sunshine." Geffen set his briefcase on the floor. He had Coach's full attention. "I called her this morning before I left Sac to see if she'd put our houses up on MLS. She didn't answer her home or cell phone. I called her office. They said she had an appointment but was a no-show. No call, no nothing. That ain't like Sunshine."

Coach turned off his CD player.

Geffen said, "Plastic Man was supposed to propose to her last night, remember? I'm wondering how that went." He quietly speculated.

Coach said, "If she ran off and eloped with that shit-head, I'ma kick both their asses."

"Elope? No, not Sunshine. She'd want us to be there." Geffen was sure about that. "Something's definitely up. Call Rice, see if he's heard from her."

Coach tapped a button on his steering wheel. The small computer screen on his console lit up. Coach spoke into the minuscule visor mic. "Dial Rice."

The sound of a phone ringing came over the speaker system, then Rice's voice message played: *"Y'all know I'm busy doing what I do, so if it ain't important hang up the damn phone and quit bothering me. If you feel it's important, leave a message and I'll decide for myself. Beeeeep."*

Coach said, "Rice, pick up the phone."

Rice answered, "Whassup, Big Zulu?"

"Geffen's back. We just left the airport."

Geffen spoke. "'Sup, dark man?"

"'Sup, Gef?"

"A whole lot of profits, my brotha, if we handle our business right. Look, have you talked to Sunshine lately?"

Rice yawned like he'd been sleeping, "Dropped by her place last night. She went somewhere. I waited, but ended up locking up and leaving. Why?" Rice intentionally left out the part about busting up Marvin's proposal.

Geffen said, "I can't get a hold of her. She didn't show up at her office this morning, either."

Rice was silent, then replied, "That ain't like her."

Coach looked over at Geffen. "I think we need to roll by her place."

Geffen said, "Definitely." He told Rice over the phone, "Peace out."

Coach and Geffen walked around to the back of Sunnie's West L.A. condo complex and stopped at the below-ground garage by the security gate. Geffen peeked inside. "Her Saab's in there, but she's not answering her buzzer."

They slipped inside the complex as another car drove out. Coach grumbled, "And they call this a secure building."

They took the elevator up to the third floor and banged on Sunnie's door. No answer. Coach pressed his ear to the door. "She's in there. I just heard her blow her nose." He yelled, *"Sunnie! Open this door, woman."*

Geffen yelled, too. "You want me to pick this lock? You know I'll do it."

Coach said, loud enough for her to hear, "Step back, Gef. I'm 'bout to break this mofo down."

They heard Sunnie scramble to unlock the door. As soon as Coach opened the door, she turned and walked back to her living room couch, her blanket dragging behind her. Coach and Geffen followed her inside, but could barely see anything. It was the middle of the day, but her window blinds were completely closed. Geffen turned on a light.

Sunnie had on a pair of orange pajamas that looked like a prisoner's outfit. Her hair was messed up, her makeup smeared, and her face was swollen and puffy. Empty Kleenex boxes littered the living room, and the small wire trash can overflowed with used tissue.

Coach stood over her and stared. "Daaamn, girl. What happened to you?"

Geffen was wondering the same thing but had more tact. He pushed aside a few stray snot rags on her coffee table and sat directly in front of her.

"Talk to me, Sunshine. What's going on?" She turned her head away and didn't say anything.

Geffen persisted. "You didn't return my call. You didn't show up for work this morning." Geffen was about to ask about the proposal, but instead he reached down and picked up her left hand, rubbed it. He made eye contact with Coach and discreetly motioned toward her empty ring finger. *No engagement ring*. He figured something went wrong but didn't want to embarrass her by saying it out loud.

Coach blurted, "Plastic Man *dumped* you?"

"Damn, Coach!" Geffen frowned and took Sunnie's

other hand, holding them both gently. "Talk to me, Amira." Geffen called her Amira because *amira* is Swahili for "princess." He wanted her to know how special she was, no matter what happened with Marvin last night. Instead of answering, Sunnie pulled the blanket up over her head.

Coach wasn't down with all that touchy-feely stuff. He cut straight to the chase. With fists balled, he demanded, "Just tell me where Buster is at. Plastic Man finally fucked up, and now it's time for me to go kick his ass."

Someone knocked on the door. Coach stomped to the door. "I hope to God it's you, 'cause yo' ass is mine." He ripped the door open.

Mother Roby raised her gold cane at him, ready to defend herself. "What did you just say to me, Franklin Brass?"

Coach backed up, hands raised, too shamed to even reply.

Mother Roby lowered her cane back to the floor and walked inside. She didn't waste any time. "Where's my Alisun? Something ain't right. I feel it in my spirit."

Sunnie lowered the blanket. The moment Mother Roby laid eyes on Sunnie, she sighed, "Um, um, Lord, have mercy." She made her way over to Sunnie. Geffen moved and let her by.

Sunnie's voice was low and hoarse. "What're you doing here, Ma Roby?"

Mother Roby smoothed her hand over Sunnie's uncombed hair. "Baby, all of hell's horses couldn't stop me from coming." She felt Sunnie's forehead for fever.

"I see it's not your body that's sick, so it must be your spirit."

She turned to Geffen and Coach. "Y'all can go, now. Alisun needs some quiet time, and I'm going to see what I can do to help her find it."

Coach and Geffen left.

Mother Roby turned back to Sunnie. "You fell off that bicycle, didn't you, baby girl?"

Sunnie nodded, leaned into Mother Roby's arms, and sobbed.

After two hours of talking to Sunnie about patience and faith, the only thing Mother Roby had convinced Sunnie of was her need for a shower.

Sunnie unwrapped the towel from her head and sat in front of Mother Roby for her to massage Vitamin E into her freshly washed hair and scalp. As a young girl, Sunnie loved this.

"Everything happens for a reason, Alisun," Mother Roby said, as she parted Sunnie's hair with a wide-toothed comb.

Sunnie wasn't in the right frame of mind to absorb spiritual truths. "Are you saying I was *supposed* to lose Marvin to Charlotta?"

"I keep telling you, you didn't *lose* anything. If God wants you to have something, nobody can take it away from you."

"I think God is paying me back for what I did to Charlotta."

Mother Roby asked, "What did you do?"

Sunnie confessed. "My friend who works at Charlotta's gynecologist's office told me that Charlotta got treated for an STD while Marvin was away at a month-long convention. I asked her if she could sneak and make me a copy of the report. She did. I mailed it to Marvin anonymously. He read it and broke up with Charlotta."

Mother Roby didn't say anything, just shook her head and moaned disappointedly, which made Sunnie feel even worse. "So I guess God and I are even now. He got me back real good." Mother Roby whacked Sunnie in the head with the comb. Sunnie cringed. "Ow. What was that for?"

"I'm tryin' to knock some sense into your head, child. Haven't you learned anything from all that Bible studying and going to church you've been doing? God doesn't work like that. He doesn't go tit for tat. If He did, we'd be in a whole lot of trouble. God's blessings *far* outweigh the disappointments he allows into our lives."

Gradually, Sunnie eased back. "I still think He's probably mad at me."

"No, God ain't mad at you, but you're starting to get me a little hot."

Sunnie glanced back, ready to duck. Mother Roby set down the comb and turned Sunnie around to face her.

"Alisun, you have a gift. It may feel like a burden at times, but just remember, God will *always* do what's best for you, even if you don't understand it. It's not your job to question God. It's your job to *trust* Him." Sunnie lowered her head.

Mother Roby asked her, "Are you listening?"

The truth was, the pain of the heartbreak she'd suffered the night before was still too new, and she was too hurt and confused to hear a thing. Mother Roby knew this, but still she hoped her words would sink into Sunnie's spirit.

"Baby, God is talking to you and showing you things, but you've got to learn to *listen.*"

Chapter

14

AFTER MOTHER ROBY LEFT, SUNNIE WANTED TO EXCHANGE the staleness of her bedroom for the fresh, watery smell of the Santa Monica Pier. Only a three-mile drive west on the 10 Freeway, the pier was the reason she had chosen her West L.A. condo. She could get to the pier fast whenever she needed to think, like today.

Things are always cooler at the pier. She and Rice used to say that all the time. And it was true. The cold wind slapped Sunnie in her face and helped clear her mind. The smell of salty water, sand, and seaweed stimulated her senses.

Sunnie parked her Saab in an all-day parking lot and started walking. The soft sand gave way beneath her loafers and made each step harder than it had to be.

The sun was setting and left in its memory a peel of orange sky on the horizon where the sky met the water. Rides like the Pier Plank Plunge and the La Monica Swing were shutting down, vendors were closing up their food stands and game booths, and people were leaving. Old men with fishing poles were packing up their dirty buckets of live bait and the few small scraggly fish they'd caught from the green water beneath the pier.

It seemed to Sunnie that the sound of the ocean waves rolling in and breaking against the rocky banks was louder than usual, that the seagulls' squawks were sharper than she remembered, and that even the laughter of two lovers with rolled-up pants frolicking down by the shore rang louder in her ears, but it could've been only in her head. *Are you listening?* Mother Roby had asked her.

Sunnie murmured into the wind, "I don't know *how*."

When Sunnie reached the end of the pier, the sun had all but gone, only faint daylight remained. The lamplights had come on. She pulled her coat together, unwrapped a stick of gum, and leaned over the rail. The ocean was black, impenetrable, and mysterious. The blackness of the water was hypnotizing. She didn't want to stare at it too long, fearing what she might see. She closed her eyes. *I don't want to be alone forever.*

Suddenly and without warning, she was attacked by sharp claws that came out of nowhere. Wings flapped violently in her face and she caught glints of a sharp, birdlike beak that was surrounded in a ghost-white feathery blur.

"*Aaah!*" She covered her head, flailed her arms, and grabbed hold of the railing to keep from falling. She felt the pull of the unwrapped gum she had been holding between her fingers and glimpsed the hooked beak of a seagull as it clamped onto it, and flew away as suddenly as it had come.

Sunnie stomped her feet, trying to shake the fright out of her wobbly legs. "Ooo—ugh." Embarrassed, she looked around. No one else had seen her. *Good.* Sunnie shoved her hands into her jacket pocket and tried to console herself. *Things are always cooler at the pier.*

That was her and Rice's favorite saying, a secret code of sorts from the first time they ran away from home together and caught the bus from Compton all the way to Santa Monica. Armed with a raggedy old sleeping bag, seven dollars and eighty-two cents, and a bag of Doritos, they came here to think, to talk, to tell each other secrets, and to cry. Just the two of them—little Alisun DeMila Clark and Rice Jordan, the skinny, shy little boy who lived down the street. They were *bestest* friends. He was a shoulder to lean on, a chest to cry on, a soft place to fall.

It was getting dark, too dark and cold to be out there alone. Sunnie was getting ready to leave when someone clamped their cold fingers around the back of her neck.

Sunnie inhaled. *"Oh, Jesus."*

She whipped around, expecting to see Freddy Krueger. Instead, she saw the familiar face of her *bestest* friend. "I'm going to kill you, Rice."

She slapped at him, but he bobbed and weaved.

"You called me Jesus. I ain't Jesus," he panted, in between ducking and laughing so hard. "Sunnie. Sunnie. Sunnie," he said, as he tried to catch both her hands and stop her from trying to strangle him. By the time he managed to catch her up in a bear hug, they both were laughing so hard they could barely stand up straight.

Sunnie was out of breath. "How long have you been stalking me?"

"Long enough to see that seagull kick your ass."

"You *saw* that?"

He started laughing all over again. Sunnie, both embarrassed and relieved, punched him two more times. She was never so glad to see somebody in all her life.

"How'd you know I would be *here?*"

"Things are always cooler at the pier," he said.

Chapter
15

THREE MONTHS LATER ON A SUNDAY MORNING, SUNNIE SAT
in Starbucks instead of in church. She was still hurt
and confused about what had happened with Marvin,
but had thrown herself into her work to keep from
thinking about it. She had slacked off spiritually, dodging Mother Roby's invitations to prayer meetings and
only attending church sporadically.

On the phone the night before, Mother Roby had
asked Sunnie, "What about your gift, Alisun? Are you
trying to ignore that, too?"

Sunnie had confessed. "I don't understand it. I go to
the mansion lately and I don't feel that strong presence
there anymore, not like the first few times I went there.
But I still feel a little weird. I'm confused. I'm just not
sure about anything anymore, Mother Roby."

The only thing Sunnie was sure of was that she
missed the guys. Geffen and Coach moved into the
mansion after their homes sold. Geffen spent all of his

time overseeing the last of the renovations, putting the finishing touches on the mansion, which had been transformed into a showplace. Coach spent all of his time working out in the gym and rehabilitating his leg so he could return to the football field.

Rice's home was in escrow when he went away on his book tour. She missed him the most. After her breakup with Marvin, she'd spent almost every night at Rice's house, blubbering about how much she'd wanted to get married. The routine was the same: She'd knock, he'd open his door, she'd lie on his couch, he'd pop popcorn and sit on the floor in front of her, watching TV in the dark while listening to her cry during the commercials until she'd fall asleep. She'd get up the next day, go to work, and do it all over again. She'd used Rice's shoulder so much lately to cry on, he needed to get it waterproofed.

After touring a few days, he had called her from Atlanta and asked, "Do you miss *me* or just my shoulder?"

Sunnie didn't understand. "Huh?"

To which he replied, "Never mind. Forget about it."

Rice's tour had ended, and he was back home, packing and getting ready to move. Sunnie couldn't wait to see him as well as the other guys, and that's why she'd called them on a four-way conference call last night. "Let's all meet at Starbucks tomorrow at noon. We don't spend enough time together like we used to."

Starbucks on Wilshire was crowded, but Sunnie managed to save three empty chairs. She'd just turned the page of her *Daily News* when she felt a tap on her shoulder. "Where's my Arabian Mocha Java?" Rice joked.

"Heeey!" Sunnie stood and hugged him real hard.

Rice looked uncomfortable with the hug, unsure what it meant.

"I was waiting for you before I ordered our coffees," said Sunnie.

"You were waiting for me so I'd pay," Rice said, always suspicious.

Sunnie blew him an air kiss. "You're cute, even when you're being cheap."

Rice went to the counter and ordered his Arabian Mocha Java and her usual Vanilla Bean Frappuccino, then returned to the table with their drinks.

Sunnie pointed to a picture of the J. Paul Getty Museum in the *Daily News*. "Look, they've added new stuff at the Getty. Let's go, okay?"

Rice sipped his java. "For what?"

"To see it."

"You see it right there in that picture."

"C'mon, Rice. It'll be fun and help take my mind off things."

Rice rolled his eyes. "You mean help take your mind off Marvin."

Sunnie closed the newspaper. "I am *so* over him."

Rice took another sip. "You are *so* lying."

Sunnie didn't deny it again. "Okay, then let's go visit your mom."

Rice put his drink down and looked off into the crowd.

"I know you don't want to talk about it, but it's been over a year since you two have talked, and that was only for five minutes when you dropped off Christmas presents. You can't just act like she doesn't exist. That won't solve anything."

Rice kept looking away.

Sunnie continued, "You need to tell her how you feel regardless of whether she accepts it or not. I'll go with you. I'll help you get through it."

Rice spotted Geffen and Coach coming through the door. He was glad for the interruption. "They're here."

Sunnie stood up and kissed Geffen's cheek. She tried to hug Coach, but he stepped back. "Back up off me, woman. You tryin' to block my game?" She slapped his arm instead. They all sat.

Geffen opened the file folder he was carrying and pulled out a work order from DynoTech Explosives along with the blueprint of the cellar. "Detonation time is scheduled for nine A.M. Sunnie, are you coming?"

Sunnie felt uneasy. She was getting that weird feeling in her stomach again. "Isn't blowing up the cellar a bit drastic?"

"That cellar is build like Fort Knox. We can't get in there any other way," Geffen said.

"But what if you damage the house?" she asked.

"Do you actually think I'd risk damaging the house after all the money we've put into it? These explosives engineers know what they're doing."

Sunnie squirmed. "Whatever's in that cellar should probably *stay* in that cellar. But I guess I'll come—at least that way I won't be at home worrying about you guys. But hey, I didn't call you here to talk about that stupid house. I called you here because we need some 'us' time."

Coach frowned. "Some *who* time?"

Sunnie repeated, "Some 'us' time. Our friendship is very special and I want to make sure it stays that way." Coach rolled his eyes and made a goofy face behind her head. "I saw that, Coach."

Geffen asked, "What makes you think we won't always be tight?"

Sunnie looked worried. "I don't know, guys, sometimes I just get this *feeling.*"

Both Rice and Coach made a face this time. Rice said, "Maybe if you cut out the pizza at bedtime, you wouldn't get all these *feelings.*" Sunnie cut Rice a look.

Geffen reassured her. "Look, Sunshine, our friendship is as solid as diamonds and nothing can change that, so stop worrying."

Rice nodded. "Gef's right. Can't nothing pull us apart."

Sunnie smiled, her eyes misting up. She turned to Coach for his turn.

Coach thought about it, then said, gruffly, "Yeah." Sunnie kept staring at him, waiting for more. Coach frowned and got defensive. "Hey, that's all I got. What the hell do you want from me?"

The next morning, Sunnie opened her blue, red, and yellow Impressionist bedroom blinds and thought about not showing up for the cellar excavation, but she'd promised Geffen. Besides, if something did go wrong, she wanted to be there for the guys.

When Sunnie arrived, the demolition crew was set up and ready to go. Bright orange cords ran from a detonator to the cellar door, where they'd strategically placed C4 explosives.

Rice and Coach came out of the house and stood by Geffen and Sunnie. She started having strange feelings again and wished she could talk them out of blasting open the cellar. It was such a beautiful clear day and she didn't want the flashes to start again, so she tried to keep her mind off things.

Sunnie asked Coach, "Have you heard from Joey yet?" She felt bad knowing that Coach's father had hurt his younger brother so much that he'd left town and hadn't called to let anybody know he was okay.

"Naw, nothing. If I don't hear anything soon, I'ma have to go find him," Coach said.

Sunnie noticed Rice watching her from the corner of his eye, but when she turned toward him, he looked away.

The foreman moved them a safe distance away. He gave the all-clear sign and set the timer. The hairs on Sunnie's arms stood at attention.

The foreman started his countdown. *"Ten, nine, eight . . ."* When he got to "one," the blast went off. A buzzing that sounded like an old man wailing exploded in Sunnie's ear. She was so freaked out, she jumped straight into Rice, banging her forehead into his chin.

He grabbed his chin. "Ooaw, Sunnie."

A large cloud of dust, smoke, and debris arose where

the cellar door had been. The foreman had misjudged the distance, and the dust cloud extended over Sunnie and the guys.

"Move back, people. Take cover," the foreman said.

While everybody stepped back and covered their eyes, Sunnie saw something move in the dust cloud in front of the cellar.

She yelled to the foreman, "Look! There's something over there."

The foreman turned and looked, but shrugged.

Sunnie insisted, "I saw something standing there and it ran into the mountains."

The foreman took another look. "Miss, it was only debris."

Gradually, when the dust cloud settled, nothing remained but a big hole in the ground leading into the cellar.

By sundown, the excavation was complete. The laborers had removed all the dirt and debris, and Geffen was deciding whether they'd use the cellar for something or board it off.

Geffen, pleased things had gone well, was in a good mood. "Once again, a brilliant plan well executed. Now I can start concentrating on the party."

"What party?" Sunnie asked.

"Didn't I tell you, Sunshine? I'm about to throw the biggest, classiest, most extravagant grand opening party of the year for our new hideaway."

Sunnie was both surprised and leery. "When?"

"In two weeks."

Geffen took Sunnie to his new custom-designed

home office and introduced her to his new assistant, Senda, a high-strung Korean college student with spiked hair.

Senda recognized Sunnie from a picture behind Geffen's desk. She jumped out of her seat. "I so happy to meet you, Miss Sunshine. Mr. Geffen talk so much about you."

Senda shook Sunnie's hand fast and hard before rushing back to Geffen's computer to continue preparing his guest list. Geffen showed Sunnie his party planner's notebook.

"Wow, Geffen. This is quite a party you've planned," she said.

"I know, and you're part of it. You're going to be the head hostess," Geffen informed Sunnie.

After they said good-bye, she headed to her car. The sun had set behind the dark, ominous trees that lined the property and at the foot of the Santa Monica Mountains. Sunnie stopped at the fountain in front of the mansion and looked back at it. The guys had really done it. They'd fixed up that old, decrepit mansion and transformed it into a stylish, modern, high-tech get-away reminiscent of a scaled-down Hugh Hefner's Playboy Mansion.

Sunnie turned and started walking toward her car. As she clicked off her car alarm, she heard a noise in the bushes near the edge of the mountains—the same spot where she saw something run out of the cellar and into the trees. She heard a weird, low buzz again, like an old man wailing.

Then she heard a woman's voice, and her stomach

erupted in a frenzy of shakes, quivers, and leaps. Sunnie jumped inside her car and locked the doors. She peered at the forest, but all she could see was dark trees.

Vixx returned from Hades feeling like a brand-new she-devil. All she could think about was getting revenge on those three bachelors for stealing her house. Though time-consuming, her trip had been a success; Queen Domina helped her hatch a plan to get rid of the guys. She was going to seduce them into destruction.

Since she couldn't penetrate the prayer covering, she'd have to go around it. She'd appeal to the guys' lust, luring them so deeply into the most tempting of deadly sins, no prayer could protect them from her. She'd shape-shift into their fantasy women and once she had them enslaved by their desires, she'd prey upon their fears and take away the things they valued most in life. Hopeless, helpless and not wanting to live anymore, they'd be at her mercy. She'd let them suffer and linger in despair while she stripped them of everything, including the house. Then she'd win.

Vixx hadn't realized just how long she'd been away until she walked up the newly paved, winding road and saw the house. It was breathtaking. The mansion had been completely remodeled and was hardly recognizable. It was tight.

She went around to the east side expecting to find her faithful ghoul sidekick, Crèp, in the cellar, eagerly awaiting her return. But what she found was a great big empty hole in the ground. The cellar had been blown up. Nothing remained but a cleaned-out pit, no place for a demoness and her ghoul to hide.

Vixx heard moaning in the trees nearby and went to investigate. When she got there, she saw Crèp sitting on a bucket.

"Crèp. What are you doing out here sitting on a bucket?"

"They put dynamite in the cellar and blew the hell out of it. Don't be mad at me. There was nothing I could do."

Vixx threw down her suitcase and started pacing. She hadn't figured on getting kicked out of the cellar.

Vixx stomped her foot. "Aw, *crap.* I've got to get situated and put certain things in place before I can start attacking the guys. Plus, now I've got to find us temporary lodging, too. Our hundred-year sentence is almost up, so I've got to destroy them fast."

Chapter
16

TWO WEEKS LATER, GEFFEN THREW HIS GRAND OPENING party. He was the epitome of coolness in his Bruno Magli gators and his midnight blue Armani suit. It was the perfect Saturday night—the celestial stars were out in the early evening sky, and a few celebrity stars had begun to arrive in their Jaguars, Benzes, and limos. Red-breasted valets lined the front entrance of the estate ready to whisk the cars away. An eight-foot-high exotic water fountain trickled down into an elaborate koi pond situated in the middle of a vast green lawn.

Geffen greeted his hand-selected guests, most of whom were VIPs from the entertainment, fashion, literary arts, political, and professional sports worlds. Geffen rubbed shoulders with some of the most influential and affluent people in Los Angeles, and his purpose in inviting a small crowd of them tonight was to promote his new venture, The Pleasure Spot.

Geffen escorted a few guests into the Grand Receiving Room with its vaulted ceiling and humongous Italian-cut glass windows, where they absorbed the avant-garde ambience created by the glowing sconces that lined the walls. He walked them through the living room, decorated in a red and black theme with a double-thick white sheepskin rug resting in front of the black rabbit-skin couch. An eclectic mix of sleek Italian-designed furniture and West Ivory Coast art conveyed both wealth and taste.

On their way to the courtyard, they passed through lounge-styled rooms illuminated by the soft glow of in-wall track lighting, some of them with their own private wet bars. Black and white tuxedoed butlers extended hors d'oeuvre trays to guests while professional caterers kept the buffet area flowing with gourmet foods and decadent desserts in the ballroom-like reception area. A live band mixed it up with jazz and neo-soul music.

Coach pulled Geffen to the side. He was decked out in a gunmetal gray Hugo Boss suit and looked like an Adonis ready to hunt down his goddess for the night. "Yo, Gef, introduce me to that pack of long-legged honeys who just walked in the door."

Geffen kept his voice low. "Those are the *Ebony* Fashion Fair models I told you about. I used to work with that one in the green."

Coach licked his lips. "I'd like to work with her myself."

Geffen checked his Rolex. "Have you seen Rice? He needs to get down here and mingle. And where's Sunnie? She was supposed to be here greeting people ten minutes ago."

"Rice is up in his room fiddling with his tie or some shit—you know how he do. Sunnie called and said she was running late. So you gonna give me the hookup?" he said, looking at the model in the green.

Geffen patted Coach's shoulder. "Can't. It's time for us to do the welcome. Go upstairs, grab Rice, and meet me in the courtyard in sixty seconds."

Geffen grabbed one of his workers. "Get the mic and PA system ready."

Coach winked at the model before going upstairs to yank Rice from his room.

Geffen stepped up on the platform in the courtyard area and greeted his guests. "Ladies and gentlemen, welcome to The Pleasure Spot. I'd like to thank each and every one of you for coming to check out this brand-new rental complex, resort, and bed-and-breakfast, where you can party in style and in privacy."

While Geffen detailed the amenities, Coach and Rice joined him on the platform. Coach stood next to Geffen, grinning and stroking his well-trimmed, jet black beard, showing off for the ladies. Even in a suit, his muscular body caught a lot of attention. Geffen's model good looks, wavy hair, and sharp attire said it all. Rice, however, stood off to the side of the platform, his back turned toward the audience. He looked good in his understated black Sean Jean. His black-rimmed glasses added an air of erudite sophistication, though he only wore them for camouflage. Several women had their eyes pinned on him as well.

Geffen continued his welcome/sales pitch. "We spared no expense because we want you to feel like a million dollars when you're here. After all, that's about what we spent."

The crowd laughed.

As Geffen talked, Rice slyly scanned the crowd and whispered to Coach, "Where's Sunnie?"

"Running late." Coach kept smiling at the ladies.

Rice readjusted his tie nervously. "I hate all these people staring at me like a damn monkey in a cage." He popped an Altoids in his mouth and put his hands in his pockets to hide his nervousness.

Geffen introduced both Rice and Coach to the crowd as co-owners and finished, "We welcome you to The Pleasure Spot. We hope you enjoy yourselves, have a good time, and the next time you need to reserve a place to—"

Geffen was cut off by a deafening screech followed by a loud boom. Before he could turn off the mic, five of the eight speakers popped like firecrackers, blowing their casings and dotting the courtyard with puffs of smoke. Then the lights went out.

Bewildered, Coach asked, "What the *fuck* was that?"

C h a p t e r

17

VIXX STOOD IN THE MIDDLE OF THE VAST LAWN AND LEANED against the koi pond fountain. She had watched the party guests as they entered *her* house. They had walked past her, but none of them saw her because she was in her supernatural form, her dark sensual body and flowing white dress invisible to the ordinary human eye.

Crèp. She called her trusty sidekick through mental telepathy. He was hiding in a cave in the nearby mountains since being blasted out of the cellar. Vixx had to beat up two coyotes to get the place, and compared to the cellar it was a shit hole. *I just turned the lights out on the men and their party guests. I wish I could take my sword, cut off their testicles, and get my house back right now.*

Crèp was rusty, so his response took longer to get to her. *You can't. Remember the protective prayer sheath.*

Yeah, yeah, yeah. I know all about that. As long as the

*girl is praying for them, I can't cut them like I want to,
but I can lead them by their own lust out of that protec-
tion, and into self-destruction.*

Vixx got excited. She was anxious to use the skills of
sexual seduction she'd learned from Queen Domina.
She remembered her instructions: "Give them what
they want and give it to them *real* good, and they'll be
ready to sell you their souls."

Crèp transmitted to her, *Time running out. . . .*

Vixx licked her lusciously sinful lips. *I know, and I
can hardly wait.*

Vixx waved her hand at the house and the electricity
popped back on. *Let's get this party started!*

As she started for her cave to get ready for the party
by swapping her invisible form for a visible one, somebody bumped into her, almost knocking her over.

"Oh. Excuse me." Sunnie was rushing so fast to get to
the party that she ran smack dab into one of the guests.
"I didn't see you standing there. Guess I was in too big
of a hurry."

Sunnie had grabbed the woman to keep her from
toppling over. The woman grabbed her back, her grip
strong and forceful. The woman looked utterly
shocked. She didn't say anything, just stared at Sunnie.

"Are you okay?" Sunnie asked. The woman looked
young, but had eyes that looked like they'd seen a lot.
She was dressed in a white gauzy-type dress with oversize sleeves that hung below her hands and drooped
unevenly at her calves, making it look like one big

uncut bandage—mummy-ish. Quite honestly, it was a butt-ugly dress.

The woman was undeniably attractive, but in a very dark, sultry, smolderingly exotic sort of way.

"You can see me?" the woman asked in a deep, gravelly voice.

"Uh. Yeah." *Duh?* Sunnie thought. *What kind of question is that?*

Her fingernails were long and dirty, and looked like she'd been scratching around in the mud. Sunnie looked down at the woman's bare feet. *What's up with that?*

Sunnie suddenly became aware of how hot and clammy the woman's hands felt on her skin. Sunnie let go of her; she let go of Sunnie. Sunnie's skin tingled where the woman had touched her, and the snap, crackle, pop that had started in her stomach as soon as she'd gotten out of her car increased.

Sunnie took a step back. The woman backed away from Sunnie, too.

The wind must have shifted because Sunnie suddenly got a whiff of the lady's scent. She smelled muggy and thick and dark, like if darkness had a smell to it.

Sunnie looked at the woman more closely. She was a dark silhouette of both beauty and evil, with a phantasmal, almost ghostlike transparency about her.

Instinctively, Sunnie knew that this woman was the threat to the guys she'd been dreaming about. Every fiber in Sunnie's body told her to run. But she stood there, her spook-o-radar practically burning up. Sunnie's heart went *ba-boom, ba-boom, ba-boom,* but somehow she managed to put words together.

She swallowed. "W-w-who are *y-y-you?*"

The woman studied Sunnie, contemplating. When she finally spoke, Sunnie could hear the venom in her voice. "I'm the *baddest,* most fierce bitch you'll ever come up against."

The woman waited to see what Sunnie was going to do.

Sunnie swallowed again. "Th-th-the guys. Y-y-you can't h-h-hurt them."

The woman's dark eyes were impossible to read. She spoke slowly. "You can't stop me."

Sunnie reached deep inside herself and pulled out some moxie. "I'll find a way."

The woman blinked her shiny, coal black eyes and said, "Not before I destroy them." She let out a loud, hawking, evil laugh that pierced Sunnie's eardrum and made her head buzz.

The woman turned and ran. Sunnie was so scared, she turned and ran, too, straight into the fountain. She tumbled forward, flipped, and landed flat on her butt in the koi pond.

Chapter

18

SUNNIE COULDN'T GO INSIDE TO THE PARTY BECAUSE HER brand-new strapless Ralph Lauren dress was dripping with koi pond water. After she climbed out of the fountain, she sat on a bench in front of the house. Her heart was still racing and she tried to think straight.

She gripped the edge of her dress and wrung it out. Fishy water splattered all over her Isaac Mizrahi sling-backs. Her heel was cracked. She'd left her phone and her purse in her Saab, so she couldn't call the guys. She would have to go inside and try to tell them what happened. But first she'd let herself dry off a bit.

As Sunnie sat on the bench wringing out her dress and massaging her buzzing temples, she heard a noise that sounded like a fender bender.

She looked up. A long, shiny purple limo rammed its way up the circular cobblestone driveway, pushing other cars out of its way. It was the longest limo she'd ever seen, boxy like a Hummer, something foreign and very eclectic. The limo forced its way in, scratching, bumping, and busting out the taillights of other cars parked there, including Sunnie's little yellow Saab.

All the valets had gone in the back, so Sunnie was the only one out front. Sunnie stood up. "Hey! What're you *doing?*"

The limo stopped directly in front of the house. Sunnie stepped closer. Every window was tinted jet black, even in the front. She couldn't see the driver. She knocked on the hood. "Hey, you just dented those cars, including mine!"

Slowly, the front door opened and the driver got out. He must've been the oldest, grayest chauffeur this side of the Mississippi. His skin was a putrid ash color, and it looked like he hadn't seen sunlight in several decades. His black uniform was so dusty it looked like he'd pulled it out of a cave, and it was more like an undertaker's getup than a chauffeur's. The crooked old guy leaned into a cane that resembled a tree branch, and used it to help him walk.

After he made his slow way to the limo's back door, he stood there stiff and silent, but he didn't open the door.

Sunnie figured the old guy was hard of hearing, so she yelled louder, "Hey, did you hear me? I said you wrecked those cars, including mine. I hope you've got insurance, buddy. You're too old to be driving anyhow."

Finally, the old man opened his mouth to speak. His teeth were rotten and looked like tiny dried-up yellow marshmallows that were barely hanging on to his gums.

"Madame wishes to speak with Señor Geffen, the host of this affair," he said in a fake, busted Brazilian accent.

Sunnie put her hand on her hip. "Oh, I'm going to get Geffen, all right. And when he comes out here and sees what you did, believe me, he is *not* going to be very hospitable."

Sunnie marched into the party, her dress damp and wrinkly and her wet feet slipping on her cracked heel. Geffen saw her and tried to find out what happened. "I'll tell you later. Right now, come with me." Sunnie pulled Geffen out the front and pointed to the damaged cars. "See? Look! This limo came barging up here like it was carrying the Queen of Egypt or somebody."

As soon as the old chauffeur saw Geffen, he opened the limo's back door. A woman got out—not just an ordinary woman, but an earthen goddess.

She put one long, sculpted leg out and gently followed with the other. With the grace of a thousand swans, she stood on her feet. Her royal blue sequined dress caught the light of the lamppost and sparkled as it moved like a curtain of diamonds around her tall, perfectly proportioned body. Her softly squared shoulders, her unbelievably tiny waistline, and her long silken legs were a sight to behold.

When she spoke, her soft, mellow voice had the melodic clink of champagne glasses. "Good evening, Mr. Cage. *Comment allez-vous? Prospère, j'espère.*"

Geffen took one look at her and his mouth fell open.

The woman extended her hand and Geffen took it.

Sunnie had never ever seen Geffen "Mr. Smooth" Cage this much at a loss for words. When he finally found a few, they were not the words Sunnie wanted him to say.

Geffen kept the woman's hand in his. "I'm—I'm sorry. Please forgive me, but I don't recall ever having the pleasure of—"

"No, you've never met me, I assure you. But I know so much about you." The woman's crystal-colored eyes sparkled with brilliant clarity. "And please, do forgive me for barging in and interrupting your party like this."

Sunnie piped in, "You interrupted a lot more than his party, toots. Your driver hit and scratched every parked car—"

The woman cut Sunnie off with a wave of her hand. "Of course, my accountant will take care of any damage we may have caused."

Sunnie whispered to Geffen, "Quick, get her insurance information before she dents and dashes."

Geffen ignored Sunnie. He was enchanted by this woman. "Don't worry about it," he said, staring into her eyes.

"I came here to meet you, Geffen Cage, an intelligent, ambitious young man who gets everything he wants." She glanced up at the house, then back at him. Geffen blushed modestly.

She continued, "I'm hoping to do business with you." The corners of her perfect mouth turned up slightly into a smirk when she said that, but only Sunnie noticed. Geffen was too blinded by the light.

Sunnie wobbled forward on her cracked heel to get a better look. Everything about this woman exuded elegance—the way she stood, the way she tilted her head, the way she talked. She oozed power, authority, class, and confidence, and yet she exuded an aura that had Sunnie's stomach doing a familiar gurgle, pop, fizzle.

Sunnie said to her, "He doesn't even know you, lady. How does he know you even *have* an accountant? Why would he trust somebody who hires a six-hundred-year-old driver who obviously can't see to drive her around in the first place? Huh?"

Sunnie rattled on, but the lady paid her no mind. She was busy holding Geffen captive. And captivated indeed, Geffen looked like a fly caught in a web.

The spider spoke. "Allow me to introduce myself. I am Dayna Devlin."

Sunnie's heel broke. She almost fell into the woman.

Geffen gently raised Dayna's hand to his mouth and kissed it lightly.

Oh please, Sunnie thought, and picked up her broken shoe.

The lady led Geffen off to the side, where they talked softly together. Geffen held her hand the whole time—like once he touched it, he couldn't let it go.

Sunnie heard Geffen say, "Just one dance? Please?" to which the lady acquiesced, and they walked around the east side of the house to the courtyard, where the live band was playing soft, romantic music. Sunnie hopped on one bare foot, following them and tripping over the lacecaps and the gardenias to get a better look.

Geffen slipped his arm around the woman's svelte

waist. They danced slowly in a private area of the garden, while Geffen gazed into her eyes as if he'd gotten lost inside.

Sunnie strained to hear their conversation. This woman was discussing the Dow Jones, trading tips, and investment strategies. *No fried green tomatoes there.*

Finally, the lady pulled away. "Oh, Geffen, you are delightful, but I really do have to go. I've got two other business matters to handle tonight, and I don't want to be late."

"Aw, do you have to rush off?" Geffen, the Doberman of business, was sniveling at this lady's feet like a poodle.

The lady laughed softly and replied, "Yes, Geffen. Punctuality is a sign of intelligence."

"Punctuality is a sign of intelligence"? That's Geffen's line, Sunnie thought.

Geffen stood transfixed, completely taken by Dayna. She lowered her lovely eyelashes and smiled at him. Geffen's PDA wasn't the only thing poking out the front of his pants. "I'll walk you out," he said.

She raised her hand. "No, stay. *Rappelez-vous moi dans vos rêves. Nous ferons votre réalité de rêves.* Think of me when you dream tonight. Good night, Geffen." She left in a cloud of mystique.

"Oh, give me a break," Sunnie mumbled to herself as she stomped to the house to find Rice. After searching several rooms, she finally spotted him wedged between the champagne fountain and an admiring fan who was getting in his personal space too much. Sunnie could tell Rice was uncomfortable. When he saw Sunnie, he excused himself.

"Where have you been, girl? And what's up with that dress?"

Sunnie tugged self-consciously on her damp, wrinkled Ralph Lauren, then pulled Rice to the side. "Never mind about my dress. I have got to tell you about the woman—"

Sunnie was interrupted by someone running past them saying, "You've got to see this. Coach is out on the tennis court in his suit."

When Sunnie and Rice heard Coach's name, they immediately went to investigate. They wiggled their way through the crowd of people who were whooping and cheering, their eyes fixed on the tennis court.

The first thing Sunnie saw was that Coach's gunmetal gray suit jacket was thrown over the edge of the tennis net and his expensive black Bruno Maglis were kicked off at courtside.

Coach was on the court, racket in hand, knees flexed in the ready position. His muscular thigh muscles bulged through his expensive dress pants, and his tight black silk shirt hugged every flexed muscle in his chest and biceps. He was sweating and grinning.

Sunnie was so busy staring at Coach she hadn't looked at the other end of the court. Rice tapped her shoulder. His mouth was hanging open. "Who is *that?*"

At the opposite end was a woman wearing the heck out of a thigh-high, slinky red strapless party dress. She had kicked off her stilettos. Every curvy inch of her five-foot, four-inch body was as fit as it was fine. Toned to a T, her flawless butter pecan skin glistened from perspiration. Her shoulders, arms, and calves were extra defined, and this girl had glutes and gams that would make Serena Williams jealous. In addition to the slinky strapless dress, she wore a sassy, sexy smile and a short Halle Berry–style traditional haircut.

"This is unbelievable," Sunnie said, as she watched the girl rear back her racket and slam the ball into Coach's side of the court with Wimbledon speed.

The sporty woman hollered at Coach, "C'mon, Big Poppa, show me what you're working with!"

She tried to divert Coach's attention with shameless, bold flirtation. He knew it, grinned, and kept his eye on the ball. He quipped back, "I'm 'bout to put it on you real good."

With a powerful forehand, he sent the ball straight back at her. She hit it back before it touched the ground. He backhanded it to her. She ran at breakneck speed, reached it just in time, and nailed it. By that time, Coach was at the net. He sent the ball sharp right court.

"Deuce!" he bellowed.

Sunnie and Rice looked at each other, speechless, then looked back at the tennis match.

With his chest heaving, Coach smiled and winked at the woman. "Am I too hard for ya?"

She replied in a sexy snarl. "That's the only way I like it. *Hard.*"

Sunnie rolled her eyes. "You've got to be kidding me."

Rice wiped his forehead. "Whew."

Sunnie looked at Rice, slapped his arm. "Why are *you* sweating? You're not even playing."

Rice chuckled.

When the sexy siren tossed the ball up for her next serve, her slinky red dress jutted dangerously high up her curvy thighs. With a quick motion, she thrust her racket forward and sent the ball straight at Coach.

Coach was ready, willing, and able. He received her serve and played off it. He whooped, "Give it to me, baby!"

She had tried to ace him, but he wasn't having it. He grunted and lunged at her small fuzzy ball. His broad chest muscles flexed and his forearms hardened as he gripped his racket real tight. With an orgiastic grunt, he swung, hurling it over the net back at her.

But the lady's athleticism allowed her to withstand the pressure. Though Coach was bringing the heat, her momentum escalated. She sucked her breath in hard, pushing her braless nipples forward. Sunnie could see them poking through her thin, damp dress like two Hershey's kisses. She jumped up and swung, sending the ball back to Coach at midcourt. Coach, grunting, reached the ball just in time and sliced it left court.

She grunted, too, but hers was a tigresslike growl through sexy clenched teeth. When they heard it, several men in the crowd shifted in their pants, including Rice.

Sunnie pinched Rice's arm. "This is insane. They're going at it like two animals in heat."

Rice kept watching. "I wish I had some popcorn."

In their final volley, Coach and his opponent locked eyes across the net. She swung, her whole body following the momentum of her racket. Coach matched her passion and gave her every bit of juice left inside of him. He thrust his body like a gladiator, unmercifully pumping both precision and power into his return stroke, and forced the ball into her court in exactly the right spot.

Breathless, she swung, pounding the ball hard. It flew over his head, out of court. Coach threw up his arms in victory. *"Match."*

Rice exhaled. "Dang. I think I need a cigarette."

Sunnie pulled Rice's ear to regain his attention. "That was ludicrous. What about Coach's injured leg? He shouldn't be out there playing like that." Rice and Sunnie walked onto the court as the crowd dispersed.

Coach leapt over the net and grabbed the woman by her waist. "Damn, Ma! You got some fire inside of you."

She threw her head back, scraped her red fingernails through her short hair. "Oh, you have *nooo* idea." Coach looked down at her nipples. She rubbed her hand across her sweaty chest in a suggestive stroking motion.

Sunnie wasn't fooled. This woman was out for Coach.

The woman curled up her glossy lips into a saucy grin. "Ooh, it feels so *good* getting beat so *baaad,*" she purred.

"Is that right?" Coach's eyes followed her hand as it moved down her breasts.

She pushed her sweaty bosom into his chest. Her small but strong, sturdy legs kept her balanced up against him.

"That's right. You really know how to work it, big

fella." Her eyes slanted with innuendo. "Is this the part where we, uh, shake hands?"

Coach threw his racket down. "We can do a whole helluva lot more than shake—"

She didn't wait for him to finish. She dove into him, pressed her plump saucy lips into his, and gave him a long, hard, deep tongue-tangling, mouth-sucking kiss while coiling her leg around his like a pretty snake.

Rice jumped back. "Damn!"

Sunnie said flatly, "Go get the fire hose. We're gonna need it."

She walked over to them. "Hey, you two!" They ignored her and continued deep tonguing. Sunnie leaned up to Coach's ear. *"Aahemm!* Hey, cool it."

Finally, Coach came up for air. Sunnie looked at Coach and looked at the girl. Something wasn't right. She was too perfect for him. Plus she had a hotness about her, and it was more than just horniness for Coach, because Sunnie felt it, too.

Sunnie ran her hand over her arm to smooth down the goose bumps. First her stomach and now chills. Sunnie tried to ignore the sensations and talk sense into Coach before he hurt his leg more. "Coach, what about your leg? And who's your friend?"

Coach grinned and smoothed down his short, neat beard. "This is—uh—"

"You don't even know her *name*, Coach?"

The woman got up on her tiptoes and whispered her name into Coach's ear while biting his earlobe.

"Evie McLure," she said, real breathy. Coach leaned down and started kissing her more, rubbing her back, causing her short red dress to rise over her firm round butt, showing a lot of skin and a little thong.

Rice stood back, ogling the two and shaking his head. *"Damn."*

Sunnie was getting ticked from all the disrespect. "Coach! This is a respectable social event, not a strip club."

Evie turned toward Sunnie. She snarled and let out a low-pitched growl that sounded just like that of a bobcat. Sunnie jumped back. Evie turned back to Coach, laughing. "I think I scared her. I was just joking."

Sunnie collected herself and straightened her wrinkled dress, embarrassed. Her headache came back again. "That wasn't funny. And you *didn't* scare me."

Instant dislike. And it was mutual. The woman pushed her lips against Coach's thick neck, planting hot kisses and sucking. Evie paused midsuck and mumbled to Sunnie, "I wasn't talking to you, bitch."

Oh, no she didn't. Sunnie said, *"Excuuuse* me?"

Evie giggled. "You're excused. Now, be out." She went back to kissing on Coach.

Sunnie looked at Coach. She couldn't believe he kept kissing on this girl even though she'd just disrespected one of his best friends.

Rice pulled her arm. "C'mon, Sunnie. They need privacy, and a room."

Sunnie jerked away. "No!" She slapped Coach's arm. "Are you going to let her talk to me like that?"

Coach kissed on Evie a little more, and finally looked up. "We're just having a little fun, ain't hurtin' nobody. Now, back off."

Evie snickered. "Yeah, back off before you gets knocked down."

Every hair on Sunnie's head rose. She felt heat coming out of nowhere and her stomach did a triple back flip. She thought she knew why—it wasn't because of her *gift*, it was because she was *pissed*. "Are you *threatening* me?"

Evie let go of Coach and stepped to Sunnie. "I'm *promising* you."

Sunnie stood her ground. Both Rice and Coach stepped between the two women. Coach said, "Ladies. As much as I love a good girl fight, y'all need to cool it."

Evie laughed like it was nothing. She turned to Coach. "Hey, Big Poppa, I gotta go anyhow. Got one more thing I gotta do tonight."

Coach tried to stop her. "Naw, don't leave. We're just getting started."

She palmed his chest, squeezed his pec. "Save your strength, Big Poppa, you're gonna need it when I come back." She winked, turned, and bent over to pick up her stilettos from courtside, giving him another peek at that red thong. She slung them over her shoulder and walked away barefoot.

Coach bit his fist. Both Coach and Rice said, *"Da-yum."*

Coach started dancing and singing Biggie's song: " *'I love it when you call me Big Pop-pa.'"*

Chapter
19

AT 2:00 A.M. THE PARTY WAS WINDING DOWN. HOURS HAD passed since Coach let that little floozy disrespect Sunnie on the tennis court, but Sunnie was still fuming. Rice was trying to get her to let it go. "C'mon, let's dance to take your mind off it."

Now, on their fifth dance, Sunnie leaned tiredly on Rice's shoulder as he rocked her back and forth—not much rhythm, but it was calming. The band played softly. It was an instrumental version of Stephanie Mills's "The Power of Love." Only one other couple danced in the courtyard next to Rice and Sunnie. Most guests had gone home. Sunnie didn't know where Geffen or Coach was, and didn't care. She was mad at them both for not taking her side over those women.

Sunnie's stomach had finally started to settle down. The incident with the dark woman at the fountain had rattled her so much that her spiritual spook-o-meter had continued to beep the entire night. It beeped when

Geffen met Dayna Devlin, and it beeped when Coach hooked up with Evie McLure. Sunnie thought it was broken. Her head still ached from when that dark woman blasted her eardrum with her loud, wicked laugh. That woman was very pretty but in an evil sort of way.

When she told Rice about it, he said, "Sunnie, quit trippin'."

She was sick of talking about it tonight. She just wanted her headache to go away.

"Let me help that headache," Rice said, and he massaged the back of Sunnie's neck as she leaned her face into his shoulder. She was glad he'd taken off those wire-rimmed glasses that he only wore as a decoy to keep women from staring into his eyes to see if he was lying.

Sunnie leaned all her weight into Rice as they danced, and he did his best to support her. She mumbled, sleepily, as he massaged her neck, "Umm, that feels so good. How could Coach let that skank dis me like that?"

"Can't you ever just be quiet and let things go? Sheesh." Rice shifted her weight to his other shoulder. He tried to justify his buddy's behavior. "Besides, Big Zulu was just smelling those panties, that's all."

Sunnie raised up. "Oh, so it's always all about the panties with you men, is that it?"

Rice gently pulled her head back. "Calm down, Sunnie. I'm just saying."

She leaned into him again, but wasn't willing to drop the subject. "No, you're right. It's true. It *is* all about the panties. The sooner I learn that, the sooner I can get on with my life." She felt Rice exhale like he knew what was coming next. Too bad, she had to get it out. "That's where I went wrong with *Marvin*."

Rice paused, temporarily losing his rhythm altogether. Sunnie knew he didn't want to hear it, but she couldn't help it. After three months, her heart was still stinging because of Marvin's indiscretions.

Sunnie went on: "If he'd just been honest and admitted that he was like *all* other men—that as soon as I looked the other way, he'd hop in bed with another woman or do it on the stairs—he could have saved me a lot of grief."

Rice asked, "So, now you *do* believe that *all* men chase the panties? That *no* man can fall seriously in love and be faithful to one woman?"

Sunnie paused, then blurted, "Yeah, I do! Just look around. What happened here tonight is a perfect example. Geffen was lusting all over that woman in the purple limo and forgot all about the fact that she wrecked my car. Coach was lusting *and* slobbering over that woman in the red thong, let her disrespect me and didn't take up for me. Yeah, men are like that. They forget what's important in order to chase panties."

Rice waited a minute. "What about me? I'm here with you, massaging your neck, listening to you whine."

Rice had made a good point. Sunnie didn't have a quick answer for that.

She said, "That's true, huh? Why *aren't* you with one of those women who were throwing themselves at you tonight?"

Rice shrugged. "Tired."

Sunnie took that to mean physically, nothing more. They danced through the end of another song with no words.

Thanks to Rice's massage, her headache was starting to dissipate. She said, "Mmmm, you smell good. What is that?"

Rice egged her on. "You like my cologne, but you don't know what it is?" She shook her head. "You bought it for me on my last birthday."

Sunnie buried her face in his chest, embarrassed. Rice cut her no slack. "Yeah, you should be embarrassed. Girl, I swear, sometimes you move so fast you don't pay attention to things."

He was right. She laughed quietly to herself. *Funny, I can hear his heart beating.*

He said softly, "Hey, remember what we talked about on the pier that Friday night, the day after Marvin broke up with you?"

Sunnie smiled. "Yeah. We talked about how that seagull had kicked my butt."

"Not that." Rice paused again, then continued. "No, I'm talking about when you said you were looking for that one true and meaningful love."

Sunnie almost couldn't hear him for his heart was beating so loud.

Sunnie nodded. "Yeah, I remember, and because I didn't find that 'true and meaningful love' with Marvin, I started crying and slobbering all over your suede jacket. I think I ruined it. I'll buy you another one."

"Sunnie, I don't need another *jacket*." Rice got quiet

again, pensive, like he was longing for something. Rice could be so private and secretive sometimes, and trying to get things out of him was a chore. Sunnie was too tired for that tonight. Maybe she'd ask him tomorrow what was on his mind. She had a feeling he wanted her to. But right now she didn't want her headache to come back, so she left him to his thoughts. Rice didn't say anymore.

After that song ended, the bandleader took the mic. "Ladies and gentlemen, that does it for tonight. It was a pleasure to play for you. We wish you all a good night and all the love you can handle. Thank you."

Rice walked Sunnie back to the table where she had left her shoes.

She mused, "It's kind of sad when the last song plays, the lights come back on, and the party's over." Sunnie sat down. Rice sat next to her and put his arm around her. She scooted down in her seat, relaxed her head on his arm. He continued massaging her neck.

She blew out a long stream of air. "You know what, Rice? I take back what I said earlier. I *do* still believe in true and meaningful love between a man and a woman."

His hand paused. "You do?"

"Yeah, I do. I really do." Sunnie could hear his heart beating again. She smiled and closed her eyes. "You know what else, Rice? I think we are really supposed to be together."

Rice's whole body froze. He cleared his throat, took the gum out of his mouth, and placed it in the ashtray. Sunnie wondered what he was thinking, because whatever it was, it made him get real nervous.

Rice said, "Funny you'd say that because . . ." Rice paused. "I feel the same way, just didn't know how to tell you."

Sunnie jerked around and looked at him, surprised. "You *do?*"

He nodded. Sunnie never saw Rice's eyes look more compassionate than they did at that moment. "Oh, Rice, then you agree with me. Marvin and I *are* supposed to be together. Charlotta messed it up for us."

Sunnie laid her head back down on Rice's shoulder. He didn't say anything.

After about thirty seconds, Rice snatched his arm from around her neck and quickly got up. "What's your hurry all of a sudden?" Sunnie asked, bewildered.

Rice yanked off his tie like it had been choking him and shoved it deep into his pocket.

"How's your headache, Sunnie? Better? 'Cause *I've* got one now. I'm going upstairs to get that Excedrin. You want some?"

Before she could answer, he'd already walked away.

Rice left his bedroom and was walking down the hall carrying the bottle of extra-strength Excedrin when he passed by his private study. A light was on inside. *I know I locked this door.* He pushed the door and it opened. A woman was standing inside with her back toward him.

Rice hated nosy people. "Excuse me. Nobody's supposed to be in here."

The woman turned around, startled. She snapped

the book in her hand closed, then nervously fumbled with her wire-rimmed glasses.

She barely glanced up at Rice. "I'm sorry, I—"

"This place is private. It's where I—It's off limits." He tried to see the book in her hand. It probably was one of his. She was probably another delusional fan.

She wore her hair in a conservative chignon. She was dressed in a dark gray blazer buttoned all the way up to her neck, with white cuffs, a plain-cut knee-length skirt, and low-heeled black pumps. She looked more like the manager of Barnes & Noble than a party guest.

She avoided his eyes. "I guess my curiosity got the best of me. I'll leave right away."

She set the book down on his desk. He glanced at it, and was surprised to see it was not one of his, but *The Perpetual Search for Identity: One Brave Soul's Journey* by Azekel Adofo Ajene.

He looked at this woman again. *Out of all the books on his bookshelf, why would she pick that one?*

She apologized, leaving his desk. "I'm sorry, Mr. Gordon, you probably think I'm some lunatic fan of yours, stalking you for your autograph or—"

Rice stopped her. "What did you call me?"

"Oh, I forgot. I guess you prefer to use your pen name, *Jordan,* as opposed to your birth name, *Gordon.* Again, I'm sorry. I'll go now. I'm very sorry I bothered you. Good night."

"Wait," Rice said. Both Rice and the woman stopped, unsure what their next move should be. Rice was perplexed; something about this woman caught him way off guard. First of all, she knew his real name.

None of his fans knew his *birth* name. Second, what were the chances of a stranger walking into his office and picking up his favorite book? About a million to none.

Rice didn't want her to leave—not until he tried to figure out this perplexing situation.

He stumbled over his words. "I don't think you're a—It's just that I always keep this door locked, and I don't know how you—"

She fumbled with her glasses again. "I wouldn't blame you if you were to have me arrested. Believe me, I understand. I'm a very private person myself. I'd hate for someone to invade my privacy. Again, I apologize—"

"Why that book?" he blurted.

She paused. "Excuse me?"

"Out of all the books in here, why'd you pick *that* one?" He pointed to the book she'd been reading.

She said matter-of-factly, "I find Ajene's work inspiring."

"In what way?"

"Well . . ." She pushed her glasses farther up her nose. "Everyone is searching for his or her own identity, but not everyone finds it—at least, not their *true* identity."

Rice listened carefully, but didn't say a word.

She continued, "The author's assertion that everyone is born with a divine identity already in place, but that exterior forces can and do impact upon it, disfiguring or destroying it, is as enlightening as it is disheartening."

Rice crossed his arms. He knew what she was saying,

but was having a hard time believing she was actually saying it. He had never discussed these theories with anyone, not even Sunnie.

She went on. "What inspires me is that the author insists we can somehow reclaim our true identity— pure and intact—despite all the dents, disfigurations, or negative impacts that have tried to destroy it. That we may indeed be impacted, but that the true essence of what we are, of who we are will not be changed— that the truth of who we are is more powerful than any external force."

She adjusted her glasses and gave a small, demure smile. "In short, it's good to know that we still are who we are."

On the surface, Rice's expression remained bland, but inside he was reeling. *This woman gets it.* But Rice cautioned himself: Even though she understood the hypothesis, did she believe it? Did she believe that a shy, skinny boy from Compton could have his identity damaged by a traumatic event, grow up unsure of himself, and somehow as an adult find his true identity again?

Rice didn't know. All he knew was that nobody was supposed to be in his office, but now that she was there, he wanted her to stay. He looked at the bottle of Excedrin in his hand. *Sunnie.* They'd been best friends since forever, but no matter how much or how long they talked, she didn't seem to *get it,* and he admitted that he was certainly not the best communicator in the world. So there they were—two people with headaches who couldn't seem to help each other.

Rice sat the bottle of Excedrin down on a table. He cleared his scratchy throat.

"You don't have to go." He pointed to his coffeemaker. "Would you like a cup?"

Sunnie waited twenty minutes for Rice to return with the Excedrin. Without his steady hand massaging the back of her neck, her headache came back.

Tired of waiting, she stood and walked up the winding staircase to his bedroom. She knocked on his door. He didn't answer, and the door was locked.

As she walked down the hallway, she noticed a light on in his study. She got closer and heard Rice talking to someone inside, a woman. They were laughing. *Um, that's odd.* Sunnie knew that Rice absolutely hated for anyone to enter his study—even her—though he tolerated her. Now, here he was laughing it up with a woman while she sat downstairs waiting for him to bring the Excedrin for her headache.

Sunnie wanted to see this lady whom Rice had allowed into his private study. She turned the doorknob. It was locked.

She knocked. "Rice. It's Sunnie."

They stopped talking, but she heard a chair move. "Rice."

Sunnie knew Rice. He wouldn't take a woman into his private study to have sex. He would have gone someplace less personal, like one of the many guest rooms. This was something else—they were *talking*. It was clear to Sunnie that he didn't want to be interrupted, and that hurt.

In fact, it hurt her so much that as she leaned into the door frame trying to listen, her stomach started to flop, jiggle, and roll again.

Not knowing what else to do, Sunnie went back downstairs. Neither Coach nor Geffen was around—only a cleanup crew. Sunnie picked up her busted shoes, got in her busted Saab, and drove back home to her lonely one-bedroom condo.

Chapter 20

ON SUNDAY MORNING, THE DAY AFTER THE PARTY, COACH
bounded down the stairs. He didn't see Geffen or Rice
around the mansion. He figured Rice was sleeping late
because he always did, and Geffen was probably somewhere on the premises tallying up his future earnings
based on the success of last night's party.

Coach left all the figuring to Geffen, and while he
couldn't quote statistics or spreadsheets or anything like
that, he knew the party had been a success. The place
had been packed with high-profile people, but all
Coach really cared about was the profile he got on that
young, hot shorty he'd met, Evie.

Coach passed a few cleanup people in the kitchen,
broke open an egg, tossed it into a shake, and drank his
breakfast. He would have preferred to sit down to some
grits, pancakes, bacon, biscuits, and gravy prepared by
one of his many honeys, but he didn't have time for
that. He had to run. Today he had to play *Cops,* and

hunt down somebody who didn't want to be hunted down.

After driving up Interstate 5 for about two hours, Coach got out, pulled his beanie down real low on his forehead, slipped on his dark glasses, and limped inside a bar. He was limping because of that game of tennis he'd played last night, but he didn't regret it. When Evie had walked up to him in that short, slinky red dress and said, real sexy, "You wanna play with me, Big Poppa?" there was no way Coach was going to refuse.

Plus, Evie really boosted his ego, and he felt it needed a boost. Dealing with being injured and sidelined, J.B., and now this shit with Joey, Coach needed someone like Evie to come along and take his mind off his troubles.

Coach handed a twenty-dollar bill to the doorman at Bam Bam's. The doorman took the cover charge. He glanced up at Coach's dark shades and beanie, probably used to seeing men disguise themselves before coming into a gay bar.

Coach walked in and picked a table in the back, away from the light. The waiter came to the table. Coach said, "Gimme a beer."

"Light or low cal?"

Coach looked at the guy for a minute, then looked away like he didn't like what he saw. He grumbled, "Regular."

"Dark, low alch, or stout?"

Coach looked at him again, but didn't reply.

The waiter shifted his weight to his other hip. "We have medium and low carb. Then there's draught, lager, or ale. If you're health conscious, you'll want to try our soy beer. We call it our 'BoyToy Soy.'" The waiter giggled.

Coach spoke real slow and low through clenched teeth. "Just—bring—me—a—fucking—*beer.*"

The waiter tsk-tsked. "Oooh, you really *scerrr* me." He blew Coach a kiss, turned on his heels, and wagged his tail off. Coach knew he wouldn't drink the beer when it arrived.

Coach didn't come for the beer anyway. He'd driven nearly two hundred miles up the California coast, and had searched a half dozen rainbow bars with names like The Back Door, Endup, The Swallow, and Moby Dick's. He had questioned a bunch of colorful characters trying to get the information he needed, and finally he'd ended up in Fresno at Bam Bam's. He was tired. He was ornery. He was pissed. But mostly he was trying to hold it together.

Coach sat low in his chair and watched the tall man in the tan and white FUBU jacket who was sitting at the bar. He was alone. That was good.

The waiter brought the beer. Coach paid for it, but didn't touch it. It smelled . . . *fruity.*

Coach lowered his sunglasses and watched the man at the bar. He was average size, well proportioned for his height, not fat, not skinny. He was good-looking, for a man, not that Coach looked at men in that way. He had also grown a beard. Coach got up and ushered his younger brother outside.

Alone in the bar's alley, the two Brass brothers avoided eye contact. Neither knew what to say. Finally,

Coach said, "Joey, Ma wants to see you, wants you to come back home."

"J.B. still alive?" Joey asked, his jaw tight. Coach frowned at his brother's question. "Then I ain't coming home."

Coach took the beanie off his head. "Your landlord evicted you from your apartment, threw your stuff on the curb. I got it, put it in storage. Looks like you lost your job at the *Daily News*, too, since you left and didn't call nobody."

Joey didn't say anything.

Coach exhaled real hard, fiddled with his cap. "Come stay with me, Joey, till you get your shit together."

Chapter 21

On that same Sunday morning, the day after the party, Geffen hadn't slept late. In fact, Geffen had barely slept at all. He had risen with the sun and was in his office before 8 A.M. The party had been a huge success, the turnout better than he expected, but the overall success of the party paled in comparison to his success on a personal level. He'd met a woman—no, a goddess—who not only blew him away in person, but when he went to sleep, she was also in his dreams.

He was so excited, he couldn't sleep. He had gotten up at 3 A.M. and checked his email. Dayna had sent him an email requesting a date. Geffen hadn't been nervous about a date in a long time. In fact, Geffen had *never* been nervous about going out with someone, but he was this time. Dayna Devlin was worth getting nervous about.

Geffen spent all Sunday morning and afternoon planning his clothes, his shoes, and his grooming for

his date with Dayna. He had to look as perfect as she
had looked the night before. But it wasn't all about
looks this time—this woman had substance. That's
why Geffen scoured the internet, briefing himself on
the current financial and business-related news. He had
finally found a woman who didn't look like a fried
green tomato and yet could talk business, so he certainly wanted to be at the top of his game.

Dayna picked him up in her foreign import Hummer-
style stretch limousine, and they were chauffeured to a
high-brow restaurant in Simi Valley. Unlike his night-
marish date with the horny bank owner/crypt keeper,
this date was a dream come true.

As they sat in a private booth with a view of the
valley, Geffen paid no attention to the glitzy décor,
the indoor fountain, or the dreamy ambience of the
restaurant created by the small live orchestra music.
He couldn't take his eyes off the divine Ms. Dayna
Devlin.

Geffen dismissed the waiter after he poured their
champagne. He said to her, "Dayna, you have the most
extraordinary pair of eyes I've ever seen. They are like
crystals, like mirrors. I swear I can almost see myself
inside of them."

Dayna didn't blink, nor did she blush the way most
women usually did when Geffen paid them a compliment. Dayna was nothing like the rest. She stared
straight into Geffen's eyes, into his soul. The more they
talked, the more he looked at her, the more she fulfilled
his fantasy.

Dayna's voice was enchanting, like music. "I see

you're a very driven man, Geffen. That you value money and intellect, and feel the two are intertwined."

Geffen replied, "We only met last night, yet you know me so well." Geffen sipped his champagne. "Ah, finally a woman not given to small talk. Confidence in a lady is like an aphrodisiac."

Dayna ran her hand across his. "You are a very confident man yourself, Geffen—at least, on the surface."

Geffen gave Dayna a look that said, *Explain.* She did. "Geffen, you rely on your intellect and your ambition to get you the material things that you desire, but there is something *non*material that you want, but you can't have it, and it erodes your confidence."

Geffen let slip a nervous chuckle, but tried to cover it up with joviality in his voice. "Oh, really, now. Is that so?"

Dayna smiled pleasantly, but her eyes remained focused. "Yes, Geffen, that is so."

Geffen took a second to adjust to the shift in the conversation. She proceeded in this subject without him asking. "That *something,* whatever it is, is always with you. It lies just beneath the surface. I see it in your eyes." Dayna picked up her glass and sipped, but her eyes never left him.

While he enjoyed her directness, this analysis was a bit hard for him to digest. She waited for a response. For the first time that evening, Geffen looked away.

She cut into her filet mignon with sharp precision and placed it in her delicate mouth, chewing with ease.

She watched him. "Shall we go back to small talk? Would you prefer that, Geffen?"

Geffen had to admire her knavish approach. She'd made him eat his own words, about admiring a woman not given to small talk, and they tasted sour.

He laughed a bit, trying to find the appropriate response to such a personal question. After all, her ability to read him notwithstanding, they had just met. "No. It's fine. To answer your question, yes, there are things that I desire, both material and nonmaterial. However, I maintain my focus on the material things, because that's more logical." Geffen picked up his glass and sipped, noticing his mouth had become dry.

She set down her fork. "What is that thing?"

He almost choked on her directness. "How about we talk about another subject?"

She picked up her fork again, but only pressed holes in her meat, didn't eat it. "What? Stock options? The Dow Jones? I can discuss those with my team of accountants, and frankly, their conversation is more beneficial. I cleared my schedule to be with you, Geffen, because I thought you would bring something unique to the table."

Geffen shifted his posture. Never had anyone made him feel so off balance. He'd been looking forward all day to seeing her again. He was not going to let the date go downhill. He patted the table once with his hand and looked her in the eye, ready to go there.

She asked him, directly, "Is it a woman?"

"Yes," he answered, unguarded. "My mother."

For the next hour, Geffen told Dayna about his beautiful mother—how she had died young, penniless, and without her only child by her side. He mentioned the father who had chosen to make *himself* absent but not his money; how his father had funneled money through Geffen's uncle to finance his boarding schools, et cetera, but how he had left Geffen's unmarried mother to scruff it out by herself.

He told Dayna how his mother didn't have money for a stable place to live or, more important, to have him come home to live with her, but that she would write him letters. He also described the disgraceful, beer-can-littered cemetery where his mother was presently buried, courtesy of his father.

"But that's about to change. My mother wrote me letters about us one day being together, and now that I have money, I'm bringing my mother home to rest on my property."

Geffen ended by pulling out a photo of his mother. It was the only one he had of her. His undying love for his mother poured from his eyes as he gazed on the photo. His mother was, indeed, a beautiful woman. Geffen shared some of her features—a softly sculpted face; smooth pecan skin; soft, curly black hair; clear and spacious almond-shaped eyes. But unlike Geffen's eyes, his mother's eyes were full of hardship and turmoil. Grief was her companion.

Geffen saw it clearly, and it hurt him deeply. He lived his life wishing he could erase that grief that was so evident in this particular photo, but this was the only one he had of her.

Dayna took it all in. She watched Geffen, his mother's photo, his yearning to erase his mother's grief while she slowly devoured her meal.

When dinner was over, they left the restaurant and Dayna had her limo driver take them high up into the mountains. They stopped at a lookout point and got out. Dayna situated Geffen near the edge of the cliff overlooking the city and made him feel like he was a prince and that the world could be his.

Chapter

22

ON SUNDAY NIGHT, THE DAY AFTER THE PARTY, SUNNIE DROVE her little yellow Saab with the busted taillight into the mansion's driveway. She used her entry code and went inside because she wanted answers—specifically, what woman could make Rice shut her out and not open the door when she knocked.

When she walked into the living room, Rice was slumped down on the black rabbit-skin couch, his feet on the white double-thick sheepskin rug, and his notebook computer teetering on his lap. He wasn't wearing his usual raggedy blue cotton karate-style pants or his faded Bruins T-shirt. He had on a decent pair of Sean John jeans and a nice blue shirt, as if he were expecting company. Sunnie wasted no time getting to the point.

"What's her name?"

"Who?" Rice acted like he was busy writing his next novel, but Sunnie looked at the screen and saw that he was surfing the internet. She picked up the Calendar section of the *Los Angeles Times* off the coffee table, rolled it up, and raised it over his head like she was going to smack him with it. He saw her and flinched, his notebook starting to fall off his lap.

Sunnie insisted, "Don't play dumb. What's her name?"

Rice kept one hand on his computer and one hand up to block the newspaper. "You make me drop this computer, you pay."

Sunnie kept the newspaper in position. "Should've bought the extended warranty, with your cheap butt. What's her *name?*"

Rice thought about it. Continuing to play dumb could get expensive, so he told Sunnie the woman's name. "Kamile Leon."

"Chameleon? Like the lizard?" Sunnie kept the *Times* in position.

Rice, half ducking, said, "No, Sunnie, not like the damn lizard. Put the newspaper down." Sunnie lowered the newspaper. "I said her name is *Kamile.* Last name *Leon.* What's so hard about that?" He closed his computer, got up, and looked out the front window.

Sunnie said, "Don't get testy with me. Ain't my fault the woman is named after a lizard."

She glanced around the living room, looking for something, she didn't know what. Something seemed different about the place. She didn't have the flip, flop, wiggle in her stomach when she entered the mansion this time, but she wasn't totally at ease, either. She still felt reasonably sure that trouble was lurking somewhere nearby.

She put her keys on the coffee table next to a book

from his study. It was about searching for one's identity, written by an African philosopher with a hard-to-pronounce name. She picked up the book and sat on the couch. "What's this book about?"

Rice heard her but didn't answer, and kept looking out the window.

Sunnie returned the book to the coffee table, and waited for him to come back and sit down. He didn't. He walked around the couch, went to the wet bar, pulled a Dr Pepper from the small refrigerator, but didn't offer her one.

Sunnie asked, "Is she coming back tonight?" Rice seemed anxious, distracted, and possibly in one of his moods toward her for no good reason that she could think of.

"Who?" Rice wandered back and stood by the coffee table. Sunnie gave him a Don't-make-me-pick-up-this-newspaper-again look. He got the message, but remained evasive. "Don't you have clients to call or paperwork to do at *your* home?"

"That comment almost sounded like you're trying to get rid of me," she said. He slid her car keys across the coffee table toward her. "That's not funny."

She glanced toward the stairs. "Where are the guys?"

"Are you the police?" Rice went back to the window.

Sunnie huffed, then asked what she really wanted to know. "Why didn't you let me in when I knocked on your study door last night?"

Rice leaned against the windowsill, looking out but being discreet about it. "Why? Did you need to cry about Marvin some more?"

"No, because I still feel like you guys are in some sort of danger and I wanted to check on you." Sunnie got up. "Why are you giving me this attitude? If anyone should be mad, it should be *me*."

Rice didn't look back. "Why?"

"Because I was practically *dying* from a brain hemorrhage while you were upstairs laughing it up with some stupid lady named after a lizard."

"You jealous?" Rice's tone was dry.

His question threw her off. "*Jealous?* Why would I be *jealous?*"

Rice, still looking out the window, said nonchalantly, "I don't know, why *would* you be?" His tone was flat, so Sunnie knew he was masking his truer emotion, whatever that was.

Sunnie stood behind Rice, peeking over his shoulder out the window, too. She said, "Look, I just want to know why you didn't open the door. I'm not *jealous* of some *trick* that will be screwed today, gone tomorrow."

He turned to face her, and said real coolly and innocently. "She's not a trick." Then he gave Sunnie this stupid, calm smile and waited for her reaction.

"She's not a trick? What do you mean she's not a trick? When have you ever been interested in anybody who *wasn't* a trick?"

Rice said, "This woman is different." He left the window, sat back down on the couch, and nonchalantly opened his computer.

Sunnie followed him. She closed his computer. "*Different?* Different how?"

"Well, first of all, she listens."

Sunnie's face registered surprise, insult, and anger all at once. She tried not to get hyper or defensive or to appear *jealous*, but it didn't work. "She listens? She *listens?* Well, just when did you decide to start *communicating?* Huh? Answer that, Mr. Mum Mouth."

The two had been friends for over twenty years, and every single thing that Sunnie ever got out of Rice she'd had to pry it out of him. That extra effort on her part took a lot of time, work, and energy, and she admitted to herself that they hadn't had a real heart-to-heart, let-it-all-hang-out type talk in a while—okay, in a few *years*—but that's because she'd been too, well . . . *busy.*

His little insinuation had ticked her off, and now they were going to have one of their all-out fights, even though Rice opened his computer and tried to act like they weren't.

Sunnie closed it, nearly smashing his fingers, and kept going. "Huh? Mr. Incommunicado? You talk about how I whine all the time"—Sunnie made a long, exaggerated, whiny face—"but at least I put it all out there and get things off my chest without you having to *pry* it out of me. You, on the other hand, keep so much stuff clammed up inside you, you need to have a 'getting it off my chest' garage sale."

Rice opened his computer again. She closed it, circled the couch, and kept going. "Now you're trying to compare me to some lizard trick, bragging about how she *listens.*" Sunnie got in front of him and made another exaggerated sarcastic, goofy face. Rice tried not to laugh, kept pretending to ignore her, and opened his computer.

She closed it. "So tell me, Mr. Closed Lipped, what is it that she's *listening* to? Huh, Mr. I've Got a Secret?"

They had a face-off. It lasted for twenty seconds and counting, until the doorbell rang.

Rice jumped up so fast, he dropped his computer. It hit the floor. Sunnie blocked him. He faked left, and ran right, dodging her. She grabbed his shirttail and stayed on his heels as they both ran to the door. She knew he'd been expecting the lizard-lady *trick* all along.

Rice grabbed the doorknob, stopped, took a deep breath, and sucked in his stomach, trying to look like he hadn't been running. Sunnie stood on her tiptoes to look over his shoulder.

He opened the door.

They both exclaimed, "Joey!"

Joey walked in carrying a duffle bag. His face looked like he'd been sparring with Tyson. His physical wounds had started to heal—however, Sunnie could tell that his emotional wounds were still fresh. Sunnie knew Rice noticed it, too, but they both faked like they didn't.

Rice helped him with his duffle bag. "Joey, man. It's good to see you, but did you know Coach's been looking for you for weeks?"

Joey's affect was flat. "He found me."

Coach came trudging up the porch carrying six plastic bags of groceries. Apparently, after he'd found Joey, they went shopping for groceries, and if Joey ate half as much as his big brother, they needed to.

Sunnie said, "Hey, Coach." She wanted to be as supportive as possible because she knew that although he'd never admit it, this was a trying time for Coach, not only because of his injured leg, but also because of his family problems. With a father as dysfunctional as J.B., Sunnie wasn't surprised.

Coach walked into the house with the bags and grunted a hello. He set the grocery bags down for a minute to speak to Rice. "Joey needs a place to stay for a minute. Cool?"

"Cool, man. No problem," Rice said without hesitation.

Coach apparently wanted to clear it with Geffen, too. He asked, "Where's Gef?"

Rice said, "Gef left a few hours ago in a big-ass purple stretch limo—some kind of foreign make, looked like it was from another world."

As soon as Sunnie heard "purple limo," she got mad all over again. "Gef went out with that car-wrecking woman?"

Rice said, "Whoever was in the back of the limo didn't get out. All I know is that Gef was all dressed up and looking happy as a fairy."

Sunnie pinched Rice's arm. They both looked at Joey. Sunnie smiled real big and said, "So, Joey, what have you been getting into lately?"

Coach purposely bumped Sunnie as he bent over to pick up the grocery bags. "Come help me put this stuff up, woman," he said.

Sunnie sucked her teeth. "What's the magic word?"

Coach said, *"Now!"*

Before they could leave, the front door opened again and Geffen walked in. "What's up, my black peeps?"

Coach, Rice, Sunnie, and Joey paused to check him out. Sunnie had never seen Geffen glow like that.

Rice said, "What's up? You look like you've been floating on cloud nine."

Coach lowered his eyebrows in suspicion. "You been sucking on the happy pipe in the back of that limo?"

Sunnie rolled her eyes. "Geffen is the *last* person in this world who'd do drugs."

Geffen kissed Sunnie's cheek and said, "At least Sunshine knows that I value my mind too much to dull it with drugs."

Coach grabbed the bags and murmured on his way to the kitchen, "If he ain't high, then he must be pussy-whipped."

Before Sunnie followed him, she heard a vehicle pull into the circular driveway blasting its horn.

She opened the front door. She, Rice, Geffen, and Joey gawked at the souped-up 4WD red Toyota truck—the kind you need a ladder to climb into—that pulled up and parked its oversize wheels on the front lawn in front of the fountain. Its suspension system was so highly modified, you could see the hydraulics, axle, and steering column. It was covered in dirt and dry mud like it had just been off-roading.

Sunnie squinted at the driver's window. "Who the heck is that?"

No sooner had Sunnie asked the question than a petite woman in a bright green tube top and yellow Daisy Duke shorts got out of the truck. She didn't use the door—she climbed out through the window, grabbed the roll bar on top of the cab, and hoisted her almost-bare booty up on the truck's roof.

Both Geffen's and Rice's mouths dropped open. Joey was only partly amused. Right away, Sunnie recognized her. She was that disrespectful hoochie from the tennis court, and just the sight of her got Sunnie irked and agitated again.

Geffen said, "Did you see that, man?" but Rice was too busy watching to see what she'd do next to answer.

And she didn't disappoint her male audience. She wrapped her bare leg around the roll bar like a stripper on a pole, and showed the guys all sorts of different angles and views of Daisy Duke shorts on the female anatomy.

Evie smiled real big and hollered, "Where's Big Poppa at?"

Coach must have caught sight of Evie through the kitchen window, because Sunnie heard potato chips crunch, jars break, and canned goods dent as Coach dropped all six grocery bags to the floor.

Sunnie could barely get out of the way before Coach came barreling out the front door, mowing down everybody to get out to the driveway.

"Hey, Evie. What's up, girl?" Coach was grinning from Indiana to Idaho.

Evie dropped her eyes to the front of Coach's slacks and said *"You,* I hope."

She jumped down off her truck, slapped the mud from her bare butt cheeks, which peeked out the bottom of her shorts, and jumped straight into Coach's

big arms. They started kissing and tonguing and sucking on each other like hungry wolves.

After they tongued each other down, Evie slapped
his behind. "Told ya I was coming back for you, Big
Poppa. I hope you took some ginseng."

Coach boasted, "Don't need no ginseng, baby, I'm
all man. What you got in mind?"

Evie didn't wait to be invited in—she grabbed
Coach by his belt buckle, led him straight through the
front door, through the receiving room and the den
toward the back of the house.

While she walked, she talked. "I'm gonna work ya,
Big Poppa. We're about to jump off into something hot
and wet, and you're about to do some stroking, baby."

Coach bit his lip, thanked his lucky stars, and pulled
her to the right toward the stairs. "My bedroom's this
way."

She pulled him to the left. "But the heated indoor
pool is this way," she said. She batted her eyelashes, real
innocent and flirtatious. "What did you think I was
talking about?"

When they got to the edge of the pool, Evie said,
"Oops. I forgot my bikini. Hope you don't mind." She
stripped completely naked and dove headfirst into the
deep end. Coach grabbed his chest and faked a heart
attack. He tore off his shirt, dropped his trousers and
everything else.

"I don't mind at all," he said, and dove in after her.

Coach put all of his strength into keeping up with
Evie. She swam like a piranha and her petite muscular
body, firm plump breasts, washboard abs, and curvy

backside made Coach's libido boil. Just like on the tennis court, their swimming and frolicking in the water was sexual foreplay. Coach was hot and more than ready, and it showed.

Coach grabbed Evie's thighs and said, "Enough swimming."

They kissed and groped, and just when Coach thought it was finally on, she grabbed his neck and said, "Let's go for a run."

She climbed out of the pool and threw her clothes on. When Coach saw that she was serious, he complained, "Woman, it's nighttime. Besides, ain't no place to run around here."

"Yes there is. C'mon, Big Poppa." She didn't give Coach time to object. She ran out the house and into the backyard. Coach put on his clothes and shoes, and reluctantly followed, grumbling.

Evie pointed to a small dirt pathway leading from the courtyard area into the dark, bushy woods. Coach had never noticed it before. "There's a path right there—let's go."

Twenty minutes later, Coach lagged behind Evie, puffing and sweating. He huffed in between breaths, "I must've been a damn fool to let you talk me into this, woman!"

They were out in the middle of nowhere. What little light there was came from the full moon, but half the time the moon was covered by tree branches. Coach didn't understand how Evie could see so well in the dark while he kept stumbling over rocks and shrubs, and almost fell on his behind with every step he took.

Evie, however, ran strong and confident, like she'd been on that narrow dirt path before.

She yelled back to him, "Can't keep up?"

Coach's pride answered, "Oh, I can keep up."

His leg was hurting like a mug. He was seriously winded, and to make matters worse, he kept thinking he saw something move in the dark trees that lined the path. But he wasn't about to punk out, so he kept going.

Finally, he got his stride. He broke loose and was jetting like a Heisman trophy winner, feeling damn proud of himself, when he took one wrong step, caught his foot on a twig, and fell on his ass.

He came down hard on his injured leg. Pain shot through his body like a bullet. When he fell, he rolled, like he'd been trained to do, and ended upright on his knees. He gave the pain a second to subside; he was used to it, but that didn't mean it didn't hurt. As soon as he got his breath, he called her.

"Evie." No answer—only the sound of the dark tree branches scratching against each other and the wind whipping through the leaves. Even though he was alone, Coach grumbled out loud, "I must've been a *damn* fool. I'ma kick my own ass for coming out here."

He stopped because he heard a noise in front of him. It sounded like a growl. *Aw shit. Here we go.* Coach froze, and listened. He took one step back, then another, then he fell into a hole.

"Aaaahhh!" Coach hollered. His big muscular behind hit the bottom of the ditch. The ditch was small and tight, and he landed in an awkward posi-

tion—his arm and legs were pinned close to his body and he was looking upward, but couldn't move. He tried to scramble to get out, but there wasn't enough space to shift his body around.

He tried to call Evie, but couldn't because the fall had knocked his wind out. His heart thumped hard and fast in his chest. Coach was claustrophobic, and this was his own personal hell.

When he tried to look up, dirt fell in his eyes. He heard footsteps, or something, moving closer.

"Evie." There was no answer. Again, he yelled, *"Evie."*

He heard a growl. It was a deep, low, rumbling growl, and real mean.

Coach looked up and saw a wolf. Its eyes were slanted and red like fire, just like in those low-budget horror flicks that Coach always talked about—the ones where the doofus brother who goes off into the dark night to investigate always gets his head bit off first.

The wolf's lips curled back into an evil grin and it bared its sharp, jagged fangs, dripping with blood and slobber.

Coach hollered real loud. *"Aaaaahh!"* His big mouth echoed throughout the whole forest.

In that moment Coach decided that if he was going to get his head bit off, it would be while he was standing up and swinging, not while his fool ass was stuck in a damn hole in the ground like a damn pig in a luau.

The red-eyed wolf growled, licked blood and slobber from its fangs, and reared back like it was about to pounce on Coach.

Coach put everything he had into getting out of that hole. His muscles strained, his body twisted, and he heaved himself up out of the hole. He swung around, ready to fight the wolf. But the wolf was gone.

Coach breathed hard and tried to calm himself, but his adrenaline was kicking. He glanced up the path. Something dark lying down on the ground caught his eye. It must have seen him, too, because it started slowly creeping toward him. *Uh-uh. I don't need this Stephen King bullshit.*

As Coach turned to take off in the other direction, he heard his name being called.

"Coach." The dark lump on the ground was Evie. She was lying in the dirt, holding her ankle, trying to crawl to him. He hustled to her. "I think I sprained it."

He looked around to see if anything was trying to sneak up on him again. "Evie, did you see anything?"

Evie looked up at him, batted her eyelashes, and said real innocently. "I didn't see anything."

How could she not see that thing—it was right here? Coach shook his head and tried to forget about it for right now. He took one more careful look around and bent over to help her to her feet.

As soon as he bent down, she screamed and pointed behind him. "It's a wolf!"

Coach didn't even glance back. He scooped her up like a pancake and took off running with Evie in his arms. Coach ran harder than he had ever run in his whole professional-football-career life. All he could think about was that bloody-fanged, devil-eyed, son of a bitch behind him.

He didn't stop until he reached the backyard of the mansion. He set Evie down on the grassy clearing in the middle of the courtyard, and he fell down beside her.

He tried to talk and breathe at the same time. "We—gotta—go—inside—"

Evie pulled herself up on him and grabbed him around his neck. She had that look in her eye. He was thinking about saving their asses, and she was getting horny. She thrust her Hershey's kisses nipples into his chest and breathed into his face.

"Coach, what you did out there took a lot of balls. It really turned me on." She pressed her mouth on his and kissed him real deep. Coach kept one eye open and looked over her shoulder for the wolf while she was kissing him.

She pulled back, bit his earlobe, and purred in his ear. "Mmm, you rescued me like Tarzan rescued Jane. Big Poppa, you are my Tarzan. Oooh, yes." She groaned and kissed him more, on his ear, down his neck.

He tried to calm her down. "Evie, we gotta go inside before—"

She growled, low and rumbling. "Take me, Big Poppa. Take me, right here, right now." She ripped off her tube top and slid out of her Daisy Duke shorts.

Coach was tired, and breathing hard, and paranoid, and his leg was aching, and now—he was horny as hell. He'd been wanting this sexy, curvy little freak from the first time he laid eyes on her at the party. He looked at her lying naked on the grass, begging him to take her.

There is a time and a place for everything, and as far as Coach was concerned, it was time to get *Monster's Ball* freaky.

He ripped off his clothes, pressed her spine into the grass, and grabbed her around her waist. His roughness brought out the freak in her even more.

"Ooohh, yes, yes. Do me, Big Poppa!"

Coach didn't care about anything else anymore. The Big Bad Wolf, Goldilocks and the Three Bears could have come out of those trees. He didn't care about anything except getting his freak on.

She pulled Coach inside of her and they went at it like two wild animals. She dug her fingernails into the grass and mud as they ground their bodies into each other. During their two hours of nonstop, rough sex in the courtyard, he made her scream so loud in ecstasy, her screams turned into a howl underneath the full moon.

He hollered, too. *"Who's the man!"*

Chapter

23

At 2:16 a.m., Rice was wide awake, sitting by the fireplace in his master bedroom suite. Of the three bachelors' bedrooms, his was the most conservatively decorated. He didn't have the wet bar, a 50-inch plasma, or the stripper's pole like Coach. He was happy with a fireplace and a lock on the door.

Rice had been waiting all day Sunday, hoping Kamile would show up or call. So when his phone rang at 2:17 a.m., he hurriedly answered it, hoping it was Kamile and that she shared his restlessness.

"Hello . . . *Kendric?*" Kamile said hesitantly. Rice didn't say anything for a moment. He closed his eyes, held his breath, and thought.

Finally, he asked, "How do you know my real name?"

Kamile had a calm, easy way about her. "Years ago, I looked it up. I found your elementary school picture."

"You're kidding!" Rice couldn't believe someone would go through the trouble just to learn his real name.

"No, I'm not kidding. You did an interview with a small, local newspaper five years ago, and you mentioned your grade school, Longfellow Elementary. Based on your age, I figured out the year you attended. I went to the school, and I found your yearbook."

"Why?"

"Because of your hero." Rice didn't understand. He waited for her to explain. "You write about a character who is so perfect, so sure of himself, who always does the right thing. No one always does the right thing. Our flaws are what make us interesting. I wanted to find out about the real man behind the fictitious character."

"No one's called me by my real name since the Jackson Five were still together and Michael Jackson was still black."

They both chuckled. Kamile made him feel like she had all night to talk. "It's an interesting name. Were you named after someone?"

"Kendra Wheats married Ricky Earl Gordon—my parents. *Kend* from Kendra. *Ric* from Ricky. *Kendric*. Lame, huh?"

"Nothing about you is lame. Be yourself around me, and I promise I'll never ask for more information than you're willing to share."

Rice closed his eyes and leaned his head back on his fireplace. Thinking about his real name brought back childhood memories.

"Kendric. Kendric Gordon!" the school nurse yelled at him. "I've got to call your mother to bring you some dry pants. What's her number, Kendric?"

He didn't say anything, just stared out the window trying to pretend he wasn't there, that he hadn't lost control of his bladder after holding his urine through five class periods because he was afraid to go into the boys' restroom. With a little more effort, he pretended that his mother didn't live in the bottom of a wine bottle. And when he squinted his eyes and tried even harder, he pretended she didn't cheat on his dad with the school's janitor, who liked to drink, too, and who sometimes liked little boys.

Later that day, little Kendric and the feisty little pig-tailed girl who lived down the street ran away together. With nothing but a raggedy old sleeping bag, seven dollars and eighty-two cents, and a bag of Doritos, they caught the bus from Compton all the way out to Santa Monica.

As they walked out to the end of the pier, Kendric tried to tug the Doritos from Alisun's hands. "Stop eating them all up. We got to make them last."

"But I'm *hungry!*"

"No, you greedy, Alisun. That's what you are."

"I'm cold, too. Why we had to come to the beach?"

Kendric and Alisun laid the sleeping bag down at the end of the pier and wiggled into it like caterpillars inside a cocoon. They zipped it up as far as it would go, and then watched the waves break against the rocks.

Alisun made a fist and stuck it up to Kendric's nose. "You better not try to touch my boobies."

Kendric pushed her fist away. "Girl, I ain't even thinking 'bout that. You ain't got no boobies anyway."

He laughed and she socked him in the nose anyway.

Then they went back to watching the ocean and the sun above it.

Alisun had promised Kendric that if that drunk man ever tried to grab him again, they'd run away together. And he did. So they did. But Alisun knew that Kendric's mother's boyfriend didn't just try to grab Kendric this time, that he'd actually caught him.

"Kendric," she said.

"What?"

"You okay?"

"Yeah. My nose don't really hurt."

"No, not that. The other thing."

The little boy didn't answer.

"Kendric."

"Don't call me that."

"Why not? That's your name. Kendric Earl Gordon."

"Not anymore." Kendric turned on his side in the sleeping bag and faced away from Alisun. Then he said into the wind, "She didn't believe me."

"You told your mama what he did?" He nodded yes. "She didn't believe you?" He nodded no.

"I don't want her name no more. I don't want the *Kend* part. I'm just Ric E. Gordon."

Alisun thought about it, then said, "Okay, Rice."

"That's not what I said. I said, *Ric E.*"

"That spells *Rice,* dummy!"

He thought about it. She was right. And that settled it. His stomach growled. He snatched the Doritos bag. "Stop eating them all up."

Alisun tucked herself all the way inside the sleeping bag and stared up at the sun. It wasn't as bright anymore. It was turning orange, yellow, and red, and spreading its light all over the ocean before it set.

Rice folded the bag closed to save the last few chips. "You better not ever tell nobody. *Ever.*"

"I won't. I promise." She leaned her head against his shoulder. "Hey, if you get to change your name, I get to change mine, too. Don't call me Alisun no more."

"Whatchu want me to call you, then?"

She looked up at the sun.

Kamile was silent. She didn't rush him, didn't question him, just listened. When he was done reliving parts of his childhood that he'd rather forget, he turned his attention back to the woman on the other end of the phone. "You still there?" he asked.

"Of course I am."

"I'm sorry. I was just thinking about—" He stopped, not wanting to give words to his pain.

"It's okay. Really," she said, as if she not only understood, but somehow had experienced that painful memory right along with him. Even when they were in his study together the night of the party, she seemed to be inside his thoughts, seeing and experiencing his secrets and ideas with him, never asking for an explanation.

She said, softly, "If you prefer, I won't call you by your real name."

"There are certain things I want to leave buried in the past."

"I understand now, and I respect that."

Rice stayed on the phone with Kamile through the wee hours of the night, until the welcoming of a new day. Sometimes they talked, sometimes they held the phone, letting silence be their communication.

Kamile said, "I've started writing a poem. I was wondering if you could help me finish it."

Rice got up and sat on his bed. His room was dark and he was alone, but he felt like Kamile was there, her presence was so strong. She began reading her poem:

> *"I searched for myself*
> *In the shadows*
> > *But the shadows kept shifting*
> *I searched for myself*
> *In the sunlight*
> > *But . . ."*

Kamile waited; she wanted Rice to complete her poem. Rice held back, doubting himself, wondering if he should show his vulnerability. After a moment, he contributed to her poem.

> *"But the glare,*
> *Hurt my eyes."*

She continued, *"I searched for myself . . ."*
Rice: *". . . I found myself."*
Kamile: *". . . Where?"*
Rice: *". . . in the beating of your heart."*

Chapter

24

On Monday, Sunnie sat in her office at Soulmates Realty thinking about Rice, as well as other things. The guys were pulling away from her, and she couldn't kick the now-constant feeling that something was going wrong.

Sunnie picked up the phone and called Mother Roby, who had been at church all day Sunday, unreachable. When Mother Roby answered, Sunnie got straight to the point.

"I *saw* her."

Mother Roby asked, "You saw *who?*"

"The dark, shadowy woman that flashed in my mind the day Rice went into the cellar."

Sunnie heard Mother Roby turn off the faucet. Concerned, she asked, "When?"

"Saturday night. I was rushing inside the party, and I ran into her at the fountain. I know exactly how she looks. She has a shadowy darkness about her. It's not natural. It's smoldering and seductive."

"Seductive?"

"Yes. She's very pretty, but in an evil sort of way."

"Did she say anything?"

"Yes." Sunnie paused, her voice trembled. "She said she was going to *destroy* the guys."

"Okay, calm down, Alisun. Let's not panic. Now, did anyone else see this woman?"

"No, we were alone. Why? Do you think I imagined it?"

"No, child, I know you didn't imagine it. It's real, and that's why it's so serious."

"There you go again, freaking me out."

"This is no time to get freaked—it's time to get focused."

"But how?"

Mother Roby paused, pondering. "Pay close attention to everything you feel because it all has meaning. God is speaking to you, Alisun, letting you see and feel things that other people can't. But you've got to learn to be quiet and listen."

Agitated, Sunnie got up, put on her headset, and walked to her office window. "Be quiet and *listen*? How can I sit by and do nothing when the guys may be in real danger and not know it?"

"I didn't say sit by and do nothing. I said *listen*."

Sunnie tugged on the blinds. "You're confusing me."

"Alisun, are you still praying for those guys?"

"Of course I am."

"Good, don't stop. But you need to use your gift, too."

"That's what I don't understand. I think the guys are

in danger, but I don't how or why or from whom. If I've got a supernatural gift and I can hear and feel and sense things but I don't know what to make of them, then how am I supposed to help those guys?"

"By learning to *listen*."

"Why doesn't God just explain everything and *tell* me exactly what to do?"

"If He did, we'd never grow up. We'd be like baby robots. We'd never learn how to have faith or how to trust him even when we don't know what's going on."

"Yeah, but it'd be a whole lot easier."

"His way may not be easy, but it's best. Remember, songbirds learn to sing in the dark."

"But what if *this* bird is scared of the dark?"

Mother Roby assured Sunnie that if God gave her a job to do, then she was qualified to do it.

Sunnie hung up and stared out the window at the traffic on Sepulveda Boulevard. She thought about the dark, shadowy, seductive woman, and how she emanated power and presence. She thought about herself, and how she felt confused and powerless. Sunnie wondered if she was any match for that woman, and if her *gift* would be enough to save the guys.

Chapter

25

TUESDAY MORNING AT THE MANSION, GEFFEN FELT OVER-whelmed by his busy schedule. He had enough items on his plate to feed Ethiopia. But Dayna had boosted his already high ambitions, giving him a new, more cutthroat perspective on business matters. Now it was more important to him than ever to succeed by any means necessary. But this particular morning, on top of having a lot of business to take care of, he had to deal with Rice being a stubborn asshole.

Geffen stood in Rice's study trying to block him from ripping out more electrical cords. A film crew stood by and watched.

"Stand back, Rice. Don't cause a scene, man," Geffen warned.

Rice, who'd slept in late that day, had come to his study to find the lock jimmied and a slew of movie production workers inside moving things around, getting ready to shoot a scene.

Rice was fuming. "Don't cause a *scene?* You got five seconds to get these cameras, these lights, and these people out of my study."

Geffen tried to justify himself. "Warner Studios agreed to pay us twenty percent more to shoot inside the study. I knocked on your door to tell you. You were asleep, so I had to pick the lock."

Rice wasn't hearing it. "Take this shit back out to the courtyard. Get out of my study." He reached around Geffen and ripped out another camera cord from the socket.

"*Your* study? This whole house belongs to the *corporation*. Its purpose is to make money!"

Rice reminded him, "You've rented out three suites for the past two weeks for over three hundred a night. We've already held two major VIP parties and charged a fortune for each one. The gym is over-booked with trainers. We're making enough god-damn money!"

Geffen slapped his forehead. "*Enough?* When it comes to making a profit, there's never *enough!* Oh, but I forgot, I'm talking to a man who won't even do live interviews to boost his book sales and increase his own royalty check."

Geffen was tired of Rice's privacy issues, and now they were getting in the way of corporate profits. "What, you got some big, dark secret?"

Rice paused. In that moment he looked like he wanted to hit Geffen. Rice had been tripping lately, and Geffen didn't know where his friend's head was right now. Violence had never been Geffen's style, but hell, this was about getting paid, so Geffen raised his hands like *Bring it on!*

Rice stepped back, his pant leg got caught on a lighting tripod, which tipped over and caused a domino effect, knocking over a camera. A cameraman rushed to try to catch it, but was too late. The expensive, state-of-the-art camera crashed to the floor and shattered into a million pieces.

Geffen nearly blew a gasket. "What the—Have you lost your mind?"

Rice looked at the busted camera. "It was an accident."

Geffen was irate. "Accident, my ass. Man, you tried to do that!"

Geffen got in Rice's face. When he did that, Rice refused to back down or apologize. They stood nose to nose, both ready to throw down.

Rice repeated, "I said it was an *accident.*"

Coach, who'd been in the gym, heard the commotion and came to see what was happening. He stepped into the study just in time to see Geffen and Rice standing nose to nose, ready to exchange blows.

He yelled like a bouncer, "What's going on in here?"

Rice and Geffen stayed nose to nose. Coach stepped between them. "I *said,* what's going on up in here?"

Finally, Geffen broke the standoff. "Your *boy* here is being trifling."

Rice responded with, "Geffen needs to check himself."

Coach looked at the busted camera. "Both of y'all are acting ill."

Geffen straightened his collar and checked his Rolex. "I ain't got time for this bullshit. I got an appointment."

As he turned to leave, the director stopped him and pointed to the busted camera. "Excuse me, Mr. Cage, but that was a *very* expensive piece of equipment."

Geffen breathed deeply and tried to maintain his composure. Making sure Rice heard, he said, "The corporation will cover the damages and deduct it from my *partner's* share of the profits."

Geffen left.

A few minutes later, he tossed his briefcase into his Hummer and jumped behind the wheel. He was backing out of the driveway when, out of nowhere, Dayna Devlin appeared inches behind his rear bumper.

Geffen slammed on his brakes and got out of his SUV. "Where'd you come from? I didn't see you standing there."

He was thrilled to see Dayna. He glanced around the driveway. Other than Rice's and Coach's cars, and the film crew's van, the area was clear. Where was her humongous purple limo?

Dayna's voice was as calm as always. "Good morning, Geffen." She looked as classy in a black designer pants suit as she did in an expensive evening gown.

"I wanted to come with you to your appointment this morning, if you don't mind my company," she said.

He smiled. "Of course not. Let me get that door for you."

With the lovely Dayna Devlin by his side, he drove

to the small cemetery where his mother was buried. Dayna and Geffen had talked a great deal, and he had given her the details about his plan to move his mother's grave to his private property, but he hadn't expected her to accompany him. Why would anyone volunteer to go on such a somber errand?

Geffen felt Dayna watching him. She said, "You seem preoccupied. Is there something troubling you?"

Geffen glanced at Dayna. He loved looking at her beauty. Everything about this woman was mesmerizing.

"It's been a hectic morning. The film crew showed up. There were a few minor problems."

"With Kendric?"

"Who?"

"I mean *Rice?*"

"As a matter of fact, yes. How did you know?"

"It's obvious, Geffen. None of your friends is as smart as you. They're not as focused, not as driven. I'm not surprised that one of them would get in your way. You should think about downsizing and cutting them loose."

"Aw, hey, they get on my nerves sometimes, but they're still my boys. If it weren't for them putting up their money and going in with me, I wouldn't have even gotten this house."

Geffen thought back on the harsh words he'd said to Rice in front of the camera crew. Sunnie had told him that something had happened to Rice in his childhood, but she didn't give the details. That's why Rice was so secretive at times, like today, when his hang-ups ended up costing the corporation a lot of money.

Geffen smoothed his mustache, thinking. Still, Rice was his *pahtna*, his *dawg*, and maybe he shouldn't have said what he'd said in the heat of the moment.

Dayna objected, almost like she had read his mind. "No, Geffen. Sentimentality has no place in an entrepreneur's mind. Everything is strictly about business; it's never personal."

Geffen had to respect her opinion. From what little he knew about her, she had to be one of the richest businesswomen in L.A., though surprisingly he'd never heard of her before the night of the party.

She continued, "You were the brainchild behind this whole venture. If it weren't for *you*, they wouldn't be part of this dynamic new corporation heading straight for the Forbes/Fortune 500 list." Geffen loved the sound of that. She went on, "There are times when every successful business tycoon has to cut his strings in order to fly higher. You do want to fly high, don't you, Geffen?"

"Of course I want to fly high."

"Well, it's lonely at the top. And there's a reason—because there's only room at the top for *one*, and that's you."

Geffen had always thought of Rice, Coach, and himself, and even Sunshine, as a team. But lately, with all the issues and aspects of running the business, Geffen felt the lion's share of the burdens had fallen on his shoulders, with little or no help from Coach or Rice.

Dayna asked, point-blank. "Did Rice cause you to lose money today?"

Geffen sighed. "Yeah, twenty percent, plus damages."

"What about Coach? Has he contributed to the benefit of the corporation lately, or taken away from it?"

Geffen thought about how Coach and his girl had ruined the grass in the courtyard during their wild animal kingdom sex episode the other night, and how much money it cost the corporation to get it replaced quickly, in time for filming.

Geffen answered, "Taken away from it."

When Geffen pulled his Hummer up the narrow, broken driveway of Kringle Cemetery, he thought about how the place never failed to disappoint him anew. That's why he'd never brought anyone with him to visit his mother's grave, except Sunshine. Sunshine had a way of making him feel as if it wasn't so bad, but truthfully, it *was* bad.

Geffen walked Dayna up to the measly, faded gray edifice they called an office. They went inside.

"Are you the manager of this facility?" Geffen asked the sunburned man who'd been working a crossword puzzle. He nodded. "I am Mr. Geffen Cage. We spoke on the phone several times regarding my retrieval and relocation of the remains of Ms. Laila Cage, my mother."

The manager scribbled on his crossword puzzle. "Right, and as I told you, moving a person's grave is a very complex matter, if it can be done at all. There are tons of legalities. There are, uh, permits that you need, clearances, zoning considerations. It's something that involves a whole lot more than just a wish."

Geffen pulled out a small, neat stack of legal papers from his briefcase and set them before the manager.

"Every *i* is dotted, every *t* is crossed. I don't deal in *wishes,* only in results."

The manager stared at the fancy letterhead from the prestigious law firm. He told his secretary, "Hey, Marge. Hold my calls. This is gonna take a while."

During their meeting, Dayna sat by Geffen's side, listening, offering suggestions at times. After the meeting concluded, Geffen walked Dayna back to his Hummer.

He said, "I need one last signature to get this process under way. My uncle's."

Dayna nodded, got inside, and accompanied Geffen to his uncle's house in Ontario. When they arrived, Geffen parked in front of the retired doctor's house.

Dayna asked, "Do you see your uncle often?"

"Not as much as I should. I try to send him a card every Christmas to let him know that I appreciate him stepping in and handling my affairs when I was a minor while my father chose to remain incognito."

Geffen walked Dayna up the steps and rang the bell. His uncle's male nurse let them in. They sat and waited in the den.

"Sometimes he'd send me a little something on my birthday when I was kid. He and my mother were never that close, though he did let her stay with him a few times when she really needed it. All in all, he's a cool guy."

Dayna placed her hand on top of his. "Then why are you so nervous?"

"I want to move his sister's grave. I don't know how he's going to react."

When the male nurse wheeled his uncle in, Geffen took one look at his uncle's face and knew why he'd had to hire a full-time nurse. His uncle had aged, ungracefully. Geffen remembered his uncle as a vibrant, robust man, always bustling. Now his once thick black hair was very thin, revealing lots of scalp. His eyes had tunneled and his light brown skin had yellowed to a jaundiced tone, a telltale sign of infirmity.

Geffen stood. His uncle extended his hand because his body was too feeble to withstand an embrace.

While Geffen talked to his uncle, Dayna's demeanor remained focused and concentrated. She shifted her eyes from Geffen to his uncle, then zeroed in on the locked antique file drawers behind his uncle's head. They were labeled "Medical Archives."

Geffen cautiously explained the reason for his visit. "I want to transfer my mother's grave site to my new property."

At first his uncle said nothing. His eyes seemed to sink farther back into his head as he stared at Geffen. As next of kin, his consent was necessary. Without it there'd be no move.

His uncle leaned forward and reached for Geffen's fountain pen. He said, simply, "You've got your reasons." Then he scrawled his indecipherable signature on the document and handed it back to Geffen.

A few minutes later, Geffen and Dayna got back into his Hummer, signed paper in hand, and left.

After leaving his uncle's house, Geffen was drained, both physically and emotionally. Though he lived for business, he felt the need to rest his mind. As he drove back to L.A., Dayna seemed to have picked up on his thoughts.

She leaned over, touched his arm. "Geffen, I'd like to treat you to an escape, something nice that will help ease your mind."

· Dayna's words were like a melody to his ears. She made a phone call. At her instructions, he drove to the Ontario airport, where they boarded a small private jet that had been waiting for them. The pilot, a navy-and-white-suited elderly man with long whitish hair and a faint Brazilian accent, closed the cabin door and left them in privacy.

Once they reached the appropriate altitude, Dayna went to the back of the cabin, where she unfolded a queen-size cot. She lowered an in-wall refrigerator and removed a vintage bottle of champagne along with a silver chalice filled with freshly cut strawberries. She turned on the sound system and soft classical music filtered throughout the cabin.

When Dayna slowly unzipped the gold zipper of her stylish jumpsuit and laid her elegant body on the silk sheets, Geffen realized that with this woman nothing was impossible. The way she looked, the way she talked, the way she moved—it all made him feel like he was a prince and she was his royal princess, and that together they could own the world.

She smiled at him as she slid completely out of her jumpsuit. She gestured for him to come lie with her, saying, "A little something to help ease your mind."

Dayna helped Geffen out of his clothes, and

together they lay upon silken sheets, kissing and caressing. As she guided him inside of her, a sweet, helpless moan escaped his lips. The sensation was intense and overpowering. He knew that sex with Dayna Devlin would be magnificent, but he had never imagined it would be this overwhelming. Ecstasy erupted like a volcano and spread throughout his body like hot lava slowly taking control of his mind.

He caught his breath and looked down at her. He saw those crystal eyes looking up at him. They were breathtaking and piercing. If she'd asked for his soul in exchange for that ecstasy in that moment, he would have given it.

Chapter

26

TUESDAY NIGHT, COACH POUNDED HIS HAND INTO THE stainless-steel refrigerator in the mansion's kitchen, ready to go off on Rice. He was already in a bad mood. Geffen had stood him up for their four o'clock appointment with his friend, a trainer, who wanted to lease the gym. Plus Evie was two hours late. He'd tried to call her, but kept getting a "disconnected" recording. Nothing was going right. His injured leg was stiff and sore, he was still going through shit with J.B. and Joey, plus he was hungry. And now, to top it all off, Rice had just pissed him off by suggesting that he accept Joey's homosexual orientation.

What began as an amiable conversation between Rice, Sunnie, Coach, and Joey as they prepared the smothered-steak dinner he'd promised his brother on Sunday had turned into a full-fledged argument.

Coach slammed the palm of his hand into the stainless-steel refrigerator again, denting it, while he yelled at Rice. "It ain't your baby brother out there doing kinky things with other dudes, so don't give me no bullshit speech about *tolerance*."

Rice took his usual approach and tried to ignore the fact that someone was standing there hollering at him. He opened a can of gravy and handed it to Joey. He said, without looking at Coach, "So, anyway, Joey, are you going to try to get your old job back at the *Daily News*? What were you, an editor?"

Coach refused to be ignored. He snatched the can of gravy from Rice and stepped in front of him. "If Kendall or Ricky Jr. was out there sucking other men's dicks, you wouldn't be all blasé about it, now would you?"

Rice forced a small chuckle, trying to stay cool. "Leave my family out of this, man."

Coach pushed his point. "Am I right, though? Admit it. Or maybe your little brothers are already out there doing weird shit like that, but you don't know because you never go home to check on your family."

Sunnie pulled the can from Coach's grip. "Hey, c'mon, Coach."

"Naw, you know what I'm sayin' is true." Coach turned back to Rice. "At least I deal with my family's problems. You hide from yours. So don't get in my face trying to tell me how I should handle things."

Sunnie held her breath and squeezed the can nervously, waiting for Rice's reaction. Rice took the can from Sunnie. His voice was fake calm and nonchalant.

"Okay, you right, Big Dude. But speaking of hiding, the next time you decide to play wild animal kingdom with your freak of the week, take it up to your room. Nobody wants to hear you two howling in the courtyard like a pair of stupid-ass wolves."

Coach walked toward Rice, his fists clenched. Sunnie dropped her dish towel and intercepted by shoving a plate of food into Coach's hands. She kept her body between theirs and ushered Coach to the kitchen table.

She tried to change the conversation. "Coach, I just love Joey's new beard, don't you? With that beard, you two almost look like twins, except you're a lot bigger."

Coach ignored Sunnie's chattering and her attempt to keep the peace. He started eating, chewing his food real hard. Sunnie ushered Joey to the table and sat him next to Coach. Rice sat directly across from Coach. Sunnie sat close to Rice, like she wanted his attention.

The doorbell rang. Coach jumped up and stomped to the door, hoping it was Evie. Her cute little caramel-apple behind would help calm him down and get his mind off this other crap.

Coach opened the door, and it wasn't Evie. And if it wasn't Evie, then he really didn't care who it was. So he turned around, walked back to the table, and continued eating.

When Coach didn't speak, Sunnie asked him, "Who was at the door?"

Coach shoved a forkful of peas into his mouth and took his time answering. He chewed, swallowed, took a drink, then said, flatly, "Nobody. Just some ho for Rice."

Rice stopped eating and looked at Coach. He looked confused, like he thought he'd misheard him. Coach stared back at him and kept on chewing.

Kamile shyly poked her head into the kitchen. "Umm, excuse me. I didn't know if I was supposed to wait at the door or—"

Rice looked at Kamile. Everybody in the room knew she'd heard Coach's "ho" comment due to her embarrassed expression. Rice looked at Coach. Coach paid him no mind, ate, burped, guzzled his drink.

Rice jumped up from the table. "That was fucking rude!"

Sunnie tried to assuage Rice. "Coach is just in a bad mood; you know how he gets. He didn't mean anything by it."

Rice pulled away from her hand. "No! *Hell* no! Negro has been fucking with me all night. Now he's gonna go and disrespect my *company* like that?"

Coach remained seated and shoved another forkload of peas into his mouth. As he chewed, he checked out Kamile, looking her up and down. She was dressed modestly in a Sears catalog-type skirt, wore thick glasses, and had her hair pinned back.

Coach sucked his tooth. "I don't see nothing worth getting all excited about. In fact, just looking at her boring ass puts me to sleep."

Rice lunged across the table at Coach, and in one quick motion, he swooped up Coach's plate of food and rammed it into his face.

Sunnie screamed. *"Noooo!"*

Joey jumped back out of the way. Steak smothered in hot gravy and buttery green peas slid down Coach's surprised face and onto his chest.

Though it had caught him by surprise, it didn't take

but a second for his reflexes to kick in. Coach jumped up and swung at Rice, who backed up just in time, causing Coach's fist to miss his face by only an inch. Coach bolted around the table to get to Rice.

"No!" Sunnie blocked Coach's path and pressed her shoulder in Coach's massive chest. "Rice, leave! Go! Get out of here."

Rice stayed, ready to do battle. "I ain't going nowhere!"

Coach knew he could hurt Rice, yet the fool was standing there about to take a royal-ass whipping, and for what? Just because he'd insulted some homey-ass trick? Since when did they ever let a *woman* get in between their friendship?

Coach moved Sunnie out of the way like she was a feather, but Sunnie kept hopping between him and Rice. Joey saw Coach's temper, knew the damage he could do, and left the room.

Kamile, on the other hand, eased closer and watched.

Sunnie started yelling at the top of her lungs, then held her stomach and grunted. "Oooh. Something is *not right!* Can't you guys *feel* it? You all are *best friends*. First Geffen blows up this morning, and now *this*. What is making you guys act like this?"

Coach was mad. That hot gravy was burning his face, and he wanted to get at Rice. "Move Sunnie," he said.

"No! I will *not* move. I will not stand by and let this happen!" Sunnie doubled over and held her stomach, but she remained positioned between them.

Seeing Sunnie like that caused Coach to calm down. He was still mad, but he said to Sunnie, "Hey, you a'ight?"

Coach tensed up a bit when Rice stepped toward Sunnie. They looked at each other but let it go, for now.

Rice put his hand on Sunnie's back. "Sunnie, don't get so upset. This ain't even about you."

Sunnie quickly corrected Rice. "Yes, it *is* about me. It's about *us*—we are friends. But ever since that party, you guys have been at each other's throats. *Why?*"

Kamile stepped forward and gently touched Rice's arm. "Um, Rice, maybe I should just leave."

"Yeah, maybe you should," Sunnie said, still holding her stomach.

Rice told Kamile, "No, you don't have to leave. This is my house, too."

Coach saw Rice throw him a look, but he dared him to do more than that. Coach knew he'd been rude to the woman, but was surprised that Sunnie was rude to Kamile, too. That wasn't like Sunnie.

Sunnie looked at Kamile, inspecting her. "Rice, let her leave. Let's you and me go somewhere and talk."

Rice studied Sunnie for a moment, then asked, "About Marvin?"

There was a silent exchange between the two of them, during which Sunnie looked guilty and Rice looked disappointed. Coach couldn't figure out what that was about.

Rice turned toward Kamile. "I'll go with you. I could use some fresh air." They left together. Sunnie finally stopped rubbing her stomach, but she didn't look happy at all.

A half hour later, Rice stood next to Kamile on the dark steps of an old downtown building and watched as she slipped a key into the lock of the door that, judging from the dust and the creak, hadn't been opened in a long time. They walked inside.

Rice looked around the large dark room, his voice trailed by a faint echo. "This is the old public library. They closed this place years ago. How'd you get a key?"

"My background in history entitles me to special privileges."

Rice stayed close to the door because he couldn't see, but Kamile gently nudged him a little farther into the darkness.

"Don't be scared," she said. "You're with me."

Kamile flipped a switch and the old light fixtures came on. The dusty shelves were filled with old books.

Rice's face lit up like a kid. "Wow. This is amazing. I love old books."

Rice's apprehension left as he walked farther into the library, gliding past sections of books cataloged by subject. He stopped at the Philosophy section, and picked up a book by David Hume.

Kamile caught Rice's hand and guided him to the cubicles. Rice picked a cubicle facing the wall, hopped up on the desk, and put his foot on the chair. Kamile leaned against the cubicle's wall.

Kamile said, "I come here by myself at night to read, to think, and basically to be alone."

"That's cool." Rice could relate. Being alone was often easier than trying to be with somebody.

Kamile ran her hand along the cubicle wall. "Most people wouldn't think being alone is cool. But I guess we're not most people." She smiled. He smiled back.

Rice liked the way their voices echoed inside the bubble-domed ceiling. It made him feel like they were in their own little world.

Kamile pointed to his book. "Read to me. Please."

Kamile leaned against his cubicle and listened to every word. He'd always hated reading excerpts at his book signings because he felt like the people weren't really listening. Not with this woman. Each time he glanced up, her eyes were on him.

As he read, Rice thought about all the women he'd been with who didn't really see him, didn't know who he was, didn't really care. He thought about how he'd always play it safe, hiding behind the façade of his fictional character, never risking the vulnerability of exposing himself. Caught up in his thoughts, Rice paused.

"Go on, please," Kamile said.

Rice continued reading, but the book no longer held his interest. He started fantasizing about Kamile. From the first night they'd met, there was something about her that made him want to touch her. Yet he was afraid, but he didn't know why. Maybe because she seemed almost like an apparition to him, and he was scared that if he touched her, she might go away.

As he read, Kamile moved closer. She pushed the chair away and wedged her body between his knees.

Rice's eyes moved back and forth from the book to her face. She took off her glasses. Her eyes were a deep, dark brown vortex. If he stared into them too long, he felt like he was falling inside. *Maybe that wouldn't be a bad thing,* he thought.

He didn't feel like being alone tonight. He especially didn't feel like agonizing over Sunnie again tonight. How could they be so close for so long, yet so far apart at the same time? Sunnie was rushing through life looking for something, but not knowing where to look, and he knew where to look, but didn't know how to get it.

He must truly be invisible in her eyes if she didn't see all the clues he'd been giving her. He'd deliberately broken up Marvin's proposal. At the pier, he'd comforted her and told her she'd probably find true and meaningful love in a familiar place, but she pretended not to understand. In that last incident at the party, when she'd said, "We really were meant to be together," he thought she'd finally realized that they had something special between them. Turned out she was talking about Marvin. That really, really hurt him.

He'd met Kamile seconds after that, and maybe it was by some cosmic plan. Whatever the case, he needed to stop thinking about Sunnie and about what could have been.

Rice turned his attention back to Kamile. She removed the pin from her hair, loosened her chignon. Her hair had a full, thick texture. He liked the way it fell, slowly grazing her shoulders. He pulled his eyes away and kept reading.

She inched closer, invading his space with her gentleness. She gently nudged the book aside and placed both her hands on his face. She turned it directly into hers.

Kamile moved her lips close to his and pressed ever so lightly. *She's about to kiss me,* he thought, but he was wrong. She didn't kiss his lips, she spoke into them.

She whispered his name. "Kendric . . . ," and pressed her lips into his so he could read her words like a blind person reads Braille, by *touch*. She spoke it again, only this time, silently, *Kendric . . .*

The way she touched him, the way she drew him in with her eyes, turned him on in a way he'd never experienced before—this was the kind of intimacy he'd purposely avoided with one-night stands. It made him feel vulnerable, but with Kamile, it was enticing.

She unbuckled his pants. Rice closed his eyes and made sure he wasn't dreaming. This was just like he'd fantasized, and this woman seemed to do everything exactly right.

With her free hand, she unbuttoned her blouse and pulled it open as far as it would go, then lowered her body until her hands fell around his waist. She unzipped his zipper with her teeth.

Without her glasses, with her hair wild and loose and her breasts spilling out over her lace bra, Kamile no longer looked like a librarian. She looked like his wildest dream.

Rice dropped the book and clutched both sides of the cubicle. His body stiffened in anticipation, especially where Kamile gently bit him. She began placing soft, feathery kisses there, never taking her eyes off his face.

She pressed her mouth into him and whispered his name, letting him feel the movement of her lips against his skin, the warmth of her breath as she blew on him, then the heat of her tongue as she licked him.

Finally, she surrounded him completely with the hot moistness of her mouth. He gripped the edge of the cubicle, threw his head back, and stared up at the bubble-dome ceiling, trying not to holler.

Just as he was about to lose control, he heard a door open. He quickly looked over his shoulder. A janitor was pushing a utility crate and dusting along the shelves as he slowly made his way toward them. *Why the heck would a janitor come into this old place?*

In a breathless whisper, Rice said, "Kamile, somebody's *coming.*"

She didn't stop, her eyes remaining on him, the edges of her lips curled up in a mischievous smile. She whispered back, "I know."

The janitor turned toward their voices and spotted Rice sitting backward in a cubicle, his head and shoulders above the top, the lower part of his body hidden.

Rice looked at the janitor with a panicky smile. The janitor was an old guy with long silvery hair and a long beard, and he was hunched over so far that he needed the cart to prop him up.

Kamile held her grip around Rice's waist and didn't seem to care that they weren't alone. But Rice did. This guy might recognize him from one of his book covers, bust him and Kamile, and spill it to the press:

"FAMOUS AUTHOR GETS BLOWED IN LIBRARY." *No way.*

With a faint Brazilian accent, the janitor said to Rice, "Good evening, señor. Have you seen Señorita Kamile Leon lurking anywhere near? She has the propensity to become sidetracked."

Kamile had mentioned that she came here a lot at night by herself, so he figured that's how the janitor knew her. Rice glanced down at Kamile, then quickly looked back at the old guy. Sweating, he replied, "If she pops up, I'll let you know."

The old janitor turned and slowly made his way out the door. Rice counted his slow footsteps, trying to hold on until he left. As soon as the door closed behind him, Rice hollered, his legs went crazy, and he kicked the chair clear across the room. Rice knew that from that moment on, he'd never look at a library cubicle the same way again.

Chapter

27

SUNNIE SAT ON THE BENCH IN THE COURTYARD, WRAPPED IN a SpongeBob blanket, munching on a peanut butter and jelly sandwich. After Coach and Rice almost got into a fight, nobody felt like eating anymore, so she gave the steaks to Coach's Rottweilers, Tabitha and Samantha. They were in their pens next to the courtyard, happy and full.

Sunnie pulled the blanket together and talked to herself while she stared up at the full moon. She had decided to stay at the mansion and wait for Rice, to make sure that he and Coach didn't get into any more food fights, but mainly she wanted to talk to him— and not about Marvin, as he had insinuated.

Sunnie took another bite of her sandwich. *So that was Kamile Leon.* It wasn't in Sunnie's friendly nature to dislike someone right off the bat, but she did. Sunnie hated Kamile from the tip of her stupid little bun all the way down to her homey pumps. Just thinking about how Kamile had stood there and watched as Rice nearly took a beating for her made Sunnie's stomach start to bubble all over again.

Am I jealous? If Rice had settled down and finally found his true and meaningful love, then she should be happy for him, but she wasn't. Rice should be with her, not some strange woman.

As soon as Kamile had stepped into the kitchen, Sunnie's stomach had knotted up. It felt the same as her internal radar, but since it had been going off sporadically since the night she ran into the dark woman at the fountain, Sunnie figured this must be what plain old jealousy felt like. *Why am I jealous?*

She and Rice had been best friends since before puberty. But lately, Rice had been sending her confusing signals. Sometimes she'd catch him looking at her, and it wasn't in a way that a friend looks at another friend. She ignored it, put it out of her mind, even scolded herself for thinking it was something more than it was. But since her breakup, Rice seemed to be doing it even more—he'd stare at her when he thought she wasn't looking, he'd start a sentence but not finish it. He'd do strange things like show up at her house unannounced when he knew she had company, and bring up the subject of true love, which was unusual for someone who supposedly didn't *believe* in it. He'd been touching her a little more lately, giving her neck massages, subtle things like that.

Sunnie wasn't stupid. She suspected that something between them was changing, but with her track record of misinterpreting a man's feelings, she needed him to come right out and say it. No way was she going to jump to any wild conclusions, embarrass herself, and possibly ruin their lifelong friendship by bringing up the possibility of romance between them.

Sunnie wanted to talk to Rice. She wanted to get things out in the open once and for all, because after seeing him with Kamile, Sunnie realized her feelings for Rice had changed.

Just as she was getting up, she heard a voice right behind her head whisper, "Sunnie."

Sunnie screamed, threw her SpongeBob blanket up in the air, and fell off the bench.

"*Rice!* You scared the sugar babies out of me. Stop doing that." She picked up her blanket and wrapped it back around her.

Rice looked pensive, his hands in his pockets. "Sunnie, I wasn't trying to scare you. Why are you sitting out here staring at the moon anyway?"

Sunnie cleared her throat. "I was waiting for you."

"And?" Rice did the same thing he'd been doing lately, waiting for her to make the first move.

"Come, sit with me." She motioned for him to share her SpongeBob blanket. He hesitated, then reluctantly sat next to her. She lifted the blanket and laid it over both of them. She scooted closer to his warmth. "You bought me this blanket for my birthday a few years ago."

Rice said, matter-of-factly, "I know."

He gave her a look like *What's this all about?* Sunnie decided to lay everything on the line and tell him she was falling in love with him.

"Rice, we've been *friends* for a long time, but now I'm starting to——" She paused. Rice's body felt more than just warm, it felt strangely hot.

"Sunnie, what are you trying to say?"

She blinked, refocusing. "I'm trying to say that maybe you and I should think about——" She stopped again. Rice's body wasn't just hot, it was radiating, and it wasn't all *his* heat. She sensed another presence on him. She leaned into his neck and felt him. "Rice?"

"What?" he snapped.

Sunnie looked deep into his eyes and saw something that resembled *guilt*. She squinted her eyes and asked, afraid of the answer, "Rice . . . did you and Kamile . . . ?"

Rice threw the blanket off and got up. "Why all of a sudden are you in my business? You never cared about that before."

Her breath got caught in her throat, and suddenly she felt a confusion of emotions—jealousy, anger, hurt, betrayal. She didn't know whether to slap Rice or to grab him in her arms. She didn't know what to feel, so she went with denial.

Sunnie stuttered. "I—I *don't* care—really—I was just—just asking."

"Since you don't care, why ask?"

"I don't know. After all, we're just—just——"

"Friends?" Disappointment reflected in his eyes.

Sunnie threw up her hands in a confusing, awkward gesture. "What else could we possibly be?"

"Right. What else could we possibly be," Rice said, flatly.

They held each other's eye a second longer. Finally, Rice said, "I'm going inside. You coming . . . *friend?*"

Sunnie searched his eyes for a clue inside his true feelings, but all she could see were remnants of Kamile, and that scared Sunnie, because if Kamile had stolen Rice's heart, Sunnie would have to find a way to get it back. She needed him—not just for a shoulder to cry on, but for a chance at the love of a lifetime.

"No. I'm going to stay out here and think," Sunnie said.

Rice looked around at the dark courtyard, then at Sunnie. He went in the back door of the mansion.

A little while later, Coach's Rottweilers started barking like mad.

Those crazy dogs. She'd given them steaks for dinner, so what were they complaining about? They were yelping and crashing into the fence surrounding their pen like they'd been doing often lately.

The more they barked, the more Sunnie became aware of the bubble, gurgle, quiver in her stomach. Her spook antennae was sounding off, and even though she thought they had a glitch, she wasn't taking any chances.

She wrapped her blanket tightly around her and prepared to make a mad dash for the back door, but paused when she heard a woman's voice.

Sunnie crouched down and peered through the trees. That's when she saw *her*—the dark, sultry woman from the party.

The woman was a dark silhouette of beauty and evil,

just as Sunnie remembered. She had a phantasmal, almost ghostlike transparency about her, wore the same white gauzelike dress, and was walking barefoot toward the courtyard, talking to herself. Before Sunnie could get her mind together enough to run, the woman had come too close. *If I run now, she'll see me.*

Sunnie crawled under the park bench, scooting in the SpongeBob comforter like a frantic caterpillar in a blue and yellow cocoon.

The woman stepped into the courtyard and stopped directly in front of the bench. Sunnie's heart went into precoronary mode, and her spook radar went into overload. All she could do was hope she hadn't left bread crumbs or anything on top of the bench that would give her away.

Sunnie knew this was no ordinary woman. She had a supernatural presence about her that was not only scary, it was downright seductively evil.

Sunnie stayed under the bench, waiting and trying not to move. After a few long seconds, the woman burped real loud and kept walking.

When the coast was clear, Sunnie quickly wiggled from under the bench. She stood up and caught sight of the woman's back as she went inside the back door of the mansion.

Sunnie ran toward the back door, leaving her blanket behind. Images of the woman wielding a humongous butcher knife and trying to make chop suey out of the guys flashed through Sunnie's mind. She had to stop her.

She tried to rip open the back door, but it was locked.

Sunnie banged on the door, yelling, "Rice! Coach! Open the door!"

A light came on inside and Rice quickly opened the door. Sunnie ran inside and grabbed his arms, checking for missing body parts. "Rice, are you okay? Where'd she go?"

Rice frowned at Sunnie. "Who?"

"The barefoot woman in the white dress." She looked around frantically.

Coach barged around the corner, looking like a grumpy bear disturbed while hibernating. "Who's that hollering like a fool?"

Sunnie grabbed Coach, checking for injuries. "That woman. She came in here."

Rice repeated, "Nobody came in here."

"But I *saw* her!"

Rice shook his head. "Sunnie, I've been standing right here the whole time, watching you in the court-yard acting crazy—crawling under the bench and scaring the dogs. *Nobody* came inside here except you."

Sunnie swallowed real hard. "You saw me, but you didn't see that woman?"

She saw the looks on their faces and felt as cuckoo as they obviously thought she was. She shut up and slumped down on a stool. *How could he not see that woman? She must be invisible to everybody except me.*

Chapter
28

SHORTLY AFTER SUNRISE WEDNESDAY MORNING, GEFFEN grabbed his Vuitton briefcase and headed out the door.

Just before Geffen hopped into his green Hummer, he removed his mother's photo from his wallet. This morning, the grave diggers would begin excavation, and Geffen wanted to be present to oversee the process. He looked at his mother's photo. *Mom, this is for you,* he thought to himself. He kissed the photo and put it back inside his wallet.

When Geffen drove his Hummer into Kringle Cemetery, he took a final deep breath and got out. It had been a long journey and now it was a dream come true to finally move his mother's grave site to his own property and give her the respectable resting place she deserved. He saw a crane and the grave diggers working by his mother's freshly dug plot, and it was a bittersweet moment for Geffen. He got out and walked to his mother's plot.

Being that close to his mother's excavated grave while the workmen hoisted her casket up on a metal gurney made Geffen feel sick. He glanced at the other casket they had to dig up in order to get to his mother's. It sat on the grass next to the hole. Kringle Cemetery buried their caskets close together, and in some cases on top of each other, to save space.

Geffen watched the crane operator shift the levers and hoist the casket from its hole. Two flat belts hugged the upper and lower ends of the standard-issue dull gray casket. Those belts were connected to the arm of the crane by two large silver clamps. Geffen heard the creaks and strain from the pull on the casket's cheap wooden frame.

Geffen hollered over the noise at the cemetery's manager, who stood next to a representative from the County Health Department and three other workmen. "You sure those clamps are going to hold?"

"Positive," the manager assured Geffen.

The crane operator moved the casket smoothly and slowly through the air toward the flatbed truck that awaited. An assistant on the ground gave him hand signals.

Geffen was so busy watching the gentle sway of his mother's casket hanging from the metal hooks that he didn't notice the operator's attention divert toward the top of the donut shop next to the cemetery. Whatever the operator saw shocked him so badly, he hit the wrong lever. The crane's arm swung the casket too far left.

Geffen yelled, "Hey, watch out!"

The crane operator grabbed the lever and, overcompensating, pulled it back too hard. The crane jerked the casket hard to the right. The jolt caused it to splinter, swing back violently, and slam into the crane's arm, breaking the metal hook and dropping the casket.

As if in slow motion, Geffen watched his mother's casket fall from the crane and crash into the other coffin on the ground. The loud clack when the two wooden coffins collided sounded like two giant walnuts cracking open.

Geffen saw both coffins break open. The rusty metal clamps popped off and their seals split, leaving a narrow slit opening to the remains inside. Geffen felt like he was outside of his body and detached from his mind.

He began yelling. *"Y-y-y-y-y-you son of a bitch! Y-y-y-you dropped my mother!"*

The sight of the broken caskets lying next to each other burned his eyes, and hot, angry tears erupted. Geffen went berserk. He yanked the operator down from the crane and clenched the man's throat. The manager and other officials rushed to Geffen and tried to pull him back, but he tightened his grip and wouldn't let go until five more workmen joined in and finally pulled Geffen off.

The cemetery workers ushered him into the small, shabby office.

Two hours passed before Geffen was composed enough to walk out of the cemetery's office. Not knowing what else to do, he had phoned his lawyers and, inasmuch as he was able to, informed them what had happened. Already there was paperwork pending to sue the mortuary for actual and punitive damages, not to mention unspeakable emotional distress.

The crewmen had worked quickly to try to correct the disaster. They'd loaded both busted caskets onto the flatbed truck and toted them to another small building used for the preparation of caskets. Geffen couldn't bring himself to go there, so he headed for his Hummer to go home.

The manager, who'd been working with the caskets, saw Geffen and intercepted him. Sweating and jittery, he sputtered, "Mr. Cage, we are sorting everything out. I assure you."

Geffen held his composure, though inside he was a hot mess of anger and despair. He opened the door of his Hummer and got in.

As Geffen drove his Hummer out the narrow, bumpy driveway he passed the donut shop that sat too close to the cemetery. It was on its roof where something had caught the crane operator's eye, distracted him, and caused this whole catastrophe to happen.

Geffen drove past but couldn't see what the crane operator had seen, nor could anyone else. Nobody could see Dayna sitting on the roof, her lips curled up into an evil grin, as she watched Geffen drive by.

At the mansion, Geffen pulled into his private home office driveway, where his assistant, Senda, was waiting for him, frantic.

"I go crazy trying to find you, Mr. Geffen. I try to call, but you don't answer your phone." She tried to hand him some insurance documents, but he walked past her without stopping.

He went inside his office, threw his briefcase on his desk, and stepped into the small bathroom, where he splashed cold water on his face. Senda followed him into the bathroom, trying to get his attention.

"Mr. Geffen, your accountant call five hundred times this morning. He say when he put you and your partners' cars under the corporation, your insurance company cancel you. They don't cover corporate assets."

Geffen looked in the mirror at his bloodshot eyes. He looked like he didn't feel like being bothered by any of that right now, but Senda ignored that and persisted.

"Mr. Geffen, there's no coverage right now for you. Your insurance company cancel you *yesterday.*"

Geffen snapped. "Then screw them!" He dried his face on a towel and went to his desk.

Senda stood there looking at Geffen, now worried about the way he looked. He had slumped in his chair and was gazing out his window.

He felt her standing over him. "Just go. Now."

Senda frowned with worry. She didn't want to upset him more, so she left.

Alone, Geffen leaned back in his chair and covered his face with his hands. He was exhausted, mentally, physically, and emotionally. As he drifted off, his arms fell down by his side.

Suddenly, he heard his mother crying. Her wails sent cold chills down his spine. He opened his eyes and saw her in a plain blue gown, like the ones hospitals use. It slipped off her thin, bare shoulders and she knelt on a cold linoleum floor, dejected, heartbroken, and crying.

Geffen tried to reach out to her, but his arms were too heavy to lift. "Don't cry, please, Mother. I'm bringing you home. I swear."

Her sobs were inconsolable. *"Geffen!"* The more she wailed, the more it felt like his heart would explode. *"Geffen!"*

He tried to answer her, but his voice escaped him. She kept calling his name.

"Gef! Wake up, man!"

Geffen's eyes snapped open, this time for real. Coach was standing over his desk, blocking out the light from the window.

Geffen sat up and ran his hand over his face, wiping away the wetness from the corners of his red eyes. He looked around the room, then looked back at Coach.

Coach's angry face jarred Geffen's memory and helped bring him back. He knew why Coach was there. Yesterday he'd missed the appointment with Coach and a trainer who wanted to lease the gym. He'd been with Dayna, making love on a jet. But he didn't feel like dealing with Coach right now.

Coach said, "You stood me up, man."

Geffen said, "Coach, don't come barging into my office unannounced. I'm trying to work."

"You were asleep. And I don't need no damn announcement to come in here. Just like you felt you didn't need to call me yesterday and tell me you couldn't make it."

"I was busy."

"That ain't no excuse. I had the guy waiting around here over an hour for your ass. He was going to bring in specialized equipment for my leg. Plus, we lost money on that deal."

Geffen stood up and faced Coach. "Don't come in here yelling at me about losing money. I spent a grip replacing that grass in the courtyard that you and some chick messed up."

"Who gives a shit 'bout some grass?"

Geffen got in Coach's face. "You would if you had a working brain cell in that thick head of yours. I'm tired of being the only *thinking* man in this partnership. Both you and Rice sit on y'all asses and enjoy a free ride while I handle everything."

"You couldn't have *got* this place without our money!"

"Speaking of money, who said your fresh-out-of-the-closet brother could stay here rent free?"

Coach's face registered sheer anger. He started to say something, stopped, then said it anyway. "Who said your mother could come here and turn this place into a graveyard?"

Geffen frowned, his voice got real low. "What did you say?"

Coach replied, "You heard what I said."

As they stared each other down, a car pulled up in front of Geffen's office playing loud music. Coach heard Joey talking real loud and laughing with another man. As much as Coach wanted to stay there and kick Geffen's bourgeois ass, Coach was distracted.

He turned back to Geffen and said, "This ain't over."

Coach parted the miniblinds and looked out. Joey

was getting out of a convertible driven by a short, curly-haired man. When Coach brought Joey home with him, he'd made one thing clear—if Joey *ever* brought a *boy*friend to his house, a whole militia wouldn't be able to pull him off Joey. That's why Coach could not *believe* what he was seeing.

Joey walked around to the driver's side, leaned over, and kissed the man on the mouth.

Coach bolted out the door and grabbed Joey by his neck before he had time to straighten up. He swung Joey around and pushed him backward over the convertible.

Coach yelled in Joey's face. "What's this, Joey? You bringing this shit to my *house* now? I told you what would happen if you did."

The driver yelled, "Get your hands offa him. You'd better not—"

Coach flung around so fast, the man didn't see it coming. Coach rammed his fist into the back of the headrest so hard that the seat broke, knocking the guy forward into the steering wheel, busting his nose. If Coach had hit him directly, he would have been road-kill. Knowing this, the guy threw his car into drive and skidded out the driveway holding his broken, bleeding nose.

Joey tried to run away, but Coach grabbed him again by the back of his neck. Joey jerked free.

Joey told his brother, "You want to do it, then do it. Go ahead, hit me."

Coach tightened his grip and shook Joey. "Don't push me, Joey."

"How am I pushing you, Frank? How am I pushing you?"

"By bringing that shit up in my house."

Joey yelled, "It ain't *shit*, it's me, man. It's who I am. Me. Your *brother!*"

Coach released Joey with a shove, and Joey stumbled.

"I came here hoping we could get to know each other. You didn't know me growing up. You don't know me now." Coach turned away from his brother. Joey added, "Don't be like J.B. Please don't be like him."

Hearing his father's name made him more frustrated. J.B. was a hard-nosed, stubborn son of a bitch. But still, he was his father, so he just accepted it, but he didn't want to be like him.

Coach's voice calmed a bit, but he continued breathing hard. "Your last warning. Don't disrespect my house."

Joey said, "I'm sorry. It won't happen again."

Joey looked hurt. He looked like he wanted to approach his older brother, but Coach's temper was explosive, so he stayed back.

Joey appealed to Coach. "I know you think this stuff is wrong, and I ain't going to try to change your mind."

"Because you can't. The shit *is* wrong."

"But that don't change the fact that we're brothers. I need you, man. Maybe if we could just talk, we could—"

Evie's voice interrupted Joey. "Hey, what's up, *boyz?*"

Coach turned and saw his new toy sauntering up the driveway. She wore a fuchsia-colored cat suit that hugged every naughty curve of her body. Coach was so glad to see her that it showed immediately in his face and in his pants.

Evie looked at Joey. She said to Coach, "Whew! With that beard on your brother's face, I can hardly tell you two apart."

She walked up close and stood directly in front of both Coach and Joey. "Wait. I know how I can tell y'all apart."

Evie grabbed both Coach's and Joey's crotches and held on firmly. Joey quickly flinched and backed away, giving her nothing to hold. Coach, however, didn't move. He stood there like Mandingo, filling up Evie's hand with every hard inch of what he had to offer.

Evie laughed and kept her hand firmly clutching Coach's crotch. "Yeah, just like I thought. Only one of you is a *real* man."

Coach, of course, was flattered anytime a woman as sexy as Evie gave him a compliment, but he did feel a tinge of embarrassment for Joey. He tried to push Evie's hand away and play down the incident, but Evie wouldn't let go.

She fondled him and aroused him even more. "Oooh, yeah, Big Poppa. That's what I'm talkin' 'bout. A *real* man, not no fag."

Evie looked straight at Joey, taunting him, making him feel worse. Joey glanced at Coach, expecting him to do something.

Coach grabbed Evie's wrist. She looked up at him, batted her thick eyelashes, and poked out her bottom lip in mock sadness.

"I was just playin'. Don't be mad at me." Then she grinned a crooked, sexy grin and said, "Unless you gonna spank me, Big Poppa."

Coach couldn't help but grin. "Girl, you are out of this world."

He yanked her to him and kissed her real hard and deep. Evie grabbed his ass to show her appreciation.

Joey watched them for a second and walked away.

Chapter 29

AFTER ACCOMPANYING RICE TO A BOOK SIGNING, KAMILE sat next to him in his car as he drove to Compton to visit his parents. During one of their many introspective talks, Rice had confided that he regretted not confronting his mother about something that happened in his childhood. He didn't tell her everything—specifically, not why he and Sunnie had run away to the Santa Monica Pier that day. Only Sunnie knew what had happened to him in his playhouse that night.

Sunnie had been trying to get Rice to go back and confront his mother for a long time, but he never would, saying he wasn't ready. He wasn't sure if he was ready now, but at Kamile's sweet insistence he agreed to give it a try.

When Rice's mother opened the front door, a thousand childhood memories came rushing back.

Kendra Gordon lifted her arms in her usual dramatic fashion. "Well, looka here. My long-lost son found his way back home."

With Kamile at his side, Rice walked into the house where he grew up. His father was slouched down in his recliner positioned close to the television. Other than an occasional cough or bronchitic wheeze, he didn't say much.

His mother put on her superhostess routine for Kamile, acting younger and far more considerate than she actually was. When Rice had called his mother yesterday and said he was bringing someone for dinner, Kendra was happy to find out he was introducing her to a woman he was seeing. Rice knew Kendra was acting supernice to Kamile only because she wanted grandchildren, preferably girls, before she got too old to swap clothes with them.

After Kamile helped his mother prepare the table, they all sat down for dinner. Kendra poured a glass of wine for everyone. When she got to her own glass, Rice watched her fill it all the way to the top. Kendra watched him back.

Kendra told Kamile. "When my son called and said he was coming, I decided to cook his favorite. Pork chops."

Rice smiled, corrected her. "That's your favorite, Ma."

Kendra gave him a look. She added more wine to her already full glass. "Well, so it is." She held the bottle up at Rice so he could get a good look at it before she set it down. That was her way of saying, *If you don't like my drinking, then don't look.*

Rick Gordon, Rice's father, asked, "Are we ready to eat or talk?"

Kendra got up. "I forgot the ice. Hold on."

When she came back, she placed the ice bucket on the table next to Kamile. "Rick, since you're in such a big hurry to eat, you get to say the grace."

They all bowed their heads, except for Kamile, who hesitated.

Rice asked. "You okay?"

She nodded. Rice's father started praying, "Dear Heavenly Father, bless this food we are about to—" He coughed and tried to continue, but he coughed more and couldn't finish.

Kendra frowned and said, "Since your father's choking like the devil, why don't we let your friend say the prayer." She turned to Kamile. "Do you mind?"

Rice thought Kamile was nervous, but she put on a smile, placed her hands on the table near the ice bucket, and started a prayer.

Kamile said, "Bow your heads, please. To the powers within the universe and rulers of legions and dominions, please hear this prayer. We dedicate this meal to you, O forces whose power and purpose is to conquer every opposing force, to destroy our enemies, and to reign supreme forever and forever, on earth and beyond. Amen."

After Kamile finished her prayer, Kendra said, enthusiastically, "Amen. Rice, that girl sho' can pray, can't she?" Kendra nudged Kamile playfully and reached into the bucket for ice. "Good gracious. How'd all this ice melt that quick?" She got up to get more.

Throughout dinner, Rice's mother laughed like a

teenager, told off-color jokes, and kept refilling her wineglass.

"Can I pour you more wine, Mrs. Gordon?" Kamile offered. Rice stiffened.

His mother threw him a smirk and tilted her glass toward Kamile. "You sure can, sweety. You're a sweet girl. Fun, not a tightass like some people I know." Kendra winked at her son.

Kamile filled his mother's glass to the brim. "If you don't mind me saying, you look quite young to have a son Kendric's age. And your dimples—they remind me of that pretty actress. What's her name?"

"Debbie Morgan? Yes, I get that a lot. And you know what, sweety? I used to act, too."

"Really?"

"Yes. Nothing big, you know, but back in the day, Mama could hold her own." Kendra bragged.

Kamile laughed with her. "Of course you can." She watched Rice's mother take bigger gulps of wine, then loosen the scarf around her neck. Kamile smiled at her.

His mother gushed. "I like to have fun, you know what I mean? Of course you do. Girls like us like to have fun."

Rice leaned toward his father, who was eating his pork chops with his head down, and nodded toward his mother's wine glass. "Pop, don't you think you should, uh—"

His father waved his hand. "She's alright, she's just being Kendra."

She threw Rice a "don't mess with me" glance, and continued on as she pleased.

"My son here doesn't take after me. Even as a kid, he never knew how to relax and go with the flow. He's always been high strung and when things didn't go his way, he'd make up stuff."

Rice quickly cleared his throat. "So, Pop, are you still rebuilding that old Mustang in the garage?"

His father drowned his roll in gravy. "No. Gave up on it."

Rice sighed and glanced sideways at his mother. "I guess you did."

Kamile asked, "Are you a mechanic, Mr. Gordon?"

"Just dabble," he said. "I'm a retired longshoreman by trade."

Kamile took an interest. "Oh, so you must have been away from home a lot."

"All the time. Weeks. Months." He drank his grape Kool-Aid.

Kamile turned to Rice's mother. "Mrs. Gordon, how did a young, spirited, attractive woman like you occupy your time with your husband gone so much?"

Rice's fork clacked against his plate.

"I kept busy." His mother tossed back the rest of her wine.

Rice said, "She did volunteer work at my school."

His mother narrowed her eyes at Rice.

He said, "Everybody knew her. Especially the janitor."

Kendra set her wineglass down hard on the table, almost breaking it. Everyone turned and looked at her except Rice.

She put on a fake smile and said, drunkenly, "Hey,

everybody. I got a joke for y'all. Okay, okay, it goes like this." Kendra leaned up and tried not to slur her words. "What's the difference between a novelist and a liar?"

She heckled. Nobody said anything. "C'mon, y'all. Ask me, *What?* So I can give you the punch line."

Rice got up from the table and left the room.

"See? What I tell ya? He's a tightass. Can't take a joke." Kendra poured herself more wine.

Kamile excused herself from the table to join Rice as he sat on the back porch in the dark, petting Skippy III, a rust-colored terrier that looked just like the one he had as a boy. Skippy sniffed Kamile, whimpered, and ran behind Rice's old wooden playhouse.

Kamile rubbed Rice's back. "I didn't realize your mother has a problem with alcohol."

"Neither does she." Rice threw a pebble, hit the side of the playhouse. "The first step of those twelve steps was way too high for her. She won't admit to anything, much less a drinking problem. I shouldn't have come back here."

"You did the right thing by coming." Kamile rubbed his shoulders.

They sat in silence, looking out at the dark backyard. "Is that your old playhouse?" Kamile asked.

Rice didn't answer. He didn't even look at it, the memories too painful.

Kamile gently asked. "Take me inside."

"No, I can't do that."

"Please, Rice, it's your old playhouse. It's a part of you. I want to be a part of you."

Rice finally looked at it, thinking back. "The only person I ever let in there was Sunnie."

Kamile got up and walked toward the playhouse. Rice hesitated, then followed her, reluctantly. She reached for the doorknob. He said, "Stop."

"Don't you trust me the same way you trusted Sunnie?"

"It's not that. That doorknob—it's rigged."

"Rigged?"

Rice smiled slightly. "Yeah. It's a dummy doorknob. If you touch it, you'll get shocked."

"You booby-trapped your playhouse?"

"I got a secret electrical chord hidden in the door frame. It runs underground into a socket inside the house."

Kamile laughed. "That's so crazy."

Rice chuckled, too, and pointed to the NO TRESPASS-ING sign still hanging on the door.

Kamile read the sign. "Except for Sunnie?"

Rice didn't respond.

Kamile poked around the door. "Show me how to get in."

Rice paused and looked at Kamile's softly pleading expression. He shook his head, saying, "I may regret this," and then showed her how to get in.

Rice took her hand and guided it carefully around the doorknob to avoid an electrical shock. He pressed her index finger into a tiny latch hidden slightly to the left on the underside of the knob.

He said, "If you pull it toward you, the door will open."

She did and it opened. Once inside, Rice stopped smiling. He fought hard to hold the memories back. Kamile hugged his waist.

"Relax, baby. It's only an old playhouse, it can't harm you." She pressed her head into his chest and held him tight, and also kept him from walking out like he wanted to. "Kendric, did something happen to you in here?"

Rice glanced at the old, torn furniture inside the dark playhouse, closed his eyes, and bit his lip. He tried to stop it, but he was thrown back twenty-odd years into the past.

In his memory, he saw the janitor, his mother's boyfriend.

"Kendric. Hey, boy! Don't run from me." The man's voice slurred. He'd been drinking, too, like his mother, who was passed out in his father's bedroom. Kendric ran barefoot across the lawn into his playhouse and slammed the door closed. Skippy nipped at the school janitor's heels, but the janitor kicked the dog, who yelped and ran. The janitor banged on the door. "Oh, so you gone try'n hide from me?" The man laughed and spit. "Since yo mamma can't finish what she started, that leaves you, boy," he said, unzipping his pants. He twisted the doorknob, trying to break the lock. Kendric squeezed his eyes shut tight, wishing for a great big giant lock that nobody could ever, ever break. The old rickety lock broke, and the man came inside the playhouse.

Rice took Kamile's arms from around his waist and walked out of the playhouse.

Once he got back inside his mother's house, Rice didn't say anything. He walked past his mother and father, removed his and Kamile's coats from the coatrack, and opened the front door.

Kamile apologized. "Mr. and Mrs. Gordon, thank you for a lovely dinner, but Rice isn't feeling well and we have to go now."

"Wait." Rice's mother jumped up from the table, clutching the whole bottle of wine, and swaggered to the door. She looked Rice up and down. "Ain't nothing wrong with this boy. He just does thangs to try to get people mad at each other. Ain't that right, son?"

Rice didn't say anything.

"Besides, y'all can't leave till you hear the rest of my joke."

Rick said, "Now, Kendra, let them go on, if they want to go."

"No, you stay outta this. I'm gonna tell my joke. This my house, my joke, and I'm gonna tell it." She wrapped her arm around both Rice and Kamile's necks, banging the wine bottle into the back of her son's head, and pulling them into her alcohol-tainted breath.

She asked, "What's the difference between a *novelist* and a *liar?*"

Rice still didn't say anything. Finally, Kamile said, "I don't know. What?"

His mother replied, "One gets paid."

No one laughed. His mother started busting up laughing, falling into Rice and spilling wine all over his clothes.

Rice didn't move. His face looked numb.

His father said, "Y'all go on home. I'll take care of her."

Suddenly, Rice spoke up. "No, wait. I've got a joke, too."

Everybody was shocked. He waited until he got his mother's full attention.

"What's the difference between a real mother, who protects her son, and a drunk, sex-crazed whore, who calls her son a liar?"

When Rice's words finally registered in Kendra's drunken mind, she reared back and slapped Rice hard across his face. Rice, who could have ducked, took the slap square on his cheek.

He looked at her. He exhaled as if he were relieved. "I'm glad we both got that off our chests. Good night, Ma."

Rice escorted Kamile out of his mother's house. They got in his car and drove off.

Thursday evening, Sunnie was working late, but her mind wasn't on real estate, it was on Rice. She clicked off her computer.

Walking to her little yellow Saab, she made a mental note to call her insurance company in the morning to get her taillight fixed. She'd called Geffen earlier to try to get Dayna's insurance company info, but he'd sounded so upset. "This is a bad time. Not right now," he'd said, and hung up. When she called Coach to find out what was wrong with Geffen, Coach said, "Ask him," and he hung up, too.

She said to herself, "I'll swing by the mansion later to check on the guys."

She knew Rice had a book signing in Long Beach because she always kept track of his schedule. She was hurt that he hadn't asked her to come with him, as he usually did.

That's why she'd left her office and was heading to Mother Roby's house in Compton, to talk about her dilemma with Rice. Maybe Mother Roby could help her sort things out. She also needed to tell Mother Roby about her latest encounter with that dark, sultry woman in the courtyard.

Sunnie pulled her yellow Saab into Mother Roby's driveway. As she went up the walkway, she noticed Rice's car parked in front of his mother's house, a few doors down and across the street. She noticed the front door was open and she could see Rice talking to his mother in the doorway. She ducked behind a tree and watched.

Rice's mother hauled off and slapped him right in his face. Sunnie's heart stopped. Then Rice walked out with Kamile. Sunnie could hardly believe her eyes. She'd been trying to get Rice to go home and confront his mother for over a year, and when he finally decides to go, not only does he not tell Sunnie, but he takes Kamile with him. *Why would you do that, Rice?*

Obviously, things had gone terribly wrong. Sunnie knew Rice had to be hurting inside—she knew how sensitive he was. Nobody understood what he was going through the way she did.

Sunnie ached all over. She ached for Rice, she ached for herself because her heart was crushed, and she ached at the sight of Kamile, a stranger, getting into that car next to Rice, her soul mate, trying to take her place.

After they drove off, Sunnie dragged herself up Mother Roby's front porch and rang the doorbell, thinking about her love for Rice and wondering, *Am I too late?*

Chapter
30

THURSDAY NIGHT, AFTER TALKING TO MOTHER ROBY FOR hours, Sunnie headed home to her West L.A. condo, but not before driving up that familiar winding road in Beverly Hills to check on her two best friends and Rice.

Mother Roby had helped her put things in perspective. She'd told Sunnie to take things slow with Rice, and that right now she needed to focus on the urgent matter at hand—in other words, this evil force that had taken the form of a sexy, dark woman who, for reasons unknown, was trying to destroy the guys.

Sunnie and Mother Roby prayed and asked God for insight. As Mother Roby hugged Sunnie good-bye, she told her again, *"Listen,"* as if she weren't completely convinced that Sunnie had learned how to do that yet.

As Sunnie drove her yellow Saab up the winding road toward the mansion, she had the strangest sensation to leave the main driveway and drive to a small clearing near the east side of the mansion.

Sunnie sat in her car with the headlights on, staring into the edge of the mountain range. All she saw were dark trees, thorny bushes, and tangling vines. She was about to leave when something seemed to whisper to her in a soft, reassuring voice, *"Listen . . ."*

Sunnie stayed and listened. That's when she heard faint voices coming from deeper inside the woods. She couldn't understand what they were saying, but she knew they were there. With nothing tangible to go on, only a strong intuitive feeling, she knew beyond a doubt that the guys were definitely in danger. Sunnie started her car and headed up to the mansion to try again to warn the guys. She used her alarm code and let herself in. The mansion was cold, dark, and empty. None of the guys were home.

Deeper in the mountains, Vixx had returned to her cave and was trampling over animal bones and other debris. She plopped down on a rock and fussed at Crèp.

"When I come home from a hard week at work, I'd like to come home to a *clean* cave, not a pigsty."

Crèp rose apologetically from his perch and tried to explain the reason for the mess.

"Vixx, Your Highness, I've been working part-time, too, this week. Plus, I have to come home and do laundry." He pointed sheepishly at the clothesline, where he'd hung the freshly laundered uniforms that he'd worn this week. There was a chauffeur's uniform, a pilot's outfit, and a janitor's, as well as her slinky red dress and other outfits.

Vixx flicked her hand. "Yeah, whatever."

Vixx had spent all day and all night working on the guys, so Crèp hadn't had a chance to talk to her much.

He asked, "How are things going with the bachelors? Are your evil plans working?"

"Of course. I learned from the best. Queen Domina taught me how to get into men's heads, seduce them, and prey upon their weaknesses, all through the power of lust."

Vixx kicked her feet up on an animal carcass. "Right now, I'm giving them what they want, fulfilling their sexual fantasies. But when the time is right, I'll turn their dreams into a nightmare. I'll exploit their fears, and make them want to die."

Crèp took a dirty cloth and dusted the animal carcass underneath Vixx's foot. "What about the girl's prayers?"

Vixx lifted her left foot so he could get a spot. "By their own free will, they have moved themselves away from her protective prayer covering."

"How?"

"By continuing to ignore her warnings and following their own desires." Vixx's smile was evil and erotic. "The power of lust is a beautiful thang."

She licked her lips, thinking about those good-looking guys. "Instead of destroying them completely, maybe I'll keep them around as slaves. They could do a few *chores* for me around the brothel."

Crèp finished dusting and returned to his perch. He knew what Vixx meant by *chores*. That had always been her weakness—getting jiggy with human men. That's what had gotten them in this mess in the first place. If Vixx hadn't fallen for Bruce, they wouldn't have lost their brothel and been banished to the cellar for a hundred years. Crèp was looking forward to getting their brothel back, but was worried that Vixx was getting sidetracked and might fail to get the guys out the mansion before the deadline. She only had a few days left.

Crèp said, intentionally, "Whatever you say, Your *Horniness.*"

Vixx narrowed her eyes. "What did you call me?"

"I said, Your *Highness.*"

Vixx threw him a warning look, then resumed thinking about Rice and how much he resembled Bruce. She began to get aroused, then frustrated.

"Rice's head is the hardest to get into. He's so secretive and so good at keeping his wounds hidden that he hides his other feelings as well. I'm a little worried."

"Why?" Crèp asked.

"Sometimes I think he feels something for that girl. But then he pushes it back and I stop worrying."

"What if he falls in love with her?"

Vixx picked up a deer skull and hurled it at Crèp, hitting him in his chest and knocking him off his perch. "Don't say that word!"

Crèp rolled over in the dirt and coughed. "What? *Love?*"

Vixx spat. "Yes! That's the only thing that could ruin my evil plan. If any one of those guys should forsake their lust and opt instead for true, meaningful love, my spell over all of them would be broken."

Crèp crawled back up on his perch. "How will you prevent that from happening?"

Vixx stood up and strutted around the cave. "I'll turn the power up a notch, crank up the heat. I'll work faster and harder. I'll hit those guys with a healthy dose of burning-hot lust, she-devil style." She walked in front of a full-length mirror and struck a sexy pose. "I'll break them off a piece of this dark sexiness. No way will they be able to resist this."

Crèp boosted her ego. "Of course, Your Highness. Under your viciously evil attack, they don't stand a chance. They are weak, powerless, simple-minded men before your awesome supernatural powers of seduction."

Vixx smiled and poked her chest out more.

Crèp went on, "After all, it's not like they have *connections* like the girl has. She, on the other hand, could whip your ass if she were to use the power she's been given."

Vixx's smile faded. "What did you say?"

Crèp went on, "Let's face it, Your Highness. Sunnie could mop up this cave with you if she trusted her gift."

Vixx fumed. "You lousy schmuck! Whose side are you on? Sunnie is no match for me. You know why? Because she's too *scared*. That's why she runs and hides under benches. She's too afraid to listen to The Voice and really trust her gift. And as long as she stays confused, she's no threat to me. I can kick *her* butt, and I can get to those guys, and I can destroy them."

Vixx smiled again, evilly and mischievously. "Spiritual ignorance is also a beautiful thang."

Chapter
31

FRIDAY MORNING, INSIDE THE MANSION'S GYM, COACH WAS working to rehabilitate his injured leg so that he could return to the football field this season. Coach strained, pushing himself beyond the limit, while his personal physical therapist, Owen, and Evie looked on.

Owen yelled at Coach to get off the leg press, but Coach kept going. He sweated, grunted, and clenched his teeth from the brutal pain of the added weight. "Coach! Buddy, you're putting too much pressure on that leg!"

Evie spurred Coach on. "He's a *real* man! He can handle it!"

Owen urged, "I'm telling you, pal, that's too much weight."

Evie snapped at Owen. "What do you know?"

"I'm a licensed physical therapist and certified athletic trainer. What are *you?*"

Evie reared back at Owen, and was tempted to do

something supernaturally wicked to him to show him who she was, but she didn't want to blow her cover just yet. "I'm his *woman*, and I say he can handle it!" She turned to Coach and cheered. "You go, Big Poppa! You da man! You ain't no punk!"

Owen jumped up. "That's it! I can't work like this. Coach, you need to choose. Who's gonna train you, me or *her*?"

Coach got up, his chest heaving, sweat pouring off his face. Panting, he said, "Owen, I want to play."

"I know, pal. We're working on that. We need to stick to our regimented program and take one day at a—"

Coach slammed the towel down. "I want to play *now!* I *need* to get back out on that field! I ain't getting no younger!"

Owen tried to reason with Coach. "But if you push too hard, you'll blow it. And you won't be able to return to the field ever."

Evie butted in. "He already blew it when he got hurt. Now he has to do *whatever* it takes to get back in the game. Until then, he's less of a man."

Owen looked at Evie, digesting that comment, then he looked at Coach. "Aren't you gonna object to that, buddy?"

Owen waited. Coach didn't object or reply one way or another. The truth was, that's how he felt—less of a man. Evie had just said it for him.

Owen tried to appeal to Coach. "Football is a game. It's not *life*. You earn your points for being a human being in real life, not on the turf."

Coach picked up the towel again and completely

covered his sweaty face with it. He exhaled. When he finally lifted the towel, he looked up at Evie, and then he looked at Owen.

He had to make a decision—either take the conservative approach and risk missing another season or bust his ass pushing his body to the limit in order to prove to himself, to J.B., and to the rest of the world that real men are measured by the size of their biceps and by the number of quarterback sacks on their year-end stats.

Coach laid back down on the bench, put his feet up in the stirrups, and said to Evie, "Add ten more pounds."

A few hours later, after Coach fired Owen, Evie slipped down into the Jacuzzi next to Coach.

Evie cooed in Coach's ear. "Baby, you didn't need that trainer anyway. You got me."

Coach tried to give all his attention to his pretty little vixen, but the tendons in his injured leg hurt so bad he wanted to holler. He was hoping the warm Jacuzzi water would massage and ease the pain in his muscles, but it wasn't enough.

As if she'd read his mind, Evie said, "Don't worry, Big Poppa, I gotcha covered."

Evie turned her back toward Coach and lowered her whole body into the water up to her neck. The water temperature instantly increased, surging 20 degrees higher.

Coach felt the heat rising. "Damn, girl! What did you do?"

She started singing Nelly's song. " 'It's getting hot in here, so take off all your clothes . . .' "

Coach laughed, snapped his fingers, and started singing with her, trying to forget about the pain. Evie reached underneath the hot bubbling water and removed her bikini top and bottom. She tossed them up in the air and they landed on top of Coach's head. He kept singing, trying to get his mind off the throb in his leg and onto sex.

Evie kept her back to him, and pressed her butt into his stomach. She spread her legs apart, and reached down and brought his injured leg up between hers, straddling it.

Coach flinched with pain. "Whoa! Careful with that!"

Evie grinned like a tigress. "Relax, Big Poppa. You gotta trust me."

Evie gripped Coach's injured leg firmly beneath the jet-streaming water, and began to massage it. Coach flexed and grabbed the side of the Jacuzzi, clenched his jaw, and breathed through his teeth.

The heat of the pulsating water and the vigor of Evie's hot hands massaging his leg slowly started to override the pain. The motion of the Jacuzzi water, Evie's body sloshing rhythmically, the feel of her nakedness rubbing against his thigh with her butt pushing into his stomach all helped to soothe him, as well as turn him on.

"Ooh, girl. Yeah, that's starting to feel *real* good." He reached around and cupped her breasts, then pulled her back onto his chest.

Evie giggled. "Baby, I'm trying to work. Quit playing."

She pulled away and started massaging his leg again, this time more forcefully.

Coach tensed up again. "Okay, babe, I said it feels good, but don't get carried away."

Evie tightened her hands around his tendon at precisely the injured spot. She twisted and pushed, working his ligaments down to his bone. The more she worked, the hotter the water became. Coach felt like he was in a witch's kettle.

"Hey, Evie. That's too much. Back off me!"

Evie ignored him and kept going. "You like it rough, don't you, Big Poppa?"

"Yeah, but this fucking hurts!"

Evie laughed a hyenalike laugh. "You think *this* hurts? Well, how 'bout *this?*"

Evie dove her whole body, face and everything, under the Jacuzzi water. She grabbed Coach's entire leg in a hooking-type motion with her whole arm. She arched her back, and in one swift movement she bent Coach's injured leg so quickly that it snapped. He heard a dull pop, followed by a muffled underwater sound of tendons ripping apart.

Coach hollered as gut-wrenching, fiery pain shot through his entire body. The pain was so powerful, it arched his back and threw his head backward over the edge of the Jacuzzi.

Coach passed out.

Evie dragged Coach, unconscious, out of the mansion. Geffen, Rice, and Joey were not around. She pulled him up into his black Suburban truck, drove him to Holy Cross Hospital, dropped him off in the emergency room, stuck his truck keys in his pocket, and left.

Some time later, Coach regained consciousness. Emergency room staff administered pain meds by IV and ran diagnostic tests, then left Coach alone in a room.

After a while, Dr. Sumkin walked into exam room B, where Coach sat nervously awaiting test results. The doctor closed the door behind him. A few seconds later, the door burst open.

Coach was hollering as the doctor backed out of the exam room. Nurses heard Coach hollering and ran to help, while other patients poked their heads out to look.

The head nurse asked Dr. Sumkin as he came out, "What's going on, doctor?"

She peeped inside and saw Coach. He was absolutely delirious with emotion.

The doctor pushed the nurse back outside and closed the exam room door, keeping Coach inside. "Give him some space. Let him calm down. We'll need to keep him overnight."

Chapter
32

FRIDAY AFTERNOON, GEFFEN WAS IN HIS OFFICE ON PINS and needles, waiting for a call from Kringle Cemetery to tell him that his mother's remains were ready to be picked up. They had also promised him that they'd transfer her to a new, temporary casket.

He'd been unable to sleep since Wednesday, when the crane operator had dropped his mother's original casket. Every time he closed his eyes, he could hear his mother crying. No matter how many times he told himself that he didn't *believe* in nightmares, and that it wasn't actually his mother crying, the visions were taking a toll on Geffen.

He'd given Senda the day off yesterday. He didn't want her up under him while he sat in his dark office. In fact, he didn't want anyone to see him in that condition.

This morning, Geffen had sent Senda out on errands, anything to get her out of the office. All she did was constantly nag him about business matters that no longer seemed important compared to his dilemma with his mother's remains. "But, Mr. Geffen, you need some insurance," she'd say, but he couldn't concentrate. He told her he'd get insurance after he got his mother home and buried.

Senda returned from her errands at the exact same time the phone rang. Geffen, already sitting at his desk on pins and needles waiting for a call from Kringle Cemetery, answered it on the first ring.

On the other end of the line the cemetery manager said, "Mr. Cage, we are sorry to inform you that we've encountered a problem with your mother's remains."

Geffen was barely able to hold the phone to his ear, his hand shook so much. "A *problem?* You already dropped her and broke her casket wide open. What *other* problem could there be?"

The manager was hesitant, stalling. "We prefer to speak with you in person—"

Geffen yelled, "No, just tell me over the phone!"

Senda set donuts on his desk and stood by watching.

There was a palpable uncomfortable silence on the other end of the line. Geffen heard the cemetery manager clear his throat. He began speaking, "The two exhumed caskets got mixed up when the nameplates popped off. Mr. Cage, we don't know which one is your mother."

Geffen's whole body started to shake from the small earthquake erupting inside of him. He kept the phone to his ear and yelled, *"Awww, fuck!"*

Senda jumped and ran around Geffen's desk. "Mr. Geffen! What happened?"

Geffen slammed the phone into his desk lamp, busting the fixture into pieces. He put his face into his hands and pressed hard. Senda stood by in a panic—she didn't know what to do. Seconds later, Geffen sprang up from his chair and kicked a dent in his metal file cabinet.

Senda was trying to grab him. "Mr. Geffen! Mr. Geffen!"

Geffen pulled away from Senda. "Leave me alone!"

Senda let go of him and started to panic, pulling on her spiked hair.

"Oh, Mr. Geffen! They did something bad to your mother? Oh, no, no. This is so bad."

Geffen could hardly speak. "I gotta go."

He grabbed his coat. Senda grabbed a piece of paper and ran in front of him. "Wait! Mr. Cage, I know you upset, but I find insurance for you yesterday and all you do is sign this paper—"

Geffen blew up. He couldn't believe, after what he'd just been told, that this stupid college kid would have the nerve to get in his face about signing a stupid piece of paper.

"Hey, did you hear me? I said, I gotta go! Move out of my way."

Senda jumped back in front of him. "But, Mr. Cage, you *have* to—"

"I don't have to do nothing!" All Geffen could think about was his mother's unidentified remains mixed up with a stranger's. "Senda, move! I'll handle it later!"

"No later, Mr. Cage, you really need to—"

"You're fired!"

Geffen jumped into his Hummer and burned rubber as he skidded off, leaving Senda outside his office crying. He had no time to think about her, he had to think about his mother. As if her life wasn't bad enough when she was alive, having to live in poverty while having her only son taken from her. Now all this terrible chaos happens to her when she's dead. And Geffen, for all his trying, couldn't seem to help her.

When Geffen pulled up into Kringle Cemetery, Dayna Devlin was already standing in the driveway waiting for him. How she got there that fast and who'd notified her of what happened, he didn't know. Right now he didn't care.

Geffen didn't bother parking his Hummer—he drove it up on the grass, turned off the engine, and jumped out. The cemetery manager, the Health Department rep, and a bunch of other people were already outside waiting on him.

Forget coolness and composure. Geffen started yelling, "You sons of bitches! How could you let this happen, you incompetent bastards?" Geffen looked like a madman, especially compared to his normal dapper, extremely well groomed appearance. He hadn't shaved in three days and he'd been skipping meals, so his already thin frame looked gaunt. His uncombed hair needed trimming, and his clothes looked like he'd slept in them, which he had.

The cemetery manager raised his palms to Geffen's chest as Geffen moved threateningly close to him. "Mr. Cage, we understand how this would be very disturbing for you."

"You *understand?* No, you have no fucking idea what this is doing to me."

Dayna touched the back of his arm, but he was already so upset he didn't feel it.

Dayna said to the manager, "How about dental records to identify the remains?"

The manager bent his head. "They were destroyed in a recent fire."

Geffen cringed. Dayna, on the other hand, was not phased.

Dayna said, "There is another solution." The manager listened. Dayna said, "DNA." Her words slowly registered with the manager, who lifted his head a bit. Geffen, however, remained distraught and unresponsive.

Dayna put her hand on Geffen's chest. "Let me help you handle this. I've got connections. Let's go inside the office and discuss arrangements."

Geffen remained where he stood, numb and hurting. Dayna motioned him toward the office. He followed.

Later that Friday afternoon, Geffen walked out of the Cellsearch Laboratories in Costa Mesa, where he had deposited his DNA sample with Dayna by his side. With Geffen's lawyers pushing them, the lab agreed to process Geffen's DNA sample quickly and to get the results back to the cemetery as soon as possible. The events of the past few days were making Geffen feel like he was losing his mind.

Geffen escorted Dayna back to his car. He had

calmed down sufficiently to drive now. Dayna had remained by his side the whole time, counseling him and giving him advice.

As Geffen got on the 405 Freeway heading back to Los Angeles, he told Dayna, "I fired Senda, my assistant."

Dayna straightened the collar of her Chanel ivory silk blouse. She said, decisively, "Good. You don't need an assistant. You have me now."

As Geffen transitioned to the left lane, he glanced over at Dayna. Her aura never ceased to amaze him. Even though they'd been in each other's company at least several hours a day, every day for a week, he still felt like she was from another space and time.

Dayna smiled at Geffen, perhaps knowing how he felt about her, her crystal icelike eyes sparkling. Then she asked the last question in the world he expected her to ask at that moment.

"Do you hear your mother's cries when you close your eyes?"

Geffen shuddered and his Hummer drifted into the other lane before he regained control of the steering wheel. "How did you know? I didn't tell you that."

Geffen had always felt as if Dayna were privy to his thoughts because of her uncanny ability to pick up on his mood, but with that question, he seriously began to wonder if strange things were, in fact, happening with her.

Dayna pierced him with her eyes for a moment, then smiled. "Geffen, you talk in your sleep."

"Oh." Geffen felt like an idiot. It wasn't in his

nature to jump to unreasonable conclusions like that, but lately he'd been doing a lot of out-of-character things. He preferred to drop the subject, but Dayna persisted.

"Tell me, Geffen, what does she say to you?"

Geffen hesitated. He didn't want to give validation to something that wasn't real by speaking about it. He told himself over and over that it was only an image and it was not based in reality.

Geffen rubbed his eyes. "She cries, she wails, and then pleads, 'Take me home . . .'"

Geffen sped up his Hummer, not wanting to hear her voice in his head again, but not being able to prevent it. But he heard it, and it seemed to emanate from Dayna. Geffen hoped Dayna wouldn't pick up on what he was feeling, what he was thinking, but she did.

Dayna turned toward Geffen in her seat. Surprise, shock, and dismay showed on her face. Since they first met, she had made it perfectly clear to Geffen that sharp mental acuity and focus were absolutely mandatory if he wanted to succeed in business, and Geffen had agreed. Now Dayna was looking at him as if he were a failure.

"Geffen, I am appalled. You actually *believe* that your mother *is* crying out to you, and that it's not simply a dream. I can see it in your face."

Geffen sped up to a dangerous 90 mph in a 65 mph speed zone. With tears welling in his eyes, he kept his face turned toward the road. His voice was hoarse and hollow as he confessed.

"I *know* it's her. But I also know that's *impossible*. I

don't believe in the supernatural, but I don't know how to stop her voice in my head."

Geffen was desperate. For a split second, he took his eyes off the road and looked at Dayna. He pleaded, "Can you help me?"

Dayna looked at him as if he were pathetic, then turned away and looked out her window. "I'll see what I can do," she said, a tiny smirk on her beautiful lips.

Chapter

33

SATURDAY AROUND NOON, KAMILE STOOD SHOULDER TO shoulder with Rice on the computer-operated tram as it ferried them from the street-level parking facility to the hilltop entrance to the Getty Center in Los Angeles. As Rice took in the panoramic view of the city's landscape—the San Gabriel Mountains, the Pacific Ocean, the vast street grid of Los Angeles—he wanted more than anything to forget about his disastrous trip home and his emotionally disruptive alcoholic mother.

Rice thought about how Sunnie had wanted him to take her to the Getty, but he didn't want to go. He didn't want to go today, either, but Kamile begged him, and when he looked into her large brown eyes, he agreed to take her. He seemed to be doing a lot of things Kamile asked him to do—like she had a spell over him—but he laughed it off, knowing that spells were not real, yet thinking they were something that Sunnie would probably believe could happen. *Sunnie*

would be pissed if she knew I brought Kamile to the Getty.
Rice had to make himself stop thinking about Sunnie.

Kamile gently leaned into his shoulder to get his attention. "It's all my fault. I'm the one who suggested that you go home to see your parents."

"Nobody's fault." Rice gazed over the city, detached, or at least trying to be. It wasn't that he wanted to shun Kamile, it was just that over the past week since meeting her, his life had been emotionally chaotic. Rice thrived on peace and the absence of conflict. That was one reason why he was so guarded with his emotions; he didn't want them to be disrupted. Unfortunately, it also backfired in that he missed out on a lot of things, too, like finding out how things could have been with him and Sunnie if he'd come right out and let her know how he felt.

Kamile bumped his shoulder again to get his attention. "I gave you my word that I'd never pressure you into telling me anything, not even what happened to you as a boy in your backyard playhouse."

Rice stiffened. He kept his head turned toward the view. Kamile continued, "But please, can you tell me just this one thing?" He took his eye off the landscape and looked at her. "Is Sunnie the only person you've ever told what happened to you?"

Rice looked back across the 110-acre hillside complex built from cleft-cut Italian travertine. He loved the way the beige-colored, textured stone caught the bright Southern California daylight, reflected it gently, and emitted a honeyed warmth in the afternoon.

He nodded. "The only person in this world."

Once inside the Getty Center, Rice walked around the museum carrying one of their iPod-type guided-tour devices. Museums were never Rice's thing; they always felt dead, closed up, and lifeless to him.

After Rice and Kamile finished touring the Getty Museum's art collections, they rolled out a picnic blanket in its Central Garden among the trimmed hedges and purple African violets and sat. Kamile opened her three-ring binder full of poems she had written.

When Rice saw it, he winced. He knew what they were because she had showed them to him before. "Oh, no, not those. Not out here," he said.

"But, Rice, you enjoy helping me write my poetry, don't you?"

The truth was, no. But he had helped her write them on a few occasions, opening himself up despite his reservations because of that mystical quality she had about her that lowered his defenses and had him doing things he would not normally do.

Rice shook his head and laughed nervously. "But that was in private. I can't be doing that out here in public. Are you trying to expose me? You trying to get me out here all sentimental and blubbering so people can point and stare, and talk about me. Uh huh, I ain't having that."

Kamile smiled. "Oh, Rice, you're such a private person."

Rice affirmed. "Yes, I am, and with good reason." Rice knew how it felt to open up and tell someone you trusted about something terrible that happened to you and be called a liar. Thanks to his mother, he had shut down after that, and refused to open himself up again.

Kamile reassured Rice as she moved a little closer. "Trust me, I would never embarrass you like that. I respect your privacy."

Kamile pushed the notebook into his hand. "There's a special poem that only you can help me write."

He was reluctant to take the notebook. "Why me?"

"Because I need to know how you *truly* feel about . . ."

Rice asked, "About what?"

"About love between a man and a woman."

Kamile waited while trepidation reflected on Rice's face.

She continued, "I need to know if you sincerely believe that true love is possible between a man and woman or if the basis for a man-woman relationship is really lust and self-gratification."

Rice was blown away by Kamile's question. Her question made him reflect on his past relationships with women. He did believe, at one time, that so-called "romantic" relationships came down to one thing—lust and self-gratification. That's why he refused to involve his heart in them. That's why he refused to put himself out on a limb by thinking there was more to it than sex. But then Rice started to won-der if a true and meaningful love was really possi-ble . . . with Sunnie. And he did, in fact, put himself out on a limb by giving Sunnie hints about how he felt. But she had ignored him. She'd made it clear that she'd never think of him as anything more than a friend.

And that hurt him, deeply, and it also justified his belief that a relationship between a man and a woman really does boil down to sex and lust, that true and meaningful love was a fairy tale.

The same was true of his relationship with Kamile. He liked her a whole lot. In fact, if he had to describe his fantasy woman, she would be it. Even though she was the epitome of how he wanted a woman to act toward him, the most powerful effect she had on him was lust.

Rice shook his head. "I don't think you really want to know how I feel about all that right now."

Kamile insisted. She handed him a pen. "Yes, I do. And be honest—*brutally* honest—and say what you feel, even if it's shallow and vain and sinful, as long as you write from your soul."

Rice swallowed hard. It was a strange request, especially the part about writing sinfully from his soul, but Kamile was a somewhat strange woman. He didn't know why she wanted him to do this so bad, but she did.

Kamile opened the notebook he was holding in his hand and turned to a blank page. She positioned the pen between his fingers.

Rice took a deep breath, gripped the pen, and began to write.

When he finished, he tore the page out of Kamile's notebook, folded it, and tucked it into his back pocket. He refused to give it to her, thinking that it might make her mad. Rice knew that although a woman might *ask* a man to tell her the truth of how she feels about sex, lust, love, and relationships, she doesn't really want to *know* the truth. And since he had, indeed, been brutally honest in the poem, he thought it best to let her keep thinking that maybe he was a nice guy.

Chapter 34

LATE SATURDAY AFTERNOON, SUNNIE SAT NEXT TO GEFFEN ON the sofa in the mansion's living room, trying to console him. He'd finally told her what had happened with his mother's casket, and she was trying to reassure him that his mother's remains would be identified and everything would turn out okay.

Geffen looked like a zombie. His eyes were glazed over, like he'd gone without sleep too long. He kept mumbling something about his mother crying, but Sunnie couldn't understand what he was saying. And when she tried to tell him things would be okay, he didn't seem to believe her.

When Rice arrived home, Sunnie jumped up, but when she saw the melancholy look on his face, she paused. He had been around Kamile, Sunnie could *feel* it. Sunnie could tell when any of the guys had been in the presence of their new women—Dayna, Evie, and Kamile. A strange aura seemed to surround them.

They'd behave differently and do things that were out of character for them. Sunnie picked up on it, and it alarmed her, but she didn't know what to make of it.

Sunnie especially hated the aura that surrounded Rice after he'd been around Kamile. He would clam up even more than usual, and he'd get this look on his face like he had unwillingly let his guard down in exchange for something she gave him.

Rice saw Sunnie, but he kept walking to the bar.

Sunnie's heart dropped. She said, "Hi."

Rice's tone was distant. "Hello." He fixed himself a drink.

Sunnie saw Rice glance at Geffen. She knew that he had to notice Geffen's ragged appearance, but she knew why Rice didn't speak to him. They were still angry with each other over the filming in Rice's study.

Sunnie had come there to try and gather all the guys together. She was hoping they could put aside their squabbles and work on repairing their friendship. It would be hard to help them and protect them while they were at odds, arguing over things that never would have broken up their friendship before.

If Sunnie could get them all in the same room and talking again, she would tell them that they were under some sort of attack. She could see the results of an attack by the way their friendships, as well as their lives, had started to unravel. But what Sunnie *couldn't* figure out was where it was coming from. Sunnie knew how the enemy looked because she'd seen her—a dark, sultry woman in a white dress—but she had never caught the woman around the guys. Try as she might, Sunnie couldn't figure it out. Her visit with Mother Roby on Thursday night had helped. Mother Roby had told her that if she was going to protect the guys she needed to focus, to quiet herself and listen to the still, small voice of God, and to trust that when the time was right, it would tell her what she needed to do.

But seeing Rice disrupted her concentration. Mother Roby had told her to focus on protecting the guys first, and that she and Rice could work out their feelings later. But Sunnie's heartstrings were pulling her toward him right now, and she hated that he didn't want to talk to her.

Sunnie walked to the middle of the living room and got their attention.

"Hey, guys, I was hoping to talk to all of you at the same time. I've got something important to tell you. Has anyone seen Coach?"

Joey, who was passing in the hallway, overheard her. He stepped into the living room. "Coach didn't come home last night. I've tried his cell phone. No answer." Sunnie knew Joey was still sulking over not being able to connect with his brother, and she could see that he was concerned that his brother hadn't made it home last night.

Sunnie was starting to get worried, too, until she heard a truck outside skid in the driveway. A few seconds later, Coach burst through the front door.

He barged in so fast and loud that both Sunnie and Joey jumped, and Rice spilled his drink. Geffen, caught up in his daze, only turned his head.

Coach walked to the middle of the room and

slammed a piece of paper down hard on the coffee table.

He hollered three words. *"I can play!"*

He threw his keys on the coffee table and proceeded to do a victory dance in the middle of the floor—the kind a defensive lineman does when he sacks the quarterback with five seconds left on the clock during the Super Bowl.

After she got over her initial shock, Sunnie picked up the paper and read it.

"It's a doctor's report. It says the X-ray report shows a healed ligament, no sign of a tear. Patient status: no further restrictions. Coach!" Sunnie jumped up and hugged his neck. He grabbed her with one arm and swung her around.

Coach was ecstatic. "I'm off the injured list! I'm suiting up!"

Sunnie screamed joyfully, sharing in Coach's exuberance. "That's great! That is fantastic! Wow! We know how bad you wanted to get back out there and play."

Sunnie turned toward Geffen and Rice. "Guys, isn't this fantastic?"

Joey's eyes lit up, but Rice and Geffen looked indifferent.

The last time Rice and Coach had exchanged words, Coach had referred to Kamile as a "ho" in front of her face. And Geffen remembered the comment Coach had made about turning the place into a graveyard by bringing his mother's remains there.

Rice barely looked up. "Yeah, cool." He poured himself another drink.

Geffen didn't bother to turn around or say anything.

Coach's elation faded. He looked at his *friends*. Sunnie saw the disappointment in Coach's face.

Sunnie said, "Guys, c'mon. He's been working his butt off for this!"

Coach's smile died off. "It's a'ight, Sunnie. It's cool. No problem."

Coach picked up his keys and his doctor's report, and looked again at Rice, then at Geffen. They still didn't congratulate him.

"So it's like that, huh? A'ight. Fuck y'all, too." Coach turned and walked away.

Sunnie's heart ached to witness such animosity between the guys, knowing what they really meant to each other. She tried to stop Coach from leaving the room feeling like that. "Coach, wait!" But he kept going. Joey followed him.

She turned to Rice and Geffen, "Guys, c'mon!" Neither responded.

Sunnie stood in the middle of the living room and threw up her hands. She pleaded, "What is *happening* to everybody?"

No one paid her any attention.

Coach jogged up the stairs and went into his bedroom. A few seconds later, there was a knock on the door. Coach figured it was Sunnie trying to play peacemaker.

He didn't open the door, just yelled, "Forget it, Sunnie. Screw them, I don't need them," and continued toward the shower.

The voice on the other side of the door said, "It's Joey."

Coach opened the door. He wasn't expecting Joey to come up. They hadn't spoken since Evie had grabbed his crotch and embarrassed him three days ago.

Joey stepped halfway inside the door. "I'm happy for you, big brother," Joey said. He sounded like he really meant it.

Coach backed up and let him in. "Yeah?"

"Yeah," Joey said. Coach's grin started to come back. Just thinking about returning to that football field made him want to shout for joy again, the way he did when the doctor first gave him the news. Coach shook his head and clasped his hands together.

"Aw, Joey, man! It's unbelievable. And how it happened. Whew!"

Joey, feeling the exuberance, too, asked, "How *did* it happen? Just the other day, you were still in pain and working on rehabilitation."

"It was out of this world! Check this out." Joey sat on the bed while Coach acted it out for him, complete with moves and gestures.

"My girl, Evie, was massaging my leg in the Jacuzzi, right? She was getting carried away, making it hot, making it hurt. Then the girl put a move on me! Aw, man! She grabbed my leg, flexed her backbone some kind of way. I don't know what she did, but it hurt like *hell!*"

"Why'd you let her hurt you?"

"But that's the trip part about it. One minute it hurt like hell, the next minute I'm waking up in the emergency room, and I don't know what the hell happened. I don't even know how I got there."

Joey frowned. Coach went on explaining. "The doctors took X-rays, ran some tests. I'm thinking, Hey, this is it, it's over—my football career, my life, my manhood."

Joey lowered his head a bit. Coach was too busy looking at his doctor's report to notice. He continued, "The doctor came back to the exam room and handed me this report. He said the tear had healed completely and that I could play."

Joey only half smiled this time. "But, Coach, that doesn't make sense. There is *no way* Evie could cause your leg to heal like that."

"Joey, did you hear me, man? I said, *I can play!* I don't give a fuck how it happened. This is all that matters." Coach held the doctor's report up.

Coach paced the floor, too excited to keep still. He went into his closet, started gathering some clothes. From the closet, Coach yelled, "I already called the team and let them know. Suckers didn't even believe me at first, so I faxed the report, plus I had the doctor call them. I am back!"

Joey was still baffled, but went along with it. "Starting when?"

"Starting next game! I'll be driving down to San Diego in two days to play in a home game."

"That's unbelievable. I'm happy for you, Coach."

"Man, Joey, I am going to celebrate tonight. Whoohoo!" Coach started dancing and pulling suits off the rack inside his closet.

Joey stood up, hopeful. "Oh, yeah? Where do you want to go? It's been a long time since we've done anything together."

Coach came out the closet holding up his favorite deep burgundy suit, admiring it. He didn't quite hear what Joey had said. "Huh, what was that?"

Joey said, "Where do you want to go?"

Coach laid the suit on his bed, a big mischievous grin slid across his face. "To the Bonaventure Hotel and get a room. A luxury suite!"

Now Joey frowned, puzzled, and said "Huh?"

"You asked me where I want to go. I'm taking Evie out on the town, and then we're going straight to the Bonaventure and celebrate *my* way." Coach started dancing again. Joey's spirits fell again.

Joey asked, "You already talked to Evie since all of this happened?"

"Yeah. She called me as soon as I walked out of the hospital. In fact, she had already made the reservations. That girl is something else. She just *knows* what I like and how to give it to me!"

Coach noticed that Joey had slouched and didn't seem as happy. While removing his suit from its bag, he asked, "So what about you? You got something to get into tonight?"

Both Joey and Coach got a little uncomfortable with that question. Coach brushed lint off his suit. Joey cleared his throat as he tried to think of something to say.

"Me? Oh yeah. I've got a job interview in the morning, and I need to prepare," he lied.

"Okay, good." Coach was satisfied with the answer and didn't push it, but his conscience did bother him as he thought about how he hadn't stopped Evie when she'd humiliated Joey in the driveway.

Joey got up to leave. Coach stopped him.

"Hey, Joey. I, uh, I just want to let you know that, uh, if there's anything you need my help on—"

Joey didn't let Coach finish his sentence. "Yeah, I do."

"You do what?"

"I need you to do something for me."

"What?"

Joey hesitated, then he said it. "I need you to talk to J.B. for me."

Coach immediately shook his head and refused. "Naw, Joey, I need to stay out of it. That's between you and J.B."

Joey pleaded, "He won't listen to me, Coach, you know that. He may listen to you."

Coach snapped, "You know damn well J.B. don't listen to *nobody*."

Joey persisted. "But *try* to talk to him—tell him to get off my back. At least so I can go there and visit Ma."

When Joey mentioned their mother, Coach softened. Even though he never had much to say to his mother, he knew how close she and Joey had always been. Reluctantly, Coach agreed.

"A'ight, Joey. I'll see what I can do."

Joey rushed over and hugged Coach. Coach told him to back up a bit, but when Joey kept hugging his waist, he didn't push him away. Coach saw how much it meant to Joey for him to talk to J.B. on Joey's behalf.

And since Joey was the only one in the house who seemed happy for him, other than Sunnie, Coach felt it was the least he could do. After all, Joey was his brother. Even though Joey was doing some things that made Coach want to bash his head in, Coach was still going to watch out for him.

Coach finally had to push Joey off, but he laughed, and he got an idea. He said to his brother, "Hey, come check this out."

Coach beckoned Joey over to his closet. He took out one of his official Chargers team jackets and gave it to Joey. "Put it on. It's yours."

Joey could hardly believe it. Speechless, he put the jacket on. It fit him about two sizes too big.

Coach laughed. "Man, you need to get your weight up. Ima have to put you in the gym."

Joey walked to the mirror. "No, I'm good. It makes me look bigger anyway." Joey did one of Coach's famous macho muscle poses, imitating him.

Coach laughed, and slapped Joey real hard on the back, intentionally.

Coach walked Joey to the door and said, "Okay, I'll talk to J.B., but I can't promise nothing."

Joey's whole face lit up as he left Coach's bedroom.

Chapter

35

LATER THAT SATURDAY NIGHT, AFTER COACH HAD TAKEN EVIE to several racy hot spots on the L.A. nightclub scene, he was ready to celebrate *his* way. He carried her across the lobby of the Bonaventure Hotel in downtown L.A., and they caused quite a scene. The plunging neckline of Evie's gown was slipping off her breasts, and when she kicked up her stilettos, men snapped their necks for a peek. Evie waved an open bottle of Cristal around, dripping champagne everywhere, while Coach whooped and cheered.

One man in the lobby said, "Congratulations! Did you two just tie the knot?"

"*Hell* naw!" Coach stepped around the man. "We're *celebrating!*"

Coach carried Evie all the way to the elevators and set her down inside. There were other people inside the elevator, but Coach and Evie didn't care. They started kissing and groping and sucking all over each other.

Evie was attacking Coach's body like he was the last rib at a BBQ.

When the elevator doors opened, they nearly fell out. Coach ran his hand up Evie's dress, grabbed and squeezed her butt like it was Charmin. People stepped aside as they made their way down the hall occasionally stopping to grope each other and wrap their bodies around each other.

Evie stopped Coach at Room 606. "This is our room, Big Poppa."

Coach slid in the card key, opened the door, and they fell inside. Before the door closed, they were ripping off each other's clothes.

"Make it rough, Big Poppa!"

Coach yanked her around and pushed her facedown on the table. She grabbed the edge of the table and braced herself. She flexed her back and popped her butt up in the air like a bright, sticky caramel apple. He bit it.

She moaned, deep and throaty, slithered over the table like a snake, and jumped off the opposite end. Coach stood up, his desire growing larger by the second.

"Oh, you gonna make me chase you, huh?"

She snapped her thong against her body. Coach faked like he was mad. "Oh, see, that right there's gonna get you spanked."

He ripped off his shirt, stripped off his pants, and leapt at her. She darted away.

"You want some of this? You gotta work for it!" She jumped over a chair. He picked up the high-back chair, flexed his muscles, and threw it across the suite like it was a feather. She licked her finger, slid it down her body, and made a sizzling sound.

He grinned, and looked up at the two red blinking lights on the smoke detector. "We 'bout to set it off up in here!"

She poked out her tongue and wiggled it at his crotch. He had on his favorite black silk briefs.

"Show me whatcha workin' with, Big Poppa," she purred. He raised his powerful biceps, grunted, and flexed the muscles all over his body like King Kong.

"Oooh, Big Poppa! I'm ready for this!"

"You ready?!"

She growled, "I'm *rrrready!*"

She stepped up on the king-size bed. He bent his knee, got into the linebacker ready position. "I'm about to sack the quarterback!"

"*Sack* me, Big Poppa!"

Coach dove at her, tackled her down on the bed. He ripped off her thong. He tore off his black silk briefs. He pounced on top of her. She braced herself and got ready to receive every big, hard inch of him. He got ready to give it to her, but when he did, something happened. Instantly, what had been thick and hard a minute ago had shrunk. It was as if someone had sung it a lullaby, put it to bed, and it had said, *Nighty night!*

Horrified, Coach looked down. "What the *f*—?"

Evie, who had been ready and in position, sat up. She looked at Coach, and she looked at it. "Where'd it go?"

Her comment jerked Coach out of his daze and sent panic through his mind. He jumped up and turned his back to her. He didn't want her looking at it in that condition.

Evie crinkled up her face. She looked *extremely* disappointed, and let him know it by the tone in her voice and the wiggle in her neck. "Hey! Is this some kind of joke? 'Cause if it is, it ain't funny."

Coach, still stunned, tried to snap back and recover. He tried to laugh it off, bragging on his past performance. He said, quickly, "Naw, naw, girl. You know how I do. I puts it down. C'mon, lay back down so we can get this show on the road."

Evie lay back down. Coach climbed on top of her. They started kissing and hugging and rubbing. Coach started getting aroused again, everything blooming and blossoming just the way it was supposed to.

Evie threw her head back and closed her eyes. She rumbled, "Ooh, give it to me, Big Poppa!"

Coach said with confidence, "A'ight, get ready. Here it comes!"

Coach grunted, sounding like a man trying to chip away at an iceberg with a toothpick. He jumped up off Evie and dashed to the other side of the room while he kept his back turned toward Evie.

Evie sat up, jumped up off the bed, and let him have it. "What is *wrong* with you?"

Never in Coach's life had he experienced anything like this before. He'd *never* had a problem with impotency. If anything, he had a hyperactive libido; he had enough testosterone floating around his body to turn San Francisco straight.

Not knowing what else to do, Coach dropped down

on the floor and started doing push-ups, then sit-ups—anything to try to get his blood flowing and his adrenaline going. He had to get some blood down there to that spot and he had to do it fast.

Evie ran up on him and slammed his head with a pillow.

"Why can't you get it up and *keep* it up?" she screamed at him at the top of her lungs in her typical loud and brazen way.

"Shhh, woman! Before somebody hears you."

"I don't care about them. I care about *this!*" Evie grabbed at him, but Coach blocked her and pulled away.

"Damn! Don't grab it." Coach frowned, already worried and frustrated, wondering if something was wrong with it.

Evie put her hands on her hips. "Well, it needs *some*thing to wake it up."

Coach hit his head with his palm. He was flabbergasted. Evie ran back over to the bed and said, "Here! Maybe this will help it."

Evie lay back on the bed and started striking all kinds of erotic poses. She twisted and contorted her body like an acrobatic porn star. She vaulted off the side of the bed and did a double somersault with a full-twist ending. When her floor routine was over, she was hoping for a perfect 10 for all of her hard work, dedication, and effort. Both she and Coach looked at the judge's scorecard inside Coach's briefs at the same time.

Evie yelled, disgusted. *"A zero!"*

Coach flinched and covered himself. He hollered, *"Shit!"*

A few minutes later, Evie was stomping barefoot through the Bonaventure Hotel's lobby, heading out the door. With her torn-up evening gown tied haphazardly around her curvy body and her stilettos in her hand, she hightailed it away from Coach, who was running and trying to keep up with her. He'd barely had time to throw on his ripped shirt and slide on his pants as Evie bolted from the room.

"Hey! Girl, c'mon. Don't leave. Let's try it one more time. It must've been something in that Cristal, that's all."

Evie jerked around, her left breast springing out of her evening gown. She narrowed her eyes and pointed her finger in Coach's face.

"I had the Cristal, too, and *I* am horny as hell. Now what's your excuse?"

Everybody in the lobby turned and looked. Coach pulled his shirt up over his face and trudged out of the hotel's lobby following a very pissed-off, horny, and disappointed Evie.

Chapter

36

SUNDAY MORNING, GEFFEN SAT IN HIS DARK OFFICE WITH ALL the miniblinds closed. The daylight hurt his eyes. They were bloodshot and watery from lack of sleep. Every time he closed his eyes, he heard his mother's voice crying and weeping, and even sometimes when he was awake.

Even though it was Sunday, the DNA lab had agreed to report the results to him today. When the phone rang, he flinched. He had been jumpy and on edge ever since they'd dropped his mother's casket. He waited a moment and tried to collect himself, then he picked it up.

"Hello? Yeah, this is him. The results? They're back?" Geffen pressed his fingers to his eyes and listened, trying to understand what the lab tech was trying to explain to him.

Geffen sat up straighter in his chair. "What does that *mean?* No. I don't understand anything about the

DNA matching process or how it works. Skip all that and give it to me straight. Did you figure out which remains are my mother's? What? *Inconclusive?*"

Geffen grabbed his wrinkled jacket off the office couch and stumbled out the door into the blinding daylight. As he backed his Hummer out the driveway, Dayna Devlin was already standing at the end waiting for him. Geffen often wondered how she would seem to appear out of nowhere at precisely the right time without any warning, but he was too tired and preoccupied to ask. He opened the door for her, she got in, and they drove away.

Geffen drove in silence with Dayna seated next to him as he headed again from Beverly Hills back to Ontario to his uncle's house. Dayna had made him feel ashamed and stupid for believing that his mother really was calling out to him from beyond the grave. With just a single glint of her beautiful crystal-colored eyes, she had made him feel dumb and foolish for believing such an outrageous impossibility. Geffen later recanted, saying that he did not really believe it, and that he was only upset and speaking randomly.

It wasn't until they were almost at the 57 Freeway near Cal Poly Pomona that Geffen felt stable enough to open up and fill Dayna in on the details. He told her that the DNA tests were inconclusive and that the lab would need a sample from the next closest kin, which would be the deceased's brother, Geffen's uncle. Geffen called his uncle as soon as he hung up with the DNA lab.

Dayna asked, "Did your uncle agree to do it?"

Geffen kept his eyes on the road. "No, he was too upset. But how can you blame him? Call a man up and tell him his sister's corpse has been dropped and her remains got mixed up with somebody else's and that you need his DNA to help identify her? He was so upset, he couldn't talk. His nurse got on the phone, told me he wasn't feeling well."

"Do you think by telling him in person he'll agree?"

"I hope so. He's the only chance I have of getting my mother back." Geffen became quiet again. He tightened his grip on the steering wheel and hoped that the faint sobbing sounds he heard coming from Dayna's side of the car would stop before they reached his uncle's house.

Geffen exited the 10 Freeway near the Montclair Plaza, and focused on the red and green traffic lights as he took the streets the rest of the way to his uncle's house. He had to focus because between the distracting voices and his tired, bloodshot eyes, he'd almost run through a red light.

When Geffen turned onto his uncle's street, they were met by rotating red lights from an ambulance and a paramedics truck.

"Oh no," Dayna said.

Geffen didn't say anything. He threw his Hummer into park and jumped out of the car.

Geffen rushed around the neighbors, who were standing along the walkway gaping at his uncle as paramedics rolled him out on a stretcher. A paramedic blocked Geffen.

"That's my uncle!"

The paramedic allowed him to talk to his uncle while they prepared to load him into the ambulance. Geffen saw his uncle lying there, the picture of illness and frailty. Geffen leaned in close to his uncle, and so did Dayna.

Geffen said, "Uncle, what's wrong?"

The frail man tried to bring his arm up toward his heart, but was too weak. A myriad of feelings rushed over Geffen. He felt sorry for the man, but he also felt extreme selfishness. He needed his uncle's DNA sample. He needed this man to be well enough to go to the DNA lab, even if they had to wheel him in on a stretcher—that's how desperate Geffen was. He could not bear the thought of never being able to positively identify his mother.

"Uncle, I need that DNA sample," Geffen said. His uncle moaned in pain.

The paramedic who was adjusting the gurney heard what Geffen said. He looked up at Geffen and gave him a reproaching glance.

His uncle's nurse stepped in. "You've already upset him over the phone. He was doing well until you called. Now you drive out here and upset him more by asking him for DNA while he's on a stretcher. That's your uncle."

Geffen tried to explain himself. "Look. I know this looks cruel, but you don't know—"

His uncle moaned again. His sunken eyes on his gaunt face closed, and his thinning gray hair stuck up on his head, making him look even more sickly and pathetic. Dayna reached over and smoothed his hair down with her hand.

"Take him to the hospital," the nurse urged the paramedics. They pushed the gurney into the ambulance.

Geffen tried to delay them. "Wait—" The paramedics shut the ambulance doors. Geffen turned to his uncle's nurse.

"You don't understand. He's the only chance I have to bring my mother home with me to rest."

The nurse shook his head. "No, I do understand. Your uncle is dying and you don't care. You're an ingrate."

The nurse went back into the house. The ambulance drove away. Gradually, the neighbors left, too, leaving only Geffen and Dayna standing in front of his uncle's house.

Geffen swallowed hard, but the hard lump in his throat remained. He nodded. "That nurse is right. I *am* a selfish ingrate."

Dayna asked, "Why do you say that, Geffen?"

Geffen gazed at the ambulance's taillights as they disappeared down the street and around the corner. "There are *two* things I *have* to have before my uncle dies."

"What are those two things?"

"The DNA sample so I can get my mother back." Geffen swallowed again, the lump growing bigger. He paused.

Dayna asked, "And what's the other thing?"

"I want him to tell me where my father is."

Geffen's eyes became more red, and his face grew intense from years of pent-up bitterness that he'd held against his father. He had told Dayna that one day he'd ask his uncle for information on his father, but he never told her why.

Geffen continued, "I want to find my father. I want to *repay* him. I want to hand him a big fat check for all of the money he spent on me, sending me away to boarding school while he left my mother to live in poverty without her son."

Geffen pressed his fingers in his burning eyes as he closed them. He continued talking.

"And then I'm going to hand him a nice, big thank-you card. Inside the card I'll write: 'Thank you, Father. I'm rich now, too. I'm a big success in the financial world, I've moved my mother to a decent burial spot, and I did it all without you, you heartless son of a bitch.'"

Dayna's clear crystal eyes looked into Geffen's face. Geffen's shoulder trembled slightly as he began to sob softly from grief, slowly realizing that he probably would get neither thing from his uncle.

Geffen kept his fingers to his eyes and shook his head. "I guess I *am* a selfish ingrate. My uncle's dying and all I can do is stand here with those two wishes."

Dayna watched him, then said in a calm and composed voice, "Geffen, in order to succeed in this world, you *must* think of yourself first, putting your own personal needs ahead of everyone else's. Now, straighten up. I have something for you."

Dayna gently opened Geffen's hand and placed something very small in it.

Geffen didn't see what it was—his eyes were too red and watery. He asked, "What is it?"

Dayna said, "It's *one* of your wishes."

Geffen cleared his eyes and tried to focus on the few, thin gray strands of hair from his uncle's head. He looked up at Dayna in tired amazement.

Dayna's crystal eyes sparkled like magic. She smiled. "Here's your uncle's DNA sample."

Chapter
37

ON SUNDAY AFTERNOON, RICE AND KAMILE SNUGGLED IN FRONT of the fireplace in his master bedroom, reading a book together. With her back to his chest and him looking over her shoulder, their eyes scanned pages, finished about the same time, and they took turns turning the page. It was so symbiotic, it was almost scary.

Kamile paused from reading. "Sunnie hates me. You know that, don't you?"

"Hates you? Why would she hate you?" Rice continued reading.

Kamile said, thoughtfully, "She's jealous, perhaps?"

Rice stopped reading. He dropped his eyes to the floor for a moment, then he concluded, "Nope, can't be jealousy. Jealousy implies that the person cared about me in the first place." Rice knew that Sunnie cared about him, just not like *that*.

Kamile waited a minute, then added, "I agree with you. Sunnie *is* a very insensitive, self-centered person."

"Aren't we supposed to be reading this book?" Rice hadn't actually said that. This was another instance where Kamile seemed to be getting inside his head.

Kamile leaned into his shoulder and they started reading again. She asked, "When are you going to give me the poem?"

Rice kept reading, playing dumb. "What poem?"

Kamile said, "You know, the *brutally honest* poem I asked you to write yesterday at the museum."

"Who says I'm giving it back?" Rice had put it in his special hiding place. He had refused to give it to her because he didn't want to disappoint her. His views on lust versus love were screwed up, turned around and backward lately, and he probably shouldn't have written the poem.

"Why won't you give it to me?"

"You may start thinking I'm a bad guy."

"How?"

"That poem explained how I really feel inside. When a woman knows how a man really feels, she changes."

Kamile assured him, "I could never think you were a bad guy, no matter what you said."

Kamile closed the book and turned to face him. "Do you think you'd ever write an autobiography?"

Rice said, unequivocally, "Never."

"Okay, that was the short answer. Now give me the long answer."

"That *was* the long answer. I can't believe you'd even ask me that."

"I didn't think you would. I was just curious."

Rice tickled her side. "Hey, do that Braille thing again with your lips."

Kamile smiled and pressed her lips softly against his. As she kept her lips touching his, she spoke soft words into them. Rice tried to decipher her words the same way a blind person would feel the bumps on a page.

Rice thought he got it, but he wasn't sure. "What was that? Say it again—"

Kamile mouthed it again, *Do you love me?*

Rice had never said those three words—*I love you*—to a woman in his whole life. And he wasn't about to now, until he caught a glimpse of Kamile's large brown eyes, which seemed to pull him like a swirling vortex. He found himself falling into her, unable to get his balance. The feeling scared him.

When asked that question many times before, he'd shake his head no, but now all he could say was: "Kamile, baby, I don't know."

Seeing Rice's bewilderment, Kamile decided to take it a step forward. She gently nudged him back on the blue chinchilla rug and lay lightly on top of him. She unbuttoned his shirt and kissed his chest softly, making his toes curl up and his mind fill with lustful fantasies about her.

When Kamile saw his lust rising, she kissed him long and deep. When he seemed unable to take any more, she raised her face an inch above his and made him look into her deep brown eyes, which seemed to expand and deepen, drawing him in more and more. She pressed her lips on his again and asked him another question in lip Braille: *Would you die for me?*

Rice was far gone. He was in the midst of swirling around and sinking in her deep brown eyes before he realized she had asked him another question. And just when he started slowly to realize what she'd asked, there was a knock on the door.

Sunnie called to him, "Rice, I need to talk to you."

Kamile stayed on top of him. "Ignore her."

Sunnie knocked again. "Rice. It's Sunnie. Open the door."

Rice, between breaths: "She'll never go away."

He got up and cracked the door open. He didn't let Sunnie inside his bedroom. Instead, he slipped out, not letting her see Kamile inside.

Rice stood between his bedroom door and Sunnie, who was pressing into him. He wanted to see what she felt was so urgent that she had to bang on his door.

Sunnie looked upset. "Rice, *what* is going on?"

"What are you talking about?"

Sunnie hit his arm. "You *know* what I'm talking about. None of you guys are acting normal and our friendships are all falling apart."

Rice shifted his feet. "You drove all the way up here, barged into my house, and banged on my door to tell me that?"

Sunnie looked like she had not slept well. She also looked more paranoid and frantic than usual. "Rice, listen to me. I came up here to tell you guys that you are under *attack*. I'm sure, I'm sure, I'm sure of it!"

Rice mocked her. "You're trippin', you're trippin', you're trippin' again."

Sunnie screamed like a madwoman. "I'm not tripping!"

Rice tried to quiet her so that Kamile wouldn't hear. *"Shhh!"*

Sunnie glanced at his bedroom door suspiciously, but kept explaining. "Look, I came here to tell you guys that there's a woman out there somewhere, and she wants to destroy you guys."

"Destroy as in . . . ?"

"Kill, I don't know."

"And the reason would be . . . ?"

"Hell if I know!" Sunnie cursed. Rice shook his head, knowing she only cursed when she was extremely upset.

"I tried to tell you guys the first day we came to this house that I could *feel* something was wrong here. Then you guys got the place, fixed it up, blew out the cellar, and then I didn't *feel* it anymore. But then I ran into *her*."

"Her?"

Sunnie spoke as if Rice should know who she was talking about. "Yes, *her!* The dark, sultry woman from my dreams. I told all you guys about her at the party, but you all wouldn't believe me."

Rice said calmly, mockingly, "Oh, right, *her*. The dark and sultry woman from your dreams. Of course."

Sunnie described the lady to Rice. "She's about yea high. She's dark, but not in a skin-pigment-melanin sort of way, but more in a shadowy-translucent-evil sort of way. Her eyes are jet black with no pupils, sort of like a lizard but not quite."

Rice raised his eyebrow. "Like a lizard, huh?"

"Yeah. She wears a flowing white gauzy butt-ugly dress," Sunnie added.

Rice looked at her, really starting to wonder now if Sunnie did, in fact, need a quick shot of Prozac. She was waiting for a response from him. He had none, but told her, "Okay, Sunnie—if I see anybody who fits that description, I'll call either you or an exorcist right away."

Rice started to head back into his bedroom, but Sunnie grabbed his arm.

"No, Rice! There's more."

Rice exhaled, rolled his eyes, and prepared himself.

Sunnie talked fast, out of breath. "When I got here to tell you guys about this and to demand that you guys stop fighting and come together so we can figure out a plan, I got that weird feeling again. I went to Geffen's office. He's not there and not answering his cell phone. I called Senda and found out he'd *fired* her Friday. I knocked on Coach's door. He's in his bedroom but he won't open the door. When have we ever known Coach to hide in his bedroom? Something's got to be wrong with him."

Sunnie stopped and took a breath. She continued, "And when I started walking down the hall to come knock on your door, my stomach started doing that jump-pop-gurgle thing."

Rice repeated, "Jump-pop-gurgle thing. Okay."

Sunnie rubbed her stomach. "The closer I got to your door, the worse the gurgle-knock-*boom* got!"

"Gurgle-knock-boom."

"Rice, stop repeating my words like I'm crazy! I

know what I'm talking about. Rice, I think the dark, sultry lady with the lizardlike eyes is hiding in your room."

Sunnie looked so serious that Rice started busting up laughing. She socked him. "Rice, I'm serious!"

Rice tried to contain his laughter and straightened up. He knew that inside his bedroom Kamile had gotten up, tiptoed to the door, and was listening. He heard her softly brush against the potted fern he had sitting by his door. He knew Sunnie didn't hear it.

He tried to placate Sunnie so that she would leave and let him get back to his company. He would find out about the weird question Kamile had asked him—something about dying, *after* they had sex.

Rice told Sunnie. "There's nobody inside my bedroom who fits that description, I assure you."

Sunnie insisted, "But, Rice, you may not see her."

"Oh, she hides under people's beds, like the big bad wolf?"

Sunnie got real serious, lowered her voice, and whispered. "No, she doesn't have to hide. She's *invisible*."

Sunnie had said the same thing that night when she was wigging out on the courtyard bench and claimed somebody had run into their house. "Okay, Sunnie. That's enough. I've got to go," Rice said. He heard Kamile brush into the fern again.

Rice turned to leave again. Sunnie grabbed his arm, this time it was with a death grip. She made a strained, crazy-girl face and grunted, "Ouhhh," just like she had in the kitchen when he and Coach were about to fight and Kamile came forward and touched his arm.

"What's wrong with you, Sunnie?"

Sunnie was wiggling and holding her stomach. "That *feeling* . . . it's getting worse."

Rice heard Kamile press against the door. The more Kamile rubbed her body against the door, the more Sunnie jumped on one leg and grunted.

Rice started getting worried. "Sunnie, stop doing that or I'm going to call a doctor—the kind with a giant net!"

Sunnie caught Rice's arm again and hung on to it, dragging him away. "Ooh, Rice, don't you feel something wrong. C'mon, I want to take you away from here."

Rice stopped Sunnie and pulled her around to face him. "You know, don't you?"

She didn't know what Rice was talking about. "Huh?"

Rice frowned, disgusted. "Stop playing dumb, okay? You know that Kamile is in my bedroom. You're trying to bust up what I've got going on with Kamile—who's *not* just another trick—not because *you* want me, but because you just want me *around*. Because you're self-centered, insensitive, and you don't have a Marvin or some other undeserving loser to keep you occupied at the moment. So you want my shoulder until you find the next boyfriend."

Rice couldn't believe he'd said it. He'd used the very same words Kamile had spoken just moments before— *self-centered, insensitive*. And it felt weird, like she'd put the words in his mouth. But he couldn't and wouldn't deny that he sometimes felt that way about Sunnie.

Sunnie stared at him, shocked. It looked like a million things were bumping around in her brain at the same time. He felt this wasn't the time to punk out.

"Yeah, I said it."

He waited for her response.

She stood there staring at him in supershock until she finally gathered her words together. And when she did, it was just a cop-out as far as he was concerned.

Sunnie said, "Rice, no, I never took you for—Is *Kamile* really in there?"

Sunnie's eyes locked onto the door. Her face looked baffled and confused and even a little scared. Here she was concentrating on Kamile when he'd just laid himself out and told her how he felt about things. That made him angrier.

"That's all you've got to say to me? 'Is Kamile really in there?'"

Sunnie kept glancing from the door to him and back to the door. She got this strange look on her face, squared her chin, and quickly reached for the doorknob as if she were going to bust in there and confront Kamile.

Rice grabbed her hand just as it turned the knob. He moved Sunnie back.

"This is stupid, Sunnie. It's childish. I don't want to play games with you anymore. Leave Kamile alone."

When Sunnie could have listened carefully to what he'd just said and focused on what was up between them, she chose to ignore him once again and squabble with Kamile, the same way she'd squabbled with Charlotta over the years. Rice was tired of participating in that game.

He told her, before going back inside, "Maybe if you'd learn to pay more attention to the *man* than you do to the *competition*, you'd actually *have* a man by now."

Rice left Sunnie, standing in the hallway as he went back inside his bedroom to spend time with Kamile.

Chapter

38

Farther down the hallway, Coach had locked himself inside his room. He didn't want to go anywhere, and he didn't want to see anybody. Coach's head was all twisted and confused.

When Sunnie had knocked on the door a few minutes ago, he'd told her to go away. He continued pacing the floor and punching the wall, thinking about what had happened to his "gear" last night in the Bonaventure Hotel suite with Evie. *Damn! What the hell is wrong with me?*

Coach had never had a problem with impotency before. In fact, Franklin "Coach" Brass got the nickname Badass Brass in college because, not only was he a bad-ass, he was also hard in more ways than one, just as his surname suggested. But now this crap with Evie was really messing with his head, as well as his pride.

As they were driving away from the hotel, Evie suggested Viagra. Coach almost hit a pole. He hollered, "I don't need no damn Viagra! I'm all man, through and through!" Evie threw a sideway glance at his crotch and mumbled, "Not tonight you wasn't." She looked out the window and didn't say anything else to him all the way back to the mansion, where she got out, slammed the door of his Suburban, hopped into her red truck, and peeled off. *Damn!* Coach punched the wall by his closet. He'd been so happy about returning to the football field that he thought *nothing* could bring him down . . . until this happened.

Coach paced the floor some more. His cell phone rang. The caller ID said RESTRICTED UNLISTED NUMBER. He knew it was Evie. He wasn't sure he wanted to talk to her—his pride could only take so much punishment. He answered it anyway.

"What's up?" he said, dryly. He heard her snicker on the other end. He got the hint. He answered another way. "What do you want?"

Evie said plainly, "You *know* what I want."

Coach barked, "I can't help you with that right now!"

Evie retorted, "Maybe you can. I've got a plan."

Evie laid out her plan to Coach. He listened. When she finished, he furrowed his brow, and asked, astonished, "You'd be down with that?"

Evie replied, "I'd be down with anything that will get you up, Big Poppa."

Coach grinned. "Okay, cool. I'll meet you back at the hotel, same suite, right away." Her plan was outrageous, out of this world and kind of crude, but that's what kind of girl she was. And maybe it *would* solve his "little" problem.

Coach hung up the phone, grabbed his overnight bag, and barged down the hallway, heading for the front door.

He practically ran over Joey on the way out.

"Hey, Coach, how're you doing?" Joey had knocked on his door twice already today, but Coach wouldn't let him in. He'd grumbled, "Not right now, Joey."

Coach said pretty much the same thing now, but sounded less grumpy. "Joey, later, man. I'm in a hurry."

Coach continued down the hall. Joey stopped him, "Hey, did you talk to J.B. yet?"

Coach couldn't be bothered with all that right now—he had much more important things he had to deal with. He shook his head and kept going. Joey stopped him again.

"Frank! You promised me."

Joey was irritating him and he wished he hadn't made that stupid promise in the first place. Coach had a lot of faults, but he made it a point to always keep his word.

"Damn, Joey! Okay. I'll do it later on, but right now I've gotta go handle *my* business."

Joey smiled. "All right. Thanks. I knew you'd come through for me, big brother."

Joey was wearing his new Chargers official team jacket—the one Coach had given him. It even had Coach's team number on it—number 58. He straightened his jacket, stood up a little taller, and went out the door behind Coach.

Chapter
39

THIRTY MINUTES LATER, COACH ARRIVED AT THE BONAVENTURE Hotel in downtown L.A. He walked into Room 606, the same one he and Evie had been in the night before. The fancy suite was dimly lit and Evie was waiting for him by the door, just as they'd planned.

Coach handed Evie three crisp new five-hundred-dollar bills, but the money wasn't for her. She took the bills and set them aside on a nightstand. She took off Coach's clothes and led him to the round kingsize bed.

Coach starting having second thoughts. He asked Evie, "You sure 'bout this?"

She laid him on the bed. "Trust me."

Coach tried to relax. Evie stretched out his big, muscular body and got behind him, wedging herself between his back and the bed's headboard with her legs spread out around him. She pulled Coach back, snaked her arms around his chest, and vigorously rubbed his nipples.

She hollered to someone who was waiting in the suite next to theirs. "Bring it!"

The door connecting the two suites opened. In walked a woman in high heels, a sheer scarf, and little else. She did a striptease for Coach while Evie massaged him from behind. The woman crawled up into the bed in one of those choreographed stripper moves, and she ran her hand up Coach's thigh.

Evie whispered into his neck, "Is it working yet?"

Coach looked down at his black silk briefs and Evie anxiously poked her head over his shoulder to look, too. No dice.

Coach cursed and sounded ready to give up.

Evie held him down.

"No! Wait, maybe it's her. I've got someone better."

Then Evie looked at the woman. "Get your sorry butt outta here. Go find a pole and practice! Skanks like you give strippers a bad name."

"What about my money?" the woman asked.

"You'll get it when I'm done here," Evie said, but the woman stood there, reluctant to leave without her money. Evie narrowed her eyes at the woman. "Don't make me get up." She left.

Coach was jittery and nervous. "I need music. And can a brotha get a drink around here? Y'all are tensing me up."

Evie got up, turned on some music, and poured him a shot. They got back into position on the bed. Evie hollered toward the same door again. "Bring it!"

Another woman walked in, a professional dancer. She took off her clothes seductively while touching, rubbing, and teasing Coach. After several minutes, both Coach and Evie checked the front of his black silk briefs.

Nada.

Coach sat up, fuming. "This shit ain't working! There must be something wrong with this bed, or the lighting, or maybe the air in here is bad and that's the problem!" Coach was ready to blame his condition on anything except his manhood.

Evie said, "I got one more."

Coach said, "Forget it!"

Evie kept him on the bed. "No. One more try and let's see what happens. I swear, this one is not like the first two."

Coach didn't feel like being humiliated again, but he had already given Evie the money for the third one. *What have I got to lose?* Coach took another shot of bourbon, lay back on the bed, and stared up at the two blinking red lights on the smoke detector while waiting for the third one.

Evie slid back into position behind Coach and shouted toward the door, "Bring it! And it'd *better* be good this time!"

The third exotic dancer *was* different. The dancer performed erotic moves with amazing skill, fluidity, and sexy rhythm.

Coach frowned at first. This dancer was dressed like one of those harem dancers with a sheer scarf around the face and head, leaving only the eyes uncovered. The dancer's eyes pinned Coach with a riveting sexy stare that silently suggested all sorts of naughtiness. Coach

stopped frowning and began to get aroused. The more
he watched the way the dancer's hips swayed smoothly
but powerfully under the low-rise wraparound skirt,
the more he liked it.

Coach started to not only relax, but to feel comfortable and confident, like his old self. He didn't even
need Evie's hand rubbing on his chest anymore. He
pushed her hands away and whistled at the dancer.

Evie asked, "Is it working, baby? You turned on?"

He grinned real big. "Awww, yeeah. This right here
is *working!*"

Evie poked her head over his shoulder and checked
his briefs. Her eyes got real big. Coach felt himself
growing so hard and strong, he didn't have to look. The
more Coach whooped, the more the dancer worked it,
and the more Coach became aroused. "Hell, yeah!"

The dancer crawled headfirst up the bed between
Coach's outstretched legs, the dancer's long hair
brushed his legs and tickled his stomach. Even that
turned Coach on more. Coach was bulging so much
beneath his black briefs that he was about to burst
through the silk. He grabbed the dancer's arm and
pulled because he was ready, willing, and able to take
things to the next level.

In fact, he was so confident, he said, "I'll take *both*
of you!"

Evie asked, *"Both* of us?"

Coach stuck his chest out, boasting, "Yeah. Might as
well get my money's worth."

Evie asked, "You sure 'bout this?"

Coach was excited and didn't know why Evie was

hesitating. She wanted this as much as he did. He pulled the dancer closer to him, and insisted, "Yeah, I'm sure. Evie, babe, you gonna watch?"

Evie moved to the side of the bed and faced Coach and the dancer. She twisted her face up in doubt and asked Coach one more time. "Are you *positive?* Did this dancer make you hard enough to go all the way?"

Coach laughed. "Evie, babe, trust me. I am jacked up hard and high enough to change the tire on a car!"

Convinced now, Evie tapped the dancer's shoulders. "Get up!" she told the dancer.

Coach held on to the dancer's wrist. "Wait! What's the matter? Let's do this."

Evie snapped, "Why'd you pick *this* one?"

"What the hell does it matter? It worked. She's got me up."

"It matters because"—Evie jumped off the bed and ripped off the dancer's skirt— "*she* is really a *he!*"

The dancer's package was strapped to the side of his thigh. Evie ripped off the dancer's face scarf. The man had peach fuzz around his mouth and chin.

Coach saw it. He buckled over and heaved his bourbon up all over the side of the bed.

Chapter

40

IT ONLY TOOK COACH TWENTY MINUTES TO DRIVE FROM THE downtown L.A. hotel back to his home in Beverly Hills because he was driving like a madman, honking at people to move out of his way and acting like a typical Los Angeles driver, only ten times worse.

When he got back to the mansion, Coach gunned his truck up the driveway, popped the curb, and hit the koi pond fountain on the front lawn. Its pipe burst and water spewed high into the air like a giant ejaculation. *Everything* seemed to be torturing Coach that night. He'd left Evie and that freak male dancer in the suite at the hotel. He couldn't say anything. He couldn't even look Evie in the eye. He just grabbed his clothes, his overnight bag, and ran out.

Coach threw his truck into park and jumped out without closing the door, leaving his keys in the ignition. He pushed open the mansion's front door so hard that the door cracked.

Sunnie heard the commotion and ran out of the kitchen. Rice, who'd heard the crash at the fountain from his bedroom window, came halfway down the stairs to investigate. Joey, who had been feeding Coach's Rottweilers out back, hurried into the living room also to see what was going on.

They all looked at Coach. He looked like a madman who'd gone berserk. He was frustrated and enraged, and had a downright panicked look in his eyes. He kicked the couch, moving it over two feet.

Rice started down the stairs toward Coach. "What the hell is wrong with you, man?"

Sunnie stepped in front of Rice.

"Don't! Let him be." Her eyes were wary, knowing it was not a good idea to approach Coach right now. "Furniture can be replaced," she told Rice. He got the message and decided to stay back.

Coach was still fuming. He looked for something else to break. He stopped, shook his head, cursed, and swung again, this time at the lamp, sending it flying across the room in pieces. Sunnie took a few steps toward him.

"Coach, *what happened?*" she begged from a distance.

He saw all of them looking at him. His lip trembled. He swore again and left the living room.

Coach immediately went down the hall to the gym, punching walls, kicking stands and tables the whole way. He jumped on the bench press, added a lot of weight, and started doing presses, leg curls, and more presses. In a matter of seconds, he'd worked up a sweat.

He needed to do something to vent his frustration and panic and take his mind off what had happened at the hotel.

He heard Sunnie outside the gym door trying to stop Joey from approaching him.

Sunnie caught Joey's arm and urged him, "Let him cool down first."

Joey shook her loose. "I gotta see if he's okay. He's my brother."

Joey walked into the weight room. Coach didn't look up. "Get out!" he shouted, continuing his manic weight lifting.

"Coach, hey. It's me, Joey."

"Get the fuck away from me!" Coach would not stop.

Joey came closer. "Coach, hey, whatever it is, let me try to help."

Coach dropped the weight to the floor so hard that the gym floor shook. He jumped off the bench, grabbed Joey by his Chargers jacket, and slammed his back against the wall.

"What'd you do to me, man? *What* did you do to me?!"

Joey struggled to talk. "I didn't do nothing! I swear. What're you talking about, Coach?"

Coach's big forearm was pressed against Joey's chest so hard that Joey's face turned red. His eyes were wide and scared, and starting to fill with tears. Eye to eye, face to face, beard to beard, Coach seethed at Joey. His expression was one of pain, confusion, and rage.

He said to Joey, two inches from his face and real low and mean, "Get your ass outta my house."

Joey begged, "What did I do, Coach? I swear, I didn't do nothin'!"

Coach's face was menacing. "Leave right now, or else."

Coach let go of his brother, and Joey's legs gave way. He slid down to the floor and started to cry.

Coach walked back to the bench and picked up the weight. Joey stayed against the wall, looking at Coach. He stepped toward Coach again, ready to plead for his brother's forgiveness, but this time both Sunnie and Rice pulled Joey back. They had been watching from the door and had entered the gym when Coach caught Joey by the chest.

Coach didn't look up. He kept doing bicep curls.

Joey jerked away from Sunnie and Rice and ran out the front door, out into the driveway. His eyes were cloudy and he wasn't watching where he was going. He bumped into Evie, who had left the Bonaventure and had followed Coach home.

"What's going on?" Evie asked, nonchalantly.

Joey's chest pumped up and down, and his face was contorted from crying.

Joey said, "It's Coach! He's gone mad. He told me to leave. He's blaming me for something I didn't do. I didn't do *nothing!* I swear it!"

"Of course you didn't," Evie agreed with him. She put her arm around him. "It's *you* he hates."

Joey wiped his eyes and looked at her.

She smiled. "You don't have to *do* anything for him

to hate you. He hates you because of what you are. A fag. A queer. A *boy bitch,* as he puts it." She giggled.

Joey turned away from her, not wanting to believe it.

She wiggled back in front of him. "Coach never wanted you here in the first place, he told me so. He was only doing your mother a favor. He wants you outta his house before your queerness rubs off on him. So leave!"

Joey started to cry all over again. He looked up at the sky. He was lost with no car and no place to go.

Evie pointed at Coach's truck, parked haphazardly by the fountain. The motor was still running and the keys were in the ignition.

She pushed Joey toward it. "Go. Leave like he wants you to. And take your queer germs with you so your big brother can get his stuff hard again for me like old times." Evie giggled and ran her hands across her hips seductively.

She pushed Joey closer to Coach's truck. Water spewing from the broken fountain splashed down on his head, getting him and his Chargers jacket wet. Joey got into Coach's truck, backed it up, and drove away.

Inside the gym, Sunnie was trying to talk some sense into Coach, hoping he'd calm down enough to hear it. Rice had gone back upstairs, leaving Sunnie to work miracles.

Coach kept pumping weights like they were going to save him from whatever had gone wrong. Sunnie was just as concerned about Joey right now as she was about Coach.

Sunnie asked Coach, "Aren't you going to go see about your brother? You hurt him. He's crying."

Coach added more weight to the press, got on his back, and pumped.

"Coach?" Sunnie didn't get too close to him for fear he'd jump up again.

Coach said, "I got a game tomorrow. I ain't thinking 'bout nothing but getting back on the field."

Chapter

41

WHEN JOEY GOT BEHIND THE WHEEL OF COACH'S SHINY BLACK Suburban, he had no idea where he was going or what he was going to do. He drove down the drive and onto Coldwater Canyon. He turned left on Sunset Boulevard and naturally gravitated to a familiar area.

Joey drove aimlessly, as if he could drive the pain away, circling some blocks twice and making erratic turns until he ended up in West Hollywood. He parked on Melrose Avenue a half block from a nightclub.

Joey was still dazed, and too quivery to get out and face people. He stayed in Coach's truck and crawled into the back of the plush, customized cab. Joey looked in the small fridge, where he knew Coach kept his stash of liquor. Coach had extra bottles of Cristal left over from his night on the town with Evie. Joey opened a bottle and drank it, then opened another, drank it, too, and lay across the seat.

Joey had parked close enough to the club to hear

music coming from its doors. He crawled from the back of the cab, tripping over the seats, and got behind the wheel again. He could barely see the gears because of all the champagne he'd drunk. Joey drove real slow directly toward the club's front entrance. He was so drunk, he popped the curb and ran the Suburban's tires up on the sidewalk. Three valets saw the big, shiny black truck, read its vanity license plate, and looked at its drunk driver.

One valet said, "Check that out. It's that football player, Franklin 'Coach' Brass from the San Diego Chargers."

The second valet didn't believe him. "Get outta here. That ain't him!"

The first valet insisted, "Yeah, it's him. Read the license plate."

The second valet read it, "BRASS 58."

The third valet said, "That's his jersey number—fifty-eight."

They watched as Joey tumbled out of the truck and straightened his oversize Chargers official team jacket. Joey smoothed down his new beard, which he hated. He'd only grown it because J.B. said he needed to look more manly.

The first valet gave Joey a ticket, hopped into Coach's truck, and drove off to park it. Joey tripped over the curb as he headed for the entrance.

"He looks smaller in person," the second valet said.

"All celebrities look smaller in person," the third one said.

"I've seen him in a few interviews. I don't think he's gay." The second one was skeptical.

"If he ain't gay, then what's he doing here?"

They watched Joey go to the door of the rainbow club. A man standing at the door recognized Joey. He walked up to Joey, hugged him, and kissed him on the mouth. They walked in together, arm in arm. The valets gave one another a look.

The second one scratched his head in amazement. "You never know who's jumping out the closet next."

A sexy lady wearing a tight fuchsia catsuit that hugged every crevice of her curvy body stood by the side of the club. They couldn't figure out how they'd missed seeing her a second ago. She called one of the valets over. "Psst! Hey you. Come over here a sec."

The second valet went over, his mouth hanging open. Just because he worked at a gay club, didn't mean *he* was gay.

He walked up to Evie, practically drooling all over her fuchsia catsuit. She asked him, "You wanna make some real money, more than you'd make parking cars for a whole year?"

The valet nodded. Evie handed him a piece of paper with a phone number on it and a disposable camera. She whispered in his ear what she wanted him to do.

She said, "When you get done, call that number and tell them what you got. They will cut you a fat check." She winked and disappeared as quickly as she'd appeared. The valet blinked, looked around the bushes, and scratched his head. Then he took off his valet vest and threw it in the bushes. He put the number in his pocket and went inside the club with the camera.

Chapter

42

THE SAN DIEGO CHARGERS' STADIUM WAS FILLED TO CAPACITY for Monday night's game. The home crowd was hyped and ready to root their home team on to victory. Coach was hyped, too. He was suited up and he was ready to play.

Coach tried to keep his mind on the game and block out everything else from his mind, including Sunnie, who had called him minutes before the game and was blabbering something about another flash she got of a white truck and him being hurt real bad. Coach told Sunnie that unless the opposite team was allowed to drive trucks out onto the field, she had nothing to worry about.

The team's head coach gave him the signal to enter the game. He'd never been this anxious to play in his whole life. He trotted onto the field, loving the smell of the artificial turf and sweating bodies, and relishing the noise from the crowd.

When his name was announced over the loud-speaker, he listened for the usual cheers that accompanied it. Coach was a popular team member, and since he'd been out for most of the season on the injured list and was making a comeback, he expected there'd be a big show of appreciation from the crowd in the form of hand clapping and cheering.

And there was. As Coach trotted out onto the field, he heard applause, but he also heard murmuring and a few jeers. *What is that about?* But Coach had to concentrate on the game.

The first play was called. *"Hut!"* Coach dove in for the tackle. He missed. The crowd jeered and murmured a little louder, and he knew it was aimed at him but he didn't know why.

His teammate, a fellow linebacker, yelled at him, "Man up, 58!"

Coach didn't like that. He yelled back, and tried to focus on the next play. He knew that a few of his teammates objected to Coach being given special treatment, missing practice and still being allowed to play. But Coach didn't care about that. He had worked too damn hard and waited too damn long for this opportunity. He had to not only get back in the game, he also had to get back into the zone. He couldn't punk out now. He needed to prove something to himself and to everybody who was watching. He was a *real* man, damn it, through and through, no matter what had happened in that hotel room.

Coach spat and tried to get that memory out of his mind once and for all. He didn't know why his girl, Evie, had set him up like that. That was messed up, but more important, he didn't know why he had fallen for it. Coach was battling internal as well as external enemies, but right now it was the external enemies on the other side of the scrimmage line that were going to pay.

Coach got into position, his heart racing, his fists tight. The play was called. *"Hut!"*

He slammed through the entire offensive line, mowed down two men bigger than he was, and crashed his body into the quarterback. He thrashed into him hard, lifted his feet from the ground, and slammed him into the turf. His adrenaline was so high, his momentum so forceful that both of their helmets flew off.

A flag was thrown on the play—unnecessary roughness. But that was okay. In fact, Coach liked it. It would give J.B. something to brag about to his cronies as they watched the game live from Compton. The quarterback couldn't get up after the play. Coach stood up, his massive chest poked out, his face intent with pride and confidence.

He shouted back at his teammate, who'd told him to man up. Coach said, "Yeah! I fucked him up good. What 'bout dat?" His cockiness on the field superseded his off-field antics; it was the psychology used by most players in rough, contact sports, and they used it to up their adrenaline and up their game.

Instead of congratulating Coach for the sack, his teammate shook his head in disgust. "Yeah, you fucked him up good and probably want to get with him after the game, too."

"What?" Coach walked toward him.

Another player stepped between them.

His teammate yelled around the other player at Coach. "Man, you're an embarrassment to the team. Shoulda stayed your fag ass on the injured list *and* in the closet!"

Coach didn't think. He reacted. He leapt over the other player, grabbed his teammate, and punched him through his face mask, knocking his mouthpiece out. Two other players jumped Coach. He fought both of them until the game officials and other teammates pulled them apart.

The referee blew his whistle. "Number 58! *Ejected!*"

Two security guards escorted Coach back to the locker room and left him there. He slammed his helmet into the metal lockers, denting two of them. He still didn't understand why his teammate had said what he said. Not until he saw the newspaper that someone had taped to the front of his locker. It was a rag, the *Globe*.

On the front page of the *Globe* there was a big color photo of Joey kissing a man on the mouth outside a popular gay bar in West Hollywood. Joey was wearing the Chargers official team jacket that Coach had given him the day before. Coach's number, 58, was clearly visible on the jacket, and Joey looked like he could have been Coach's twin. The headline read: "SAN DIEGO CHARGERS DEFENSIVE LINEMAN IS MUCH LESS DEFENSIVE OFF THE FIELD." Beneath the photo was Coach's name.

At that moment, Coach's cell phone rang inside his locker. He slammed open the locker and answered it, thinking it was Joey. It was Evie.

She talked fast. "Coach, I don't know what is going on, but I have to tell you that I ran into Joey last night. He was on his way to a club. He said that you had kicked him out of your house and that he was going to do something to get you back. I don't know what, but watch out." She hung up.

Coach left the stadium in a fit of rage. He jumped into the rented jeep he'd picked up from Hertz because Joey had taken his Suburban last night and kept it. Coach sped 113 miles up Interstate 5 from San Diego to Compton with his teeth clenched and his fists balled around the steering wheel the whole way. When he reached Costa Mesa, he called his parents' house.

"Ma, where's Joey? He's there, isn't he?" Coach could tell by the way his mother hesitated. She knew, and she was going to try to protect her favorite son.

"But, Franklin, now wait a minute. He says he didn't mean for that to happen. He says it was—"

"Put Joey on the phone, Ma." Coach could hear Joey in the background, pleading, trying to apologize. Joey got on the phone, his voice shaky.

"Frank, I—"

"Shut the fuck up and listen to me. Stay there. If you run, if you make me come looking for you—" Coach's lip trembled so badly from anger he couldn't finish. He slammed the phone onto the dash.

It took him only a half hour more to reach Compton. All the highway patrol cars must have been parked at Yum Yum Donuts because nobody pulled him over despite the fact he was running yellow lights and rolling through stop signs.

When Coach reached Dwight Avenue, where his parents lived, along with Mother Roby and Sunnie and Rice's folks, he was still driving so fast he almost hit another car.

He pulled up to the curb in front of his parents' house behind his black Suburban. Joey had stayed there like he said. Coach got out and ran up the driveway. J.B.'s old white Ford truck was gone. Coach thought, *Good, because Joey's ass is all mine this time!*

Coach banged on the security screen door, and when his mother opened it and tried to block his path, he brushed by her forcefully, almost knocking her down.

She called after him, "Franklin! Franklin!"

Coach headed straight to the back room where he knew Joey was—in his old bedroom. Joey had locked the door. Coach rammed the door with his shoulder and broke it off the hinges.

Joey was sitting on the floor in the corner, crying. "Frank, I didn't mean for that to happen. I was drunk."

Coach snatched Joey up like he was a rag doll.

"I go find your ass, I let you in my house, and this is how you repay me?"

Coach crammed the *Globe* into Joey's face. With his free hand, he grabbed Joey around his neck. "You stole my truck, you pretended to be me, and you went kissing on men in a fag club!"

Joey pleaded, "I didn't know they'd think I was you. I swear!"

"You *knew!*"

"I didn't know!"

"You knew, goddammit! Don't play fucking dumb! Evie told me! You told her you were going to pay me back for kicking you out!"

"I didn't say that," Joey cried. He squinted his eyes shut and grabbed his head like it hurt. He moaned, "I *swear* I didn't say it."

Coach tightened his fist around Joey's collar. His patience had run out. He was going to hurt his brother now, and nothing was going to stop him this time.

"Go ahead! Do it! Kill me! I don't care no more!" Joey sobbed without restraint. "Evie told me what you said. She told me you *hate* me!"

"Quit lying!"

"She told me, Frank! She told me!"

Coach's fist stayed cocked. He wanted to hit him so bad, but Joey kept sliding down the wall.

Joey said, "I knew you hated me, just like J.B. hates me. You ain't no different from J.B. He told me he wished I was dead, so go ahead and kill me."

Joey would have crumbled to the floor if it weren't for Coach's hand wedged around his neck.

"Yeah! I did it!" Joey blurted out, admitting to something he didn't really do. He laughed pitifully, like he was delirious or suicidal. "It's kinda funny. Huh? It's ironic. Now everybody thinks Badass Brass is the *real* fag of the family!"

Coach punched Joey in the face with a right hook that almost knocked him out. Coach reared back and was about to punch him again, but J.B. surprised him from behind.

J.B. threw his arm around Coach's neck and caught

him in a choke hold. Thrown off balance, Coach fell to the floor. J.B. wrestled him down and punched Coach in his jaw. The force banged Coach's head into the floorboard. Both his mother and Joey started screaming at J.B., who looked like he was trying to kill Coach.

Surprised by the attack, Coach barely blocked his father's punches. He managed to grab his arm before he threw another punch.

"Pop! What's wrong with you?" Coach's mouth was bleeding.

J.B. stayed on top of Coach, ready to swing. He spit saliva into Coach's face as he spewed out his words.

"I already got one fag son! I don't need *two!*" J.B. punched Coach in his face again. Coach didn't know how strong J.B. was until that moment. He couldn't get J.B. off him.

J.B. continued to spew saliva into Coach's face. "I thought you was a *real* man, not another soft-dick pussy wimp like your brother! I thought you was a son who was going to make me proud! Not embarrass me in front of the whole world!" J.B. slammed his fist into Coach's eye.

Coach rolled over and threw J.B. off. "Stop! Listen! It ain't *true!*"

"It *is* true! You a faggot! Some woman in a tight dress just played me a tape of you in a hotel room last night about to let a *she*-man suck your dick!"

"What? *Evie?*"

"She hid a camera in the smoke detector!" J.B. was done talking. He came at Coach again. This time Coach ducked and swung back. His left jab caught his father in his chest. J.B. lost his wind, but stayed on his feet. A second later, he was swinging at Coach again, exchanging blows.

Joey and his mother scrambled out the room to get help. Joey tried to call the police, but his mother stopped him. She knew the police would have to shoot J.B. before he'd let them take him to jail. She ran out the front door to get a neighbor.

Coach and J.B. tore up the back room fighting and falling into furniture. They crashed through chairs and broke tables. They knocked each other around like two gladiators, with the older Brass man fighting like a dying tiger. Coach was bleeding badly from his eye. He punched J.B. and pushed him hard enough to give himself time to run out the room.

J.B. caught up with Coach in the hallway. Coach ran to the front door. J.B. dove after him. Coach spun J.B. around using his own momentum against him and threw him out the front door, breaking out the cheap security screen door as he went through it. J.B. scrambled up, pushed away his wife and a neighbor who were trying to stop him, and tried to lunge back through the door.

Coach slammed the door closed and locked his father out.

He stumbled into the kitchen, found a towel, held it to his bleeding, burning face. When Coach went through the small house to the back room, he didn't see Joey there anymore and figured he'd run away during the fight. Coach went to the back door to lock that, too, in case J.B. tried to get in through the back.

He wanted to keep his father out, because if his father hit him one more time, Coach swore, he'd have to kill him.

When he got to the back door, he heard J.B. start up his white Ford truck and rev the engine. He heard his mother and a neighbor trying to stop J.B. from leaving. Coach went out the back door. J.B.'s truck was backed up halfway into the backyard, with J.B. behind the wheel.

Coach yelled to his mother, "No! Let him leave!"

J.B. yelled back at Coach from inside the truck. His face was bleeding, too, his eyes swelling. His right arm hung limp, like it'd been broken. "Fuck you, Franklin! You ain't my son! You ain't no Brass man! You ain't shit!"

Coach stepped up to his window and pointed his finger at J.B. "You ain't no father! You ain't nothing but an old-ass bully and you always have been!"

J.B. revved his engine real loud, then glanced in his rearview mirror and saw Joey behind the truck. When J.B. threw his Ford into gear, Coach jumped back, but instead of putting it in forward like Coach thought he would, J.B. hit reverse. His face was deranged, his eyes wild, and he yelled at Coach. "One damn queer son is enough! I don't need *two!*"

J.B. floored the pedal. Coach looked back just in time to see his brother, who'd been hiding near the BBQ pits behind the truck.

Coach screamed, "Joeeeey!"

J.B.'s tires screeched and burned rubber sailing backward in the driveway and headed directly at Joey.

Coach hollered. "No! That's my *brother!*"

He dove behind J.B.'s truck and knocked Joey out of the way.

J.B.'s tailgate rammed into Coach's right hip. His taillight clipped his leg. The force spun Coach around and sent him flying backward, straight into J.B.'s pits.

Coach lay on the ground, his body broken underneath J.B.'s steel drum BBQ pits. The weight of them crushed him even more. He struggled to stay conscious as his body threatened to go into shock. The sounds around him faded into background noise. He could hear Alejandro, the little boy from down the street, crying and calling him. *"Señor Coach! Señor Coach!"*

Coach could hear his mother calling him, and J.B. cussing him. He could barely open his eyes through the blood and the swelling. He made out the blurry tailgate of the old white truck that Sunnie had tried to warn him about.

Suddenly the evil woman that Sunnie had tried to tell them about had a face—and she looked exactly like Evie, whom Coach saw standing behind J.B. She'd been his girl, his freak, and his destruction all wrapped up in one pretty, sexy little package. Evie crawled up on the white truck, swung her legs seductively over the tailgate. She winked at Coach.

Weakness forced Coach's eyes closed, and his hearing slipped away completely as his body went into shock. The last faint sound Coach heard was Joey crying. *Crying*—something J.B. never allowed Coach to do. Coach wouldn't cry even now, no matter how bad the pain was or how scared he was of dying, because he was happy—

happy that he'd stopped J.B. from killing his little brother. He wanted to ask J.B., "Who's the real man now?" but he couldn't move and he couldn't feel his body anymore.

Vixx blew her whistle loudly, like a referee, and shouted, "Game *over!*"

She made a gesture in the air with her hands like she was keeping score and declared, "Vixx one! Men zero!"

She pranced around the cave doing a touchdown victory dance as Crèp watched and cheered as loudly as his one-hundred-twenty-year-old body would allow, which wasn't very loud.

"You should've seen it, Crèp. It was better than the Super Bowl half-time show when Janet flashed her tit at the world!"

The old ghoul sidekick said, "Yes, Your Highness, it appears as though you have destroyed one man, but what about the other two? You only have one day left before our deadline."

Vixx stopped her victory dance and calmed down a bit.

She sighed, thinking. "Right. I've still got two more guys to destroy. I'll put my victory celebration dance on hold and get to work. I've got only one inning left and two more touchdowns to score."

Crèp corrected her. "*Innings* are in baseball, *touchdowns* are in football."

Vixx rolled her eyes. "What*eva!*"

Chapter

43

TUESDAY AFTERNOON, GEFFEN SAT IN HIS HOME OFFICE WITH his blinds closed and the lights out. Calls had not been returned, bills had not been paid, documents had not been signed, and without Senda there to help him, he didn't even know how far behind he was.

But he had Dayna. The elegant and beautiful Ms. Dayna Devlin always managed somehow to be around Geffen at his most crucial moments. She was there at his side, advising him, instructing him, and even aiding him in almost mystical ways, like when she cunningly provided him with the DNA sample he needed from his uncle by indiscreetly stroking his head and pulling off strands of his thinning, gray hair.

Not only did Geffen admire Dayna's fiercely intellectual mind, he also appreciated the active role she had taken in both his private and personal affairs, because at this critical time in his life, he needed someone he could trust.

Geffen's so-called best male friends had let him down. Rice didn't understand the fundamental rules of making money—profit over privacy. Coach had turned out to be a financial basket case and big liability. He'd destroyed the courtyard's grass, the fountain and koi pond in the front. But it was Coach's comment about Geffen's mother that had broken the camel's back and sent their friendship crashing to the ground.

Sunshine was still a friend, but when it came to having a sound mind and being able to think rationally, Sunshine was seriously lacking. These last few days, all she wanted to talk to Geffen about was her gut feelings and a dark ghostlike woman who wanted to destroy Geffen, along with Rice and Coach. Sunnie even told him about a premonition she had had in a "flash," as she called it. It involved a crosswalk full of kids. That's all she could tell him. "Thanks, Sunshine, but I'll be just fine," he had replied, and let it go at that. When she asked if he knew where Coach was, he said he didn't, and quickly got off the phone with Sunnie.

The last thing he needed was more mental unbalance around him. He was having a hard enough time dealing with his own irrational emotions. Geffen had been hearing his mother crying out to him so much lately that several times he had had to catch himself to keep from answering her back.

Geffen keeled over on his desk and dozed off. It was midday, but Geffen had lost so much sleep in the last few days that his body didn't know night from day. Just as he heard his mother start to cry and saw her on her knees on a hard, linoleum floor, reaching out her hand to him, the phone rang.

Geffen jerked his head up and checked the caller ID. It was the DNA lab. Geffen listened to the lab technician as he started explaining the results of the last tests.

While Geffen listened, Dayna walked in. He was glad to see her, and again marveled at her ability to show up at precisely the right time. He whispered to her, "This is the DNA lab."

The laboratory technician said, "Mr. Cage, I have two pieces of very important information to give you. First, the person's DNA you submitted to us is of no relation to your mother. Therefore, we are still unable to confirm your mother's identity."

Geffen held the phone and closed his tired eyes. He was exhausted and confused. "I don't understand. That person was my uncle, my mother's brother. What's going on?"

The lab tech asked, "Mr. Cage, are you sitting down for this next bit of information?"

Geffen grew agitated. "Yes. Just tell me what's going on?"

The lab technician cleared his throat. "We ran a cross check between all three DNAs."

"And?"

"The person you thought was your uncle is actually your father."

Geffen dropped the phone. His smooth pecan-colored complexion turned ashen gray as the blood drained from his face. He felt faint. He tried to get up to go into his bathroom for cold water, but as soon as he stood up, his legs gave way and he fell on the floor.

Dayna got up calmly and walked to Geffen. She didn't have to ask him what was wrong—she already knew.

Geffen said it aloud not only for her, but for his own benefit, to try to come to grips with it. "My uncle is really my . . . my *father?*"

Geffen had trouble saying the word *father*. All of his life he'd hated his father, resented him for neglecting his mother and sending him off like a piece of luggage. All of his life he'd wanted to meet his father and get the chance to repay him, and to tell him what a selfish son of a bitch he was. And now, today, he found out that his father had been right under his nose this whole time.

Dayna stood over him. She ran her hand gently through his wavy hair.

She said to him, "Geffen, if you really want to know why your father did what he did, go to his home and look inside the file cabinets that he keeps behind his chair."

Geffen looked up into Dayna's crystal eyes. He didn't know why she said that or how she knew where the answer lay, but he knew that he would follow Dayna's instructions. He almost felt like he had no choice, like this woman had cast some sort of spell over him.

Dayna helped Geffen to his feet. She helped him gather his things and walked him to his Hummer. He asked, "Aren't you coming with me?"

Dayna replied, "I've got other business to tend to, but I'll get back to you later."

Geffen drove to his uncle's house and waited for his uncle's nurse to leave for the evening. Geffen watched as the male nurse turned off the lights, locked the front door, and got into his car. Geffen waited until the man drove away, then pulled his Hummer up to the front of his father's house and got out. Geffen picked the lock on the front door and went inside.

Once inside, Geffen went into his den, where they had signed the cemetery papers last Tuesday, one week ago. Dayna had been with him then. Geffen could not, for the life of him, figure out how Dayna could possibly know what was in these file cabinets, but she said he'd find the answer inside them, and that's what he had come to do.

Geffen set about his search for the truth. He picked the lock on his father's antique file drawers labeled MEDICAL ARCHIVES, and he searched the manila file folders until he found one with his mother's name on it. He opened it, sat down and read it, and slowly learned the truth about his mother and father.

Immediately after reading his mother's medical archive file, Geffen left his father's house in Ontario and drove eighteen miles west to Glendora, where he parked in Foothill Presbyterian Hospital's parking lot. He got out and walked through the automatic double doors. Dayna was standing inside the doors waiting for him.

"I knew you'd come here," she said, and offered her

hand. He accepted it, and they took the elevators up to the sixth floor.

Geffen walked in and stood at the bedside of Dr. Herv Brentanbrock, his father. Life-support machines clacked and whizzed, but all Geffen could hear were the incessant cries of his mother echoing through his mind.

Geffen said to his father, "My mother had schizophrenia. You were her doctor."

His father's eyelids fluttered. The nurse told Geffen, "He may be able to hear you, but he may be too weak to respond."

Geffen went on. "You had me address the letters I wrote my mother to the State Hospital. You told me it was because you worked there, and she didn't have a permanent address. You lied. It was because she *lived* there."

Dr. Brentanbrock's eyes fluttered more intensely. Geffen turned to Dayna. "He can hear me. I know this son of a bitch can hear me."

Dayna rubbed his back and asked the nurse to give Geffen some private time alone with his father. The nurse left the room. Dayna stayed.

"You never married her because you were already married. You treated my mother—your mental patient—like a whore. She was *sick!* You got her pregnant, snatched me away from her, shipped me off to boarding schools, and didn't even have the decency to admit I was your *son*. You didn't want to claim a crazy lady's bastard child as your own."

Geffen's shoulders trembled. The weight of his turmoil combined with the pressure of Dayna's hand on his back caused him to sink to his knees. When his knees hit the cold linoleum floor, the image of his mother flashed before his eyes—she was on her knees also, on a cold linoleum floor, and now Geffen could see that the plain blue gown she wore had black ink on the front: ATASCADERO STATE HOSPITAL.

Geffen blinked his eyes and tried to tear himself away from that sorrowful image. He went on, "She was crying for me, her baby! You tore me from her arms."

He reached into his pocket and pulled out the crinkled hospital report he'd taken from his father's archived file cabinets. He read it: "June 16, 1983, patient Laila Cage jumped to her death from the ninth-floor window, deceased on impact."

Geffen stood up. He laid the report flat on Dr. Brentanbrock's chest. He said, "You had money, but no heart. You killed my mother."

Geffen turned around, and Dayna embraced him. Behind Geffen's back, Dr. Brentanbrock's eyes fluttered and opened.

"Look," Dayna said. "He's awake."

Geffen jerked around. His father's sunken eyes shifted and focused on Geffen's face. He moved his lips.

Geffen quickly lifted the oxygen cap off his father's face. Geffen's hands shook as he held the mouthpiece. "He's trying to talk."

His father struggled to get enough breath in his collapsing lungs to speak. Geffen knelt down close and watched his father's lips move, hoping words would come that would help ease all the bitterness and pain Geffen felt. He was hoping his father would tell him something that he could take with him the rest of his life, that would give him a sense of peace—tell him he really did love his mother, tell him he'd planned to one day bring his family together, tell him he was sorry.

His father opened and closed his mouth, swallowed, and tried to open his mouth again. Geffen stood still and quiet, listening, waiting, and hoping against all hope.

Dayna knelt close to Geffen's father, her steely, sharp crystal eyes darting from Geffen to the old man and back to Geffen.

His father continued trying to speak, but nothing came out but heavy, laboring breaths. Geffen put his face down so close that he could smell the old man's medications in his breath. Geffen didn't care—he wanted to hear every word that his father would speak on his deathbed.

Geffen said, "Say it, please. Tell me something. You *owe* it to me."

The sick man licked his dry lips with his tongue. Geffen lowered the oxygen mask so that he could refill his lungs. When he'd had enough and his eyes refocused on Geffen, Geffen removed the cap once again. The old man looked determined to tell his son what he'd been keeping to himself for over thirty years.

Geffen tried to hold his composure, at least long enough to hear what his father had to say, but he was losing hope.

Then his father said, in slow, labored breaths, "I—will—tell—you—*son* . . ." His father began, but then he stopped and coughed as if it might be his last breath.

Dayna clasped Geffen's shoulder. "He's dying, Geffen. I'll use the button to call the nurse."

Geffen leaned his ear even closer to his father, sharing his breaths. "Tell me. *Tell me*," Geffen whispered, his fingers clasping the bed rail tightly.

His father started talking again, with great determination. "You, Gef-fen, have . . ." He stopped again and coughed.

Dayna said, "The button doesn't work."

Geffen snapped, "What?"

Dayna lifted the white nurse's button that was on a white cord. She said, "Geffen, you need to run down the hall and get a nurse."

"I can't leave right now—he's about to tell me something."

"You have to. I can't run as fast as you. I'll stay here with your father, you go," Dayna said. Geffen kept his face close to his father's. He didn't want to go. Dayna said again, "Run and get a nurse, Geffen. Now, before it's too late."

Geffen looked at his father. The old man's eyes were open, and for the first time since Geffen had been standing there, he looked awake and communicative. His father opened his mouth again, his voice was stronger and he was ready to tell Geffen something.

Dayna raised her voice, "Geffen, *go*, now!"

Geffen left his father's bedside and shot down the hall. He practically broke the sound barrier getting down the hall to get a nurse.

The second Geffen stepped out, Dayna pulled the plugs on the life-support machine.

Dayna watched with sparkling crystal eyes as the old man's face registered first shock and denial, then death. But before he died, he spoke. Dayna heard him clearly, then watched him die in only a matter of seconds. She quickly plugged the machine back in.

Geffen barreled back through the door pulling a nurse with him.

Dayna looked at Geffen, her crystal eyes as calm as always. She said, "Geffen. I'm sorry."

Geffen looked at his father. His father looked even grayer and more ashen than he'd looked moments ago. Geffen raised his hands to his head, but words escaped him.

Dayna saw that Geffen was about to lose his composure. She walked quickly to his side and took his hand.

She said, "Geffen, he spoke before he died."

Geffen's face changed from despair to hope, and lit up with anticipation. He swallowed real hard and asked in a shaky voice, "What did he say?"

Dayna lowered her beautiful crystal eyes momentarily, as if she was reconsidering telling him, then she lifted them again and looked directly at Geffen.

"He said you have the schizophrenic chromosome, too, just like your mother."

When Geffen heard that, he completely lost it. He raised his hands, dug his fingers into his wavy hair, and pulled. He let out a scream that was so long and so pitiful that he began to sound exactly the way his mother sounded when she cried and wailed in his head.

Chapter

44

GEFFEN LEFT THE HOSPITAL IN A BLAZE OF GRIEF AND
devastation, refusing to sign any paperwork or assume
any responsibility in the handling of his father's newly
deceased body. He got in his car, Dayna hopped in,
and he took off, trying to get as far away from his
father and the news that he was carrying the chromosome for schizophrenia as he could.

Geffen sped his Hummer down the freeway heading
back to L.A. Dayna held on to the passenger's seat bar.
"You're driving too fast, Geffen. Way too fast."

Geffen pounded the steering wheel. His hands were
shaking and sweating. "Why didn't he tell me sooner?"

"If he had, what could you have done? Nothing. If
you've got the chromosome, then there's nothing you
can do. You are genetically predisposed." Dayna sat
back in her seat and took in the sights.

Geffen jumped in and out of lanes, and flew around
other cars.

"I've got the chromosome. What the hell does that mean?"

Dayna's voice was calm despite the fact that he was going twenty miles over the speed limit. "Geffen, you're upset right now. We can talk about this later."

"No! I need to know *now!*"

Dayna was the voice of reason and practicality. "Perhaps you should go back to your office and try to get your business matters in order first, and settle your affairs."

Geffen jerked the wheel and almost clipped the car in front of him. Her words carried a tone of doom, and he picked up on it. Geffen, who had always valued mental intellect above all else, had been feeling like he was sliding down a slippery mental slope lately, what with the sound of his mother constantly crying in his head. But he thought he'd be able to pull it all back together. *I can't be losing my mind!*

Geffen exited the freeway and turned left on Wilshire Boulevard. He ran his fingers through his wavy hair and tried to think straight. *I'll rehire Senda. We'll tie up loose ends and get back to business.*

Dayna asked, "Geffen, are you going to try to hold on to your corporation?"

Geffen gripped the steering wheel so tightly that his knuckles turned whitish. He didn't know why Dayna would ask such a question. "Of course, I am! My corporation is all I've got!"

Dayna looked calmly ahead at the traffic lights. "You will need your mind to run it."

Geffen frowned, turning to look at her. How could she be so calm and so elegant when he was going through such hell and anguish? "What do you mean by that, Dayna?"

Dayna remained silent. She looked straight ahead. Geffen asked again, "What do you mean, Dayna?"

She kept her eyes straight. "It's obvious."

Panic flew through Geffen's whole body. Dayna finally turned toward him. She placed her hand on his arm. "Geffen, you're losing your mind."

Geffen's whole body stiffened. He grabbed his head, and his foot hit the gas pedal. *"Nooooooo!"* he wailed.

Dayna leaned into him. "You have the chromosome. You hear voices in your head. It all makes sense now. Geffen, you are schizophrenic."

Geffen tried to grab the wheel. His Hummer was careening out of control toward a red light at Curson Avenue near La Brea Tar Pits. He tried to slam on his brakes, but he was too late.

Dayna said insensitively, "Geffen, you are crazy, too, just like your *mother.*"

Geffen shouted again, *"Nooooooo!"*

His Hummer hurled through the red light, skidding out of control.

Dayna shouted, "You're suicidal. You're going to kill yourself, just like your mother did!"

Through his red, watery, burning eyes, Geffen saw the blurry image of kids on a field trip crossing in the crosswalk on the other side of the intersection.

He was seconds away from hitting them. *"Nooooooo!"* Geffen cut the wheel left so sharply that the Hummer hit a school bus, clipped a Mercedes, then flipped on its side.

Everything went black for a second, then blinding white. Geffen was still belted inside his Hummer, dazed but conscious and not seriously injured. His body was bent and pushed up against the dash and the truck was flipped on its side. He heard his name.

It was Dayna. She called him in a calm, cool, and collected voice. "Geffen. My dear, schizophrenic Geffen . . ."

He struggled to turn his head. He saw her. She was sitting in her seat perfectly upright, no seat belt, not a scratch on her lovely, calm face, not a hair out of place. But to Geffen, who had been thrown against the side door and dashboard, Dayna seemed to be suspended in midair, defying gravity.

Dayna smiled at Geffen and said, softly, "You see that school bus you just hit?"

Geffen squinted. He peered through his cracked front windshield and saw the school bus with a dented fender. People were running around in a panic, getting the kids off the bus one by one until they were all standing by the curbside. Geffen heard sirens and an ambulance approaching.

Geffen exhaled, and turned back to Dayna. "But they're all okay."

Dayna shook her head. "It doesn't matter, Geffen." She pointed to the Mercedes that Geffen had also clipped after hitting the school bus. "Read the license plate. It says: 'SUE EM.' That's Fred Gertz's Mercedes, he's the famous PI attorney from the commercials. He was driving his pregnant wife to her prenatal appointment. Tsk-tsk—too bad you fired Senda before she could get you that insurance coverage."

Geffen saw the attorney get out and usher his pregnant wife to the curb, where she sat down, holding her stomach, but apparently okay. Fred Gertz looked around the crash site. He looked at the school bus, the schoolchildren, who were frightened but okay, about fifty witnesses standing around chattering, and at Geffen's Hummer, which had run through the red light.

The famous attorney walked over to Geffen's overturned Hummer, read Geffen's vanity plate: CORP BIZ. Fred scratched his short stubby chin.

He peeked inside. Through the cracked windshield, he looked directly at Geffen, but didn't notice Dayna, who was suspended and hovering above Geffen.

Fred made eye contact with Geffen. He asked, "Are you all right?"

Geffen, dazed, scared, and bewildered, nodded. Fred smiled. "Good. Now, tell me, what kind of corporation did you *used* to own, because I'm going to sue you for every penny you've got, good buddy."

Fred turned around and shouted to the EMTs who had just arrived on the crash scene, "Neck braces for everybody!"

Geffen remained dazed and frozen, staring out his cracked windshield, until Dayna tapped his arm.

Geffen jumped. He jerked around. "Who *are* you? *What* are you?"

Dayna feigned hurt. "Why, Geffen, you know who I am. I'm your *fantasy* woman." She winked at him.

"No you're not. You're that—that *woman* Sunnie was talking about. You made all this happen. You did all this to me. You're *evil*."

Dayna smiled. "Evil? Don't call me evil. Call me *Mama*."

In a blinding flash, Dayna changed herself into Geffen's mother. She looked helpless, tears streamed down her face, her hospital gown falling off her shoulder. "Heeelp meee, Geffen, heeelp meee before I killll myself!" And she disappeared.

Geffen screamed. He scrambled fast to unbuckle his seat belt, twisted his body, and crawled out the passenger-side window. He jumped down off his Hummer, looked around at the crash site, at the attorney who was about to take his corporation away from him, and over by the traffic light, where someone had called his name.

"Geeeffffennn!" Geffen turned and looked. It was Dayna's voice, but she still looked like his mother. Geffen screamed up at the sun, then took off running down Wilshire Boulevard. He couldn't see where he was going, he just ran, and thought about his mother, and about committing suicide, just like she did.

Chapter
45

SUNNIE RAN THROUGH THE MANSION'S KITCHEN LIKE A tsunami. She bolted out the back door, ran through the courtyard and up to the edge of the garden, where the Santa Monica Mountains began. She held her cell phone to her ear and pointed her face toward the trees blowing in the wind. She listened.

Sunnie heard the sounds of laughter and celebrating again. She quickly told Mother Roby, who was waiting on the phone.

"I hear it! I hear that laughing again, like they're celebrating, but it's not good. It's, like, *evil.* Oh, Mother Roby, I can't explain it—it's just freaking me out." Sunnie put her hand on her forehead and closed her eyes.

Mother Roby gave her instructions. "Alisun, this ain't no time to be *freaked,* it's time to fight!"

When Sunnie heard the word *fight,* her heart jumped up into her throat. "But Mother Roby, I'm not *ready.*"

"Then you'd better *get* ready because evil plans don't wait." Mother Roby cleared her throat. "And now is not the time to doubt your gift, Alisun."

Sunnie had spent the last two nights at the mansion because she knew something bad was about to happen. She could *feel* it.

She didn't want to leave because she wanted to be there to help the guys if something happened, but she was afraid to stay because she didn't know exactly what she'd do if something terrible *did* happen.

Sunnie's voice quavered. "Mother Roby, I think it's already started. I feel like bad things have already happened."

Mother Roby's voice sounded alarmed now, too. "Alisun, go back inside and close the door."

Sunnie did as she was told. As she left the courtyard, a bone-chilling breeze wiggled up her back and put chills in her spine. As she locked the door behind her, she continued talking.

"For the last two days, my spiritual radar has gotten more intense. I could be just sitting in the mansion's living room, and it will go crazy for no apparent reason."

"But I told you to pay closer attention to it, to look and see what's happening around you when it gives you that warning."

Sunnie sat down at the kitchen table. "I did, and that's what's scaring me."

"Why?"

Sunnie pulled in a deep breath. "It goes off whenever the guys' girlfriends drop by. The other day, it was going off like crazy when I went to Rice's bedroom. I thought for sure the dark, sultry woman was around, hiding under his bed or something, but it turned out that *Kamile* was in his room." Sunnie paused.

"What do you think that means?"

Sunnie swallowed. "Mother Roby, I'm scared."

Sunnie thought about how she'd tried to tell Rice that there was something weird about Kamile, but instead of believing her he'd said hurtful things. Sunnie *knew* that Kamile was somehow influencing Rice, but she didn't know *how* she was doing it.

Shortly after Kamile left, Dayna had come and gotten Geffen from his office, where he'd been sitting in the dark. Each time Geffen left with Dayna he looked a mess, and he was getting worse. Also, Coach had bolted out of the house several times over the last few days, saying he was hurrying to meet Evie, but after he'd played in the Monday night football game, he hadn't come back. Geffen had left today, too, and hadn't returned. Sunnie was worried about all of them.

"And, Mother Roby, I got those flashes again, only this time they were worse."

Mother Roby asked, "When did they occur and what were they?"

Sunnie kept looking out the kitchen window toward the mountains.

"Yesterday, after I saw Coach get ejected from the game on TV, I saw him again in a flash. He was on the ground, hurt real bad, and there was an old white truck close by. And only a few moments ago, just before I called you, I flashed on Geffen again. There was a crosswalk full of kids, then I saw him yelling and crying. It doesn't make sense."

Mother Roby listened. "What about Rice?"

Sunnie paused. "Nothing. He hasn't been in any of these strange flashes, but that doesn't mean he's not in any danger."

Sunnie stood by the refrigerator and banged her head back against it. She grabbed her stomach. "Oh, Mother Roby, I can feel it right *now*. It's happening again!"

"What, Alisun? What's happening?"

"My stomach. It feels all hot and bubbly, and I know it's close. Wait!" Sunnie walked to the hallway and listened. She heard Rice come in the front door. She whispered to Mother Roby over the phone. "It's Rice. He's not alone. I hear a woman's voice. I think he's with Kamile."

Sunnie listened as Rice walked up the stairs. Sunnie tiptoed to the edge of the staircase. She heard his bedroom door open and close, then it opened again and he went down the hall to his study. Sunnie's heart was beating a mile a minute. Her hands were sweating and she could hardly hold the phone.

"Mother Roby, Kamile is in Rice's bedroom. I can *feel* it. Oh, Mother, my stomach is in knots, and I'm scared. But I've gotta *do* something!"

Mother Roby's voice was alarmed, but she tried to keep her tone even and not upset Sunnie more than she already was. "Alisun, listen to me. If that small voice inside is saying to go up there, then you go. But you pray as you go, and Alisun, remember one thing."

Mother Roby paused. "Love is greater than any other force out there."

Mother Roby's words brought both comfort and fear. Sunnie quickly closed her cell phone. Her stomach was telling her exactly where the *other force* was—Kamile had stayed in Rice's bedroom while he went to his study to get something.

Sunnie knew that if Rice returned to his bedroom before she got up there, he wouldn't let her inside. Sunnie said a quick prayer and rushed up the stairs. She ran past Rice's study and went straight to his bedroom door. With each quick step she took, the higher pitched her alarm went. Kamile was inside for sure. Sunnie could hear her in there moving things around, breaking things.

Sunnie turned the doorknob. She was going to burst in and take Kamile by surprise, maybe throw her down on the floor and step on that stupid chignon she wore on the back of her head. Sunnie was never fooled by Kamile's homey little wardrobe; Sunnie knew that deep down inside Kamile's little Sears catalog panties, she was a superfreak, as freaky as they come. Sunnie could *feel* that, too.

Sunnie laid into the door with her shoulder, planning to bust it open fast so she could bum-rush Kamile, but the door was locked. She heard Kamile pause inside. She heard her laugh, only it didn't sound the way Sunnie imagined Kamile would laugh, it sounded much more dark and sinister. Kamile went back to throwing things around and opening Rice's drawers and closets like she was looking for something.

Sunnie kept turning the knob and banging on the

door. "Kamile! Open this door. We need to have a little woman-to-woman talk and I think you know why. Open this door!"

Rice heard the commotion and came out of his study. As soon as his study door opened, his bedroom door came unlocked and Sunnie fell inside. Sunnie jumped up quickly and looked around. It was empty.

Rice came running in. He saw his room. It was ransacked. All of his drawers were opened, his personal affects had been pulled out, closets were opened, and even his mattress had been pushed to one side. His window was left wide open, and the wind blew his curtain up.

Sunnie stood by his bed looking around, confused. She knew she looked guilty to him by the way he stood there looking at her.

He looked pissed. Nobody knew better than Sunnie how much Rice *hated* for people to look through his things, *especially* his bedroom or his study.

"What is your problem? Why are you going through my stuff, Sunnie?"

"Rice, I didn't—"

Rice stomped past Sunnie and closed the window to stop the wind from blowing the curtain up. "Don't lie. What were you looking for?"

"Rice, I didn't do this. *Kamile* did it. After you left her in your room and went into your study, she ransacked your room. She must've climbed out the window." Sunnie ran to the window and looked out. All she saw were the trees leading up into the mountains.

Rice said, *"Kamile* ransacked my room? Kamile wasn't even with me."

Sunnie's eyes got big. "Yes, she was. I heard her talking when you came in the front door. When you went into the study, I heard her in here."

Rice said, flatly, "I haven't seen Kamile all day. Get out of here." Sunnie stuttered, trying to explain. Rice held up his hand—he wouldn't listen. He said, "Now."

As Sunnie walked down the stairs, she felt her spirits going down, too. The way he had accused her of tearing up his room and then dismissed her like that made her feel so bad. She thought about going home and giving up. But she remembered that *laugh*. It was evil and it was mocking her. Instead of going home, Sunnie headed back to the kitchen. She gazed out the window and thought about what had just occurred in Rice's bedroom. *You think you'll get rid of me that easy? This battle is just beginning.* Sunnie folded her arms. She wasn't going to leave. These were her friends and she loved them. She was going to stay and *fight*.

Chapter

46

AFTER URGING ALISUN TO CONFRONT THE EVIL FORCE threatening the guys, Mother Roby decided she needed to do more than just advise Alisun. She said aloud as she turned off her television, "Evil plans don't wait. And neither do I."

Mother Roby didn't waste any time. She immediately got on her phone and started calling her *posse*, as she jokingly referred to them when she was around Alisun. Her *posse* was her prayer group—a group of seven no-nonsense, Bible-believing men and women from her church who not only believed in the power of prayer, but knew how to use prayer to kick the devil's butt.

"Hello, sister. Listen up, because it's time to kick the devil's butt," Mother Roby said. One by one, she told her prayer friends the situation. Her prayer partners were already familiar with the matter because Mother Roby had put Sunnie and the guys on her prayer list a long time ago, but Mother Roby explained why right now *urgent* prayer was needed.

She told them, "Right this very minute, as we speak, two of the guys are missing—Coach and Geffen. And the third one, Rice, is in danger right now, but doesn't know it."

The prayer team members who lived close to Mother Roby's house rushed over immediately. The ones who lived too far or were physically unable to come stopped whatever they were doing to pray right where they were. Mother Roby knew that it didn't matter where they prayed, it only mattered that they did it, because all of their prayers were going up to the same place.

Mother Roby gathered her prayer team in a circle in her living room. She took a picture of Alisun off her fireplace mantel and set it on the coffee table in the middle of them. Mother Roby bent her knee and started off the praying: "Lord, help these three young men, and help Alisun, too, because whatever she's about to come up against is either going to scare her to death or it's going to make her stronger."

Vixx crawled into the cave on her hands and knees, dragging her dark sexy legs in the mud and dirt. She looked confused and pathetic. Crèp jumped up from his ghoul perch.

"Vixx! Your Highness, what's wrong?"

Vixx crawled farther into the cave and stopped near a pile of deer bones to rest. "Aw, Crèp, I can hardly move my legs, and my arms feel like lead. I'm sinking in quicksand!"

Crèp looked at her body, puzzled. "Vixx, that's dirt, not quicksand."

Vixx slapped his knee. "You can't see it. It's *supernatural,* you fool ghoul!"

"How did you get stuck in 'supernatural' quicksand?"

Vixx dragged herself a little farther and leaned her back against the wall. She looked at Crèp, her eyes filled with dread. "Because they are praying!"

Vixx rolled over on her back, out of breath.

Crèp tried to prop her up. "But Queen Domina said that a person's free will overrules the prayers of others."

"I *know* what she said. But those fools are praying like crazy. They're quoting Scripture left and right, and even cheating with stuff like oil and holy water." Vixx made a barfing gesture. She added, "And it's not just Sunnie praying, it's that old geezer friend of hers who up and called her whole doggone prayer group. All that crap is slowing me down."

"But we only have twenty-four hours left to get them out of the house."

"I know! But I can't *move!*"

"But if those guys aren't dead by midnight, we won't get our house or brothel back."

"But—I—can't—*move!*"

"But—but—" Crèp tried to hurry and think of what would give Vixx the strength to overcome the quicksand. He ran to his bucket and took out an old photograph that he'd been secretly saving for a hundred years. He put the photo in Vixx's face.

Her eyes bulged. Her face grimaced, her lips curled up. She spit out the name like venom. *"Bruce!"*

Vixx pulled herself up by a twig in the wall and struggled to her feet. She repeated the name. "Bruce! That no-good, two-timing, self-loving, woman-chasing, man dog!"

Crèp kept the photo in front of her face. It was working like a charm. Vixx's whole body was reenergized by her hatred for Bruce, the human man who'd taken her goodies and then kicked her to the curb a hundred years ago. Vixx jumped to her feet, pulled the back of her white dress up like a hood over her head, shadowboxed, and starting humming the theme song from *Rocky.*

If Vixx couldn't get revenge on Bruce, she'd take it out on the three guys, especially Rice, who resembled Bruce around the eyes.

Vixx was sweating now from the adrenaline high. She punched-jabbed-ducked and shuffled her feet like a boxer. Crèp ducked, too, because she'd been known to get carried away at times.

Vixx panted. "I'm gonna get them! I'm gonna rip their heads off!"

Crèp kept the picture in front of her. "What about the prayer quicksand?"

"It's slowing me down, but I'm going to find a way to put a stop to it."

Vixx was pumped, and kept throwing air jabs and bouncing in place as she updated Crèp. "Two of them are already down for the count. I just gotta finish them off and that won't be hard. One's unconscious and the other one is suicidal."

Vixx did two quick leg stretches, then popped back to her feet, bouncing.

She said, "Coach, the handsome hunk, is all banged up and broken. Since he idolized his body and manhood, he won't want to live. Pretty boy Geffen is about to lose his corporation as well as his mind. He had made money and intellect his gods, so without them he thinks he has nothing."

Crèp kept the picture of Bruce held up in front of Vixx like a mirror. She glared at it.

Crèp asked, "What about the third guy?"

"Rice? Yeah, I'm saving writer boy for last. I got something real special for him."

Vixx had a sexy smirk on her face, which Crèp didn't like. Her horniness for men was always getting them in trouble. Crèp only hoped that her man fetish wouldn't get in the way of her finishing them off, now that they were so close.

Vixx popped her neck like Mike Tyson. "I tried to find that poem he's hiding, but couldn't get it."

Crèp asked, "But, Vixx, I thought you could read their minds."

She snapped, "I *can!* But that Rice is so damn secretive, he even keeps secrets from *himself.*" Then Vixx threw her arms up in victory. "But I'm going to annihilate those guys. I'm the champ. *Nothing* can stop me."

Crèp reminded her. "Except if one of them falls truly in love. Then your spell will be broken."

Vixx froze. As soon as Crèp had said it, he realized it

was a stupid move. Although it was true, it wasn't what Vixx wanted to hear at that moment, and before he could duck, it was too late.

Vixx knocked Crèp out with a solid right hook straight into his old ghoul nose.

Mother Roby's prayer meeting in her living room was going well. They had been praying for hours. Sometimes they'd sing those good, old-fashioned gospel songs, then they'd go back to praying. They were about to call it a day and go back to their respective homes while staying in a prayerful mode when Mother Roby's phone rang. She excused herself, went into her bedroom, and answered it. The person on the other end sounded strange and muffled.

Mother Roby squinted, and asked again, *"Who* is this?"

"It's *Sunnie!"*

"Baby, what's wrong? You just don't sound like yourself," Mother Roby said. Sunnie asked if the prayer meeting was over yet. She said she needed to come by right away, but that she didn't want to come until everybody left.

"Why, baby?" Mother Roby asked.

"It's personal."

Mother Roby didn't understand, but she thought it best that she clear out the prayer warriors and let Sunnie come, because there was obviously something wrong.

After the last prayer warrior left, Mother Roby sat on her couch and waited for Sunnie. She heard a knock on the *back* door and got up to look. She opened the door.

"Alisun?"

Sunnie came in. She was wrapped up in a thick wool blanket, even though it was summertime, and was wearing what looked like a scuba diver's suit underneath that. Her face looked troubled. Mother Roby started to ask her about the clothes. Sunnie stopped her.

"Please, Mother Roby, can we just sit down and talk? I'll explain all this later." Sunnie walked past Mother Roby and went to sit on her couch.

Mother Roby followed her. When she sat on the couch next to Sunnie, Sunnie turned her back.

Mother Roby laid into her. "Now, Sunnie, what's wrong with you, child? You come in here acting all peculiar, you won't turn and face me, you've even got me feeling all heebie-jeebies now. What's going on? Did you face off with that *Kamile* person?"

Sunnie kept looking at the wall. "Mother Roby, I have some confessions to make. I just don't want you to be mad at me."

"Spill it, child."

Sunnie hesitated and clammed up. Then she said, "I can't talk like this. I'm too nervous. Let's eat first and then talk."

"Eat? Well, I haven't cooked anything. I could fix you a peanut butter and jelly—"

Sunnie whipped out a box of gourmet brownies from under her wool blanket. Mother Roby looked at them. She was surprised, then chided Sunnie. "Now,

Sunnie, you know I can't eat those. All that sugar will put me in a diabetic coma."

Sunnie jumped off the couch. Her voice got higher, sounding insulted. "Now, Mother Roby, you know I would *never* bring you regular brownies. These are from that diabetic nonsugar gourmet bakery on Rosecrans—you know, the one I told you about. How could you *think* that?"

Mother Roby felt kind of bad for upsetting Sunnie. "Oh, baby. I didn't mean to imply that—"

Sunnie popped the box open. "Got milk?"

Mother Roby went to the kitchen to get milk, and when she returned she tried to get to the bottom of Sunnie's strange behavior, but Sunnie insisted that they eat first and talk later. Mother Roby had been fasting all day and praying, and really wasn't in the mood to eat brownies, but just to appease Sunnie, she took a few bites.

Mother Roby raised her eyebrows. "You know, Alisun, for a no-sugar brownie, these really are quite good. But let's get down to business. What is it that's making you behave so strangely?"

Sunnie held the box to Mother Roby and waited for her to take two more brownies before she started telling her what was wrong.

Sunnie said, "Guilt."

Mother Roby put her brownie down after taking a few more bites. "Guilt?"

Sunnie started crying and falling all over the couch. "Oh, Mother Roby, I've been such a bad girl. I know you think I'm an angel since I started going to church with you and Bible study and all that. But really I'm a little ho."

Sunnie sniveled and **blew** snot into her blanket. Mother Roby's eyebrows raised. She was speechless.

Sunnie went on. "I led you to believe that me and the three guys are only friends, platonic, no nookie." Sunnie shook her head and drooped her shoulders. "I lied. I've been banging them every day, three times a day, sometimes twice with Coach because he's such a big freak."

Mother Roby leaned forward to try to get a good look at Sunnie. Sunnie made a guilty, puppy-dog face, then turned back toward the wall.

She said, "There's more. On nights when I'm not at Bible study with you, I go down to Drop It Like It's Hot, that strip joint in San Pedro. And you know what I do there, Mother Roby? I drop it like it's hot. I pop it, I bounce it, I shake it, and I even make it clap."

Sunnie clapped her hands two times real hard and loud.

Mother Roby almost jumped out of her skin.

"So, you see, you and all your friends need to stop praying for me because I'm going straight to hell anyway."

Mother Roby's face dropped into a deep frown. She got up slowly off the couch and leaned into her cane real hard. She moved away from Sunnie, went and stood by her fireplace mantel, facing Sunnie, keeping her eye on her carefully. She was stooping over more than usual, looking like she'd been punched in the gut.

Mother Roby pulled in a deep long breath of revelation, and her face fell in disappointment—she was disappointed in *herself*. She said what she should have known when this woman first knocked at the back door. After all, she had the gift, too, though hers was not as strong and vibrant as Sunnie's.

"You're *not* Alisun."

Vixx smiled and said, "And those *aren't* sugar-free brownies."

Vixx bounced up from the couch, full of energy. She threw off the wool blanket, which she'd used to try to camouflage her supernatural demoness scent. She peeled off her scuba diver's suit and fluffed out her white gauzy dress. Vixx dug her dirty bare feet into Mother Roby's soft living room carpet.

Immediately, Mother Roby's heart raced, her blood pressure shot up, her insulin levels plummeted, and her diabetic body began to react to the high sugar intake from those *regular* brownies. But still Mother Roby gripped her gold cane with all her strength. She gripped the mantel with her left hand to steady her body. She raised her gold cane and pointed it straight into Vixx's face, holding it there to keep her at bay. Mother Roby was ready to pray and fight Vixx at the same time.

Vixx stepped closer. "Oh, lookie! The old lady is ready to fight me. If this were a physical fight, I guess you know who'd win."

Mother Roby squinched her eyes, her voice came out hoarse. "It's a *spiritual* fight."

Vixx applauded. "Correct! It *is* a spiritual fight. And since you spend so much time in church and on your knees, you should know, old lady, that if there's one thing us evil ones *don't* do, it's fight fair."

Mother Roby's eyes started flickering, the room started to spin.

Vixx cooed, "Ooh, don't blame me. I didn't *make* you eat those brownies. I only set the temptation before you. You ate of your own free will."

Vixx pranced around Mother Roby's coffee table. She looked at the picture of Sunnie that Mother Roby had placed in the middle of the prayer circle. Vixx kept taunting her. "Hey, this is sorta like what happened to Adam and Eve in that garden, huh? That snake got a bad rap in that story. All he did was point to the apple, he didn't shove it down Eve's throat." Vixx giggled. "He's really not a bad guy once you get to know him." Vixx knocked Sunnie's picture off the coffee table with her bare foot.

Mother Roby wobbled. Her blood sugar sky-rocketed and she slumped down low from the dizziness, but she still used all the strength in her body to keep her cane pointed up at Vixx like a sword.

Mother Roby tried to keep her eye on Vixx, but things started to blur, and Vixx's haunting image began to slip in and out of view. Mother Roby coughed, and tried to move closer to the small stand where she kept her daily insulin shot. "Why'd you come here?"

"I came here to put an end to all that stupid praying." Vixx poked her nose around Mother's Roby's living room.

Mother Roby tried to stay focused. "You can't hurt Alisun."

Vixx smiled. "I can try." Vixx opened Mother Roby's drawer in the small stand next to the chair. "I can scare poor little Alisun so bad that I make her hurt herself. That's always fun."

Vixx pulled out Mother Roby's little blue pouch that contained her next dose of insulin. She held it up. "Ooh, what have we here?"

Mother Roby squeezed her eyes shut. She needed that insulin badly, but she refused to panic. Instead, she prayed, silently.

Vixx saw her reaction but kept talking and taunting. "You and the girl should have stayed out of it. This is between me and the guys."

Mother Roby breathed heavily. "Alisun loves those guys."

Vixx snapped. *"Love?* What's love got to do with it?" she sang, mocking Tina Turner. "This is about *lust,* and those guys are full of it. Lust—that's all I needed as an opening."

Mother Roby struggled. "Love overpowers lust."

"Right. All it would take is for one of them to fall truly in love, and I wouldn't have any more power over them. But that ain't gonna happen. You want to know why? Because all men are *dogs!"*

Vixx let out a loud, hawklike laugh and unzipped Mother Roby's medicine pouch. She flung it upside down. A syringe and an insulin bottle crashed to the floor.

Vixx giggled. "Oops."

Mother Roby's vision blurred completely. She bent down only as far as her knees, and started praying out loud while Vixx listened: "Yea, though I walk through the valley of the shadow of death, I will fear no evil . . ."

"Fear no evil? How about fear *no insulin?*" Vixx laughed and slapped herself on the knee. "Sometimes I crack up my damn self."

Vixx stepped on the insulin bottle and crushed it with her bare foot. She quickly snatched the phone out of the wall.

"I hate to eat and run, but I got to get back to work. I only have a few hours left to destroy those guys. You try to have a good night. And hey, try to lay off that chocolate. You're getting a little hippy. Ta-ta!"

Vixx smiled, pretty and evil, and left.

Chapter

47

SUNNIE SAT AT THE KITCHEN TABLE TRYING TO FIGURE THINGS
out. She knew that something wasn't right about
Kamile, and for that matter, Dayna and Evie, too. She
also knew they were connected somehow to the sultry,
smoldering woman in the white dress. The next time
she got the chance, she planned to confront Kamile
and ask her what she knew about the dark lady in the
ugly white dress.

But right now Rice and Sunnie were alone in the
mansion, though Rice was not speaking to Sunnie. As
for both Geffen and Coach, she'd called them a zillion
times. Both were still missing. Geffen had no family
that she could call, other than an uncle out in Ontario,
but Sunnie didn't have his number. Sunnie did call Joey
and Coach's parents' house, but no one answered the
phone. She prayed someone would call her and let her
know what was going on.

Sunnie got up and walked to the kitchen window.

She gazed out at the mountains for the umpteenth time. She'd heard moaning, then talking, then something that sounded like a boxing match coming from there today. She'd tried to call Mother Roby again, to update her on what happened when she tried to catch Kamile in Rice's bedroom, but Mother Roby didn't answer her phone. *Maybe she's praying and turned off the ringer.*

Sunnie decided to use sweet temptation as a weapon to get Rice downstairs. She took out a package of chicken and started preparing Rice's favorite dish—sweet-and-sour chicken with the pineapple glaze and brown sugar. He'd smell it, get hungry, and *have* to come downstairs.

She heard his bedroom door open. She dropped the chicken breast and it slid down the garbage disposal. Sunnie ran to the bottom of the stairs, stood there, and tried to act like she'd been standing there all along.

She just wanted to talk to him, wanted them to be close like they were supposed to be, like best friends if nothing else. But she could tell by the way Rice kept his head down and walked around her when he reached the bottom of the stairs that he was still mad at her.

Sunnie caught up with him in the hallway. He was headed out in an attractive dark blue suit. His hair was neat and brushed, and he had on his distinguished-looking glasses, the ones he wore as a decoy.

"Rice, I know you think I messed up your room, but I didn't, really."

He didn't look at her and didn't stop. "I know, Sunnie. The tooth fairy did it."

Sunnie decided to try a different subject, since she wasn't getting anywhere with that one. "Have you seen Coach or Geffen? They seem to have disappeared. I call but neither answers his phone."

Rice kept walking down the hallway. He only stopped briefly to check himself in the mirror and readjust his tie, self-consciously. He gave her the short answer. "Nope."

His cavalier attitude regarding two of their best friends frustrated Sunnie. "Rice, I think something's happened, something *bad*. I can feel it. You may think I'm crazy, but trust me on this. We should go out and look for them."

Rice retied his tie. "They are big boys. They can handle themselves. I've got other things to do."

Sunnie felt plain old jealousy rising in her bones. She tried not to show it, but she was never very good at hiding her emotions. "A date with *Kamile?*"

Rice left his tie alone, deciding it was his collar that was the problem. He pulled at it. "As a matter of fact, no."

Sunnie perked up. "No? Then where are you going all dressed up like that?"

"I'm doing an interview. I'm going to be on television, live—not that it's any of your business."

Sunnie couldn't believe it. Rice *never* did live interviews. He hardly ever did interviews period. He had this big fear that the interviewer would ask him something too personal, or that he would say something that he wished he could take back.

"I've been trying to get you to do an interview since *forever*. What made you decide to do this one?"

Rice didn't answer. He pulled the right side of his collar lower than the left. Sunnie knew by the way he was acting that a *who* was involved. She coped an attitude again. "Kamile?"

His silence confirmed her suspicion. Sunnie lost whatever front she was trying to maintain. She grabbed his arm, jerked it away from his collar. "What is it about that woman? She's got you doing all sorts of things you would *never* do before!"

Rice pulled away. "I gotta go." He walked out the door.

Sunnie ran after him. She didn't want him to leave for a lot of reasons. She didn't want him to be with Kamile. She didn't want him to do an interview just because Kamile had asked him to. She didn't want him to leave the house because she was scared something was going to happen to him. She already didn't know where Geffen and Coach were, and she sure didn't want to lose contact with Rice, too.

"Rice, wait!" Rice kept walking around the bushes toward his car. Sunnie caught up with him as he was opening his car door. She pushed it closed. She was desperate. "Stay here, don't go. *Please!*"

Rice huffed. "What is it with you, Sunnie? Are you really that *needy?*"

"You don't understand. There is something going on."

"Yeah. Not only are you still trippin', I'm starting to think I really don't know you anymore."

Sunnie took a step back. His comment was like a slap in the face. "How can you say that? After all the things we've been through together and all the years we've known each other, how can you *say* that?"

The way Rice looked at her made hot tears well up in her eyes. Sunnie knew that Kamile had done something to Rice to make him change, but Sunnie thought nobody would ever come between them.

"Rice, I thought we'd be friends forever. Now you're letting a strange woman come between us."

Rice hit his palm on his car's hood. He snapped, "This has nothing to do with nobody but you and me. You always bring other people into it. If it's not Marvin, it's somebody else you're crying to me about. And now that I got tired of listening to you cry, now that I got somebody who listens to *me*, you blame it on her. Your *selfishness* never ceases to amaze me, I never really noticed it before. What else is there about you that I don't know about?"

"Rice, that hurts."

Rice sunk his hands deep down in his pockets and looked away. She'd never felt a distance like this between them before. It made her want to grab him and shake him, or pull him and hug him until that distance evaporated and they were close again, like soul mates.

Rice took his hands out of his pockets and opened his car door. He didn't look happy about that distance, either, and Sunnie knew he felt it, too. "I gotta go."

"Wait, Rice, please don't leave. Please."

Sunnie begged. She had no shame. To her, friendship was more important than pride. For a brief moment, Rice looked like he wanted to stay, but he shook his head. "I gotta go."

He closed his car door. Sunnie shouted through the window, hot tears melting the backs of her eyes. "At least tell me where you're going."

Rice started his car and put it in drive. He cracked his window. "BET's satellite station on Cahuenga."

Sunnie swallowed. "What time is the interview?"

"Nine o'clock." Rice drove away.

Sunnie stood in the parking lot for a few minutes, until the chill in the wind drove her back inside. Plus, it was getting dark.

Sunnie went into the kitchen and got her cell phone off the table. She called Mother Roby again, but there was no answer. If Mother Roby was praying, she must really be moving mountains. Sunnie wandered back into the living room.

The only good thing that had come out of all this— everything from finding the mansion to getting nearly engaged to breaking up with Marvin to Rice meeting Kamile—was that now Sunnie knew how she really felt about Rice. Before, she was always too busy running after guys whose love she thought she needed, when all along, she had enough love right here. For all his quirks and pecu- liarities, all his insecurities and hang-ups, he was the only man she really wanted to be with, the only one she could really *trust* with her feelings. She hoped that somehow, despite what he'd said, he still felt the same way about her.

Sunnie went up to Rice's bedroom and stood at the door, even though she knew it would be closed and locked. When she leaned her head against it, to her sur- prise, the door opened.

Sunnie knew how much Rice hated people inside his personal space, but she couldn't help it. She was drawn inside.

She walked around his bedroom, sat on his bed. Rice had cleaned things up since the ransacking earlier that morning. Sunnie lay down gently on his bed, trying not to disturb the pillow. She wanted it to be exactly the way he left it so that she wouldn't get in trouble again for being in there.

Sunnie had made a mistake with Rice, a big one. She'd taken him for granted, and he knew it. Now, if she had to pay for her mistake by losing him forever to another woman, it would be the hardest thing she'd ever have to do in her life. If he had simply grown tired of being taken for granted, and rightly so, she had no one to blame but herself. If he simply did not love her in that way, she'd have to make herself understand it and accept it.

Sunnie felt so comfortable lying in Rice's bed, she began to drift off. Somewhere in that mystical space between wakefulness and slumber, she heard a small voice.

She woke up, not knowing for sure if she'd actually heard a voice or if she'd dreamed it. She remembered what Mother Roby had said about listening carefully and paying close attention to that small voice.

Sunnie got up. She walked over to Rice's fireplace. She sat down in front of it and reached her hand up the chimney. Just as the small voice had said, there was a piece of paper there. She had no idea what it was. She opened it. It was notebook paper with Rice's handwriting. She read it.

After Sunnie finished reading it, she had to sit there with her back against the fireplace and think about what it said for a good long time. Rice's poem was brutally honest and made her wonder if after all these years, they didn't *really* know each other at all.

The warm tears were about to start rolling down Sunnie's face. The only thing that stopped them was her cell phone ringing.

She wiped her eyes and answered. It was Joey. He was upset and crying, too. It was about Coach.

"What Joey? What happened to Coach?"

"He was hurt real bad. They don't know if he's going to make it. He's in the hospital."

Sunnie's heart froze. "Which hospital?"

She heard static and a clicking sound, and they were disconnected. She immediately called Joey back, but his cell phone's service had gone down. Sunnie was on the verge of panic, but she forced herself to think straight. She had to find out where Coach was. She called Coach's parents' house, but there was no answer again. She'd drive down there—maybe a neighbor knew. Sunnie folded the piece of paper quickly and put it in her back pocket. She ran and got her purse and car keys, then ran out to the driveway as fast as her legs would carry her.

When she hopped into her yellow Saab and started backing out of the driveway, she had to slam on her brakes because she almost ran over Geffen. She jumped out of her car, calling his name.

"Geffen!"

She couldn't tell if Geffen heard her or not. He was in a daze. He was sitting in the driveway in the dark, mumbling to himself like he'd lost his mind or something.

"Geffen!" She ran to him, and immediately wrapped her arms around him. He was cold and shivering, and his eyes were far away. "Geffen, sweetie, what *happened?*"

His words didn't make sense. She looked around for his Hummer, but didn't see it, and wondered how he'd gotten there.

Sunnie had never seen Geffen like this before. He had always been the sharpest-minded one out of the four of them. She tried to take his face in her hands. "Geffen, look at me. Talk to me. What *happened?*"

"Schizo," Geffen murmured, and turned his face away from Sunnie again.

"What?"

"Crazy, nuts! Can't catch it like AIDS, but you can get the chromosome. Like me. I'm crazy, like my mother."

"No! You're not crazy, Geffen. You're the smartest, sharpest-minded person I know."

"Not anymore, Sunshine." He started laughing. "Wait till you hear this: I just lost the corporation!"

"What? No you didn't, Geffen. Everything's fine— you just need to catch up on some paperwork."

"Insurance! None! I wouldn't sign the papers. Ha! I'm too late, and you know what they say—punctuality is a sign of—" Geffen stopped laughing midsentence and started to sob.

"Oh, no, Geffen, it doesn't matter. The corporation doesn't matter. You've got people who love you. That's all that matters."

"Nobody loved my mother. My father didn't." Geffen chuckled pitifully. Sunnie didn't know exactly what had happened, but she knew something must have absolutely devastated Geffen since she'd last seen him. She wanted to get him up and out of the driveway and into her car. No way was she going to leave him alone like this.

Geffen resisted her tugs—he wanted to tell his story, most of which made no sense to her. "Sunshine, my uncle wasn't my uncle."

Sunnie kept trying to get him to stand up.

"My father was right under my nose the whole time. Now that son of a bitch is dead." Geffen started sobbing and convulsing. Sunnie finally got him to his feet and to her car.

He said, "I ran away, you know, from the accident. None of them could catch me. I ran into an alley and hid. Caught a bus up to Sunset and walked. It don't matter, though, they've got my car, my license plate, my ID. They know how to get me. Just like Dayna knew how to get me."

At the mention of Dayna's name, Sunnie paused. She knew those women were somehow responsible for the things that were happening to the guys, but she hadn't found out how yet. She asked Geffen, "What did she do?"

All of a sudden, Geffen hugged Sunnie tightly to his chest. "You were right, Sunshine. I should have listened to you. You were right."

"Right about what?"

"She's not Dayna. She's the evil woman you tried to warn us about. Because of her, I've lost everything—

my money, mind. I have nothing left. Just like my mother, I should kill myself."

"No. No! Never give up, Geffen!" Sunnie's head was spinning. She didn't know exactly what had happened to Geffen, but at least she had him with her. Now she had to go get Coach. Sunnie shoved Geffen into her yellow Saab as fast as she could and closed the door. She ran around to the driver's side, hopped in, and sped down Coldwater Canyon to Sunset, and to the 405 Freeway.

Sunnie drove straight to Coach's parents' house on Dwight Avenue, the same street where Mother Roby and Rice's parents lived, and where her adoptive parents used to live before they moved out of the country.

Geffen kept muttering stuff about schizophrenia, the state hospital, his uncle, his father, Dayna, and the dark woman the whole way. Sunnie was starting to realize that Dayna and the dark, sultry woman were more than just sorority sisters—they were probably the *same person* but in different disguises.

She parked in front of Coach's parents' house and told Geffen, "Stay here. I'm going to see what I can find out." Sunnie rang the doorbell, but no one answered and the house was dark. Sunnie noticed that the front security screen had been completely broken off its hinges. She peeked inside the window. The curtains had been left open, and even though it was dark inside, Sunnie could see that the house was a wreck, like people had been fighting. On her way back down the walkway, Sunnie caught a glimpse of something from the corner of her eye—it was what she'd seen in her flashes, an old white truck. That was Coach's father's truck. She had seen it a million times before but hadn't connected it to the one in her flashes until now. Panic rushed through her body.

Sunnie ran to the next-door neighbor's house and rang the doorbell. She knew the family, though not that well—they were new to the block. They told Sunnie what she'd already sensed in her spirit. Coach had gotten into a fight with his father. His father had hit him with his truck and Coach was unconscious when they took him to the hospital.

"What hospital?" Sunnie was shaking so badly her knees were growing weak. They didn't know. Sunnie left there and ran four doors down to Mother Roby's house. She hadn't answered her phone since earlier that day and Sunnie wanted to check on her anyway.

When Sunnie was two doors away from Mother Roby's house, she got run over by a little boy in cut-off jeans riding a scooter. Sunnie caught her balance and caught the boy from falling off his scooter, too.

"Alejandro, you've got to watch where you're going."

He looked sad. Sunnie knew exactly why. Alejandro was one of the little boys Coach had taken under his wing at a summer camp he helped sponsor. "You know about Coach?"

Alejandro nodded. Sunnie gave him a quick hug, turned, and continued hurrying toward Mother Roby's house. He called after her, "Señorita Sunnie, they took Señor Coach to Gardena Memorial Hospital."

Sunnie whirled back around. She couldn't believe it. Without her asking, the little boy had told her exactly what she needed to know. She ran and gave

Alejandro a quick kiss on his head, which he promptly wiped off. "Thank you!" She had the information she needed, and now she needed to get to Coach.

Sunnie headed back to her car, where Geffen sat waiting for her. As soon as she put her hand on the car door, she heard a voice say, "Go to Mother Roby's house." Sunnie didn't need to. She knew where Coach was now, and she was in a hurry. She jumped in the driver's seat and started her car. She figured she could call Mother Roby on her cell phone on her way to Gardena Memorial Hospital. Sunnie pulled over when she heard the voice again. *Now.*

She slammed on her brakes. Mother Roby was the one who'd told her, "Listen, child, always listen." Sunnie got back out and ran up to Mother Roby's porch. As soon as she got there, she knew something was wrong. Her stomach started to quiver.

The door was open. Sunnie didn't want to go in, scared of what she might find, but she rushed in anyway. To her horror, she found Mother Roby face down on the floor by her fireplace. She was holding Sunnie's picture in her hand. Her insulin bottle and syringe were smashed on the floor next to her. Sunnie was no doctor, but she knew in one instant that Mother Roby had already slipped into a diabetic coma.

She grabbed Mother Roby. "Mother Roby, wake up!"

Sunnie kept one arm around Mother Roby and reached for the phone. She saw that it had been ripped out of the wall. She fumbled with her cell phone, opened it, and called 911. She quickly gave the information to the dispatcher and hung up. Sunnie had a foreboding sense that the ambulance might be too late.

Panic blinded her and the fear of Mother Roby dying consumed her entire body. "Oh, Mother Roby!"

Sunnie rubbed Mother Roby's cotton-soft steely gray hair. She looked bad. Her usual brown sugary color had faded to a dull gray, her body was way too cool, her lips were parched, and she was barely breathing.

Sunnie felt for a heartbeat. It was faint. Perhaps the worst thing was that she'd lost her usual rosy smell. Sunnie cried, "Please don't leave me. Not now, not like this." Sunnie buried her face in Mother Roby's chest. "You've got to stay. You've got to keep on being my mother."

She prayed and cried, and prayed some more. *Listen, Alisun. Be quiet and listennn.* . . . Sunnie wiped her eyes.

Suddenly, she heard a beating sound. It sounded like a small drum. Sunnie knelt down close to Mother Roby's chest. It was Mother Roby's heart, and it grew louder and louder, until Sunnie thought she was imagining it. She quieted every other thought from her mind and listened. . . .

Mother Roby's heart began beating loud and strong, like a powerful African drum.

The strong fragrance of roses began to emanate not only from Mother Roby, but throughout her whole house. The aroma was warm and vibrant, and it encircled both Sunnie and Mother Roby. Mother Roby's body wasn't cold any longer, it was warm and vibrant. Her skin color grew rich and sugary brown and glowing again.

Mother Roby opened her eyes, and as soon as she did, a thousand rose petals—small pink, soft, velvety rose petals—floated upward, one after another, with no end. Sunnie knew then what she was seeing was not physical but spiritual. She knew that whatever it was, it would not last, and she hesitated to embrace it.

Mother Roby saw Sunnie holding her and her eyes lit up. She smiled up at Sunnie. "Alisun? Don't ever doubt your gift, baby. Embrace it. Let it guide you."

Sunnie could barely move. She nodded, and tried to smile back, but her tears got in the way.

Mother Roby spoke again. "Alisun? Are you finally *listening*, baby?"

Sunnie said, "Yes." This time she didn't try to stop the tears from falling down her cheeks.

"Good, because that's God talking, baby, and you'd better listen!"

She nodded.

Mother Roby's voice grew urgent. "The enemy is after those boys. It wants to destroy them—mind, body, and spirit."

Sunnie closed her eyes and listened to Mother Roby's words. "They need you because they don't have what you have. The enemy is crafty, it won't play fair, but you have everything you need inside of you. You just got to trust it, got to pay attention. If you do, then you'll learn how to see, even in the dark."

Mother Roby stopped talking. When Sunnie

opened her eyes, she saw that Mother Roby's were closed again. Sunnie got scared. "Mother Roby?"

Only Mother's Roby's mouth moved, her voice lowered to a faint whisper. "Shhh. I'm listening, too. God is calling me *home*."

Sunnie grabbed onto her tighter, squeezing. "No, Mother Roby, you can't leave me! You've got to stay here. You've got to help me fight!"

Mother Roby's voice grew fainter. "Hush . . . child . . ."

Sunnie started shaking uncontrollably. The sound of the ambulance sirens approaching made her tremble more. "Don't leave me, Mother. Please, don't leave me."

Mother Roby's glow was fading; her body grew cold again.

"Mother Roby, please, you've got to help me through all this."

". . . Songbirds are taught to sing in the dark. . . ."

Sunnie bowed her head. "Please . . . Mother!"

Mother Roby's voice mellowed down to an echo. "Listen . . . hear it? It's beautiful. . . ."

Sunnie begged, "Please. You're the only mother I've got."

". . . You'll never be alone. . . ."

Chapter

48

LEAVING MOTHER ROBY IN THE HANDS OF THE PARAMEDICS was one of the hardest things Sunnie ever had to do. Sunnie never wanted to remember the way Mother Roby had looked when they tied her to the stretcher; she only wanted to remember the way she'd looked when the rose petals were floating up to heaven and she was glowing like a full moon.

Sunnie left Geffen in the car and ran into the ER lobby at Gardena Memorial Hospital. The head nurse informed her that Coach had already undergone emergency surgery and was now in the ICU, but that she couldn't enter. Sunnie rushed through the double doors anyway.

When she found Coach's room and rushed in, she had to pause. Coach's whole body was broken up, bruised and swollen. Tubes were coming out of his nose and IVs out of his arm. His handsome face was dark and bloated and scratched up. Instead of that big old grin of his, he looked like he'd lost all hope. He didn't look like Coach. The nurse who'd followed Sunnie was about to force her out, but backed away when she saw Sunnie's grief-stricken expression.

Sunnie whispered, "Coach. Oh, Coach."

He cracked his eye open. When he saw Sunnie standing over him, he tried to turn away from her, but his body was so imprisoned by medical apparatus that he could barely move.

Coach tried to speak; his voice was hoarse and dry. He grunted, "Not—like—this. Don't look—"

"Coach, it's okay." Sunnie noticed that he was wrapped up from his hip all the way down both legs. She covered her mouth.

His eyes may have been swollen nearly shut, but Coach still saw her. He tried to offer some of his usual brash style to cheer her up. He said through a clenched jaw, "You—know—I—like—it—rough."

But that courage only lasted a moment. He knew he was in bad shape and that his chances of walking out of that hospital were slim to none. Sunnie could see it in his eyes.

Coach coughed. Sunnie heard fluid in his lungs. He said, "Tell them—unplug—me—let—me—die—"

Sunnie stopped him. "No. Don't say that. Don't *ever* say that." Sunnie couldn't help it, she shed the tears she'd been trying to hold back. She bent her head and leaned into what used to be Coach's big, strong body.

He didn't cry, but he spoke his tears. "How'm I gonna be a real man like this?"

Sunnie leaned in close and looked Coach in the eye. "Now you shut up and you listen to me, Coach. You're a *man* because of what's *inside* of you, not your exterior. No matter how big your head and your mouth was, your heart was always ten times bigger. *That's* what has made you a man, Coach."

Coach's expression changed, his voice hollowed out. "You right . . . 'bout Evie. She's not *normal.*"

Sunnie nodded. She was surprised to hear Coach admit that—she only wished he hadn't had to find out like this. Sunnie was going to square off with "Evie" later. Right now she had to concentrate on Coach. She prayed that these wouldn't be the last words they would ever say to each other.

She told him, "This game's not over. You've got to believe that."

A nurse came in. She told Sunnie she had to leave. Sunnie squeezed Coach's hand. "Don't you give up, Big Zulu! Don't you never give up on yourself, 'cause I ain't never gonna give up on you."

Sunnie left her cell phone number with the head nurse of ICU and told her to call immediately if there was even the slightest change in Coach's condition. Sunnie had to get back to Geffen because his frame of mind was so fragile that any little thing could push him over the edge. She also had to let Rice know what had happened to Geffen and Coach. Once he heard about them, he'd *have* to believe Sunnie about Kamile. He'd *have* to be convinced that he was in danger, too.

When Sunnie got back to her car, Geffen was gone. "Geffen!" She ran through the dark parking lot looking for him. "Geffen!"

She heard a noise two rows over. When she circled around a van, she bumped into Charlotta. She hadn't seen Charlotta since the day she'd told Sunnie in the church's parking lot that Marvin was not going to marry her.

Charlotta was very pregnant, and apparently loving it, judging by the way she kept rubbing her swollen belly. She made sure Sunnie saw the big fat diamond on her finger, the one that Marvin had originally bought for Sunnie.

"Hello, Sunnie." Charlotta was all smiles.

"What are you doing out here?" Sunnie asked. The sight of her old high school rival, pregnant and gloating, made Sunnie feel sick to her stomach.

She patted her pregnant stomach. "Gotta check on Little Marvin, here, and get an ultrasound. Hey, maybe I'll get prints made and send you one. We missed you at our wedding. Did you get the invitation I sent you?"

As much as Sunnie had been through lately, she couldn't understand why those old feelings of high school rivalry still flared up whenever this woman taunted her. Like Rice had said, "Get over it."

"Good night, Charlotta." Sunnie turned to leave and find Geffen, but Charlotta kept talking.

"Hey, Sunnie. You want to know why you'll never beat me when it comes to getting a man?"

Sunnie stopped but didn't turn around.

Charlotta went on, "It's because you don't *deserve* a man's love."

Walk away, Sunnie. Just walk away.

Charlotta continued, "You know why you don't deserve a man's love? Because you're a phony."

A phony? Sunnie turned around.

Charlotta said, "You're all smiles, but no substance. You pretend to be all loving and caring, but you're basically low down and dirty like the rest of us. That's why you sent a copy of my STD report to Marvin. But I found a better way to get Marvin back." Charlotta patted her pregnant stomach.

Sunnie took a deep breath. Charlotta's words pierced straight through her. For over twenty years, this woman had brought out the worst in her, but now Sunnie was determined to finally get over it. Sunnie closed her eyes and prayed.

"Charlotta, listening to you right now, I finally realize something—you're just as scared about never finding true love as I am. We had the *same problem*—neither of us knew how to recognize true love when we saw it. But I'm learning."

Charlotta waved her hand. "Oh brother! Gimme a br—"

"Shut up and hear me out, because I'm only going to say this once. I forgive you for every dirty, backstabbing thing you've ever done to me over the years, including the way you got my ring. I'm asking you to forgive me, too, for sending Marvin your STD report."

Charlotta rolled her eyes. Sunnie explained, "I'm doing this for me, not for you. I refuse to go on hating you or Marvin. I wish both of you the best."

Charlotta tsk-tsked, like she didn't believe that.

Sunnie went on, "And you know something? You're right. I don't *deserve* love. Love is a gift. All I can do is receive it if it should ever come my way." Sunnie turned to leave.

Charlotta said, "Wait!"

When Sunnie turned back around, things looked clearer. Maybe it was because after years of bitterness, she'd asked her longtime high school rival to forgive her, or maybe because that was what letting go of your anger does—it makes you see more clearly.

Either way, Sunnie was glad because, when she *really* looked at Charlotta standing there and thought about what was *really* happening at that moment, calmness and peace began to fill her body and her mind. Those old gnawing feelings in her stomach finally began to subside.

Now Sunnie knew why she'd run into Charlotta, and she knew why Charlotta was trying to distract her and delay her from getting to her friends.

Sunnie laid it out. "I *love* those guys. God loves them, too. And I *refuse* to believe that anything in hell can trump God's love."

Sunnie fully embraced and trusted her gift. She was not afraid anymore. Just as Mother Roby had said, when the time comes, she would be able to see, even in the dark.

Sunnie said, "One more thing, Charlotta." Charlotta looked at her questioningly. Sunnie took a step closer. "Your bandages are showing."

Vixx let out a loud bellow. Now adorned completely in a white gauze dress and barefoot, Vixx laughed in Sunnie's face.

"You want to fight me? Do you really want to fight *me*, Sunnie, girl?"

Vixx flicked her wrist and instantly a long, sharp, shiny dagger appeared in her hand. She pointed its tip at Sunnie's face, right up close to her nose. Sunnie didn't flinch—she held her ground.

Vixx said, "Because, I'm warning you, I am one *bad* bitch!"

Sunnie quoted Scripture. " 'God has not given us the spirit of fear, but of power, and of love, and of a sound mind. . . .'"

"Save it for church! Right now you're in *my* world and I don't fight fair. I fight real dirty." She grinned, her jet black eyes dripping with hate.

Vixx bragged. "I really stuck it to your boys, didn't I? Big Man went toe to toe with a truck, and guess who lost? And Pretty Boy's done lost his natural born-mind, just like his schizo mammy." She cackled. "And Rice, oooh, I'm about to give him something that's going to feel real good." Vixx checked her watch. "Gotta run, it's *showtime!*" Vixx disappeared.

Sunnie jumped, a bit startled. A feeling of frustration tried to come over her, to make her panic and make her doubt her gifts, but she quieted herself, and listened. Rice's words came back to her: "BET's satellite station on Cahuenga. . . . Nine o'clock."

Sunnie ran back to her Saab. Geffen still wasn't around, but she couldn't wait for him. She jumped in, started her car, and backed out. A head popped up in the backseat. Sunnie screamed. It was Geffen.

Sunnie caught her breath. "Geffen, where'd you go?"

"Had to go take a leak."

•   •   •

When Sunnie pulled up in front of the TV station on Cahuenga Boulevard, it was two minutes to nine. She didn't have time to park. She didn't have time to do anything but jump out in the loading zone. She left her keys in the ignition, told Geffen to get behind the wheel, and she ran inside.

Sunnie ran past the night guard as he leaned against the reception desk. She ran straight into the back, where a camera crew, a makeup artist, and a director surrounded Rice and the show's host, who were on a small shiny stage. Rice sat in a bar-stool-type chair while a makeup lady finished powdering his face.

Sunnie ran to the edge of the sound stage, but when she tried to step up onto it to get to Rice, a crew member held her arm and motioned for her to step back and stand to the side of the camera. She was too late to talk to Rice. The director had already begun his count-down.

"Five seconds to airtime!" the director called out. "Four, three, two . . ."

Sunnie looked to her left. Kamile was standing there, conservatively dressed, with a modest-looking face, evil incarnate.

Rice looked nervous and very uncomfortable under the bright stage lights. Sunnie still couldn't believe that he had agreed to do this all because Kamile had asked. Sunnie knew now, beyond a doubt, that Kamile's and the other two women's power and influence over the guys was not normal but supernatural.

Sunnie didn't know what Kamile, if that was her real

name, had planned for Rice, but Sunnie knew whatever it was, it was intended to destroy him.

The host of the live TV show began his spiel.

"Good evening and welcome to *Live Talk,* where we talk with the most talented and inspirational people in our community. Tonight we have Rice Jordan, popular novelist of many bestselling books."

Rice put on his paper-thin smile and did his best to try to fake like he wasn't as nervous as he was. The show had only started seconds ago, and already Rice was sweating.

Sunnie saw Rice glance out the corner of his eye at the side of the stage. He looked at Kamile, and he looked at Sunnie, who was standing next to Kamile. Sunnie had no idea what Rice was thinking right now, or what he was feeling about her, but she hoped he had reconsidered what he'd said in the parking lot before he left the mansion. If Rice didn't know her or trust her, then who did?

"Tonight's show is going to be quite different from our usual show. We were notified a short while before airtime that Mr. Jordan wants to use tonight's platform for a special purpose. Since we agreed with the idea behind it, we decided to break the norm and do it at the last minute. So bear with us."

Rice looked surprised. It was clear to Sunnie that he didn't know what the host was referring to. Rice shifted on his chair.

Sunnie became uneasy, too. This whole thing started making her nervous and suspicious. She glanced at Kamile. Kamile stood there, looking innocent and picture perfect.

The host continued, "Mr. Rice Jordan wants to come clean tonight about an issue that has haunted him for most of his life. He hopes that by doing so he will help other young boys who have suffered similar abuse."

Sunnie's eyes got big. She didn't know what to expect next. Neither did Rice. She could tell by the way he froze and held his breath. Neither Sunnie nor Rice could believe the host's next words.

"Mr. Jordan was molested as a child by his inebriated mother's boyfriend."

A hush fell over the studio. Quiet murmurings among the crew and makeup artists whooshed over the stage and over Rice. As Sunnie watched the host speak, the enormity of the situation hit her—an entire vast TV audience had just heard Rice's secret because it was broadcast *live*.

Sunnie stiffened and sucked in her breath.

She took one look at Rice's face and she realized *this* was the evil plan of attack. This was how the forces of evil were going to destroy Rice, by making his biggest fear in life come true—exposure of his abuse.

Kamile stood by, calm, cool, and quiet. But Sunnie detected a tiny smirk curling around the edges of Kamile's mouth.

The host continued reading from a set of index cards.

"One reason why Mr. Jordan has been so secretive about this incident is because his mother, an alcoholic who refused to get treatment, *denies* that it ever happened. Though young Rice Jordan, whose birth name is Kendric Gordon, confided in his mother the day after the incident, she didn't believe him, and to this day she calls him a liar."

Sunnie didn't know what to do. She looked at Rice. The shock of it all had paralyzed him. His privacy had been stripped away, and he'd been exposed to the entire world. For any person this would be traumatic, but for Rice, an obsessively private and guarded individual, Sunnie knew that this type of exposure could utterly destroy him.

Sunnie decided she'd run on the stage and grab Rice. She'd knock the cameras away and hold him, cover him, protect him, and tell him that everything was going to be all right. She stepped around Kamile and headed for the stage, but the director, who saw what she was about to do, caught her arm.

Sunnie jerked away from him. "Let go of me!"

Rice heard the commotion from Sunnie tussling with the director. The noise jarred him out of his shock and paralysis. He said quietly to the host, "I'm leaving."

Rice stood up, unplugged his mic, and was about to walk off the stage when the host stopped him. "Wait! We're about to roll tape and we want your comments afterward."

Rice could care less about the tape, he was going to get out of there. He fumbled with the clip mic. It wouldn't come off easily so he ripped it off, tearing his shirt collar. As he threw the mic in the chair and turned to leave, the host began speaking to the camera.

"We sent our film crew to Compton, where Mr. Jordan grew up, and we interviewed his closest childhood friend, Alisun DeMila Clark, better known as Sunnie."

Rice froze. The host said, "Roll tape."

The stage lights were turned down. The large monitor next to the stage came on, and it zoomed in on Sunnie. She was standing in Rice's parents' backyard talking to the TV camera.

In the studio, Sunnie gasped. She took two steps toward the monitor to get a better look. It was her face, her voice, her body—but she didn't do it!

Sunnie immediately ran over to Rice and grabbed his arm. "That's not me. I swear, that's not me."

Rice looked at Sunnie, at the monitor, and back at Sunnie as if to say, *It's you, plain as day.* Rice's face went blank. The way he looked when the host first shocked him was nothing compared to the way he looked as he watched Sunnie—his *best* friend—giving an interview outside his old playhouse.

Sunnie saw his reaction and wanted to scream. She repeated over and over, "That's not me. I swear, that's not me."

Rice tuned her out. He sank his hands deep into his pockets and watched the monitor. He was in such total shock to see his closest friend betray him.

The whole studio quieted and watched the monitor.

In the taped footage, Sunnie stood in front of the door of the playhouse. She looked directly into the camera and told everything she knew about Rice's molestation.

She said, "Rice's mother would wait until his father left for his longshoreman job. As soon as her husband was gone, Kendra would send all three of her boys down the street to play, but Rice never wanted to go. He was shy and introverted, and preferred to stay in his room and write than go play with the other children. Kendra would get drunk and call her boyfriend over. He was a janitor at Rice's elementary school."

On the monitor, Sunnie walked closer to the playhouse. "One night, Kendra passed out. The janitor, who not only liked drunk married women, but also liked little boys, went into Rice's room. Rice had been typing on the electric typewriter he'd gotten for Christmas, but had gotten so tired he fell asleep across its keys. When he woke up, the drunk janitor was trying to grope him. Rice ran and tried to wake up Kendra, but she was out cold in a drunken stupor. So Rice ran out the back door in his pajamas in the middle of the night to try to get away, but the janitor chased him."

On the tape, Sunnie put her hand on the playhouse door. "Rice ran inside this playhouse, thinking he'd be safe here. The janitor broke the lock and came inside after Rice, and what happened after that is—well—too horrific and embarrassing to put into words."

In the studio, Sunnie clutched Rice's arm. She pleaded quietly for him to listen to her and to believe her. "Rice, I didn't do that. I would *never* betray you."

Rice didn't seem to hear anything Sunnie was saying. He kept his hands deep in his pockets, and watched the monitor, where Sunnie told the cameraman, "Let's go inside so everybody can see where it actually happened."

Sunnie turned her back to the camera and touched

the door's handle. She jumped from the shock. A little embarrassed, she explained to the camera how after the incident Rice had booby-trapped the door so nobody but him and her could ever come inside.

On the monitor, Sunnie turned back around and pressed the tiny lever hidden behind the handle to override the booby trap, and they went inside and filmed the old broken-up green furniture where Rice was molested.

After the tape ended and the stage lights came back on, Rice had nothing to say. He didn't even look at Sunnie, he just started walking with his hands still sunk deep into his pockets. The director and studio crew were confused, and didn't know what to do. The host, who had thought Rice had agreed to all of this beforehand, tried to stay in control of the situation by ad-libbing.

Kamile stood back and watched.

Sunnie ran in front of Rice. She refused to let him leave until he believed her. "You know me, Rice. I would never do that to you. That was not me in front of that camera."

Rice looked at her, his face blank. He was too stunned to even feel anything at that moment, but Sunnie could see in his deep, pensive eyes that he didn't believe her. She saw what he was thinking, *That was you.*

Sunnie swallowed and tried to remain calm, but inside she was slowly coming unraveled. Not only had the dark forces destroyed Rice, but they were threatening to destroy her as well, because the way Rice looked at her was hurting her.

Though a studio full of people listened, Sunnie didn't care. She tried to explain everything to Rice.

"Rice, listen. That may have looked like me, but it wasn't me. It was *her*." Sunnie pointed at Kamile. Rice looked at Kamile standing by the stage looking at Sunnie as if she were crazy. Rice shook his head and started walking away again.

Sunnie ran in front of him again. "She's not normal, Rice. Neither are Dayna or Evie. Rice, they can *change*. Kamile made herself look like me and sound like me, and *she* did that interview. Not me. I would *never* do that to you, you *know* me."

Rice laughed lightly. "I *know* you, Sunnie? Naw, I don't think I really do. You've done some things lately that have me thinking maybe I never *really* knew you."

"Rice, you do—"

Rice cut her off. "You've ignored my feelings, you've taken me for granted, you've shown me how selfish you really are. You've tried to break up me and Kamile just so that I can pay more attention to you. You went through my stuff, trashed my room, then lied about it. You've been lying about a lot of stuff, saying crazy things that aren't true. But *this* . . ." Rice gestured toward the monitor. He shook his head like he'd lost all hope and trust in Sunnie. "This right here is too much for me."

"But I'm telling you, I didn't do *this*. Kamile did this to you."

Rice told Sunnie why he knew it was her. "It was you, Sunnie. It had to be you because besides my mother, who doesn't believe me, I've never told another soul what happened to me in that playhouse, not even Kamile."

Sunnie looked at Kamile. Kamile's smirk increased by a half centimeter, but Sunnie was the only one who saw it.

Rice said, "You were the *only* person in this world I trusted."

Kamile walked up and took Rice's hand.

Sunnie screamed, "Rice, she's evil! Rice, Kamile *is* that dark woman from my dreams. She changes form. She can look like Dayna. She can look like Evie. She destroyed Coach and Geffen. Rice, if you don't believe *me,* talk to them. They are in trouble right this very second, and so are you, Rice. If you leave with her, she's going to finish destroying you. She's going to make you lose all hope. She's going to make you want to die."

Rice looked at Sunnie. He didn't believe a word she said. Kamile squeezed his hand. His voice was flat, emotionless. "I can't stand to even look at you."

Rice turned to walk away.

Sunnie reached in her back pocket and pulled out the piece of notebook paper she'd found inside his fireplace. She held it up. "What about this?"

Rice saw it, knew what it was. Kamile's eyes zeroed in on it, too.

Sunnie opened it, but she didn't need to read it again. She had already read it ten times. She knew very well what it said.

Sunnie smoothed it out. "Your poem says you love me."

Kamile narrowed her eyes. She looked at the piece of paper that she hadn't been able to find, and she bit her lip. Her smirk faded.

Rice shifted his weight to the other leg. His expression remained flat.

Sunnie said, "Your poem says you *do* believe that true and meaningful love is possible, but not between you and *any* woman—only between you and me."

Kamile's smirk slipped into a snarl. Sunnie saw it, but she didn't care anymore. She was going to lay it all on the line and let Rice know exactly how she felt about him.

Sunnie stepped close enough to Rice to look deeply into his eyes. She could also feel the mad, hot body heat vibrating off Kamile's evil flesh. But it didn't matter now. What used to be a quiver in her stomach letting her know when evil was near was now a subtle *peace* put there by God, letting her know that love always trumps hate.

Sunnie looked into Rice's eyes and tried to put this one doubt in his mind to rest. "Rice, I *love* you. I love you as *more* than a friend. I've loved you for quite some time, but I've been too blind to see it."

Sunnie watched Rice's face. He swallowed hard and let go of Kamile's hand.

Sunnie wasn't finished. "Rice, you are my best friend, my soul mate. You are more than a shoulder to cry on, you are my rock. I love you for who you are. I love *us* for who *we are together*. I don't need to search anymore. We have everything we need right here in each other to build the love affair of a lifetime."

The studio was dead quiet. The only thing Sunnie could hear besides Rice's heartbeat was her own.

Rice moved toward her. His dark brown eyes never looked as reflective as they did at that moment.

He started to speak. Sunnie's heart stayed still and listened.

"Sunnie, I've been waiting probably my whole life to hear you say what you just said. I share some of the blame, too, for not opening up and letting you know how I felt, like I opened up when I wrote that poem."

Rice looked at the crinkled notebook paper. "It's true. Over this past year or so, I started believing that I was capable of being truly in love with one woman, but only if that woman was you. I'd give anything for us to be more than friends, because you were the only person in this world that I trusted with my feelings and with my secrets, until now."

Sunnie didn't follow at first. She saw everything in his face that began to look like love crumble into something that looked like hurt, disappointment, and despair.

Sunnie frowned. "Rice, what do you mean?"

Rice gestured to the monitor. "I told you, you were the *only* person who knew."

Sunnie tried to explain again as she pointed to Kamile, but he stopped her. "And nothing else you've told me makes any sense."

"Rice—"

Rice shook his head. His eyes were completely filled with hurt now and clouded by utter dismay. "I can't for the life of me figure out what I did to you to make you want to hurt me so bad."

Rice turned and left with Kamile. There was nothing Sunnie could say now to stop him. Even if there was something, Sunnie didn't have the strength to say it because her heart had stopped beating the moment she knew he didn't trust her anymore, and she was having trouble making it start again.

After Rice left with Kamile, Sunnie stayed on the set a few minutes longer to give her body time to adjust to the impact of Rice's words. When she could, she folded his poem and returned it to her back pocket, and exited the building.

The street in front of the TV station was empty and dark. Sunnie quickly scanned the parking lot and the street hoping to catch a glimpse of Rice driving away with Kamile in his car so she could follow them. She didn't see anything, not even her yellow Saab or Geffen, who was supposed to be outside waiting for her. Sunnie ran to the other side of the building and back around again. Geffen had driven off and left her. His mind was probably still a fog, and he didn't realize what he was doing. She blamed herself for telling him to get behind the wheel and leaving her keys in the ignition.

My keys, my purse, my phone! Sunnie stomped her feet on the cold, dark pavement as she remembered that she was in such a rush to get inside the studio, she had jumped out of her car with nothing but Rice's poem and some change in her back pocket.

Sunnie went back inside. The night guard sitting at

the reception desk stopped her. "Sorry, miss, I can't let you back in here."

Sunnie said, "I just need to use the phone. My ride left me."

"Sorry. Manager is on my case for letting you slip through here before. They say you disrupted their show and upset their guest. I can't let you back in, not even to use the phone. Sorry."

Sunnie went back outside. Not knowing what else to do, she started walking south on Cahuenga Boulevard. With each step, she tried to remember the things Mother Roby had told her. *At the right time, you'll know exactly what to do.*

Sunnie needed a sign now—a voice, something— because all she could think about was how bad things were. Coach was in ICU, Geffen suicidal, driving around aimlessly, Mother Roby in a coma or worse.

Sunnie stopped. She could no longer put one foot in front of the other. The catastrophe of it all came down on her hard, and she went down on one knee at a bus stop bench. How could she fight the enemy when self-doubt and despair had brought her to her knees on a cold, dark, lonely street with no phone, no coat, and not even enough money to catch a cab?

Sunnie stayed on her knees and placed her hands on the bench seat. The only thing she could do in that position was pray.

Sunnie never thought the day would come when she couldn't even pray. *Forgive me, Lord.* She stopped praying and started sobbing. She wanted to do something—run, scream, fight—anything except stay there, bent over a street bench, sobbing. *Quiet yourself, child, and listen. . . .*

Sunnie sucked back her tears. After her sobs died down, she heard the sound of a bus. It stopped at the bus stop where she had been kneeling.

Chapter

49

AFTER RICE LEFT THE TV STATION, HE AND KAMILE GOT IN his car and headed back to the mansion. He hoped Sunnie would not follow him. He didn't want to see her face anymore—it was too painful. She couldn't have planned a better revenge if she'd had a magic wand.

One day, he'd try to figure out what he had done to her to make her hurt him so bad, but for right now, he just wanted to run away and not look back. Rice planned to pack a bag quickly, book a flight, and board a plane. The destination was unimportant. What mattered was that he get far away from Sunnie and the hurt she'd caused.

Rice hoped that Kamile wouldn't want to come with him because, truthfully, he was growing tired of her. Whatever spell she'd cast on him was wearing thin. Even though things had turned out badly between him and Sunnie, Sunnie had undeniably changed him. Lust was no longer as appealing to him as it once was. And lust was basically the only thing he and Kamile had.

Rice drove and tried not to think. He sensed Kamile sitting next to him trying to figure out what was going on inside his head. He hoped that for once she would not intrude on his thoughts. He used to think it was fascinating and a big turn-on, the way she intuitively knew how he felt. Now he simply found it annoying.

Sunnie never did that. In fact, most of the time Sunnie didn't have a clue what Rice was thinking. That was obvious, but even with that quirk between them—his secretiveness, her inattentiveness—they could have been good together. He thought about what she'd said, that theirs would be "a love affair to last a lifetime."

Rice shook his head silently as he drove. He didn't want to think about it, and he couldn't get his mind around it. It simply didn't make any sense for Sunnie to do this to him. If she had done *anything* else in the world to him, he could have forgiven her. This was the *only* thing she could do to make him take his love back. If there were a way he could take a giant eraser and erase this one thing, he would do it, and he would keep right on loving her.

Rice turned right on Coldwater Canyon and left the bright street lights on Sunset Boulevard for the dark, winding canyon road leading toward the mansion.

Kamile broke the silence. "Rice, you must be hurting so much right now. I tried to warn you about Sunnie. I knew she hated me, but after what she did to you tonight, it's obvious she hates you, too."

Kamile ran her hand down Rice's arm. Rice tried to tune her out.

She said, "The whole world knows your secret now. No matter where you go, people are going to point at you and laugh behind your back. Your privacy will be nonexistent."

Rice drove, silently, but his mind burned. *We were best friends for over thirty years. This just doesn't make sense.*

Kamile said, "Even when people read your books, they'll be thinking about the author—the abused child of an alcoholic whore."

Rice tugged on his ripped collar, but kept his eyes on the road. *This was the only thing she could have done to make me never want to see her again.*

Kamile continued, "Because of Sunnie, your professional life is over, as well as your personal life."

Rice tapped his finger on the opposite side of the steering wheel. *If she hadn't done this, I'd still trust her, and I'd still love—*

Rice said out loud, "The booby trap."

Kamile heard him, but didn't know what he was talking about. "What?"

Rice repeated, "The booby trap. I never showed Sunnie how to open that door."

Kamile shifted in her seat, her voice measured. "Rice, surely you showed her. You said that you and she were the only two people allowed inside."

"Right, but she couldn't get inside without me. I never wanted her to go in there alone. It was my way of protecting her. I never wanted anything like what happened to me to happen to Sunnie."

Rice was calm, but he kept thinking. His sudden realization changed his whole perspective on everything. He had to backtrack and figure this out. Sunnie had asked him a million times to tell her how to override the electrical shock to open the door, but every time, he had refused. The only person he'd shown that to was . . . *Kamile*.

But what did this mean? If Sunnie had not done this, then he could still trust her; if he could trust her, then he could believe her—no matter how crazy it all sounded.

Rice told Kamile categorically, "That wasn't Sunnie on camera. It was you."

Kamile looked at Rice from behind her glasses and raised her eyebrows. "Me? Rice, that's preposterous. You can't believe all those outrageous things Sunnie said."

Rice was calm, but adamant. "I believe her. Based on our friendship alone, I never should have doubted her."

But now Rice had something much more urgent on his hands to deal with. If what Sunnie said was true, then—

Rice asked Kamile, point-blank, "Who are you?"

Kamile took off her glasses and cleared her throat. Her voice was lower now and less patient.

"C'mon, now, Rice. Don't start freaking out on me before it's time. You know who I am—I am *Kamile*, your *fantasy* woman. Now, let's go back to my house and have sex one more time before—"

"*Your* house?" Rice's mind was clicking and connecting the dots. All the crazy out-of-this-world things that

Sunnie had tried to tell him, Coach, and Geffen from the first day they saw that mansion came rushing back to him. But this time he believed them.

Kamile exhaled. Rice looked at her. Her eyes had darkened, her innocent facial features became sharper and more exotic. She was starting to look different physically.

She checked her watch. "Yes, *my* house, but we'll get to that later. Right now I want to have sex one more—"

Rice interrupted her. "You're that dark woman Sunnie was talking about."

Kamile huffed, her patience all but gone.

Rice pulled his car over. He turned to Kamile and said, "Get the fuck out of my car."

Kamile laughed, mildly amused. "I don't think so."

Rice rubbed his chin, figuring he was going to have to throw this woman's butt out of his car, and it wouldn't be the first time he'd had to throw a woman out. But first he needed to know exactly what he was dealing with.

He asked, "What are you? Are you human or what?"

Kamile pushed her head back against the headrest. The conservative clothes she wore whenever she played Kamile for Rice were starting to bother her. She unbuttoned the collar, pulled the jacket open a bit.

"Oh, Rice," she said breezily, her voice changing. "I can be anything I want to be, sweetie poo. But if you don't drive this car back to *my* place so that we can get busy one last time before midnight, when I have to destroy you, I'm going to be something you really, really don't want me to be."

Rice refused to drive on. "What? Is that a threat?"

Kamile had had it. She said, "The first time I laid eyes on you was when you came down into my cellar. You reminded me so much of Bruce."

Rice had no idea what she was talking about. "What?"

Kamile twisted in her seat and faced him. "Here, I'll help you remember. Watch carefully."

In a flash, Kamile changed into a gigantic hairy tarantula. She spread her eight legs out on the dash and opened her mouth at Rice.

Rice hollered. He jerked back so hard, the back of his head cracked the door window. He lunged for the door handle to get out, but Kamile locked him inside with her. Rice squashed himself against the door, too scared to move, and put his hands up to block and kept his eyes pinned on the giant spider.

Kamile changed again, but this time she was Vixx.

Rice looked at Vixx. Her whole body was shadowy, sultry, and erotic. Her cleavage pushed against her white gauzy dress. Even sitting, Rice could see that her legs were long and curvy, and her whole being oozed potent female sexuality.

Rice sat back in his seat, but leaned away from Vixx.

His voice was airy, but still relatively calm. He tried another approach. "Get the fuck out of my car, *please*."

Vixx laughed. Her voiced turned smolderingly sensual. "Not only do you look like Bruce, you kinda act like him, too. And oooh, even after spending a hundred years in exile because of him, it still turns me on."

Vixx ran her hand down her breasts and rubbed,

making a hot moaning sound. "I can't have Bruce any-more, but I can have you."

Rice had no idea who Bruce was, and he wasn't about to ask—not after the way she had answered his last question.

Vixx leaned into Rice. He moved away until his back was pushed up against the door and he had nowhere else to go. Vixx stroked his chest and blew on his neck. Her voice was almost sympathetic, but not quite.

"I'm going to have to kill you, Rice. That's the only way I can get my brothel back. You've proven to be a harder nut to crack than those other two, who I've suc-cessfully put on the brink of suicide. They are out of my house for good and sufficiently dealt with. I don't know why I couldn't get to you as easily. Maybe because you run a little deeper, maybe because you hide so much, maybe because of that stupid little Sunnie girl." Vixx scowled. "Anyhow, now I'll have to assist things along by running my dagger through your heart. But first, it'd be a shame to let all of this sexiness go to waste without hitting it one last time."

Vixx straddled Rice right there in the car. She pushed his seat all the way back and began licking his neck and grinding her body into his. Rice struggled, trying to turn his head and wiggle away from her, but Vixx was strong.

After a few minutes of what Vixx considered fore-play and Rice considered torture, Vixx probed his crotch. For all the sexual oozing and all the luscious lusting Vixx brought to the party, Rice had other things on his mind, so his little pal didn't get the memo that there was a party going on.

Vixx was irate and a bit self-conscious. She sat up. "What's the matter with you? Don't I turn you on? Don't I look good to you?"

Rice thought about it. "Um, do you mean now or when you had eight legs, a minute ago?"

"Don't get cute with me. All men respond to good old-fashioned ear-biting, hair-grabbing, nipple-squeezing lust, and you are no different. So get with the program and let's go."

Vixx lowered herself on Rice again and cranked up the heat. She bit his earlobe, grabbed his hair, and squeezed his nipple, but Rice didn't respond to any of it.

Vixx jerked herself up. "Look, we don't have much time left before I have to destroy you. There's nothing wrong with you—you're resisting me on purpose." She climbed off Rice.

Rice was glad she was off until she said, "Well, if we can't have sex, then I'll go on and kill you now."

"Wait!" Rice had to think of something quick. He didn't like what was behind door number one, but he *hated* what was behind door number two. So, he came up with a door number three. "I know what the problem is. It's not you, it's the setting."

"The *what?*"

"You know, the atmosphere, the ambience. I need inspiration."

"Inspiration? What the—?" Vixx started to slice him right then, but her own lust held her back. She wanted him in a bad way, especially with him sitting there looking so much like Bruce. "So, what are you saying?"

"I'm saying, we need to go somewhere more, um, romantic. I know just the right place. Then I'll be able to give you exactly what you need."

Vixx thought about it for a second and agreed. She did *need* it. After going a hundred years without it, she needed a whole *lot* of it.

Rice put the car back in gear and drove. He couldn't let himself think about what he was planning to do because he knew that this crazy bitch could read his mind. All he could do in this situation was hope that his plan would work. For the first time in his life, he seriously thought about going to church, *voluntarily.*

Rice parked his car in the closed all-day parking lot. Vixx was anxious to jump his bones, but he had to keep her off him until they got to the right place. The hardest thing was staying calm. He had been with a lot of freaks in his day, but *this* woman took freakdom to a whole new level.

Vixx's tone was sharp and no-nonsense. She wanted to get down to business. "Are we there *yet?*"

She kept checking her watch. Vixx's plan was to have incredible sex and then slit his throat. It was twenty minutes to midnight. She had to make sure that Rice was still under her spell, that he had removed himself from Sunnie's protective prayers. By following his own lust and not falling truly in love with Sunnie, Vixx could kill him.

Rice kept walking until finally Vixx yelled, "Okay! Stop! That's far enough."

Vixx ripped open Rice's shirt and unbuckled his belt. She pushed him down to the ground and straddled him.

Rice complained, "Can a brother get a little fore-play?"

Vixx checked her watch. "Okay. You got sixty seconds, starting now."

Vixx immediately started kissing and biting and sucking on Rice's neck while grinding and groping him, giving him time to get ready. Rice remained remarkably calm given the circumstances.

Vixx started cooing and whispering sweet nothings in Rice's ear, pretending he was Bruce and exposing her weakness for human men once again.

Starting to feel a bit romantic herself, Vixx whispered in Rice's ear, "Ooo, babe, why'd you pick this place?"

Rice answered her with a smile on his lips. "Because things are always cooler—"

Sunnie walked up behind Vixx and finished Rice's sentence. "—at the pier."

Vixx heard Sunnie's voice and jumped up. She whipped around. "How did you find us here?"

Sunnie smiled. "I listened."

Vixx frowned. "You *what?*"

"I knelt at a bus stop, and I listened. I heard a bus coming. I had two things in my back pocket—Rice's poem and enough change for bus fare. I got on the bus. Then I listened to my heart, and it led me here."

Vixx grimaced. "You wasted your bus fare. This no-good man dog doesn't really love you, he only thought he did." Vixx whipped out her dagger and pointed it at Rice's neck, daring him to object.

Rice stood up and with courage and love as his guide, said, "Sunnie, I love you more in this very moment than I ever did before."

Vixx reared back and swung at Rice's throat, but the instant her dagger touched Rice's skin it crumbled into dust. Vixx jumped back. Her hand was full of dagger dust where she'd been holding its handle. She balled it up and threw a dust ball at Rice.

Rice dusted off his shirt and stepped around Vixx to get to Sunnie. He took Sunnie into his arms and looked directly into her eyes.

Sunnie said, "I'm sorry I took you for granted."

Rice said, "I'm sorry I held back."

Sunnie smiled. "So, is ours going to be the love affair of a lifetime?"

Rice pulled her closer. "Short answer? Yep."

Vixx looked at Rice and Sunnie staring into each other's eyes and saying all that Harlequin romance-type crap. She put her hand on her hip, and muttered, "Well, ain't that a bitch?"

After Rice and Sunnie finished kissing, they looked at Vixx, who had slumped down on the pier.

Sunnie heard Vixx muttering something about more years in exile, not being able to destroy the guys, and something about a guy named Bruce.

Rice saw that Sunnie seemed to know exactly what Vixx was saying, while he only saw her lips moving with no sound coming out.

He asked Sunnie, "What's she saying?"

Sunnie shrugged. "It's really not that important. All that really matters is that we're together, and I've got this really strong feeling in my stomach that Geffen, Coach, and Mother Roby are all going to pull through. In fact"—Sunnie looked up at the sky. The full moon in all of its glory shined down directly on her face, and her face lit up—"I'm *sure* of it."

"Yeah? How can you be so *sure* of it?" Rice asked. Sunnie smiled. "It's a gift."

Chapter

50

ONE MONTH LATER, SUNNIE SAT NEXT TO MOTHER ROBY IN the front row of First Angeles Church, waiting for the service to start. Sunnie leaned into Mother Roby to get one more whiff of that fresh rose smell that always emanated from her.

"Mmmm." Sunnie kissed her cheek. She could hardly believe that she'd almost lost this precious woman to a diabetic attack. Mother Roby had spent two weeks in the hospital, and though she remained a bit weak, she absolutely *insisted* on coming to church today.

As Sunnie straightened Mother Roby's hat, she remembered a question she'd been meaning to ask her, but never had. "Remember that night when I was holding you in my arms and you were slipping away? You said, 'God is calling me home,' but you're still here. How did that happen?"

Mother Roby giggled. "I said He was *calling* me. I didn't say I answered."

Sunnie laughed. "Well, I'm glad He let you stay here with me because I'm not ready to let you go yet, not for a long, long time."

Mother Roby smiled and squeezed Sunnie's hand. "Are they here yet?" she asked Sunnie for the third time.

Sunnie turned around and looked. She spotted Geffen walking next to Coach, who was rolling himself in a wheelchair. Rice was behind Coach trying to push him, but Coach wouldn't let him.

Sunnie turned back around to Mother Roby. "Yes, the guys are here. Now tell me what's going on. Why are you so anxious to see these guys?"

Mother Roby grinned like she had a secret. "Oh, no reason."

Geffen kissed Sunnie's cheek, greeted Mother Roby, and sat on the other side of her. Rice kissed Sunnie's lips and sat next to her on the front row.

Sunnie turned to Coach, who had stopped his wheelchair at the end of the second row. "Hey, Coach, come up here and sit with us."

Coach grumbled. "Naw, that preacher may spit when he preaches, and I ain't trying to get spit on up in here."

Sunnie shook her head and turned back around. Coach was back to his normal grumpy, lovable self. His football career was over after he suffered a broken hip and other injuries, but he was healing well thanks to his self-motivated physical therapy. Joey moved into J.B.'s house to look after Coach's mother since J.B. was serving time. Coach wasn't going to have time to miss football, because he had already found himself an empty gymnasium on Rosecrans where he was opening a year-round camp for physically challenged boys, teaching them self-defense techniques as well as character-building skills.

The guys gave up the mansion, and even if they hadn't voluntarily left it, they would have lost it in the corporate bankruptcy that Geffen was forced to file. Fred Gertz, Esquire, sued the corporation and won, but thanks to Geffen's business savvy, he found a few loopholes that protected the guys' personal assets, as well as their reserve cash in the bank, and prevented them from losing everything.

Although things didn't go exactly as Geffen had planned, he did eventually recover his mother's remains, buy her a new casket and headstone, and lay her to rest in the beautiful and tranquil Forest Lawn Cemetery in Cypress, California. Geffen was tested for the so-called schizophrenia chromosome, which has never been definitely proven to cause schizophrenia. When his tests came back negative, he realized that that had been one of the many lies that Dayna had told him. Geffen never will know exactly what his father *did* say when Dayna tricked him into leaving his father's bedside at the moment of his death, but Geffen had learned, with the help of Sunnie and friends who loved him unconditionally, to let things rest. As for his financial aspirations, he would get to pursue moneymaking, but on a smaller scale for now. Geffen was Rice's new business manager.

And Rice really needed a business manager after

being offered three times more than his usual book advance for his much-anticipated nonfiction book on adolescent molestation and its effect on developing one's own identity. Sunnie could hardly believe he had agreed to write it, but after all the years of shielding his emotional wounds, Rice was ready to open up and start the healing process.

Sunnie was so proud of Rice. Over the past month, they had spent time together working on their relationship, which included learning how to communicate effectively and how to stay sensitive to each other's needs.

Sunnie was also elated to have her three best friends back together. After Sunnie explained to them the dynamics of being under a spiritual attack the guys made their apologies and reconnected. As they helped one another start to put their lives back together, the bond between them grew even stronger than it had been before. It warmed Sunnie's heart to know that not even the forces of hell could tear apart the love the four of them had for one another.

As far as the guys' hit-it-and-quit-it philosophy with women, after all they'd gone through, they'd finally changed their perspectives. Rice was with Sunnie now, dedicated and loyal. Geffen had a new respect for women, especially after finding out how his father had mistreated his mother. In honor of his mother, Geffen vowed to give women the respect they deserved and always place greater value on their feelings than on any material thing. Coach—well, he needed a little more working on. One of the first things he did after leaving the hospital was make sure all the ladies knew that it was his *hip* that broke, and everything else was working just fine. Even though he didn't come right out and admit it, Coach was glad to still be alive and he had a new, healthy perspective on spiritual matters and controlling one's lustful desires.

Out of curiosity, Sunnie had driven back to the mansion yesterday. The house was empty, but someone had rolled a huge boulder to where the cellar door had been and sealed it up again. Sunnie heard voices inside fussing and complaining.

On her way back to her car, she saw a moving van pull up. Fred Gertz, Esquire, from those personal injury commercials, and his pregnant wife got out of the van. Sunnie just looked at them, smiled, and said, "I pray that you two have a whole lot of love for each other, plus a little faith, because you're going to need it." Sunnie hopped into her little yellow Saab with the brand-new taillight, said a final good-bye to the mansion, and drove away.

Ten minutes before the service was scheduled to start, Coach reached up and banged the back of Rice's seat. "Hey, Mustafa. What you waiting for?"

Rice ignored Coach and kept looking up at the stage as if he were suddenly deeply interested in the floral arrangements. Geffen and Mother Roby both peeked at Rice.

Geffen checked his watch and told Rice, "Punctuality is a sign of intelligence, King Tut. As your business manager, I suggest you go ahead and make that investment before time runs out."

Rice heard Geffen, but he ignored him, too, and nervously popped a TicTac in his mouth.

Sunnie frowned. "What in the world are you guys talking about?"

Mother Roby grinned. Sunnie knew that Mother Roby was in cahoots with the guys, but Mother Roby wouldn't clue Sunnie in. Instead, she took Sunnie's right hand, placed it in her lap, and squeezed it tight.

Sunnie turned to Rice. "Okay, what's going on? I know you're not going to start keeping secrets again, not after all we've been through."

Rice finally took his eyes off the floral arrangements and looked at Sunnie.

He said, "Do you remember how you found that poem? You were lying on my bed and a small voice told you—"

"To look up in the fireplace. Yeah, why?" Sunnie was on pins and needles. She wanted to find out what was going on.

"Well, you missed something." Rice pulled out a small square velvet box from his pocket and held it in his hand. "This was taped right next to that poem."

Sunnie started hyperventilating. "Ohmygod, Ohmygod, Ohmygod."

Mother Roby squeezed her hand and said, "Hush, child, and *listen*."

Sunnie calmed down. The organ music started playing as the service started. The choir started marching in.

Rice nervously tugged at his collar and took Sunnie's left hand. "Sunnie, whatever love I have inside of me, you put it there. Now I want to give you something back."

Rice opened the box and took out the ring. The choir began to march up the aisle toward the altar, singing loudly and joyously.

Geffen and Mother Roby leaned in close to Sunnie and Rice. Coach rolled his wheelchair up to the front row and gave Rice a supportive pat on the back as Rice got out of his seat and down on one knee in front of Sunnie.

Other people standing near them noticed what was happening. They stopped clapping with the choir. They craned their necks, shifted their bodies, and watched Rice as he took the ring and slipped it on to Sunnie's finger. Sunnie's knees were bouncing up and down, and she looked ready to leap out of her seat.

Rice asked, "Sunnie, will you be my wife?"

Sunnie asked, "You want the short answer?" Rice nodded. Sunnie leaped up and shouted, *"Hal—le—lu—jah!"*

Everybody around them, but especially Mother Roby, Geffen, and even grumpy but lovable Coach, started clapping and singing and rejoicing with Sunnie as she flung her arms around Rice's neck and refused to let go. She planned to hang on to that man for the love affair that would last a lifetime.

Not sure what to read next?

Visit Pocket Books online at
www.simonsays.com

**Reading suggestions for
you and your reading group
New release news
Author appearances
Online chats with your favorite writers
Special offers
Order books online
And much, much more!**

EXPERIENCE PASSION, SEDUCTION,

AND OTHER **DARK DESIRES** IN BESTSELLING PARANORMAL ROMANCES FROM POCKET BOOKS!

Discover the darker side of desire
with bestselling paranormal romances from Pocket Books!

Master of Darkness
Susan Sizemore
She thinks he's helping her hunt vampires.
She's dead wrong.

The Devil's Knight
A Bound in Darkness Novel
Lucy Blue
A vampire's bite made him immortal. But a passionate
enemy's vengeance made his hunger insatiable....

Awaken Me Darkly
Gena Showalter
Meet Alien Huntress Mia Snow. There's beauty in her
strength—and danger in her desires.

A Hunger Like No Other
Kresley Cole
A fierce werewolf and a bewitching vampire test the
boundaries of life and death...and the limits
of passion.

Available wherever books are sold
or at www.simonsayslove.com.

POCKET BOOKS
A Division of Simon & Schuster
A CBS COMPANY

POCKET STAR BOOKS
A Division of Simon & Schuster
A CBS COMPANY

14179